PLAGUE

PLAGUE

CAROL BALIZET

Chosen Books

A Division of Baker Book House Co
Grand Rapids, Michigan 49516

© 1994 by Carol Balizet

Published by Chosen Books
a division of Baker Book House Company
P.O. Box 6287, Grand Rapids, MI 49516-6287

Printed in the United States of America

Library of Congress Cataloging-in-Publication Data

Balizet, Carol.
    Plague / Carol Balizet.
      p. cm.
    ISBN 0-8007-9213-0
      1. AIDS (Disease)—Patients—United States—Fiction. I. Title.
PS3552.A4536P57 1994
813'.54—dc20   93–44722

For my own Sarah,
my own Angela,
and my own ten-year-old boy

1

Thursday, September 9, 1999

Aaron Tyler parked the van under the spreading oak trees that embraced the Stoddard home. This house, like Will Stoddard who owned it, was substantial, gracefully aged and intrinsically Southern. It had been Olivia's home until her marriage to Aaron, and she was still different somehow when under its roof. The Tyler children exploded from the rear of the van as soon as the motor stopped, racing around the house toward the pasture. Aaron and Olivia sat in silence, marshaling their strength before facing the scene they knew awaited them inside.

"No sense putting it off," Aaron said in a reasonable voice. "Won't get any easier for waiting."

"True," Olivia agreed. They continued to sit.

"Maybe he can help," Olivia added.

"I'll just be glad if he doesn't blame me for the whole thing," Aaron responded. He took a deep breath and opened the van door slowly. "Let's get it over with."

The house was traditional, two-story, constructed of wide, horizontal timbers with large, deep windows. As they approached the front door of Will Stoddard's home, Aaron recalled the hundreds of times in the past, before their marriage, when he had walked this same path to meet Olivia or bring her home, and he felt some of that old, familiar apprehension. Willoughby Stoddard, like no one else in the world, had the capacity to make Aaron feel inadequate.

Olivia opened the door and walked in. "Mama! Daddy!" she called. "Company!" She turned to Aaron and spoke softly. "Just tell them, calm and matter-of-fact. If we're not emotional, maybe it'll help."

Sure, Aaron thought. *No emotion. Your eyes are still red from your own crying.*

"Back here," they heard Will shout.

They walked through the house to the kitchen, where the Stoddards waited. There were smiles, hugs, beer or coffee offered and served, and as this flurry ended Aaron spoke out abruptly: "Olivia's got to go to Belle Glade. She's been drafted."

There was a moment of silence, then an explosion.

"I won't allow it! Not my daughter, they won't! It's kidnaping!" Willoughby Stoddard banged his beer can on the table and glared at Olivia. "You hear me, girl? I won't allow it."

Will was a brawny man in robust middle age. His waistline had spread a little and his thick hair was frankly gray, but he was still tall and handsome, still a forceful presence.

"I don't know how you can stop it, Daddy," Olivia protested. "I'm a licensed nurse and they recruited me. But we do want you to try."

Although her voice was controlled, Aaron knew she was frightened; only a little while ago she had been crying and clinging to him. But a lifetime of training kept her voice calm in the face of her volatile father's distress.

Aaron sat where he always sat at his in-laws' long kitchen table—facing the big windows, his back to the hall. He could look past his wife's face into the backyard and beyond, into the pasture where the horses grazed. He could see his children, Philip following the horses as always and Sara following her brother. The golden September sunlight slanted over the gently rolling hills, bringing a twilight beauty that was almost painful.

He took a drink of beer, now getting warm, and listened as Olivia continued. "We thought you could talk to Joe Jenson."

Aaron heard his own voice, as reasonable as his wife's. "Olivia ought to be exempt a dozen times over; she has kids, she's working an essential job and she's never done that kind of nursing. Plus I know there are new infected people all the time and they're supposed to go first."

"But the point is, Daddy, we need to get it straightened out right away. I'm due to be in Belle Glade, ready to start work, before the end of this month." Olivia sipped from a glass of water.

Aaron knew she hated beer and avoided her mother's coffee. No wonder! It was strong and black and seldom hot.

Olivia took another sip of water and shuddered slightly. "I don't think God Himself could get me off the list after the start date."

Charlotte Stoddard walked behind Aaron to take her own place at the table, patting his shoulder as she passed. She carried her usual cup of the vile-looking coffee. "We'll work it out, Olivia, honey. Somehow. Won't we, Will?"

Willoughby Stoddard had turned to look at the horses. He nodded in response to his wife and Aaron sensed his pain. Behind Will's bluster and anger, beyond the loud and vain words, were sorrow and bewilderment. Aaron knew his father-in-law would like to walk away from the problem, out into the reddish glow of the dying day, into the calm and gentle world of the children and the horses.

"I'll call Joe Jenson later," Will said. "If he can't fix it, he'll know who can."

"Here's the notice." Aaron handed over the official document, and with it some of his own burden. Will was far better equipped to fight city hall—no, it was more accurate to say Capitol Hill—than Aaron was, and Aaron told himself firmly that it didn't make him less of a man, less a protective husband, because he sought help. He was just using wisdom.

"Mrs. Olivia Tyler, 8806 River Drive, Pine River, Florida, is conscripted for a six-month period of service as a Licensed Practical Nurse at the Roy Fitzgerald Memorial Hospice, Belle Glade, Florida, such service to begin 6:00 A.M., Monday, September 29, 1999. And so on and so forth." Will read the rest of the document to himself, the details of transportation, housing, duties, compensation. "I remember a time when guys headed to Canada when they got this kind of letter. 'Course, that was when only guys got this kind of letter. Now they can draft women, even mothers. . . ."

Charlotte interrupted her husband, speaking with forced cheerfulness. "I heard on TV there're a lot of people challenging these conscriptions. I mean, they may not even be legal."

"I'm afraid that's a moot point, Charlotte," Aaron said. "It won't help us even if it's true."

The back door opened to admit the Tyler children. Philip was a ten-year-old replica of his father. Both the Tyler men were medium-sized, well-built and agile. They had brown hair and brown eyes that were quick to laugh, and their smooth skin was browned from the sun. They were serene, confident and competent. Father and son alike were popular and respected by their peers.

Six-year-old Sara was a sunny, extroverted child in whom the dark blonde beauty of her mother and grandmother had been magnified. Charlotte was lovely, Olivia was quietly beautiful, but Sara was stunning. Like the Stoddard women, she had dark brown eyes and curling, honey-colored hair, worn long. She moved with a grace and self-confidence surprising in a child. The delight of the family, she had such an abundance of charm that Aaron feared she might never feel the need to develop character. She was the apple of his eye and she adored him in return.

"Ginger's pulled up lame, Grandpa," Philip told Will Stoddard. "I checked for a stone and didn't see one."

"I'll go look at her, Flip. Thanks for telling me." Will Stoddard rose, effectively closing the meeting. He put a beefy arm around Olivia's shoulder and hugged her. "I'll call you later, let you know what Joe Jenson says. And don't worry. Your old daddy can still take care of his little girl."

The car was more comfortable than most Army vehicles, and Ed was satisfied with Paul's driving. In fact, the major was satisfied with everything about the sergeant. The two men had been together almost four months and developed a friendship as well as a working relationship. Their comradeship bridged differences in age, education, rank, religion and politics.

"What do you think, Sergeant? Hungry yet?"

"I can wait, sir. Another thirty miles will put us out of the Lake City sector and into the Gainesville sector. It'll probably be a lot safer to stop then."

The major grinned. "Fine with me. I like being safe even more than I like to eat." He opened the map and flipped on the dome light to supplement the dwindling daylight. "We're on 247, right? Won't that take us right by the park?"

"I'm not sure, Major. One of their favorite things is switching highway markers. Whatever the road, we're heading southwest, and we ought to hit 129 before we get to the Suwannee River."

"Miles to go before we sleep, right?"

The sergeant smiled. "Before we even eat, I'm afraid, sir."

Major Ed Shearson was Semitic in appearance, dark and stocky, just beginning the middle-aged battle against a re-

ceding hairline and an advancing waistline. A good Army officer, bright, well-trained, motivated, he loved the milieu of
good-guys-versus-bad-guys. The life's work he had chosen
was, he believed, a virtuous, important occupation; but even
more than that, he thoroughly enjoyed it. Hurtling through
the twilight with his faithful comrade-at-arms, skirting the
danger zone (in this case, Ichetucknee State Park, which had
been taken over by God-only-knew which group of rebels),
plotting the safest route to their assigned rendezvous—it was
glorious fun to the major. And one of the reasons he was so
fond of Sergeant Paul Cordray was that he sensed in Paul this
same little boy, cops-and-robbers, cowboys-and-Indians men-
tality. At any rate, the sergeant seemed mighty eager to get
on with the mission.

The two of them could go for hours, even days, without
thinking about the AIDS epidemic. They were too busy dealing with the results of the disease. AIDS itself, with its hundreds of thousands of deaths, had almost become secondary
to the multiple ramifications within the structure of society
that were the outcome of the epidemic. The government, including its military arm, was busy trying to hold the country
together despite the deaths, the increasing number of those
infected, the riots and violence. To the military mind, AIDS
had ceased to be a disease and had become simply an enemy
that was devastating America.

"Do we still have some of that trail mix?" asked the major.

"In the glove compartment, sir."

"Mind getting me a handful?"

"Glad to, Sergeant."

For more than a hundred years, the name Jenson had meant
the law—and political clout—in Pine River. For almost as
long as there had been a town, there had been an attorney
named Jenson to advise, caution, organize and instruct the

townspeople. As often as not, a Jenson had been mayor, and several men by that name had been sent to the state government in Tallahassee. They never achieved high office; they hung predictably, contentedly and prosperously around the middle rungs of the state's Democratic Party power structure.

In 1999 Pine River's current crop of Jensons was a father-son combination: Carl Joseph Jenson, Senior and Junior. They continued to occupy the family home on Lafayette Circle and still used the old-fashioned suite of offices on First Street. The legend emblazoned on the street-front window, *Jenson & Jenson, Attorneys-at-Law*, had actually been painted there forty years ago in 1959 when Carl Joseph, Sr., had passed the Florida bar and joined his father in practice. And now *he* was the father, the senior partner.

This particular Jenson was called Joe. He was now sixty, with thick, white hair, still in the pink of health, still full of fire and enthusiasm for the machinations and manipulations of small-town politics. He was smooth and subtle, hiding his intellect and education behind a facade of folksiness and the poor grammar typical of Southern men of his generation. On this Thursday evening as the cocktail hour approached, he gave his face its public visage—an expression of benign wisdom—then opened his office door. No one was in the outer office but the two-girl staff (although one secretary was 34 and the other in her 40s, the Jensons always referred to them as "girls"), and Joe's face relaxed. "Where's Carly?"

"He's in his office, Mr. Joe."

"Tell him I'd like to see him." The girls knew the Jensons had drinks every evening, of course, but Joe never spoke of it to them. *None of their business*, he thought.

"Hi, Dad." Carly entered smiling and Joe warmed with his customary pleasure. Carly was an eminently satisfactory son. He was tall and handsome, a charmer, a sharp dealer and a rising attorney. He was Joe's immortality. "Heard about the mess over in Branford?"

Joe handed his son a glass and smiled. "No, been in the books all afternoon. What's happening?"

Carly shook his head. "I don't know myself for sure. The news was confusing, but there's a state of emergency over there, curfews and the like. I gather some group took over the power station, cut phone lines. That kind of thing."

"Branford's getting too close for comfort," said Joe uneasily.

"The Lake City forces don't seem to have much control of anything," Carly continued.

The phone rang. "This is Joe Jenson. Oh, hello, Will. How's it going? Really? Tell me about it. Of course I'll do whatever I can."

As Joe spoke, his voice became deeper and more soothing. As he had a public countenance, so he had a public way of speaking. He pushed a button and Willoughby Stoddard's voice was amplified through the room. Both Jensons listened to the story of Olivia Tyler's notice of conscription.

"Ah, just to make it official, Will, I have to ask: Olivia is testing clean, isn't she?" Joe's smooth voice was almost a purr.

"'Course she's clean! She works right in the school, in the clinic. She gets tested so often she's practically anemic from the blood loss!"

As Will's strident voice quieted, Joe spoke soothingly. "I know it seems like the end of the world, Willy, but people *do* come back. It isn't a sentence of death, you know."

"Same thing as. How can you stay with those people all the time—live and work right in an Infected Zone and not get infected? And Olivia's a nurse. She'd be touching them, giving them baths and God knows what else!"

"I'll call around, Will. See what I can find out. Ah, I hesitate to mention this, but—ah, what if I *could* work it, but I had to sort of, ah, show some appreciation in certain quarters? How would you feel about that?"

"You talking about a bribe, Joe? Buying somebody off?"

"That's a pretty blunt way of—"

"I'm a blunt guy, call a spade a spade. But sure, I guess so, if it's the only way. How much we talking about? Thousands? Tens of thousands? More?"

"I have no way of knowing, Willy. I haven't even talked to anybody yet. I'd like some idea of how far you're willing to go."

"I don't know." Will spoke more quietly. "I don't have much cash, don't have much of anything but land. Never thought I'd need to be buying off a bunch of crooked politicians to save my girl's life. But I will if I have to. Whatever it costs, I'll get it somehow."

"I'll make a few calls and get back with you." Joe hung up and turned bright eyes to Carly. "How about that? I'm sorry about Olivia, of course, but Will Stoddard just wrote us a blank check, by jingo!"

"Has he got enough to get excited about?" Carly asked.

Joe Jenson was thoughtful. He knew, of course, that Will had inherited wealth; both the Jensons and the Stoddards had lived in Pine River for generations, and as an attorney, he was in a position to know something about who owned how much of what.

"He's got plenty. He said it; he's got land, miles of it. Lots of river front, land the Stoddards been sitting on since Depression days." Joe smiled a smile of pure pleasure. "Now maybe you and I can sit on some of it."

Carly drained his glass and left his father's office. The outer office was empty now, the girls gone for the night. The street-light outside cast a shadowed duplicate of the window's legend, *Jenson & Jenson*, across the carpeted floor. Carly stepped delicately across their names, his thoughts racing. Olivia Stoddard Tyler was Iris' older sister, the quiet, settled, decorous, unquestionably clean older sister of Iris Stoddard, Carly's current inamorata.

Olivia had been drafted! And old man Stoddard had enough money to set Joe Jenson's eyes agleam with greed. This required thought. It took something exceptional to excite old Joe this way. How could Carly use this information, these relationships? For surely information was power, and power was meant to be *used*.

The sign read,

> ## Pine River Diner
> ## 60 Years in the Same Location
> ## Under New Management

For some reason Iris Stoddard always read the sign as she entered, wondering, *Same location, new management. Am I the same or am I new?* She was never able to answer.

Waitressing here was an ideal job for her: It paid well, she worked around friendly people, and covering the dinner shift meant she was often gone from home when her father, Will, was there.

Not that she had a problem with her father; no, it was more that he had a problem with her. It seemed as though from the time Iris was born, something about her had bothered Willoughby Stoddard, and after 28 years she was sick and tired of trying to fix it.

Most men had no problem with her at all. Like the other females in her family, Iris was a brown-eyed blonde, but smaller and more lush, much more self-aware, and she used more cosmetic assistance. Iris had an open, friendly nature. Her goal in life, the very star she steered by, was *fun*. An early marriage had ended after three years, and two later liaisons had died because they had ceased to be fun. But even in tiny Pine River there were still plenty of men who were glad to have *fun* with Iris Stoddard.

It was quiet for a Thursday night and by 9:30 only two tables were still occupied. Iris had bussed her station, refilled the condiments and was rolling silverware in napkins when the two uniformed soldiers entered. They avoided the tables by the windows and moved to a back booth.

Iris picked up menus and approached them engagingly. "What'll you have?" The bigger the smile, the bigger the tips.

The older of the men, who looked like an officer, smiled back and asked, "What do you recommend?"

"The chicken and dumplings are good. There's a dinner plate with turnip greens, biscuits, homemade applesauce and dessert."

"Sounds very Southern."

"Well, this is the South, honey." Iris drawled out the last word; she was having a good time. Two new men, both friendly and good-looking, especially the younger guy. He was a typical matinee idol type—tall, slender, dark, handsome.

"Chicken suit you, Paul? O.K., give us two of the dinners. And coffee right away." The older man opened a map and spread it on the table.

They were still poring over the map when Iris returned with the coffee.

"You know this area well?" the officer asked her.

"I've lived here all my life."

"Look, I'm Major Shearson; this is Sergeant Cordray. We need to meet some people in Cross City and we need the quickest, safest route. Can you help?"

"Sure. It's pretty quiet over there. You shouldn't have any trouble." Iris pointed to the map. "Take 51 down to 27 and go left. It's about 25 miles south."

The sergeant spoke for the first time. "But it gets tricky in the dark when the road signs are either missing or wrong."

Iris smiled brilliantly. This younger one was a prince. She had already noted that he wore no wedding ring.

"What's happening in Cross City?" she asked.

Major Shearson answered. "We're putting together a new Finger Squad, slated for duty in Belle Glade. Our medical consultant is in Cross City and we're picking her up first. We collect the others in Tampa."

"Well, you ought to see some excitement. Tampa's bad enough but Belle Glade is horrible." Iris made a face.

"Have you been there?" the sergeant asked.

"No, but—you know, you hear things."

"Well, wish us luck," he smiled.

Iris floated to the kitchen pass-through window to pick up their dinners. What a glorious man, this young soldier! Too bad he was heading into the worst section in Florida—some said in the whole Southeast.

Suddenly she realized she'd forgotten to scan their finger-prints to assess their health status. An official declaration of negative blood testing was required to eat in a "clean" restaurant, and the almost total computer connectivity now in place made it possible to contain, regulate and report all blood test results from one central computer.

An Army uniform alone used to be enough to verify a clean bill of health, since all the military services tested every three months and anyone infected was separated. But now some of the escapees from Quarantine Zones were wearing stolen Army uniforms, and regulations required restaurant personnel to see each customer's current readout, checking identification numbers and pictures carefully. No problem. She would just ask now. It only meant there would be more talk—a great way to pass the hour till closing time and her date with Carly Jenson.

✧   ✧   ✧

No electricity again, no way to cool things down. Everything was hot—the air, his drink, the patients, tempers. And here it was *September!* Fall, for cripe's sakes! Burton Chancey wiped the sweat from his brow with a paper towel and pitched it into the wastebasket. *Sweat is a body fluid,* he thought. *You can almost certainly grow a virus in sweat. I wonder if there are any growing in mine.* He often said he didn't fear infection; he expected it.

A large, pale man, Burt had thinning hair and a reddish complexion that warred with the Florida climate. He took another swallow of his Scotch without rocks. Was it possibly his destiny to be the last gay man in America *without* the dread HIV?

He could see a glow in the eastern sky. West Palm Beach had lights. Of course, they always did. All the nice, clean, healthy *straight* people in West Palm had their air conditioning, their television, their blasted *ice cubes.* But not Belle Glade. Why waste energy on a bunch of worthless people who were dying anyway?

Almost time for the call from Atlanta. Why was his call always scheduled for evenings? He always had to face these calls when he was tired, discouraged and often just a little drunk. He rehearsed in his mind.

"I don't mind the hard work. I don't mind the danger of disease. I don't mind trying to give decent terminal care to almost ten thousand men, women and children with totally inadequate facilities and staff. But you *must* arrange to police this area and make it at least safe enough to function in." He warmed to his message. "It's like trying to run a hospital in the inner city slums, with gangs, violence, drugs and crime. Can't we get some soldiers? National Guard troops? Something. Boy Scouts! *Girl* Scouts! Anything!"

Dina Hawks knocked once and stuck her head around the door. Her head was strangely round, capped with short, shaggy

hair. Her body was also round. She was shorter than average
with sloping shoulders and very short arms. In fact, she almost
looked like a caricature until you saw her eyes; they were sharp
with intelligence and at variance with the soft, round body.

She spoke. "Did you finish with Atlanta?"

"They haven't called yet. I've been practicing what I'll say
when they do. Come on in." Burt nodded toward the Scotch
bottle. "Help yourself to a drink. Sorry, no ice."

Dina found a cup, filled it halfway, took a swallow and shuddered. "How I hate this stuff! To me, Scotch tastes the way
dirty feet smell."

"That's picturesque."

Dina chuckled and sat down heavily. The "Office of the
Director" of the Roy Fitzgerald Memorial Hospice was a par-
titioned corner of a steel shell building, the rest of which
served as warehouse, supply depot, armory and overflow for
patient care. The office was furnished sparsely. There were
desks for Burt (who was the director), his secretary and his
assistant, Dina. There were file cabinets, a telephone switch-
board, a bookcase, extra chairs and a long table that had supported their computer until it was stolen. The office was neither cozy nor comfortable, but it was familiar.

"Have things calmed down in Post-Op?" Burt asked.

Dina nodded. "They started singing, of all things. Somebody from that new batch got them all singing. They settled
right down."

Burt smiled. "Music hath charms to soothe the savage
patient."

"It was pitiful, in a way. Some of those guys didn't know
any of the words to songs like 'I Been Working on the Rail-
road.' You wonder what kind of background they come from,
there are so many holes in their knowledge. In their whole
lives, I guess."

Burt eyed the older woman with curiosity. *Talk about back-*

grounds you wonder about, he thought. *Talk about lives with holes in them . . .* But he said simply, "Yeah, I guess so."

Dina Hawks was an interesting woman. She had been an executive with a large department store chain, a gloriously successful '90s woman, happily meeting and beating men on their own turf. When her commitment to her career destroyed her marriage, she hardly noticed. When her two daughters married, she was relieved. It meant that now, at age 49, she had even more time to give to her vocation.

Then she tested positive for HIV and within 72 hours was inside the "Infected Area" of Belle Glade—quarantined for the rest of her life. She had unpacked her inappropriate clothes and gone to work. She was tireless and efficient. Purposeful. No job was too lowly or unsanitary for Dina. She was an enormous help to Burton Chancey. But no one, not even Burt, had seen one inch below the surface of her calm efficiency.

"They're late calling, as usual," she observed. "Doesn't that aggravate you?"

"I'm fine. Ready to say all the things I always say and hear how sorry they are, but keep up the good work."

"You *are* doing good work, Burt. Nobody could possibly do it better."

"Then how come all I see is people dying?"

"Cause that's what these people do."

The telephone rang.

Iris smiled when the sergeant approached the counter. "Need something else?"

"We wondered if you'd rinse out this thermos and fill it with coffee, please." He handed over a battered two-quart thermos.

"Sure. I just made a fresh pot. Late as it is, I figured I'd pour half of it away, but now you come along and solve my problem." She began running water into the thermos as she continued. "I'm mighty sorry you all have to go to Belle Glade. You must really hate the Army for sending you there."

"Sorry, but you're wrong. Twice. I love the Army, and they aren't sending me there; I volunteered."

"You *volunteered* for Belle Glade? What's the matter, got a death wish?"

He shook his head and laughed softly. "No, it's more what you might call a life wish."

"You'll have to explain that one."

"Did you ever hear of the Moravians?" The sergeant sat down on one of the counter stools and leaned toward Iris. "They're a religious denomination and they really loved God. This was back a hundred years or so ago. I don't know what's going on with them now, but back then they *loved* God. They went out soulwinning, not because they wanted to help the people—though I guess that was part of it. But mostly they did it for God. They had a motto: 'To win for the Lamb the reward of His suffering.' They even sold themselves into slavery to witness to the slaves, to evangelize and minister. They were simply magnificent."

The handsome face across from Iris was radiant, but she saw little of the beauty of this young man's zeal. She saw a fanatic, an extremist, a frightening radical.

"So that's why I'm going to Belle Glade. Almost everybody there is a slave—a slave to one thing or another. Disease, drugs, crime; they're all outcasts from society. They need to be set free. They need to know Jesus."

"Well, that's . . . nice."

Paul Cordray laughed heartily and Iris recognized the weakness of her response. She smiled with some embarrassment.

"No, honey. It's not 'nice.' It's either godly and glorious or it's damn-fool stupidity. I'll admit there are times I favor the latter viewpoint."

She handed him the thermos with genuine liking. As he

returned to his superior officer in the back booth, her eyes followed him. Such a gorgeous man, and he had to be a religious fanatic. What a waste!

From June to November of each year, somewhere between sixty and a hundred low pressure waves are formed off the west coast of Africa and begin traveling eastward. About ten of them become strong enough to be rated as tropical storms, and six, on average, develop into hurricanes.

The hurricane is widely acknowledged to be nature's most destructive force. It is a tropical cyclone, an area of low pressure around which winds flow counterclockwise in the northern hemisphere, spawned and nurtured in the tropics. In the Atlantic, the eastern half of the ocean within a few degrees latitude of the equator is a choice site to birth a hurricane.

The easterly trade winds from Africa flow over water that is usually warmer than 80 degrees Fahrenheit; a low-pressure disturbance may divert part of this warm easterly wind toward the north. The air is constricted; it rises—sometimes as high as 40,000 feet—and heat and moisture are released. The earth's rotation can impart a twist to the rising column of warm, moist air until it becomes a cylinder, whirling around a core of relatively still air.

On Thursday, September 9, 1999, these conditions existed off the coast of the Cape Verde Islands. The Geostatic Operational Environmental satellite, passing over at a height of 22,500 miles, transmitted images of the phenomenon to the National Weather Service. It would become one of the sixty to a hundred or so storms they watched each year.

It was a time of day Aaron always enjoyed, that little window of serenity between the children's bedtime and the time the adults went to sleep. He sat with Olivia on the living room sofa, their four bare feet resting on the coffee table, watch-

ing the news on television. The distressing accounts of the
world situation usually contrasted with the peace within their
own home, but now the horror had invaded their personal
lives. Olivia had been singled out, and in some obscene way
the precious, unquestioned circle of protection around their
family had been broken. Aaron was sick with dread and anger.
How could this possibly be? Could lawful, elected, sanctioned
authority really mean to abduct his wife?

Olivia took his hand. "We might as well go to bed," she
said. Her voice, her face, her posture spoke exhaustion.

"You really need some sleep."

"I don't think I'll be able to."

"Livvy, honey, try not to be too upset. We're Christians,
and there's comfort and grace available if we can just receive
it."

"I'm not upset, Aaron. I'm terrified and furious and bro-
kenhearted and sick to my stomach and in the worst pit of depression I've ever imagined. I'm not upset."

Aaron could identify. He had all these, too, plus guilt that
he was unable to protect his woman. "I know, honey. But there
are still all the promises of God to sustain us."

"I don't want to hear about receiving grace, counting it all
joy, yielding to the will of God—none of that. I want God
to stop this thing! If He can't, or won't, I don't know what
I'll do."

"Maybe it's all still so new—"

"No, Aaron. Don't you understand? I don't want grace to
stand this, or God helping me live through it. I don't want a
God who just sustains me through disaster. I want a God who
prevents disaster."

Aaron caught her to him. "Oh, Livvy, sweetheart, I don't
know if there are any gods like that."

Olivia buried her face on his chest and sobbed.

✢   ✢   ✢

Carly Jenson never came into the diner to get Iris. He always parked around the corner, away from any streetlights, and waited in the car. He wondered if Iris resented this—did it look like he was ashamed of her, of having a relationship with her? But what else was he to do?

He was listening to music with his eyes closed, his head resting on the headrest, when she knocked on the window. He reached to the control panel on the console and clicked open the lock on the passenger side. "You're late tonight."

"A couple of military guys came in late and we got to talking. They're headed for Belle Glade."

"So what was the attraction, the soldiers or Belle Glade?"

Before Iris could answer and they began their sparring— that ageless, ritualistic, male-female role-playing with the predictable exchange of accusation, protestations of innocence, jealousy, flirting—Carly remembered Willoughby Stoddard's call and spoke with rare emotion. "Oh, Iris, I'm sorry. You were thinking about Olivia, weren't you?"

Iris could play the verbal mating game with the best of them, but now she looked plain confused. "What's Livvy got to do with anything?"

"Haven't you heard? She's been drafted. She's ordered to Belle Glade in a few weeks."

"You're joking!" Iris looked stunned.

"No, it's true. Your dad called the office for help."

"Nobody called *me*. I guess it never occurred to anybody. I'm only her sister."

Carly smiled in the darkness. This was to be expected. It wasn't unheard of for bad things to happen to Olivia, but it was rare. Livvy was the lucky one and the Stoddard family favorite. Carly could even anticipate Iris' response. First she would be annoyed with her father. No matter how he handled things, she would find something to criticize. She always did. Next she would be glad. Oh, she would hide it, say all the right things about poor Olivia, how dreadful, what can we do to prevent such a terrible thing, but underneath Iris would be happy as a clam that such a catastrophe had struck her sister.

"Well, can you all help her? Will she have to go?"

"I don't know. Dad's going to handle it. But even if he can get her off, it still might mean she'd have to leave Pine River."

"You mean go in hiding somewhere?"

"Maybe."

"That's almost as bad. No, that's silly. Nowhere is as bad as Belle Glade. But she'd still have to leave her home, the family. I guess Aaron and the kids would go, too."

Carly waited a few moments, then asked, "Does this mean we can't go out tonight?"

"I guess so. I guess I ought to go on home." She opened the door. As the dome light came on, Carly examined her face. He saw some shock, some confusion, but also just a hint of pleasure.

"Will I see you tomorrow night?"

"Oh, I don't know, Carly. I'll have to see." She shut the door without kissing him and walked back toward the diner. He started the engine and followed her slowly until she was inside her own car with the doors locked.

He wasn't much of a gentleman and did not know the meaning of the word *chivalry*. But in 1999 it was part of the game for the male to protect the female, and no sane female resented it.

2

Friday, September 10, 1999

It was a clear night in northern Florida; the temperature was in the mid-60s and a light wind was blowing. It had not been easy to fall asleep with her mind so full of tomorrow's big adventure, but by 3 A.M. Dr. Cassandra Kovaks slept as soundly as a tired child, beside an open window in the bedroom she had known since her childhood. The familiar room, the intimate murmur of the wind sighing through the limbs of the massive oak tree outside her window, the ordinary night sounds of this old house, all sang a lullaby that finally hushed her excitement.

She was the second Dr. Kovaks in Cross City; her father had practiced medicine here for nearly thirty years. Soon she would join him, as they had always planned—a family of doctors practicing family medicine. But first she had this term of service to work out to pay off the last of her student loans. For six months she would serve as medical consultant for one of the U.S. Army's Emergency Investigative Teams—the so-called Finger Squads. And it would all begin in a few hours.

Across town, in a medium-priced bed-and-breakfast, Major Ed Shearson and Sergeant Paul Cordray slept in adjoining rooms. Ten years earlier they would have found lodging in a

motel, but the precipitous decline in automobile travel had
rendered those establishments unprofitable. So an old enterprise had been revitalized by the need to replace motels, few
of which had enough business to stay open anymore. Private
homes opened to paying guests, a return to the practice customary earlier in the century before automobile travel became so commonplace.

The men slept lightly, never unaware of conditions around
them. A step outside their door, a whisper of motion in the
hall, and both men would awaken instantly; listening intently,
evaluating. They enjoyed no breeze; their windows were
locked, heavy drapes drawn. These men knew far more than
young Dr. Kovaks that danger roamed abroad, even in the
peaceful town of Cross City. The universal target of the lawless ones was *authority*, and who personified authority better
than the military?

The violence and anarchy that had germinated in the inner
cities had now spread like a malignant fungus across the face
of America. In many locations, chaos reigned. Laws were
flouted, enforcement was lacking and penalties were inadequate. Pockets of peace and security like Pine River and Cross
City were designated "clean." But appearances could be de-
ceiving, and professional soldiers know that vigilance often
spells the difference between the quick and the dead.

Aaron slipped carefully out of bed. Olivia had finally fallen
asleep and he did not want to waken her, but he was restless.
Maybe warm milk would help.

He flipped on the small light over the stove, poured milk
into a pan and turned on the burner. The kitchen felt strange.
He was never up at this time of night.

"The thing that makes or breaks you isn't the circumstance
you face," he quoted to himself. "It's the nature of your response." But that kind of thinking implied you could control

your response; it assumed some sort of choice. Aaron felt no such luxury in his dilemma. It took all the control he had not to run shouting into the night. Was he going to lose his wife?

Even five years ago this situation would have been unthinkable. There had been AIDS, of course, but it had not yet so radically, irreversibly altered the structure of American society. Aaron thought about what he knew of the development of AIDS from the early days when it was called GRID, the Gay-Related Immune Deficiency disease. Back then it was simply news; it was *their* disease and held no threat for mainstream America. It became instead a civil rights issue, a point of political conflict masking the fact that for the most part it was a formidable, aggressive, adaptive, species-threatening, incurable, one-hundred-percent-fatal disease.

From the beginning, news releases about AIDS were not aimed primarily at disseminating information. No, there was another agenda to which the media had adhered faithfully: to calm the public, play down the danger and educate society to tolerate the homosexual lifestyle. For a long time the number-one weapon used against the threat of AIDS was education. The primary goal was never to curtail the spread of the disease; it was to control the public's response.

But this campaign was effective only temporarily. As the disease spread, multiplying geometrically, alarming statistics battered the media's theme that "these sick people are victims." Now Americans were bombarded with statements like: *For every known HIV carrier there are a hundred who are unknown;* and *Each AIDS case costs approximately $150,000 to treat, and these funds are taken increasingly from tax moneys;* and finally, *The human race will be extinct within fifty years.*

The individual's right to privacy and protection from discrimination slammed against other individuals' rights to remain uninfected. One of the first of these confrontations—

and undoubtedly the most flamboyant—was the conflict between health care workers and their patients. The laws concerning who-has-to-tell-whom, and who-can't-refuse-to-deal-with-whom exacerbated the conflict as policemen, food-handlers, morticians, schoolteachers, cosmetologists and barbers, childcare workers, even tattoo artists refused to work in close contact with anyone who could not produce proof of cleanliness. The AIDS activists howled, the ACLU cried foul and laws were passed, but these were increasingly ignored.

Gay-bashing now became AIDS-bashing against those considered responsible for bringing the disease into American society. The legal clout, the entitlements, the laws protecting AIDS carriers from discrimination and defining AIDS as a disability, the media bias toward the infected as victims—all these began to erode. The uninfected began to clamor for their rights, too. The AIDS epidemic had cost the taxpayers of America over $800 billion and carriers were no longer the underdog to be pitied and succored. They were now the adversary.

For several years carriers claiming a violation of civil rights had won handily in the courts. But things had begun to change. Teachers removed from classroom duties when they tested HIV-positive, who had consistently won legal appeals for reinstatement, began to lose. Infected children who claimed the right to be educated with other children within the school setting were denied entrance. Juries now refused to award large settlements to plaintiffs who claimed discrimination by employers, insurance companies, the medical community or providers of services.

The public as a whole discounted the proclamations of the experts. The previous errors were too glaring, the lies too obvious. As late in the AIDS game as 1984, the executive director of the Council of Community Blood Centers argued that testing would create "unnecessary anxiety" among donors whose blood might be rejected. In February 1984 the Task

Force of the Centers for Disease Control stated for publication that "no evidence exists that this is an infectious disease." Many remembered that the medical community had known as early as 1982 that AIDS could be transmitted via blood transfusions, but that no testing was done until the spring of 1985.

It was widely publicized that in August 1982 the officials of the New York Blood Center had claimed, "There is no evidence that AIDS can be spread through blood transfusions. The legal protection of donor confidentiality cannot be breached." That message was amended to: "The risk of getting AIDS from a transfusion is about one in a million." These odds were later altered to one in 10,000, later still to one in 5,000. Even after that, the Secretary of Health stated, "I want to assure the American people that the blood supply is 100 percent safe."

The public remembered all this in the face of over 100,000 deaths from contaminated blood alone.

In 1984 the American Hospital Association's official recommendations had required all healthy hospital employees to work with AIDS patients, stating, "There is no scientific reason for healthy personnel to be excused from delivering care to patients with AIDS." After thousands of health care workers were infected, they began to ignore the recommendation.

Stories were spread of falsified death certificates, of slanted statistics, of adjusted records. The AIDS "experts"—the men and women of the medical community and media who had denied the infectious nature of the disease, discounted the risk of blood transfusions, suppressed the information that the AIDS virus was present in tears, saliva and sweat, and censored information about the spread of the disease through household contact—had lost all credibility. They still maintained that casual contact was safe, but few listened anymore to their pronouncements. The public knew their agenda—

don't inflame the gays, don't alarm the healthy—and was no longer buying.

Then came the phenomenon of Critical Mass, when the AIDS situation became a new ballgame.

Aaron remembered the first time he had heard of Critical Mass, on a talk show featuring a debate between panels of doctors concerning Critical Mass. What was it? Was it real? Had it been documented in other epidemics? If it happened, how would it happen?

Critical Mass, one of the doctors explained, was that process by which the increased incidence of a disease, with its concomitant increase in the number of pathogens extant, evoked a change in the methods and facility of transmission of the disease. Simply speaking, it meant that the more cases of AIDS there were, the easier it would be to catch it. An inflammatory statement indeed!

This doctor claimed that this process had been evident in past pandemics, and cited the Bubonic Plague in Europe in the 1600s as a case in point. In the beginning, he said, the disease was spread only to those actually bitten by a flea that had previously bitten an infected rat. But after significant multiplication of the number of cases, it was possible to catch the disease by way of droplet infection—by inhaling the tiny drops of moisture sneezed out by an infected person. Critical Mass had made it easier to become infected.

The other panel of doctors denounced this theory. They claimed there was no evidence to support droplet contagion and that only an idiot would trust medical records from the 1600s or base an opinion on such documentation.

The next testimony cited by the "Pro" panel on behalf of Critical Mass was evidence of transmission of the AIDS virus by vector (by an organism that could transmit a disease-producing microorganism). They based this claim on good old twentieth-century scientific evidence. The "Con" panel laughed them to scorn. A totally unwarranted assumption, contrary to the best current medical opinion. Mosquitoes carrying the AIDS virus from human to human? Ticks? Bedbugs? Ludicrous! The opposing panels battled to a draw; no consensus was formed that the public could take as truth.

But *something* had happened. The number of AIDS cases seemed to explode. They were everywhere: Eighty percent of hospital beds were given over to AIDS patients and the medical system staggered under the weight. Many insurance companies went under as a result of the cost of their care. Increasing numbers of patients remained outside of the usual AIDS categories—they were monogamous or sexually inactive, not users of intravenous drugs, not exposed via blood transfusions. How had they been infected? The medical community argued different theories with increasing hostility. But all agreed on one point: Something had changed.

The epidemic raged and America changed. It was no longer possible to ignore AIDS. Now they could come into your home and take your wife away.

The milk was boiling and Aaron poured it into a coffee mug. It tasted unpleasant but he drank it down, burning his tongue in the process.

I can't imagine that'll help, he thought as he rinsed the cup and pan.

He decided to check on the children. It wasn't something he usually did, but the situation with Olivia had altered his emotional climate. His unspoken assumption that nothing would go wrong had been shattered.

Sara wasn't in her bed; she often slipped into Philip's room, sleeping at the foot of his bed like a puppy. Olivia did not approve of this and Aaron knew she would want Sara returned to her own room. So he crossed the hall and opened Philip's door.

The room, bathed in light from the hallway, looked as it always looked. The walls were decorated with Star Trek posters and pictures of horses; the desk was a clutter of books, baseball cards, CDs and copies of *Sports Illustrated;* the bookcase was overflowing with puzzles, rocks, electronic games and model cars. The bed was messed up. The pillow was on the floor.

There was no sign of the children.

Burton Chancey lay quietly, eyes closed, consciously relaxing his muscles. It was hideously late and his mind groaned in anticipation of the headache, lassitude and irritability he would harvest in the morning from another night of too little sleep. But he was literally too busy to think during the day; it was only during the dead of night that his mind roamed so despairingly over the barren fields of his life. He laughed without humor. What a phrase—*the dead of night!* And accurate, for the forces of darkness and death reigned during the night hours. It was then that grievous thoughts overwhelmed him.

Of the 40,000 AIDS patients living in the Belle Glade Quarantine Zone, about a quarter were classified as terminal, meaning death was imminent. These people were Burt's special responsibility and he felt it keenly.

Many, of course, chose the suicide machine, but even so, the patient load was staggering. The ratio of worker to patient was totally unacceptable and the body count, as always, was rising. The whole place was a failure. His precious hospice was nothing but a tired, miserable finger in the dike in the battle against AIDS.

In the small picture, his glorious sacrifice, his daring choice to leave his New York success to head this brave endeavor, had accomplished exactly nothing. All his abilities and compassion had done nothing to slow the ghastly toll of torment and death. He could hardly even consider the big picture. He could not wrap his mind around what might happen in the future.

But his talk with the powers-that-be in Atlanta had produced one tiny ray of hope. They had finally agreed to send an investigative team to Belle Glade. That much they would do.

So they were on the way—a Finger Squad of soldiers, medical personnel, sociologists and maybe other types coming to see what was needed in Belle Glade. Burt could tell them if they would listen. Of course, they had to get there first, to make it through the dangers that were becoming more and more commonplace in Florida life.

Aaron sat at the table by his wife. There were lights and sounds from outside, people and cars gathered in the driveway and on the lawn. Their tidy, homey kitchen was crowded. Both Joe and Carly Jenson were there; Aaron had no idea who had called them. There were two sheriff's deputies, a man from the Highway Patrol and two other men in suits who were probably some kind of federal officers.

Will and Charlotte Stoddard were there, along with Iris, and Aaron noticed that his mother-in-law had fixed coffee and was forcing it on everybody. Typical of Charlotte. Her immediate—and often her only—response to crisis was making coffee. Too bad she did it so poorly.

Iris was perched on the stool next to the stove watching everyone around her. Her expression was unreadable. Carly Jenson stood near her, looking as though he needed a cigarette. Aaron's anguished mind wondered dully if the rumors about these two were true: Had Iris really been foolish enough to become Carly Jenson's latest lady?

Will Stoddard was talking to the investigators. Aaron listened to their quiet conversation and felt the old resentment rising. This was Aaron's home, Aaron's family. Where did Will Stoddard get off acting like he was in charge? But in the face of catastrophe, this jealousy of his father-in-law seemed suddenly petty.

Olivia had aged ten years in the past hour. She was huddled at the table, apparently unaware of the activity around her. Aaron reached for her hand but she ignored him.

The uniformed state patrolman approached and stood respectfully until Aaron acknowledged him. Will Stoddard and Joe Jenson joined them. For the first time Olivia looked up. "Daddy, do you know where they are yet?"

"Livvy, this is Captain Ruiz." He nodded at the uniformed highway patrolman. "He has some ideas."

The captain cleared his throat. He seemed to have trouble meeting Olivia's eyes and addressed his remarks to Aaron.

"Well, to begin with, we think we know their vehicle. Your neighbor was in your yard about two; his cat was tangling with a gopher. There was a panel truck in your driveway at that time." He consulted his notebook. "A white panel truck with the sign *Otto Krause, Tip-Top Painting*." He shook his head in amazement. "Can you beat that? Committing a capital crime in that kind of vehicle!

"Anyhow, they must have come in through the back door there; that lock is sprung. They seemed to know which rooms to hit. Shows they cased things at least a little. Or maybe just got lucky. They used some kind of inhalation anesthesia and it could be they were in and out in five or six minutes." He looked at Olivia. "Your mother doesn't think they took anything, clothes or possessions. She checked for us."

"Didn't they worry that we were here?" Aaron felt such anger and horror that it was hard to breathe. The effrontery of these people! To walk right in and drug and kidnap his children, confident he could do nothing to stop them. As it turned out, they had been justified in their belief; he had almost certainly been awake during the crime and had heard nothing.

"I imagine they'd have killed you if you'd discovered them," the captain said quietly. "That's the kind of people we're dealing with."

"But why?" Olivia pleaded. "Why did they want *them?*"

"We don't know all the reasons, ma'am, but we know some. None of them's decent and you'd do well not to be thinking about it."

"Captain, I don't want to be protected. Please tell me anything you know."

The captain looked at Aaron and he nodded in consent. "Well, there's some men who want to use them for pictures, that kind of thing. Maybe rent them out, but they usually keep them pretty healthy. They feed them and all. These men are what's called chicken hawks. A bad lot, but not the worst. Your kids are blondes, right?"

Will Stoddard answered for her. "The little girl is blonde. The boy's hair is browner."

The captain hesitated. "There's more demand for blondes. Other groups sell them. There are people who use them in rituals—"

Olivia gave a strangled cry and Aaron shook his head. "That's enough, please." He felt bile rising in his throat and thought for a moment he was going to vomit. Then the sensation subsided.

One of the deputies spoke. "Whatever their reasons, I'll bet they're heading for Belle Glade."

"Why would they go there?" Aaron asked.

"Belle Glade has what you might call a free trade market," the deputy explained. "Anything you want to buy or sell is there—drugs, guns, women, forged passports and certificates of health. Whatever makes a good profit is for sale there. And that includes kids."

Will turned to the captain. "Is that right?"

"Oh, yes. If those kids are still alive, they're on their way to Belle Glade." Now he addressed Will. "You know, there's just a chance you might be able to get them back; snatch them away from the kidnapers. It's not an easy trip to Belle Glade nowadays. They can't just hop on the interstate and tool on south. It takes planning and weapons and connections, plus a good bit of money, and if they're dumb enough to use a truck with a *sign* on it, for Pete's sake, they may just be dumb enough to keep the same vehicle. And it might be that a couple of smart guys with the right connections could catch up with them."

"Tell us the truth, Captain," interjected Will. "Is there really a chance?"

"Not much of one, but there's no chance at all if you don't try. There's not enough law left down there to put your faith in. It'll take money and a good car and some good weapons. And somebody who knows the kids. They change them right away, probably already have. Cut the hair, dress boys in girls' clothes, things like that."

"You know any men who do this kind of work?" Will asked.

"I might get some but it'll cost you."

Aaron stood up. "No, no, we don't want to hire anybody. I'll go myself." His words were addressed to the captain, but he was facing Willoughby Stoddard. "These are my children. I'll go get them."

"You know what you're doing?" the deputy asked.

"I can drive a car and I know the kids. I'm a fair shot with a handgun and I can blow the eye out of a squirrel at three hundred yards with my rifle. I was born in this state and I know it as well as most locals. And I have one other thing going for me. I love those kids better than life itself. That's something we'll never get from a mercenary."

The three men stared at him. The captain, the deputy and Will Stoddard stood in silence as Aaron faced them. His breathing was labored and he was crying, but for the first time he felt a tiny flutter of hope.

"I don't know . . ." Will began but Aaron broke in.

"It's my decision, Will. I don't need your permission."

There was silence for a moment. Then the captain spoke. "What kind of weapons you got, son? You gonna need any ammo?"

Now there was feverish activity. Will Stoddard had turned over four or five credit cards and his personal debit card to Aaron, then left to get cash for the trip. Both the Jensons noted the fact that he would apparently have no trouble getting his hands on thousands of dollars in cash—or something else as negotiable—at five o'clock in the morning.

Charlotte began packing food—canned drinks, fruit, packaged crackers and granola bars. Aaron could not count on finding restaurants open south of Orlando.

The two sheriff's deputies were checking Aaron's small arsenal of weapons. He owned two matched .38 revolvers, a small .22 automatic, two shotguns and his prized rifle, a .30–.06 Mauser. His supply of ammunition was low and they were discussing what to add.

Aaron, Captain Ruiz and one of the federal officers were gathered around the table, studying a map of Florida. Aaron's face was intent, still tear-streaked but no longer shattered. He was alive with purpose and determination.

Iris Stoddard had been through a searing change in the last hour. Her not-quite-admitted pleasure in Olivia's conscription now seemed a hideous blasphemy. This present horror overwhelmed her lifelong resentment of her older sister and filled her with tenderness and sympathy. Her mind was brimming with memories of her niece and nephew: the years Flip had called her "Irith" because he couldn't pronounce an *s;* this past Thanksgiving when she had taught Sara how to do a cartwheel; the unconditional, wholehearted love both children had demonstrated for Iris all their lives—and how often she had looked on them as an irritation.

Suddenly the sight of intent men huddled over a map kin-dled a memory. She rushed over to Aaron. "I almost forgot! There's an investigative team going to Belle Glade; I met the soldiers at the diner last night. Maybe you can hook up with them."

The captain responded first. "That would be a good idea, but aren't they already gone? What time did you see them?"

"They were going to Cross City for the night. They're picking up their medical person. They'll be there till after breakfast anyhow. Can't you call? You could tell them to wait."

The captain suddenly grinned at Aaron. "Son, it looks like maybe you're being dealt one decent card after all. Miss Stoddard, do you have any idea where they were going to stay or the name of their doctor?"

"I know it's a woman and she's just finished medical school."

"That ought to be enough. Cross City isn't that big." He hurried to the telephone and Aaron gave Iris a hug.

They were still arm-in-arm when Olivia walked into the kitchen carrying a suitcase and a small, dirty stuffed bison. She was dressed in jeans and a University of Florida sweatshirt and her golden hair was tied back in a ponytail. Her face, devoid of makeup, was set in grim determination.

"I'm going with you, Aaron. I'm your second man." He began to protest but she kept talking. "I can drive, too. Maybe I can't shoot as well as you, but I can shoot. I know this state, too, and I can read a map. And—oh, Aaron, I can't just sit here and do nothing but worry while you all are gone. I have to *do* something. I have to help."

"Livvy, it's dangerous. There's all kind of evil—"

"But don't you see, I don't *care!* I don't want to be safe if you're all in danger! If you all die, I don't want to go on living. Please, can't you understand that?" Suddenly she smiled, a smile of real amusement. "Anyhow, I was *ordered* to go to Belle Glade, remember? I have a paper to prove it."

Aaron looked at her dubiously. "So you're all packed and ready to go?"

She nodded. "I brought Buffalope." She held up the dirty little bison. This was Sara's most beloved toy, a homecoming gift brought by the Stoddards from a trip to Montana. His name was a combination of *buffalo* and *antelope*. "Sara will be so glad to see him!" she added softly.

Suddenly all three were crying—Aaron, his wife and her sister, sobbing in an awkward three-way embrace. Buffalope was hugged among them because somehow he represented the stolen children. "If I could, I'd take Ginger along to give to Flip," Olivia sniffed.

"We can't stick a horse in the back of a van, Livvy." Aaron disentangled himself from the women and wiped his eyes. "Besides, Ginger belongs to Will."

"You said *we*, Aaron. *We* can't stick a horse in the van. Does that mean I'm going?"

"I think it's a bad idea, and it's wrong of me to take you into that kind of risk, but I do understand how you feel. I know I couldn't just sit home and go crazy worrying about everybody else. Yeah, you can come with me." Aaron pulled his wife close to him. "I'm always a better man when you're with me. You bring me luck! Sure, come on, honey. Let's go get the kids!"

"I'm coming, too." Iris felt almost as surprised as the Tylers looked as she made the announcement. "Look, it'll take two people awake all the time, one to drive and one to navigate and ride shotgun. I can drive. I want to go."

"I can't let you risk your life."

"Aaron, I want to do this. I *need* to do it—for Livvy and for the kids. And I need to do it for *me*. Please, Aaron, let me come with you."

It was almost certainly her appeal to his authority that won his favor. That was Aaron's soft spot and Iris knew it. But it was also the flow of the moment, and she knew as she spoke that he would agree.

What she did not know was why she wanted to go so badly. She was not turned on by danger; there was no thrill in high-adrenaline situations for Iris. She preferred comfort and safety like any normal person. Nevertheless, she felt an irresistible call to join this gallant little caravan of rescue. It appealed to her as nothing she had ever done. She felt as strongly as Olivia did that she *had* to go.

Was it the gorgeous sergeant? Was she fool enough to risk her life just to see him again and be with him? How could that be? He was a radical, Bible-thumping fanatic and there was certainly nothing appealing about *that*.

Carly had gone outside into the Tylers' backyard to smoke a cigarette and talk with his father. He always found he could think better, evaluate and form opinions better, after talking with his father. It wasn't that the old man told him what to think; it was just that things got clearer.

"We really fell into the sugar bowl this time, Carly." Joe laughed softly. "We got lucky!"

"How so?"

"Well, for months now I been trying to figure how to sell some silver. I got almost seventy pounds of silver in bars, and I think it's time to sell. And the best market in the world is in south Florida. I just couldn't figure how to get it there, and now we have the answer. The United States Army is going to protect us and our silver! Government troops with federal passes, and we'll just travel along on their coattails." He chuckled. "And if that don't work, we'll have Aaron Tyler and his squirrel gun."

"Dad, how can there be such a great free market if people can't get to it without risking their lives? Seems like that would limit their customers."

"Most of the people who buy and sell there sort of have their own law. Who needs the Metro Dade police if they got a hundred Colombians armed to the teeth?"

"Oh, I see." Carly dropped his cigarette and ground it out with his toe. "So you and I are going to Belle Glade?"

"Well, I don't think we both need to go. Somebody has to take care of Pine River." Joe smiled sweetly, a sure sign of devilment. "Maybe you're ready to go it alone on this one."

"You're staying here and I'm going to Miami to sell the silver? Do I have any choice about it?"

"Come on, Carly, it'll be an adventure! We'll never find a safer situation. And folks will never forget what a brave and unselfish thing you did, helping the Tylers."

"And we keep the silver deal quiet, right?"

"Well, that's nobody's business but ours, is it? You run on home now and get your things. They'll be pulling out pretty quick."

Carly walked obediently, disbelievingly, to his car. All his life he had known approval and affirmation. And despite the fact that his father was an almost totally selfish man, Carly had known love. Now, at age thirty, he realized with a shock that there might be things his father loved even more. Was it possible that Joe loved gold and silver and power more than his own son and heir?

Had he been a clearer thinker, Carly might have enjoyed the paradox of the situation: Aaron Tyler was risking his life and braving dangers in order to rescue his son, while Joe Jenson was sending his son into the same dangers for that all-American purpose—to make a buck.

Every Friday morning Burton Chancey and his assistant, Dina Hawks, made rounds through the hospice. They were usually accompanied by the Director of Nursing Services and the various unit supervisors. It was the only time they saw every patient and it was always a wrenching task to Burt. He had been here almost two years and was still not used to the reality of death.

They began with the admission ward. There were over a hundred new patients being worked through the admittance routines—mostly males, mostly adults. Many opportunistic diseases were in evidence; some patients were still fairly healthy while some appeared close to the end. But they shared one thing in common: an emotional climate of fear and anger.

As Burt walked among them, they watched him silently. Sometimes he spoke to them but more often said nothing, avoiding eye contact where possible. Suddenly one man stepped forward and faced him.

"I know you. You're Burt Chancey. I remember when you came here. You were a senator, right?"

"Congressman, actually."

"And you started the Gay Liberation Front, didn't you? You were going to put *us* in control of everything—treatment, research, money, all the laws on AIDS." The man was leaning toward Burt, aggressive in tone and demeanor. "So tell me, what happened?"

"We accomplished a lot. We have full governmental subsidies for treatment, full handicapped rights, full minority rights, affirmative action, full—"

"I was picked up, quarantined, shipped off down here with no hope of ever getting out, just because a bunch of bigoted, so-called upright citizens are scared they might catch something. Like I'm a leper or something! Like I have no rights at all."

Burt was uncomfortably aware of increasing interest from other patients. This was the kind of thinking, the kind of talk, that led to riots. And often the new patients were the most likely to rebel. America was becoming more and more polarized into *us* and *them,* and both camps were moved to excesses when they concentrated on the opposite side.

Burt spoke quietly. "They're still the majority, and they're becoming more and more concerned with self-preservation. But we must apply our efforts to the things that pertain to us and our needs and try not to concentrate on *them.*"

"But I get really boiled when I think they have the power to pick me up, practically *kidnap* me, and lock me—"

"And they get just as boiled when they think about the tax money spent on medical care for you. It's not like it used to be, friend." Burt smiled with all the charm he could muster. "But this isn't the time to talk. We'll have to get together later on and have a good chin-wag about it. I'd really enjoy hearing what you have to say."

The other man smiled sardonically. "Anytime you say, Chancey. I'm not going anywhere."

Iris chose her clothes for comfort—jeans and sweatshirts as well as shorts and T-shirts. The calendar said autumn but she knew south Florida would still be hot. She took two suitcases, one for clothes and one for cosmetics, curling iron and such. She wanted to be beautiful as well as attired. She threw her own pillow, a portable radio with new batteries, headache pills, the novel she was reading and her camera into a separate carry-all.

When she drove back to the Tyler home, Aaron was loading the van in the driveway. Most of the crowd was still there—policemen, the neighbors and the curious. In the kitchen Olivia and Charlotte were closing and taping the food boxes that Charlotte had filled, and one of the deputies was packaging shotgun shells at the table. The house was chaotic, the kids' rooms still sealed off by the police, clutter and mess everywhere else. Iris had never seen her sister's home in such disarray. But then, never had Olivia's life been so disordered.

Willoughby Stoddard was furious. When he had returned from his expedition to get cash and found out Olivia was going on the rescue, he had not believed it at first. Never had this compliant, virtuous daughter defied his authority. But the bulk of his anger was directed at Aaron for agreeing with her mutiny. When Will learned that Iris was going, too, his rage was truly frightening. Almost his entire family would be in critical danger and he could do nothing to change it. Now he was sitting on the steps to the back porch and had not spoken for more than an hour.

Iris approached him. It was not unusual for her to feel her father's angry disapproval; it was the climate in which she lived. She felt some small satisfaction at his present distress, much as she had enjoyed Olivia's call to work at the Belle Glade hospice. Years of painful trial and effort, her failure to please him, and her resentment at being so consistently inadequate had flavored her love for both her father and her sister with resentment.

But minimizing the residue from past problems was the enormity of the present and the uncertainty of the future. She spoke to him with tenderness. "It's going to be all right, Daddy. We'll all come back safe, and we'll get the kids, too."

Will looked at her intently, studying her face as though trying to memorize every line. Suddenly her hugged her to him almost painfully, and she could feel his heavy body shaking with sobs. It had been literally years since they had even touched, let alone hugged, and Iris was not comfortable with the intimacy, but she patted his back comfortingly and murmured gentle words.

Will drew back and stared at her through red-rimmed eyes. "You all better come back, you hear? Your mama and me, everybody we love'll be in that van and we just couldn't survive to lose all of you."

Iris nodded without answering. Her heart was singing and an incredible spring of well-being was bubbling up within her.

Why, he does love me, she thought in surprise. *Maybe not as much as Olivia, but he does love me. And for the first time I can remember, I'd rather be me than her. Right now, today, I'm the lucky one!*

Carly Jenson owned few clothes that were appropriate for a trip like this. He selected his expensive workout garments, some casual slacks and the oldest of his shirts. He paused in his packing to consider what else he might need: shaving gear, shampoo, his vitamins. . . .

Joe Jenson entered, breaking into Carly's thoughts. He was struggling under the weight of a small suitcase. It was dull aluminum with a black handle and large, efficient-looking locks. Joe heaved it onto Carly's bed and the springs sank under the load.

"Here's the silver. Seventy pounds almost exactly." Joe caressed the case with a loving hand. "I tried to catch the Tokyo price but I was too late. It doesn't matter much since it'll be at least a week or ten days before you get there and who knows what it'll be going for then."

"Dad, I'm not sure I can do this. How do I make contact with the buyers? I can't just put an ad in the *Miami Herald*."

"You look for an opportunity, boy. You expect things to work for you and they do." Joe poked through Carly's suitcase with interest. "Things'll open up. You meet somebody who strikes you as kind of interesting, you get a certain feeling about him and you drop a hint or two. He responds, you open up a little. That's how it works. Time you learned. Say, you don't have anything decent here. You need a good suit, you need to dress rich for this kind of operation."

"Well, I don't need to dress rich for the trip down." Carly was fighting his anger at his father. "Remember, I'm supposed to be helping find the kids. I'm not going to wear an Armani suit to fight rebels and INFECTEDS."

Joe chuckled. "I guess you're right. But take something along."

"I can only take two bags, and one of them is full of silver, leaving only one for *me*."

"You'll be fine." Joe smiled his happy smile and Carly turned away. He walked into his large closet to select a suit. What did one wear to sell silver on the Miami black market? He chose a dark gray.

They did not get away till almost eight in the morning. Considering that four different people had to plan and pack and about eight different people were making decisions about the trip, it was remarkable they moved as fast as they did.

Aaron was driving, and Olivia took the passenger's seat. Iris and Carly were in the swivel captain's chairs behind them. The van was bulging with luggage and supplies—guns and ammunition, sleeping bags, food, water, ten five-gallon cans of gasoline, a radio, maps, first-aid kit, Coleman lanterns and flashlights and tools. And right on the dashboard, in the role of mascot and ship's figurehead, was Buffalope. Olivia had held it close all morning for comfort.

Captain Ruiz was issuing last-minute instructions. "They promised to wait till noon and you have the address of their bed-and-breakfast. Even if you have trouble, you should make it to Tampa in a couple of days, and you can telephone home from there. I wouldn't count on it much farther south. Check with the Hillsborough County sheriff about the kidnapers' truck. I put the description on the wire."

Charlotte Stoddard was crying. Will stood with his arm around her shoulder, his expression bleak. He had kissed both his daughters but he did not speak to Aaron. Joe Jenson had changed clothes and was looking cool and dapper as usual. He shook hands with Carly through the van window and winked cheerfully.

"Well, wish us luck," Aaron said. He started the motor and began to back out. Then he paused. "No, I take that back. Don't wish us luck. Pray for us."

3

Friday, September 10, 1999

Paul Cordray was always an early riser, and this morning was no exception. He had showered, shaved and eaten by six o'clock. Like many military men, the sergeant was groomed meticulously. His dark hair was regulation short, and even though he wore fatigues, his uniform was immaculate. Tall and lean, he looked somewhat older than his 28 years. He was an Army brat, the second of four sons, born to a love of military life. Two of his brothers were also Army men, the third a Naval officer. Their parents, retired now to California, had weathered the storms, separations and instability of service life to raise sons with character and purpose who were a credit to their name.

Major Shearson joined the sergeant after seven in the kitchen of their bed-and-breakfast. They listened to the national news on the radio as the major ate his breakfast. None of it was an aid to digestion.

There was more controversy about conscriptions. An altercation had occurred between the Oregon State Militia and a gang of escaping INFECTEDS, with high casualties on both sides. The water supply in Baltimore had been polluted by vandals and an investigation was underway. More highways were closed in Virginia; the governor had issued a warning to any groups hiding within the Shenandoah National Park. Border skirmishes along the Rio Grande were increasing as the INS attempted a crackdown on illegal aliens. Rioting at Tulane University had resulted in hostages being taken; the campus police were powerless. And the dollar was down slightly against most foreign currency.

Another good start to another good day.

"That was a great meal," Major Shearson said approvingly. "I must say I could get hooked on this sausage and gravy thing. How about you?"

"Well, I didn't have any sausage, sir."

"The doctor should be here by nine, but I told the people from Pine River we'd wait till noon if needed," the major explained unnecessarily. "You get the car ready and I'll see what I can learn about conditions between here and Tampa."

"Yes, sir." The sergeant downed the last of his coffee and walked out to the driveway.

Aaron Tyler had had no formal schooling past the twelfth grade but he was a well-educated man. He had that thirst for knowledge that is the hallmark of a scholar, along with the initiative to study and learn. He was widely read on any number of subjects, but his special interest was history. In particular he knew American history, and it was natural to compare his current circumstances to situations in his country's past. He thought of the westward expansion of America in the mid-to-late 1800s. How similar the experience of those pioneers was to that of travelers in the late 1990s!

Because the pioneers had faced dangers in their journeys across plains, mountains and deserts, they had banded together in wagon trains for safety and mutual assistance. It was exactly the same today. A caravan of many vehicles would intimidate all but the most determined adversary. And like the

Conestoga wagons of old, the Tylers' van could carry the provisions they would need (and might not be able to obtain along the way) for their journey.

But the American pioneer had no monopoly on the idea of a caravan. Travel had been dangerous in many societies; if not Indians, then highwaymen threatened the wayfarer. Likewise today only the foolhardy traveled alone. The enemies might be different but the peril was the same: armed men preying on travelers. The solution: banding together to travel and using guards. The large trucks that delivered most consumer goods around the country now drove in convoys, and most had a backup in the cab "riding shotgun." Despite gun-control laws, this was an increasingly literal description of the second man's function.

Aaron drove at a steady 55 miles per hour. There was almost no other traffic but he was vigilant, especially for roadblocks ahead. This was a common ploy of the rebel gangs, and Aaron had no reinforcement built onto the front of his van that might help him batter through such a barrier. Iris and Carly were talking quietly behind him, but he tuned them out.

Glancing at Olivia, he was pleased to see her alert, watching the road ahead. She held the shotgun carefully. Like most country girls, she had been raised around guns and was trained to handle them properly.

"How're you holding up?" he asked softly.

"I'm doing O.K. I get a bad spell every now and then, but I can function. Don't worry about me. I can do what I have to do." Her voice and her face were determined.

"That's good, Livvy, because it's up to us, you know. Not those Army guys or anybody else. Us."

"I know that."

"But we can do it. We know their truck, we have people to travel with, we have the Lord on our side. We can do it."

"We *have* to. We couldn't stand it if we lost them."

Aaron reached across and squeezed her shoulder. Yes, that was the goad, the whip: How could they endure life without the children? But people did. Other people lost loved ones and they lived on—even achieved a degree of healing and moved beyond the pain. But *how?* He could barely handle the present, while there was still hope to buoy him, spur him. What if hope were gone? How do you endure the unendurable?

He looked at his wife, this quiet and gentle woman who had always radiated peace and tranquillity. Now she was stony-eyed with purpose, emotions sternly under control, shotgun gripped tightly—a lioness robbed of her young. The female of the species was truly more deadly than the male.

He drove on in silence.

Dr. Kovaks helped his daughter unload her baggage from his car, kissed her goodbye and left without meeting any of her colleagues. She approached the olive drab car where Paul Cordray was cleaning the windshield, stuck out a friendly hand and smiled. "Hello, Sergeant. I'm Dr. Kovaks. There's my stuff; hope I didn't bring too much. Mostly it's books, textbooks and all. I mean, you can't have too many books ever, can you?"

Paul was surprised at her. He knew she was thirty, two years older than he, but she looked incredibly young. She also looked too innocent, too wholesome, to be so educated. She looked as if she had just stepped off a bus from the farm. She was tall, athletic in appearance, with an open, sunny face bare of makeup. Her dark, curly hair was tied back casually in a ribbon, and she seemed as happy as a kid at Christmas. Cheer and enthusiasm were rare attitudes these days.

There was a pile of luggage: three expensive leather cases, a duffel bag and two large boxes—the books, no doubt. Paul opened the trunk and began rearranging the bags already packed. No way would it all fit; some things would have to be carried inside the car.

"Where's the major?" she asked. "He seemed nice on the phone. Do you know when we'll leave? Don't we have some troops to, you know, guard us?"

"Major Shearson is on the phone with the highway patrol, assessing the best route from here to Tampa." Paul spoke as impersonally as possible. Until relationships were established, and even after, he enjoyed the security of military protocol. He would treat her with every courtesy, but maintain a distance. "We'll drive there as directly as possible and pick up a squad of APs—Air Police—at MacDill. Meantime we have another vehicle to caravan with us, a family traveling south to try to rescue their children who have been abducted. We'll leave here as soon as they arrive from Pine River."

Her face clouded at the mention of the children. "Well, two cars are better than one, right? How long do you think it'll take to get there? You know it isn't but a couple of hundred miles. To Belle Glade, I mean. Tampa's only what, like a hundred, maybe?"

"Something like that, I believe, but we can't always take a direct route. We have to avoid the danger points, if we can."

She nodded. "Well, I think I'll go use the restroom. I always need to go real often when I'm, you know, like, excited, and I bet the major wouldn't like having to stop."

She trotted off toward the house and Paul watched her curiously. She was not your everyday medical consultant, that was for sure. A different breed of cat, indeed. But how would all that cheer and good will stand up to the reality of the torment and death she would face?

The Pine River contingent pulled into the driveway of the bed-and-breakfast at exactly nine o'clock, and within a few minutes the seven travelers were sitting around the major's room, reserved and awkward in forming these new and vital relationships. They were committed to a common cause, and their very lives might depend on the faithfulness and competence of the others, but for now they were strangers. They observed each other covertly as the major examined the Certificates of Health printouts for the Pine River group.

Aaron liked the soldiers on sight and whispered to Olivia that maybe their luck was holding. But it was more than liking; both military men impressed Aaron with their air of competence. They radiated professionalism and assurance. The doctor was another matter. She seemed flaky, and her enthusiasm was almost an affront. For now, though, Aaron would give her the benefit of the doubt. Olivia maintained her icy control, and Aaron could tell she was indifferent to her companions.

The major mapped out their strategy.

"There are two ways of looking at it," he began. "We could get on 19 and barrel on south; it would take us within fifteen or twenty miles of Tampa. It's four-lane, limited access, and sometimes that's the safest thing to do. But when they block a major road like that, it's usually a disaster. They don't try it without twenty or thirty guys, at least, with some heavy-duty weapons, and the motorists don't stand a chance. I've been on the radio and the phone to get an idea of what's safe, and I've got us routed through for the first leg."

He spread a well-creased map across the bed and motioned Aaron closer. "You know this area, right? So anything you want to suggest, speak right up."

Aaron and the doctor bent over the map to follow the major's finger. "Dixie County's pretty quiet, so let's say we take 27 over to Old Town, then go south on 349. I know that's the kind of road they like to ambush, but so far as anybody knows there aren't any gangs around there, and there are two cars of us and plenty of weapons. We can handle anything minor. We'll cross the Suwannee River south of Manatee State Park and take these secondary roads through Levy County. If we're lucky we ought to make it to Lebanon Station, maybe even Dunnellon, by afternoon. Highway Patrol tells me we can buy gas there, and they still have restaurants."

Aaron nodded thoughtfully. "Sounds good, given the original decision to avoid main highways."

"You don't agree?"

"I don't know enough to say."

"It's not just a question of does somebody blockade us, and do they get control of us," the major explained. "It's also a question of who they are. There are different kinds of gangs. Some of them would just take our vehicles and guns and supplies and let us walk away, alive and unhurt. But there are other gangs that might want to infect us or even kill us. These people are so full of anger and hate, they lash out and hurt anybody they can get hold of. They might leave us our cars—maybe they don't especially want our possessions—but they'd give us a little IV before they let us go, especially Sergeant Cordray and me. They hate authority and anything even resembling the law.

"And that's the kind of gang that operates mostly on the big highways, interstates and turnpikes. We might drive right through without a hitch, but if they did blockade us, we'd end up either dead or dying."

The whole room was silent. Was this what faced them as they drove south? Each person reacted as the words hit.

Carly and Iris, sitting side by side on the other bed, were exchanging looks of consternation. The trip sounded more like a gauntlet to be run than merely an adventure. Carly fought new feelings of fear as well as anger against his father, while Iris wondered what had happened to her enthusiasm for the enterprise.

Olivia was thinking of the children, battling one of her

What is happening to them right this minute? attacks. *Are they hungry, cold, together? Are they being brutalized?* No threat to her own person had the power to torment as these questions about the children.

The sergeant was standing by the dresser, idly polishing the glass of the major's binoculars. He was peaceful. He had no fear such as he sensed in the lawyer and the young lady sitting on the bed, and no urgency like the parents of the kidnaped children. Nor did he have an opinion about the route; that was the major's call. The sergeant simply believed his steps were ordered by God. What might appear to an observer as military discipline was in reality spiritual tranquillity.

"Whatever you say," Aaron said, yielding about the chosen route.

"You planning on using debit cards or what?"

Aaron hesitated. It seemed illogical to withhold information about their financial situation when they were trusting these men with their lives. But still he felt uneasy. He compromised. "Yeah, mostly."

"Right. Our car'll go first, at least for now. How's your rear vision?"

"I got a big back window and two side mirrors. They can't sneak up that way."

"Regular glass in the windows?"

"Yeah. I never thought I'd need anything more. I wasn't planning a trip into the Quarantine Zone."

"Mostly you need something to keep the shattered glass from flying around if it gets hit. Even a blanket or something can help. 'Course, then you can't see." The major grinned and Aaron smiled back.

"If there's a roadblock ahead, we'll do everything we can to push through. We don't stop unless it's absolutely necessary, a genuine blockade or tires shot out or some such. Remember, they usually come up behind—also with some kind of barricade, maybe just a car, but they try to get you caught between two barriers. So if we see an obstruction we'll signal you, and you cover the rear."

"I understand." Aaron hoped he sounded more confident than he felt.

"You signal if they come up behind. Sound the horn: *Beeeep, beep-beep, beeeep.* That's long, short, short, long. We'll do the same." The major indicated Aaron's group with a wave of his arm. "Can any of you shoot?"

"Yeah, all of us, but I'm the only one really good." Aaron's words were a declaration of fact made without pride.

"So let somebody else drive, you ride shotgun. Keep one in the back armed, and that means holding the gun in their hands. All the time."

Aaron addressed the Pine River people. "Okay, Carly, you take a handgun and sit in the back. Livvy, you too. Iris can drive."

"What about you, Doctor?" the major proceeded. "Can you handle a weapon?"

"Not at all. I'm sorry, but I just never had, like, an occasion to learn. I mean lots of people around here do hunt, you know, but I never did." Dr. Kovaks had pushed her mirrored sunglasses up into her curls, and she carried a large shoulder bag made of patchwork quilting. She looked eager and earnest, like a college kid leaving for spring break. "My father was, like, real anti-guns, so there was that, too, I guess. I can drive, though, and that'll mean—"

"Fine." The major stood and looked around the room. "We got everything, Sergeant?"

"Yes, sir." The major and the sergeant were both wearing a sidearm; there was nothing of bright-eyed, youthful excitement about them. They were purposeful and professional.

"Let's do it, then." The major looked at himself in the mirror and adjusted his hat.

It was becoming dreamlike to Aaron, like a movie. This couldn't be real. Soldiers and caravans and guns and danger? But the major's next words broke the spell: "We'll all use the bathroom again before we go. It's pretty awkward, using a can in the back of a car in a mixed crowd." That didn't sound like any movie Aaron had seen.

But then, it didn't sound like his normal life, either.

For months now, Burton Chancey had followed the course of the patient he knew as Ken. Burt had noticed him as he was being admitted. Ken was typical of the patients Burt had come to rescue—young, still on the sunny side of forty, well-educated, cultured, gifted, handsome, full of promise and potential. And full of ginger. No placid victim, this one. Ken was a fighter.

He had addressed the admissions group that first day, Burt remembered.

"We must fight for our lives as we have fought for our rights," Ken had said. "We must *not* go gentle into that good night. Rage, my brothers, I exhort you, rage against the dying of the light."

It had all been said before, and better, by others. It was rhetoric, posturing, but it was also gallant and remarkably appealing.

Now Ken was dying—a few more days, a week at the most.

The cots in the ward were so close together there was barely room for the attendants to walk between them, but Burt managed to fit a chair beside Ken's cot. He sat down and observed the effects of eleven and a half months of AIDS.

For some reason, the diseases had fairly galloped in their conquest of Ken's body. There had been no quiescent periods, no remissions. After the original invasion by the Human Immunodeficiency Virus, there came an almost immediate onset of the first symptoms—coughing, night sweats, fever, weight loss. Quickly thereafter, Ken had been attacked by multiple enemies, by almost every pathogen known to strike AIDS patients. He was assaulted by parasites, fungi, viruses, bacteria, bacilli and protozoa. He was infected with herpes, salmonella, toxoplasmosis, encephalitis, hepatitis and tuberculosis. He had been blinded and deafened. He had severe lymphandenopathy, and a white fungus in his throat now made breathing difficult. He could no longer eat. He had no control of his bodily functions. He lay febrile, comatose, wasted. An IV dripped into an arm as shrunken as that of a corpse.

And thus would end all that glorious potential, battered and beaten by the Human Immunodeficiency Virus.

It seemed so remarkably *personal*, that virus. It was alive, of course, a living entity. Only the most materialistic scientist denied the thing had life, but it was more than that. It was full of evil intent, malicious, almost as though it possessed emotions.

Burt often fantasized: This was no mere germ they were dealing with. It was more like an alien, some outer-space being trying to cleanse the planet of intelligent life prior to taking over. Or maybe it was a demon from hell dispatched to impose the searing judgment of some hideous, homophobic god. It had attacked Ken's shield of bodily defense not only with astonishing efficiency and triumphant power, but with malevolence, anger and violence. The vigor of this enemy surpassed a mere biological dictate to grow and multiply; it demonstrated a conscious, almost deliberate rationale as it advanced toward its objective. And its goal was to destroy.

Burt took hold of Ken's withered hand. It wasn't clean, but with the current ratio of workers to patients it hardly seemed to matter. The hand was blotchy with the purplish-brown lesions of Kaposi's sarcoma. The fingers were curled inward and the nails long and yellowish. Burt had a sudden vision of his own hand ravaged as Ken's, the enemy's victory banners flying for all to see.

What more could I have done? What more can I do? I have achieved almost every goal. We completed the agenda and won all our points. But they still die! With all the money, all the control, all the political clout we demanded, we still lose. Almost all the young ones are gone now, the beautiful, gifted ones. All dead.

Burt lifted the ugly, waxen hand to his lips. "I'm sorry, Ken. I tried to save you. I cared. I tried." He was almost crying now. "I didn't want you to die."

Then a blaze of realization hit him. A shudder passed through his body and he dropped Ken's hand.

I did all this to save me! *All the young ones, all the good-looking, smart, accomplished ones—they're me. I'm the one I really don't want to die.*

His hatred of this enemy and his wholehearted pledge to battle with every resource available had been little more than self-interest.

"Never send to know for whom the bell tolls," he quoted softly. "It tolls for thee." Certainly.

After the whirlwind of preparation and excitement of the military-style briefing, the drive southward was anticlimactic. The road was two-lane blacktop, traversing flat terrain with only occasional curves and turnings. Routine highway maintenance, like much in these days of political and social upheaval, was inadequate. This neglect had allowed the profuse Florida vegetation to invade the easement, and as a result the highway verges were increasingly narrow. Given the number of large, flourishing trees, this produced an almost claustrophobic effect.

Iris was frustrated and bored, and the tension of the sleepless night just passed had left her with a raging headache. She had been driving for only a short time when she asked Olivia to replace her. Now the Tylers manned the front positions, and Iris and Carly Jenson again shared the seats behind.

Carly had swiveled his chair around until he faced the back window. Now he stared with a glum expression at the receding road behind them, holding one of Aaron's .38s limply.

"This is a hoot, isn't it?" he asked. "Gonna get waylaid any minute, get ourselves blasted to kingdom come."

Iris murmured something indistinct and he fell silent.

That had been their pattern, Iris observed, since leaving Cross City: silence, then one of the four would speak, usually receiving no answer, when silence reigned again. The intensity of emotion was oppressive. To feel so strongly and be able to do nothing about it was bizarre; to impose tedium on top of fear, anger and grief felt grotesque.

Suddenly Carly spoke. "Whoa, look out! Somebody's coming up behind us!"

Iris whirled around to see a rusty red truck approaching from the rear, closing the distance crazily between the two vehicles.

"How many in the cab?" Aaron asked.

"Two. Second man's got a shotgun."

"Give them the signal, Livvy," Aaron said, and immediately their ears were blasted: *Beeeep, beep-beep, beeeep.* The van wavered and plunged ahead, following the brown Army car, as Olivia accelerated. Aaron moved to the back of the van. The truck was close now, only a few yards behind the van.

"Hey, he's gonna shoot!" Carly screeched, pointing wildly behind them. The second man had shoved a shotgun through the side window and was leaning out to take aim. The driver was hunched over the wheel and Iris could see his teeth flashing white in a grin.

"Kill him," Aaron said quietly to Carly. He crouched down

on one knee between the two captain's chairs, his own shot-gun in his hand. "I'll get the driver, you take the second man."

A sudden burst of noise exploded the rear window. Iris felt a hot spray of something—glass? shot?—across her face and arms. She was shocked: The men in the truck had fired at them!

"Now, Carly. It's them or us." Aaron raised his gun smoothly. "Try and hold us steady, Livvy." Olivia was driving raggedly, still sounding the horn.

Carly raised the .38 and fired several times through the broken rear window; the sound of the shots compounded the din of the horn. His fist was white-knuckled with tension and Iris felt a flash of passion. Carly was more aggressive, assertive, protective than he had ever been.

He fired again. "Did I get him? Can you tell?"

Aaron squeezed the trigger of the shotgun and the explosion rang through the van. The rusty truck veered wildly across the road and plowed into the undergrowth, its horn blaring steadily.

"You got him!" Carly shouted. "He slumped over the wheel. I don't think I got my guy."

Aaron moved quickly to the front seat and put a steadying hand on his wife's shoulder. Iris, fascinated, saw her flash him a grin of pure delight. "Good for you, honey! Way to shoot!"

Then Iris turned again to catch the scene behind them. No one emerged from the cab of the truck but three men jumped from the bed of the pickup and were opening the driver's door when the van sped around a curve in the road and her view was blocked. Her mind was reeling, not only from the assault and her superficial but painful wounds. There was also the fact that her brother-in-law had shot and probably killed a man, and Olivia was delighted about it.

"Look out, Livvy," Aaron said sharply.

Iris swiveled forward again. The brown military vehicle

was still in front of the van with Sergeant Cordray at the wheel.
She could see Major Shearson at his side and the young doctor in the back seat. The sergeant was blowing his horn, the
same *Beeeep, beep-beep, beeeep* code. Beyond the Army car was
a confusion of cars, trucks and armed men. The road itself
was effectively blocked by a large furniture van parked across
the pavement. Other parked vehicles blocked the shoulders.
There was no way around; they would have to stop.

Aaron was gripping the shotgun. "Try not to let them see
you're armed, Carly. Put the pistol in your belt and cover it
with your shirt."

Carly obeyed with shaking hands. "How many men you
see?"

"Only six or seven out in the open. That don't mean that's
all there is."

The sergeant had braked and swerved to a halt about twenty
feet short of the blocking van. Olivia slowed down behind the
Army car.

"Pull up right next to them," Aaron said. "Close as you can
get." Olivia pulled over into the left lane and brought the van
to a stop beside the Army car. They were less than two feet
apart. Like the sergeant, she left the motor running.

"Livvy, the other .38 is right on the floor beside your seat."
Aaron sounded very calm. "You can just reach down with your
right hand and pick it up if we need it. You still got a gun,
Iris?"

Iris, terrified, murmured an assent.

Olivia picked up Buffalope from the floor where he had
fallen and replaced him on the dashboard. She rubbed a hand
along his back as though he were a cat.

Six of the waiting men approached.

"Y'all stay sharp," Aaron whispered. "Remember, if they
stop us from going on south, the kids'll surely die."

The sergeant rolled down his window and turned an unruffled face toward Aaron, not two feet away in the van. He nodded a greeting. "Let's try not to shoot each other, O.K.?"

Iris saw Aaron nod slightly. She could not see his face.

Willoughby Stoddard had lived all his sixty years in Pine River. He lived on family land, farmed the same acres his father had farmed, and held almost exactly the same opinions and attitudes his father had held. Will liked to say he was from good peasant stock, and certainly the Stoddards were men of the soil. But the Willoughbys were high-toned Atlanta folk, educated and cultured, the best of the Old South.

Lydia Willoughby, Will's mother, was university-educated; she had come to Pine River in 1934 to teach, newly graduated from the Georgia State College for Women. Within six months she had married Ed Stoddard, moved onto his farm and begun a demanding life as the wife of a dirt farmer with never a sign of regret. She acknowledged the social strata she had so willingly abandoned only in the naming of her son. Willoughby was a pretty highfalutin name for a country boy.

Will considered himself a good American, a patriot unashamed to wave the flag and love his country. He remembered the attack on Pearl Harbor in 1941 and the maps his parents kept tacked up on the dining room wall to help them follow war news on the radio. He remembered V-E Day, the Bomb and later V-J Day. It had been proper then to feel pride in America, and it was great to be a citizen of the best country in the world.

Then came the changes—wars America did not win; too many people with too many complaints and demands; betrayal by those in positions of trust; anger, protest and violence from young people presuming to instruct their elders. Women had railed against the roles of marriage and motherhood, seeking to be fulfilled—whatever that meant!—in men's functions.

The grief continued: a liberal oligarchy in Washington running the nation into a ditch; crime on the rise and criminals coddled; prices soaring and banks failing; welfare rolls swelling; and now the Japanese (of all people!) owning most of the country. The public schools graduated classes with more than half the students functionally illiterate.

Gone were Frank Capra and Sam Goldwyn. Movies, like books and music and television, were getting dirtier and more depressing. The nation had over five million *known* HIV-carriers, most of them still loose in society, and every dang-fool group in the country was demonstrating for its rights. It was harder and harder to be proud to be an American.

But only *now*, this day, had the forces Will had lamented so loudly actually reached his inner sanctum. Now his own family faced whatever evil had perverted American society, evil that had once been outside the familiar, the safe. Outside Pine River.

After the kids had left for Cross City, Charlotte had taken two sleeping pills and slept most of the morning. Will both envied and resented her oblivion. He himself was full of nervous energy, augmented by a dozen cups of black coffee. There was no question of his resting. Finally he decided to investigate what might truly await them.

He thumbed mentally through his potential sources of information. He considered Joe Jenson, the lawyer cum politician. Joe knew all that was worth knowing. Or maybe Baxton Burney, an award-winning newsman at Gainesville's leading television station—not a personal acquaintance but a possibility. Journalists always knew things. Or maybe his old beer-drinking buddy Jory Tinkman. Jory had retired from the Florida Highway Patrol and worked as a ranger at Ichetucknee Park. He was still hooked into the law-enforcement network, but more than that, Jory was nosy as an old granny and always had the latest gossip on everything.

In the end Will discarded them all and called Micah Boyd in Pine River. Micah was a long-haul trucker and made more trips to south Florida than anyone in the county. Micah was not a buddy; he did not hunt or drink or play cards. He did not raise horses and was gone from Pine River about half the time. But Will had known him for more than fifty years and realized with some surprise that he considered Micah a friend, someone he could count on.

He called the Boyds' home and Micah himself answered. It took only a few minutes to explain the situation and Micah agreed to meet at once.

"Come on over, Willy," he urged. "The wife's shopping and we can talk in private. You know where I live?"

"You're off Mill Drive, right? Beyond the high school?"

"Right. First place after you cross the tracks."

"See you in ten minutes."

Will left a note for Charlotte on the kitchen counter and drove off. His spirits lifted ever so slightly at this semblance of purposeful activity.

Sergeant Paul Cordray kept both hands visible, curled loosely around the steering wheel. He watched the men advance toward the cars, dividing into two groups of three each. They were white, poorly dressed, ranging in age from late teens through early forties.

"See any more?" the major asked quietly.

"Maybe a couple behind that blue Nissan," Paul answered. "I can't see your side."

"I don't see anybody, but that doesn't guarantee anything." The major turned to the back seat. "Doc, you keep down, there's going to be shooting. And keep your mouth shut."

Dr. Kovaks nodded. She looked ready to explode.

The two trios of highwaymen, meanwhile, had slowed their approach and were huddled in conversation fifteen feet away.

"Seems they're thinking it over, Major," murmured Paul. "They don't look real enthusiastic."

"Must have heard the shooting. Or maybe they're waiting on the guys in the red truck."

Aaron Tyler spoke quietly from the van idling next to the car. "Three more men near the blue car on this side—can't see what kind of guns they're carrying—and one man with some kind of automatic weapon behind that gray station wagon. We need to get him right away, soon as the shooting starts."

"Can you hit him?"

"Prob'ly. Wish I had my rifle out."

One of the highwaymen took a step forward and called out, "You guys Army?"

Major Shearson answered loudly. "That's right, United States Army. We're on official business."

Well, now they know we're not the army of Mexico or China, Paul thought irreverently.

"What about the van?" the highwayman demanded.

"They're traveling under our protection. We're a convoy." Everyone knew what that meant: All for one and one for all. If they attacked the van, the soldiers would defend them.

"Two cars ain't much of a convoy."

"Maybe you ought to count guns, not cars," the major said calmly.

"We got no quarrel with the Army. We're waiting for another bunch."

"Does that mean you'll let us pass?"

"I reckon." The man turned back to his cohorts and there was more huddled discussion.

"I think we just got lucky," Major Shearson breathed.

"Do you think the red truck was part of this gang, sir, or were they the target?"

Too many unanswered questions, Paul thought. *Do these*

guys even know about the red truck, and if so, do they know we took it out?

Two of the highwaymen walked closer and squeezed in between the van and the Army car. They peered inside, making sure no one was hidden within. They nodded knowingly at the shot-out back window and murmured approval of Iris. Then one stepped back and shouted at the armed man who now stood openly beside the gray station wagon.

"Hey, Vernon, move them vehicles out of the way over yonder. Clear a path." He turned back and spoke to Paul. "On your way, now. And don't think about coming back. It wouldn't be healthy."

The other highwayman grinned and nodded toward Iris. "You can leave that one here if you want to."

Paul said nothing and turned the wheel sharply to his right. Olivia was pulling the van around to follow him through the new opening in the barricade. They bumped down onto the shoulder of the road and swung wide around the furniture van. As soon as he had skirted the obstruction, the sergeant stepped on the gas, eager to put the roadblock and armed men behind them.

Dr. Kovaks spoke urgently from the back seat. "We have to stop, Major. I need to use the bathroom and there's, like, no way I can use that can. I mean, can you just pull over and—"

"What the heck was *that* all about?" exclaimed Major Shearson, ignoring her. He still gripped his gun. "I can't believe they were scared of us."

"I don't know, sir. I know the Army has a public relations problem, but maybe we still have enough of a reputation that they thought we could handle ten or fifteen men."

"The two of us?"

The sergeant grinned. "Why not? 'Our strength is as the strength of ten because our hearts are pure.' Maybe they were afraid."

"Well, I don't know about your heart, Sergeant, but I'd hate to put much confidence in mine." Major Shearson laughed. "Let's pull over, first good spot you see. We'll let the doc do what she needs to do and then she can take a look at Miss Stoddard's injuries. I don't get it, though. Why did they let us go? They didn't even take our guns. It's crazy!"

Paul considered briefly telling the major about the power of prayer. But it wasn't the time.

4

Friday, September 10, 1999

S ocial historians have asserted that in every documented
plague in human history, society has eventually imposed
quarantine to separate the infected from the healthy. These
historians further claim that there is a well-defined process
to chart the public's response to the danger of an epidemic;
and that after denial, anger and seeking a scapegoat, after civil
disturbance, violence and other predictable stages, those still
free of disease will eventually demand separation. Certainly,
these experts say, this stage would come in a plague that is
100Δ percent fatal.

It turned out, at least with the AIDS plague, that they were
right. Fidel Castro's Cuba began practicing mandatory testing and quarantine in the late 1980s. Even the harshest crit-
ics in America had to admit Cuba's program was successful in
one sense: It curbed the growth of the disease. Finally in the
United States, in response to rising public demands, a gar-
gantuan new governmental department, the Agency for
Relocation Policies and Procedures, was established by
Congress and given the daunting task of formulating and im-
plementing a quarantine program.

Under existing laws, however, it was an impossibility. The problems of trying to balance public health concerns against the legally established rights of privacy and freedom produced a chaos of red tape. It appeared that by the time quarantine came to America, in the plague named Acquired Immune Deficiency Syndrome, it was probably too late.

There never was a federal law mandating universal testing; there were, instead, literally dozens of federal statutes, state regulations and local ordinances, and hundreds of regulations decreed by various governmental bureaus, all aiming at different groups and activities. Prisoners, the military, health care workers, health care recipients, food-handlers, athletes involved in contact sports, students—more and more groups were ordered, as time progressed, to be frequently and repeatedly tested. But never was there blanket legislation that covered all citizens.

In addition to the legal confusion, there were not enough laboratories or trained staff to test millions of people. And millions of people were unwilling to be tested. Many who suspected they might have HIV simply refused; those ordered into quarantine almost universally resisted. To them, the right to life, liberty and the pursuit of happiness far outweighed the right of others to protection from the disease. To a society that for thirty years had emphasized its rights and deemphasized personal responsibility, testing was an infringement of personal freedom.

The problem of law enforcement was enormous; certainly there were not enough police to compel testing, and only the military had resources to enforce the quarantine. For the armed services to play a role in enforcing the law, however, required the repeal of the *posse comitatus* act, which forbade the use of military force to administer civil policy. This complicated issue had been tested in the '80s with military assistance to the counternarcotics effort. The law still maintained that the armed forces were limited to providing support and advice; only the DEA, FBI, border guards and local authorities could make arrests.

The question of the military's authority, like everything else, was bewildering, and the outworking of the answer varied enormously from one location to another.

Quarantine Zones were huge, often as large as several counties. The right of imminent domain was invoked and all the land, buildings and infrastructure within the zone were purchased to provide homes, schools, business opportunities—all the framework necessary for the functions of society.

Major concessions were granted: the INFECTEDS were guaranteed full support, the best medical care, opportunities to pursue whatever interests they had. Recreational and educational facilities were available. Loved ones who chose to join them were allowed to do so. The INFECTEDS had everything they might want, except the freedom to travel outside the Quarantine Zone.

The plan might have worked. It had a kind of logic: a self-contained community, much like other American towns, with schools, libraries, hospitals, museums, sports arenas, businesses, restaurants, markets, except that its inhabitants were all infected with HIV. It was the best solution, the *only* solution short of civil war. But not even those wearing the rosiest of glasses could call it effective, for none of it was successful. Almost no one submitted to quarantine.

So a whip was added to the carrots. It was decreed that medical care for AIDS patients would be given only within the Quarantine Zones. This had the effect of a final straw; it polarized the infected from the healthy with a finality and hatred no one could have foreseen.

Then the seeds of destruction that had been germinating for a generation sprang to life. The nation that had been the melting pot of the world became a hotbed of racial and ethnic hatred. Throughout the country, various-sized enclaves sprang up, each vehement in its hatred for the others and demanding sovereignty over its own destiny. What had begun with groups of so-called "hyphenated Americans"—those who were something else before being "just plain Americans"— had ended in polarization.

Burton Chancey had been part of it all. He spoke for the more moderate homosexuals and had never embraced the goal of destroying American society. He wanted gay rights, political clout and all the resources of government turned to the AIDS problem, but was wise enough to see that hatred and destruction would destroy his group, too. So he encouraged no malice toward straight society.

Many of the new admissions at the hospice, by contrast, bragged on the number of straights they had infected. They could die more easily, it seemed, knowing they had caused others to die. Burt could not agree with their thinking, although he would not judge them. For Burt, passing judgment was the worst possible offense. The highest virtue was tolerance.

He usually ate lunch with Dina Hawks. The hospice's cafeteria was housed in another of the large metal buildings, with high ceilings and huge windows looking out on a landscaped area. The acoustics were poor, the sounds loud and difficult to understand. At least today it was cooler; the air conditioner rattled along cheerfully.

Dina sat across the table from him, and as usual she had assembled a lunch of vegetables only. She was spearing Brussels sprouts with relish. "This meal is better, Burt, definitely up to adequate."

"I think they do pretty well, all things considered."

"I suppose so. Say, do you think they spit in this food? They do on the outside."

"Why would they here? *We* aren't the ones they hate."

"I don't know, Burt. I just think if you feed hate long enough, it gets to the point where it doesn't discriminate. It just hates."

"Well, maybe some of them. But I know most of the guys in the kitchen and they're not like that."

Dina spoke around a wad of spinach. "They had three deaths in the past week. That always stirs things up."

Burt stared at his plate, suddenly sickened. They were still saying the virus could not easily be spread through saliva, but what if it were mucus from lower down, coughed up from the lungs? So many of these fellows had pneumocystis, were always hacking and coughing, and their sputum would most certainly have the virus.

But far more than the disgust at what they might do to his food was the horror that one person could deliberately defile another. Not merely to take pleasure in the misfortune of another, but to cause it. That mindset was even more deadly than AIDS.

He pushed his plate away.

The rest of the day passed without incident for the two-car convoy from Cross City. Even Dr. Kovaks had little to say. She had dug a book from one of her boxes and was reading with every evidence of enjoyment. The soldiers shared the front seat in silence.

Aaron was driving the van. He ached with exhaustion and recognized the same state in his wife. He prayed they would be able to sleep—wherever they might be—when night came, but he doubted they could turn off the haunting of their thoughts.

In one of the back seats, Carly dozed through the afternoon, while Iris sat in thought. Her injury from the shotgun blast was minimal, and the ointment Dr. Kovaks had applied had taken most of the pain away. Iris was reacting more to shock than to physical trauma. As she reviewed the morning, she reexamined her opinion of her companions.

She had known Olivia all her life, of course, and despite her resentment and jealousy, Iris had to agree with the universally held belief that Olivia was wonderful. She was pretty and wise and wholesome; goodness oozed from every pore. Iris often said dryly that Livvy had read *Gone with the Wind* and become Melanie Hamilton.

Even in childhood Olivia had had her act together. Her room was neat, her chores done, her grades good, her obedience complete. She managed her allowance well and seldom wasted time. She was well-liked but impervious to peer pressure. Olivia was a hard act for Iris to follow.

Aaron Tyler had been Livvy's best friend in grade school and her boyfriend from junior high on; there was never any one else for either of them. He was nearly perfect, too, of course. Iris had tried hard to dislike him; later she had had an excruciating crush on him. Through it all he remained constant in kindness and brotherly affection.

Olivia and Aaron had traversed the rocky shoals of adolescence with grace. They kept the rules, said no to drugs, stayed innocent. Iris considered them an anachronism, more typical of her mother's generation than their own.

So Olivia grew from girl to woman. She attended a one-year nursing program in Gainesville after high school, at her father's request, but came home every weekend to spend as much time as possible with Aaron. Finally Will surrendered to the inevitable and Olivia and Aaron were married. They had a son two years later and a daughter four years after that. They were—predictably—wonderful children. The Tylers attended church regularly, but never offended anybody with their religion.

And now Aaron Tyler had killed a man, with his wife's enthusiastic endorsement. Iris had to fit this new information into her perception of them.

O.K., she thought, *Aaron is a hunter; he owns guns and they aren't for target practice. He really kills things.* But she knew he never hunted for sport; he killed only what they could eat. It was just one more thing that put the Tylers out of sync with modern life: He actually hunted game, and they actually ate what he shot.

Another idea occurred to Iris: Aaron favored the death penalty. She had overheard him talking to her father about it. He had even told Will it was what the Bible advocated. So maybe he considered execution a legitimate option. Whatever the rationale behind the act, Iris was too conditioned by their mutual history not to succumb to comfortable ways of thinking. If the Tylers did it, it must be a good thing to do— even the deliberate killing of another human being.

Carly, on the other hand, was a leaf in the wind. When he fired at the pursuing truck, Iris realized—though she had been stirred by the unexpected show of strength and protectiveness—he was neither following nor violating a pre-existing code of ethics; he was acting by instinct. Like a child or an animal, Carly did at any given moment what seemed expedient, what was good for Carly.

Well, no surprises here. The Tylers always acted in accord with an internal value system; Carly had none. His acts were based on personal advantage.

Which brought Iris to the question of what motivated *her*. Where did she fit in? And why in God's name had she come on this trip?

Will Stoddard had no trouble finding the Boyd home. It was a small house on about five acres, well-tended and comfortable-looking. This far from the river the land was gently hilly, and Boyd's property abounded with large water oaks.

Will climbed the three steps to a deep and shady porch. As he knocked, he read a shiny metal plate screwed into the wall next to the door:

> *As for me and my house, we will serve the Lord.*
> *Joshua 24:15*

This made him uncomfortable. He was here for straight talk and had expected to find a man who would relate to the crisis the same way Will himself did. How much did he really have in common with a man who would stick that kind of sign on his front porch for all to see?

Micah Boyd opened the door and smiled warmly. "Come on in, Willy. We'll sit in the kitchen. Coffee or iced tea?"

"Tea, I guess. I'm about coffeed out."

The kitchen was sunny and cozy, cluttered but clean. Micah poured from a pitcher of strong, dark tea, and roused one of Will's strongest aversions by serving it in a plastic tumbler. A glass ought to be made of glass, Will thought. They took seats at the round wooden table.

"I heard about the Tylers, Willy," said Micah, stirring sugar into his tea. "Can't tell you how sorry I am. We prayed for them."

Will looked up in surprise. "There's church on Friday now?"

"No. I mean Nora and I prayed. Here at home."

"Much obliged." Will tried to push aside his discomfort. "I thought maybe you could give me an idea of what they'll be facing. 'Course, the Highway Patrol guy and the deputies had some information, but you're the only man I know's actually been there."

"I'll tell you whatever I can. And it's interesting you should have thought of me. I've been keeping a kind of notebook about it. I been real interested in how things have developed down south."

"There're Haitians in the Everglades, right?"

Micah nodded. "Among others. But your kids won't be going that far south, will they? I thought Belle Glade."

"Depends. They'll go wherever the children are."

Micah rose. "I got a map in the den; be right back."

Will closed his eyes against the dull pain across his fore-head. At some point the tension would ease. The situation would resolve itself one way or another, and the emotional climate would change to either rejoicing or intolerable griev-ing. But they would be set free from the ache of not know-ing. Will was a fighter; he wasn't good at simply enduring.

Micah returned and spread out a Department of Trans-portation map of Florida, scaled at one inch for every sixteen miles. "In thinking about how these gangs operate, there's two main factors, what you might call underlying principles, they consider. This is true everywhere, not just in Florida. All these groups, from the Klan to street gangs and illegal aliens, they like public parks—the bigger the better—and they don't like being near military installations. The safest place to be south of Lake Okechobee is right around Homestead. From Perine on down to Florida City, it's quiet and peaceful be-cause they rebuilt most of the Air Force base."

"Not too safe for the airmen, from what I hear."

"Oh, they get an attack every now and then, but it takes something bigger than what's operating there now to handle the U.S. military."

Micah said it with pride, and Will recalled that Micah had served in the military, maybe the Marines.

"But let's get to the particulars. No great problems in Tampa; they've got the base at MacDill and plenty of cops, and they're tough. They have crime, sure, and there's some gang activity, but for the most part Tampa's safe. You know, back in the early '90s, Tampa had the highest per capita crime rate in the nation, but not now."

"They're going to call us from Tampa. Captain Ruiz of the state police said that'd probably be their last chance."

"They'll have a military police escort with them after Tampa, right? Maybe they can take 75 to Fort Myers, then take 80 east. They don't want to get into the Everglades. That's really bad news."

"Is that the way you go?"

"Not usually, but then, we're not aiming at Belle Glade. We're heading to the coast, cities like Palm Beach, Lauderdale, Miami. We take the Turnpike or 95. But we travel with at least six trucks, we all have at least one man riding shotgun, and we have the reputation of making it cost anybody who attacks us. And too, they know they need us. If it ever gets where trucks can't get through, that'll be the end of American civilization."

"Sure is different from when we were kids."

Micah nodded. "I can remember when this was a Christian country. Then for a while it was just secular. Now it's truly evil. The wind we sowed in the '60s is a whirlwind in the '90s."

Will could think of no answer to a statement like that; he did not even know what it meant. So he pointed to the map and asked, "You say they like parks; anything here at Withlacoochee?"

"There's some survivalists. No real problem; you leave them alone and they won't bother you. And a bunch of different gangs from up north." Florida's semitropical climate had attracted many inner-city groups, especially from the Northeast. "They can be vicious. But mostly they hate gays. If you're white and straight, maybe they'll let you go. But they go trolling for gays over in Orlando or down in Tampa, and they kill 'em. You don't want to know how they do it."

Will grunted. "So the gays hate the straights, and the Klan hates the blacks, and the survivalists hate the ones escaped from prisons, and the Haitians hate the Klan, and the rednecks hate Orientals, and the Hispanics hate the Yankees, and everybody hates AIDS carriers."

Micah nodded. "That says something about the condition of the human heart, doesn't it?"

The human heart? "Be nice if they all just killed each other off, wouldn't it? Get rid of the riffraff."

Micah became suddenly still and his face was stern. "You don't really mean that, Willy."

"Why not? Get rid of all the troublemakers. Like blacks. They want to run things in this country because they're a minority, and they want to run things in Africa because they're the majority. Go figure! And I always like to say I'm a native American, more than any Indian. Both parents and all four grandparents born in this country. You can't get much more native American than that."

Micah offered no reaction and Will began to feel uncomfortable. "Hey, we're the endangered species here, Micah. White American males. We're *everybody's* target. They get together, study their culture, their history, it's fine. *We* do it, it's sexist and we can get arrested. They protest and lobby for their special rights, wonderful. They get special laws passed. But let a bunch of white guys try something like that, and you hear 'hate crime' and lawsuits."

"There's truth in what you say, Willy. The pendulum has swung too far back. But I don't think we can say, 'Just kill 'em all.' No group has a corner on injustice, and white American men—well, we have a long way to go before we're the underdog."

Will shook his head. No use talking if Micah had that kind of attitude. Anyhow, he hadn't meant *murder* them, exactly. "No offense intended," he muttered.

"None taken," Micah responded.

There was an awkward silence, then Will spoke again. "Lots of little enclaves around Orlando, aren't there?"

"Oh, yeah. There's all that empty land Disney owns, same as a park. And they still have hotels there. One skinhead group just took over a hotel. Chased everybody out and moved their group in. But the police took it back. Bad publicity for tourists—as if it wasn't bad enough already."

"How do people still take vacations there, in all this mess? How do they travel?"

"They come mostly by train. Trains and, of course, planes are safer than cars. You know Disney; they do all things well. Maybe they're not as big, but still operating. It may cost an arm and a leg, but you can still have the all-American family vacation at Disney World if you got the money."

"Lots of outlaw groups on further south, right? All through that flatland." Will gestured across the middle third of the peninsula.

"Dozens. Some have escaped from the Q. Zone, and they're out to infect anybody they can get their hands on. There's one big South American enclave who are even farming, I hear. Talk about peaceful! Another group, they have what they call a Sanctuary, a place people can go—for a price—if they don't want to be tested, or if they're positive, or if they're wanted by the law somewhere. For a price you can stay there, and they'll protect you, feed you, house you. They built cabins where you can stay. Real entrepreneurs. That's about all the groups I know of. But there's not much law down there and you travel at your own risk."

"Well, I can't say I'm happy about what you've told me, but I appreciate your time." Will gulped his tea and rose. "I better get home in case Charlotte wakes up."

Micah walked with Will to his truck, where Will shook his hand a little self-consciously.

"I wish there was something I could say to help, Will. We'll keep praying."

"Much obliged," Will said. More of this religious slant. But there was some consolation in it, too. Micah seemed to believe that prayer might actually accomplish something. It couldn't hurt to have this man praying for the kids.

They reached Dunnellon by mid-afternoon, a pretty, peaceful little town on the Withlacoochee River. The major suggested they stop for the day, primarily so the van's back window could be repaired. No one resisted the proposal, not even the Tylers, who were driven by dreadful urgency. The whole group from Pine River was ragged with fatigue.

They found a guest house and worked through the complications of registering. Their thumbprints were scanned, their Certificates of Health were displayed on the screen, and Aaron observed the computerized transfer of funds from Will Stoddard's bank account into the account of their host.

In the late afternoon they all had a hot meal in the dining room, but they were too overwhelmed to enjoy it. They reviewed the morning's episode from every angle, reaching no new conclusions. And they discussed plans. Aaron overheard Carly suggest halfheartedly to Iris that they explore what action the little town might offer and sound relieved when she stated her preference for a long shower and a rest. Aaron, still wondering what was up between Carly and his sister-in-law, was relieved, too.

"Let me get Olivia settled," Aaron said to Major Shearson, "and we'll find a body shop for the van."

The major nodded.

Dr. Kovaks approached Olivia as she and Aaron climbed the stairs to the room assigned to the Tylers. "Do you think you'll be able to rest? I mean, I know you're tired, but it may be hard to, you know, shut your thoughts down. I have some sedatives if you think you might need something. It's been a very hard time for you, I know. . . ."

Olivia shook her head. "That's very thoughtful, but no, thanks."

"Well, if you change your mind, I'm in with your sister. It's, like, right at the top of the stairs."

The room was clean and cool. Olivia sank onto the edge of the bed. "I have never been so tired, honey, so totally undone, in my life. I just pray I can hang on."

Aaron sat next to her and pulled back the bedcovers. "Stretch out there and I'll rub your back."

She sank down onto the pillows. "I'm not so selfish I don't realize you're just as devastated as I am, but there's nothing in me to help anybody else, even you. I simply don't have the resources to do anything but endure."

"That's all right, Livvy. I'm O.K. All I want's for you to get a little nap." His strong, brown hands moved soothingly across his wife's shoulders and back, and he could feel the tension diminish. She was asleep within ten minutes.

He covered her with the sheet and rose slowly, careful not to awaken her. It reminded him of when just recently he had left his sleeping wife, making every effort not to wake her, praying she could continue in a dreamless sleep, unaware of the horror of the real world.

Had it been only last night?

Either by coincidence or by some unrealized phenomenon by which our lives and events are linked, at the very moment Olivia Tyler fell asleep, her son Philip awakened. He was confused, headachy and nauseous. There was very little light and he had no comprehension of his surroundings.

Gradually he oriented himself: He was in a moving vehicle, lying on his back amid all kinds of litter, covered with a stiff cloth. He pushed it off his face and peered around. He was on the floor of a van or enclosed truck, and now he was assaulted by smells. He had evidently vomited, which smelled sickening, and even worse, he had wet and soiled himself. Overpowering both these smells was the powerful odor of paint and turpentine. There were cans, boxes, ladders and more cloths in disarray all around him. *What in blazes?* he thought in indignation. Where was he? His vision was adjusting and he could make out the silhouettes of two men in the front of the truck.

He realized two things instantly: These men were strangers and they were dangerous.

He tried to remember how he came to be lying under a painter's tarpaulin in the back of a truck, but the last he remembered was going to bed at home, in his own room. He was still in his pajamas, he realized, and barefoot. He was also thirstier than he had ever been.

One of the men laughed suddenly, and Philip closed his eyes again, feigning sleep. He wanted desperately to avoid confronting those men.

There was a sudden stirring next to him. The laughter had aroused someone—or something— still under the tarp. Philip was horrified, but he feared the men more than the unknown thing, and he stayed still. Then he heard a soft voice: "Mama?"

It was Sara. At first he was elated to learn he was not alone in this strange and terrifying situation. Then he was dismayed to realize his sister shared whatever danger he faced.

He moved the tarp off her face and spoke in a whisper. "Don't be afraid, Sara. I'm here. Go back to sleep."

"I want a drink, Flip. And I need to go to the bathroom."

"There is no bathroom. You'll have to wait."

"It stinks in here. Where are we, anyhow? I don't feel good, and I want to see Mama." Sara's voice was getting louder. Although the truck was noisy, Philip feared the men would hear her.

"Mama isn't here right now. Go back to sleep. I'll wake you up when we get to a bathroom."

"My head hurts, and I feel like I'm gonna throw up."

"Well, don't do *that*. Just go to sleep."

Philip was about to scream. He knew in his very depths that some unspeakable catastrophe had happened, and he felt keenly the responsibility for his sister's welfare. She was always a tagalong, always under foot, and his folks always said—unfairly, in Philip's opinion—that his role as elder brother was significant. Now, in the absence of their parents, Philip felt responsible for keeping her safe and happy. The burden was overwhelming and he didn't know how he would do it.

"*Please*, Sara!" He moved even closer to her and hissed in her ear. "You have to be *quiet!* If you don't make any more noise, next time we go to Grandpa's I'll let you ride Ginger the whole time. I won't even get on her."

"You promise?"

"I promise. Now go back to sleep."

Sara settled herself more comfortably, eased somewhat by her brother's concession. "Where's Buffalope?"

"He isn't here. Just go to sleep."

Sara pushed at him in annoyance. "You should've brought him!"

He groaned inwardly at the injustice of this.

"I just want you to know, Philip Tyler, I'm not happy about any of this."

He almost laughed. Through the fear, confusion, resentment and physical distress came a ray of pure amusement.

"I don't blame you at all," he whispered.

5

Saturday, September 11, 1999

A aron slept through the night, but when he awoke at 5 A.M. he knew he was awake for the day. He dressed quietly and left the room in search of coffee.

The host's wife was busy in the kitchen; he smiled without speaking and helped himself to coffee and two bagels, exiting through the back door. He wanted to be alone. His inborn need for privacy had been sorely denied him these past few days. Since the arrival of Olivia's notice of conscription, in fact, he had had almost no time alone; despite that sleepless night, no time to deal with the assault. In view of the far more overwhelming disaster of the loss of the children, of course, the letter had been forgotten.

He found himself on a concrete lanai with plantings, umbrellas, tables and chairs. A small oval pool was empty of water now in this time of AIDS, filled instead with sand. His mind went back four years to the summer of '95. Philip was six and already a strong (if ungainly) swimmer, and had mounted a campaign for a pool. Aaron and Olivia were in accord: no pool until Sara, then a toddler of two, could also swim. Then Philip shrewdly approached Will Stoddard, and that summer Will installed a 36-foot in-ground pool, complete with slide and

diving board. Aaron was furious at both his son and his father-in-law. Actually, a residue of irritation had remained till
the present.

How trivial it seemed now! In the face of his children's abduction, how greatly his ideas had changed, his concepts of
what really mattered in the long run. He was suddenly grateful that Will loved the children; the years of Aaron's strife and
competition with Will seemed offensive.

He sat down in a lawn chair, its plastic cover slightly wet
from the morning dampness. He sipped the coffee and took
a bite of bagel. It tasted good, and he felt ashamed he could
enjoy even this small thing when his children were undergo-
ing no telling what kind of hardship. Probably *hardship* wasn't
nearly strong enough a word.

Now I'm alone, he thought. *Now I can think, plan, pray.* But
his mind was skittish, running after trivialities and diversions.
It would not, or could not, wrap itself around the reality of
the children's kidnaping; in fact, it was expending all its effort to avoid facing that fact.

And prayer was a mockery. If he so much as lifted his mind
to God, he dissolved into tears. His total prayer had been a
mindless, wordless cry of pain, pleading for help. He was without strength, without reason, almost without hope.

The door opened behind him and Sergeant Cordray approached. "If you want to be alone, I can find another spot."

"It's O.K. Have a seat."

"Been a rough couple of days for you. I'm impressed at
how you're managing. My first name's Paul, by the way." The
sergeant shifted his coffee to his left hand and stuck out his
right. Aaron shook it self-consciously.

"Major Shearson told me last night he'd call around to see
if any of the local law has spotted the kidnaper's truck," Aaron
said. "Does that sort of thing still work? All Points Bulletins
and things like that?"

"Sometimes. You'd be surprised. There aren't as many law-men as there used to be, but what's left are really dedicated."

"Everybody's been telling me I can't count on the law. Captain Ruiz, the deputies at home, even the major. They all say it's up to us."

"That's true, in a way, but in another way it's not. We still have law; we still have men and courts and jails to enforce the law, protect society. As a nation, we haven't quite come to true anarchy."

"Just here and there, in spots," Aaron responded.

"Maybe so." The sergeant took a chair next to Aaron. "We still have an hour, probably, before anybody else gets up. Feel like talking?"

"Yeah, I guess so. If you feel like listening." Aaron found to his surprise that he *did* want to talk to this quiet, confident, self-contained man. "I came out here to pray but I can't. Probably never in my life have I needed prayer so much, and I can't."

"Maybe knowing you need to pray is a prayer in itself."

"Maybe."

"Knowing you can't handle life without God, acknowledging you need Him."

"Yeah, well, that's sure true."

"And if there's one thing our God knows about, it's having a Son abused by evil men."

Aaron looked at him in surprise. This was a new side of Paul Cordray and a new perception of the Father's role in the atonement.

The sergeant took a sip of his coffee. "You know, I've wondered since our little encounter at the roadblock yesterday: You have any problems with the idea you'll probably have to kill some people to get your kids back?"

Aaron chuckled. "When you want to talk, you mean it, do you? But, O.K. Let's talk about that. I think I may have killed the driver of that truck; I know I hit him, at least. And it doesn't bother me a bit. I was ready to kill again—those men at the blockade."

"Yet you're still a good man, a law-abiding citizen."

"I always was. I don't know now. If it's a choice of some stranger—a crook, an outlaw, somebody keeping me from getting my kids back—then I'll blow 'em away and dance on their grave."

"No turn-the-other-cheek, resist-not-evil?"

"I always thought I lived by that code, but I'll do anything—I mean anything at all—to rescue my children. I'm not even thinking, is it right or wrong; I'll just do it, no matter what."

The conversation seemed suddenly bizarre to Aaron—to be sitting in the pearly pre-dawn light, serenely discussing the ethics of killing with this stranger, a professional warrior, while enjoying coffee and bagels. Life had gone completely mad.

He turned to his companion and asked with interest, "What about you? You ever have to kill anybody?"

The sergeant was quiet for a while. Then he spoke softly. "Yes. First time, I'd been assigned to protect some people and they were attacked by a gang. The way it fell out, somebody—a lot of somebodies—were going to die. Either the people I was there to defend would die, or the attackers. It was up to me and I made a choice. I still have to make that choice, fairly frequently. I figure this way. The ones who bring death in, they're the ones to die. The Bible says that they that take up the sword shall die by the sword."

"So you moved to protect the weak from the aggressors?"

"To protect the innocent from the guilty. That's what the law is supposed to do." The sergeant turned to Aaron, and in the golden glow of the light coming through the kitchen window, his face was somber. "If the law fails, then each man must defend his own family."

"So you think it's right for me to kill the men who took my

kids? You think it's in line with the Bible?" This had to be one of the strangest conversations he had ever had. Too intimate by far.

"Well, I can't cite you chapter and verse, but I don't see any clear word telling you to let your kids die, either."

"Well, that's good, because I'm going to do whatever it takes to get my kids, and if that means killing somebody, then so be it."

Major Shearson had set breakfast at seven sharp, so the wake-up calls came at 6:30. Olivia woke instantly at the knock on the door. Her mind jumped back onto its treadmill, the same questions and fears returning to plague her after the night's rest. She dressed quickly, paying little attention to grooming.

She wore no makeup, though she seldom did. Her beauty was the result of good bone structure, abundant health, clear skin and an inner serenity. All her life Olivia had been told she was beautiful, and she believed it as surely as she believed that she was female, Caucasian, Southern. But this morning the face that stared back at her from the mirror was haggard, gaunt. She shuddered and turned away. She ran a brush through her golden hair, pulled it back into a rubber band and left in search of Aaron.

In the room at the top of the stairs, the physician and the waitress greeted the day and each other with little enthusiasm. As the two passed each other in the room, taking turns in the bathroom, they smiled and nodded but hardly spoke. Despite similarities in background, age, sex, race and nationality, not to mention their commitment to the same hazardous journey south, they had almost nothing in common.

Cassandra Kovaks plugged in a small cassette player, inserted a tape and spent twenty minutes in fevered exercise. That left ten minutes for showering and dressing, and it was enough. She merely brushed her damp curls back from her face. With heart rate steady and endorphins active, she was ready for the day.

Iris Stoddard used a debit card to purchase coffee from an automatic dispenser attached to the wall in the hallway, and drank it black. She used mousse, a curling iron, then spray on her hair; she applied cosmetics to her face with skill. It took almost a half-hour to produce results that satisfied her—the look of simple, natural beauty.

Iris looked much like her sister—a brown-eyed blonde with lovely skin and fine bone structure. But where Olivia was cool, Iris was warm. She was shorter, more rounded, more vivid, somehow. And whereas Olivia radiated composure, Iris transmitted a restless hunger for life. The older sister could appear almost stuffy with satisfaction; the younger was almost breathless in her quest for stimulation. Thus, Olivia had the kind of beauty women admired, while Iris had the kind of beauty men desired.

Cassandra Kovaks and Iris Stoddard finished their preparations and left the room together, fortified to face the day, each feeling innately superior to the other.

The group met precisely at seven—neither soldier had referred to it as a "rendezvous"—and were taken up immediately with food and newspapers. There was little discussion: Olivia Tyler ate mechanically; Carly Jenson huddled stiffly against any conversational attack, the editorial section of *The Tampa Tribune* raised as a rampart; Iris and Cassandra scanned the rest of Carly's paper; Aaron and the Army men talked.

"I can't get any word about the kidnapers' truck, but I really didn't expect to till Tampa," the major told Aaron. "But the local police told me about a truck convoy leaving here about eight. They say we can join them, and of course that means we can hit 41 and barrel on down. Get there sometime this afternoon. We can leave as soon as we eat and load up."

Aaron nodded. "Ready when you are."

❖   ❖   ❖

Will Stoddard ate his usual breakfast Saturday morning. He wasn't hungry, but he thought it might help Charlotte if he ate the food she had prepared and they maintained their customary morning routine. So he faced a plateful of eggs (from his own chickens) scrambled lightly, with grits, bacon and toast. He ate in silence, staring through the kitchen windows at the bucolic scene in the pasture behind the house.

The horses were in high spirits, trotting along the fence line, tossing their manes in the morning breeze. Ginger showed no sign of lameness and Will thought how happy this would make Philip. Then he groaned. How could he survive another day of not knowing?

Charlotte, wearing a faded robe, was drinking coffee and nibbling a piece of toast. Her light hair, still long and thick and usually pulled back into a knot, now tumbled down her back. She leaned over the table, shoulders hunched as though to withstand a blow. He felt great tenderness for her. "What are you going to do today?" he asked.

"Oh, the regular things. Clean the house, do a couple of loads of clothes, fix meals. The usual."

"Let's go riding first. Just the two of us." He regretted that last phrase, an unfortunate reminder of their current status.

"We'll see. Finish your eggs first." Charlotte poured more coffee, her third cup.

Will thought how often Olivia chided her mother about caffeine. In her gentle way, Olivia could be as stubborn as a mule. "You drink ten or twelve cups of coffee a day, Mother, then wonder why you don't sleep well. That's just silly." His heart constricted with grief.

"Please, Charlotte. Come riding with me. I know you think you got to do all these chores, but I need you." Unusual words for him, a little awkward, but undeniably true.

Charlotte looked at him intently as though seeing him for the first time. "If you like. I'll get dressed." She left the kitchen and Will dutifully finished his food, tasting nothing.

What were the others eating? Aaron and the girls were probably in Dunnellon, maybe Inverness, and there were still restaurants there. But the grandkids. . . . His thoughts danced dangerously toward the forbidden areas before he clamped a firm grip on his mind.

It's all a matter of endurance, he thought. *Living through the time. Just getting through each passing minute without going mad.*

Charlotte came back, hair smoothed into its subdued knot, now wearing jeans and boots and a bright green shirt. Even now, with her haggard countenance, he found her attractive. He had always liked the way she looked in jeans, just as he had always admired her competence with horses. He had been over thirty when they married and had almost given up finding a wife. There had never been another significant woman in his life.

He smiled at her.

"O.K., Willy. Let's go." She forced a smile and he took her hand.

It had been a long time since Charlotte had left dirty dishes on the table.

Even as recently as three years ago, there had been cafés and truck stops along the highway. Before the explosive increase in crime, places where a traveler might eat were almost as common as gas stations. Now there were virtually none outside the urban areas, especially in regions as lawless as the peninsula of Florida. So when Otto Krause and his sidekick Stoney Hickman decided they were hungry, they had to rely on what supplies they had brought along.

Otto found a likely spot and pulled the truck off the road. Otto was the decision-maker, Stoney an adaptable combination of employee, friend, acolyte and fan. It was a long-time and workable relationship.

The two men had much in common. Both were in their mid-40s and unmarried. Both were from the same neighborhood in Jacksonville. Both were citizens in good standing of that city's criminal subculture. They worked sporadically as house painters but sustained life by craft and guile and petty thievery.

And all their lives they had suffered devaluation on account of physical unattractiveness. Otto was vaguely porcine in appearance—large, soft and fair, with a square, balding head. Stoney was short with a pockmarked face, small, dark eyes and gaps between discolored teeth. Both men expected to be rejected and were seldom disappointed.

But they survived.

A psychological profile on either man would have indicated an immature personality structure, citing "inappropriate affect" and "poor impulse control." Stoney was marginally retarded; Otto would have been identified as a borderline sociopath. Neither man could predict or even recognize the consequences of his behavior.

These were the men who had kidnaped the Tyler children. Not major criminals, not pedophiles, not part of a gang. They were men simply trying to get along, men who had not the vaguest perception of an objective standard of right and wrong.

"You want the kids to eat, too, Otto?"

"Mize well. We got enough. Twinkies and chips."

"O.K., Otto. I'll wake them up."

Philip Tyler had always resented the fact that his mother made him sleep in pajamas. Nobody wore pajamas! Nobody but girls, anyhow. Not Grandpa, not Daddy, none of the guys he played with—nobody but Philip had to wear dumb old pajamas. It made him feel stupid whenever one of the guys slept over. But right now, as he climbed shakily out of the painter's truck into the light of morning, he was glad to be wearing more than his underwear.

They were parked about ten feet off the road in an uninhabited stretch of two-lane highway. There were no signs of life anywhere, no buildings, not even other cars. The two men were walking around, stretching their legs, talking to each other. Philip stood by the truck, blinking in the light.

He was weak and dizzy, unexpectedly nauseated, headachy. He had a raging thirst. He was also filthy; evidently he had wet his pajamas repeatedly and soiled them at least once. He had no idea where he was or how he got there, and he was terribly afraid he was going to cry. Then he heard Sara: "I can't open the door, Flip!"

Her tone of voice made it clear that it was all his fault and that it was his duty to make it right. He managed to open the truck's back door, which exhausted him.

Now Sara stood beside him, blinking. The truck was dark within. "Where are we? Who are those men? Where's Daddy? I want to go home!" She looked as though she were tuning up for a good cry. Then the men approached and she fell silent.

Philip couldn't decide which of the two looked worse. The larger, blondish man had a flat and distant look in his eyes with no expression at all. The small, dark man was bright-eyed and interested, but his eagerness made Philip nervous.

The smaller man spoke. "You kids hungry? There's food in the front. Drinks, too."

"Who are you?" Sara asked.

Too dumb even to be scared, Philip thought.

"I'm Stoney. This here's Otto. What's your name?"

"I'm Sara Angela Tyler and this here is my brother, Philip." Philip looked at his sister in amazement. She was being Missy Cute Stuff, expecting these men to think she was wonderful as everyone else did. *They might shoot her if she acts too cute,* Philip thought. But Stoney smiled.

"Here, come here." He led them around the side of the truck and opened the side door. There were two large grocery sacks on the floor behind the front seat. "You like Twinkies?" Stoney asked. "We got sodas, too. Help yourself."

Suddenly Philip was ravenous; he pulled out an unopened box of Twinkies and extracted two. Opening the cellophane of the first, he took an enormous bite. Nothing had ever tasted so good! As he chewed it in almost obscene pleasure, he opened one for Sara and popped the tops on two cans of ginger ale. He drank almost a whole can, then took another bite of Twinkie.

White sugar, white flour and animal fat—forbidden fruit! He had tasted this kind of treat before, of course. Once he started school, it was simply a matter of time before he threw off his mother's prohibitions against processed sugar, preservatives, monosodium glutamate and very much fat or salt. Away from home Philip had tasted sugared gum, white bread, even Tootsie Rolls—but never without feeling defiled. This non-nutritious breakfast, on the other hand, evoked no negative emotions; it was sensual bliss.

Stoney was laughing at them. "Coupla chow hounds, Otto. Look at 'em eat!"

Philip grinned, forgetting for a moment that these were enemies.

Then Otto broke in. "You kids go to the bathroom. No more stinking up my truck." His voice was cold and there was no trace of amusement on his face.

Sara was also eating ravenously, but she said around her Twinkie, "I want to go home, please."

Otto did not bother to answer. He walked a few feet away, turned his back and urinated onto the ground. Sara stared at him and giggled with embarrassment.

Philip spoke to Stoney. "Where are you taking us? You kidnaped us, right? Why? You think you'll get a ransom for us?"
He had ripped open another Twinkie.

Both men ignored Philip's questions.

"You better be careful. They'll come get us and my dad'll
beat you up. You can't get away with this." He wanted them
to know that every effort would be expended to rescue them,
that he and Sara mattered.

Otto zipped his pants and walked back to the truck. His
expression was still passive but his jaw had tightened. Philip
stepped back until he bumped into the truck.

"You got a big mouth, kid," Otto said quietly. He drew back
his hand and smacked Philip across the face, splitting his lip
and causing his ears to ring. "Keep it buttoned, y'hear me?"

Sara screamed and ran to her brother, whether to give or
receive comfort Philip could not tell. He was overwhelmed
by shock, unable to stop the flow of tears, emotionally devastated. His parents were far stricter than any other family he
knew, and firm advocates of corporal punishment. But even
when he chafed under their discipline, he recognized that it
sprang from love. He had never been attacked before, and
this man did not even show any emotion.

"Ain't nobody gonna find you. No daddy's gonna beat me
up, you got that? You just put a sock in it, hear?" Otto's voice
was still calm. He pushed Philip away from the truck. "Now
you get through going to the bathroom and we'll get started.
You, too, girlie."

Philip patted Sara on the back and nodded. He had little
capacity to minister comfort, but he tried. "It's O.K.," he said.
"Go on and do what he said."

Then he followed her, walking unsteadily along the verge
of the road, trying desperately to control his fear. "Dad will
too come," he muttered through his tears. Suddenly he recalled a Scripture memory verse from Sunday school. He had

forgotten the reference but remembered the words: "I will not leave you as orphans; I will come to you."

He looked over his shoulder; he wanted to be sure Otto was diverted before he made himself even more vulnerable by taking down his pajama pants. The two men were by the truck talking, and Sara was squatting about fifteen feet in the other direction. Philip cautiously lowered his pants.

"He *will* come," he whispered through gritted teeth. "Dad is coming to get us."

6

Saturday, September 11, 1999

By now the volatile area of low pressure that had formed off the coast of the Cape Verde Islands was growing and moving westward on the prevailing easterly winds of the tropics. Warm, moist air was drawn into it from the surface of the sun-warmed sea, feeding energy to the rising, spinning column of air and increasing its speed as it came. It was upgraded to the level of a tropical depression by the National Weather Service, at which point the six-man team at the National Hurricane Center in Miami went into action. They telephoned the appropriate people at the Air Force base and the Naval station, and reported the latest data to the High Seas Broadcast in Washington, D.C., a worldwide network for disseminating information concerning marine conditions. This agency related the situation to concerned nations via code. The various news agencies and private weather forecasting services were notified via the weather wire of the National Oceanographic and Atmospheric Association.

A bigger storm. A greater threat. A closer watch.

They rendezvoused at 8:00 at a truck stop just outside town on Highway 41. Paul Cordray surveyed the scene: Eight trucks were parked and idling, tractor-trailers used for over-the-road hauling. Each had a team of at least two, who looked calm despite the danger. They wore jeans and boots, for the most part, with cowboy hats or baseball caps. The air was thick was diesel exhaust.

Major Shearson joined the clutch of drivers and guards who stood by the gas pumps talking and smoking. Paul knew they would be discussing the route, the order the trucks would take, and where and when they would stop.

The Tylers, Iris Stoddard and Carly Jenson were traveling in Aaron's van as before, while Cassandra Kovaks sat in the back seat of the Army car reading. The shattered rear window of the van had been repaired and both vehicles were topped off with gas.

"There time for me to call home?" Aaron called above the sound of the idling motors.

"Sure. There's still another truck to come."

Aaron walked from the van to the public phone booth which, though obviously vandalized, still stood attached to the side of the building.

Paul followed him and waited at a distance, pondering the young man hunched in the phone booth. Aaron was medium in height, more slender than average, with strong, ropy muscles. He moved with controlled energy, graceful and quick. His smooth, brown face was tranquil; laugh lines enhanced his brown eyes. His speech had a deep Southern flavor, flat and humid and, to Paul (who enjoyed regional accents), strangely inflected. Aaron Tyler gave an impression of dignity and composure.

Now he hung up the phone and joined Paul. "I tried to call my father-in-law, but they're not home; I got the machine. Maybe for the best, though. He probably couldn't stand talking to me. He didn't think the women should come."

"How's Olivia?" Paul asked. It was the first time he had used her given name.

"Just this side of catatonic. I've about run out of things to say to her."

"And you? You O.K.?"

"That depends on how you define O.K. I'm functioning but that's about it. I can't figure out why all this is happening, you know? All our lives things have been pretty smooth—not perfect but good. Now, in three days, my whole life has fallen apart. I feel like I've got a sign on my back saying *Kick me*, only it's worse than being kicked."

"I can see how you'd feel that way."

We talk personally for guys who have only known each other a couple of days, Paul thought. He recognized, as Aaron had earlier, that their familiarity and lack of reserve were unusual.

"I just wonder what's next." Aaron began walking stiffly towards the vehicles. "And I wonder why Livvy and I are victims all of a sudden."

"You're trying to see cause and effect?"

"Well, something like that. I don't want to think it's just—a fluke. They call it 'random violence,' but I don't believe in a random universe. It's supposed to make *sense*."

Paul nodded. "And if you see the cause, maybe there's a cure, right?"

"I guess."

"There might not be a simple answer. Lots of times in the Bible, there was no clear reason why some calamity happened, just an emphasis on how to respond, to get the grace to handle it."

Aaron shook his head. "I know sometimes we have to just stand things, live through them without cursing God and dying. But I want to know if I did something wrong and made God mad."

Paul felt an overwhelming compassion for this gentle,

wounded man. How few in his place would be concerned that they might have angered God! Most would be angry at God instead.

"That's not necessarily what happened, Aaron. We live in a sinful world and sometimes the evil rubs off on us. But there *are* patterns, general cause and effect. Because you're right; it's not a random universe."

Aaron looked up and gave a pathetic little smile. Paul took that as encouragement. "Start with this. What's the root cause for kidnaping?"

"I don't know."

"Well, think about it: Why the recent escalation in crimes against children in this country? Not just abduction; let's include child abuse, incest, teen suicide, homicide, even deaths from drugs. And, of course, AIDS. I think they're all part of one enterprise, one project, that the enemy is working on right now."

Aaron frowned. "The enemy being Satan?"

"Yes. And it all comes under the heading of child death. Satan's been loosed to kill children in this country, legally sanctioned, because our government has legalized abortion. Do you see the connection?"

Aaron was just staring at him.

"Look, if our legal, mandated authority has said, in effect, that it's O.K. to kill babies, then that decree has loosed the enemy to kill. And now that he's free to kill, he isn't limiting himself to killing just through abortion."

"That's certainly an interesting point of view."

"He's been loosed like that a couple of times before. In Egypt at the time of Moses, he killed all the baby boys. Pharaoh was the legal authority and he opened the door for a spirit of child death. Then again in Bethlehem, at the time of Jesus' birth. Then it was Herod. Now it's *Roe v. Wade.*"

"Go on."

"That's the way the universe operates; cause and effect, seed and harvest." Paul paused a moment. "Think about Pharaoh. Why was the final plague on the Egyptians the death of the firstborn son? I think it was because Pharaoh had decreed to kill all the Hebrew baby boys. He sowed it and he reaped it."

"Hey, that's true."

"Remember how King Saul threw javelins at David? Tried to pin him to the wall? So how did Saul wind up? His body was pinned to the wall of Bethshan. Whatever a man sows, he reaps."

"So you're saying I did something to allow the enemy to steal my kids? Come on, Cordray! I never kidnaped anybody."

"No, I'm not saying that. Lots of those Hebrews—and Egyptians, too—lost sons, and they were innocent. I guess I'm just saying there *is* a cause, and if we knew it, it'd make sense."

Another long semi had pulled off the highway toward them, and the driver waved a friendly hand. The other drivers and guards broke out of their circle and began walking to their trucks.

"We're getting ready to leave," Paul said. "Talk again later?"

Aaron nodded and walked toward the van, apparently deep in thought.

"Let's head for Tampa, boys," the new driver called.

One by one the men climbed into their cabs.

Most men tasked with managing a multimillion dollar enterprise, as Burton Chancey was, care little about the number of hours they work. Burt, a typical workaholic, actually sought reasons to stay at the job. Busyness masked the aridity of his personal life.

So he sat this dreary Saturday morning working on his list of suggestions for the Finger Squad. The hospice was quiet on the weekend with many departments closed. Dina Hawks sat at her own desk, preparing records for the accounting section. She, too, preferred activity to leisure.

The hospice was huge. It had been spacious when built and had been enlarged several times as the number of AIDS infecteds grew. Still, it was inadequate for the number of patients.

Whether by design or happenstance, all the supply rooms had been placed in the central core of the hospice: medical stores, kitchen provisions, central supply, all the articles needed for housekeeping, the business office and pharmacy. This location provided *de facto* protection and there was remarkably little theft. Pilfering from within, yes, but so far not much robbery.

This may have made them careless.

It was mid-morning when Burton's door opened to admit a uniformed security guard. Like almost everyone else in Belle Glade, this man was HIV-positive but without signs of infection. He was tall, robust, full of energy and currently quite agitated.

"Got a problem, Mr. Chancey," he said urgently. "Somebody's broken into the storerooms, killed one guard and wounded two more."

Burt was on his feet and running. "Lock the office, Dina, then come on."

He pounded down the hallway behind the guard, aware of his own fierce anger.

Always the overload, he thought. *Bloody impossible job to begin with, then this total lack of security.*

The guard slowed as they reached an intersecting corridor that led to the storeroom area. "I don't think there's any of them still in the building, but let's don't take any chances." He drew his gun and walked cautiously forward, hugging the wall. "Hey, Pete! All clear down there?"

"That you, Ski? Yeah, they're gone." Far down the hall,

another guard poked his head around the corner. Burt and Ski trotted forward.

Pete was standing in a large holding area furnished with flimsy plastic chairs and metal filing cabinets. This was requisition. Handtrucks, dollies and a small forklift were parked along the far wall; doors on the right opened into the various storerooms. A long counter ran along the left wall, where a handwritten sign proclaimed curtly *Wait your turn. Take a number.*

An older man leaned against the counter, holding a handkerchief against his left shoulder. Bright red blood flowed steadily around and through the handkerchief, and Burt felt the jolt he always felt these days at the sight of blood. Any blood in this place could spell death to those few like Burt who were still uninfected.

He found it hard to turn away from the sight of that bright scarlet assassin; it mesmerized him as the snake did the mongoose. With effort he wrenched his eyes away and looked at the other two victims.

One was obviously dead. He was face-down on the floor, a bullet's ragged exit wound in his back. The other guard was female. She sat on the floor, both hands gripping her right knee. She was making a ghastly sound, a high keening, rocking back and forth in agony.

Pete was talking into a mobile phone. "Three of them, yeah. They just left, can't have gotten far, but for God's sake be careful! They're wired on something and got all kinds of firepower! They killed Stan, shot Bertie in the arm and got Maisie in the kneecap. Look, I gotta go, Mr. Chancey's here. Get back to me."

He handed the phone to the other guard. "You get the emergency people in here, Ski, get these wounded tended to. I'll take Mr. Chancey around."

Dina Hawks entered from the corridor and, after an expressionless glance around, joined Burt as the guard Pete led him through one of the doors on the right.

"They must have started in the pharmacy, sir, because it's cleaned out, but they were in dietary stores when they got caught."

"Have you checked the other storerooms?"

"Haven't had time yet," Pete answered. "We can look now."

Burt took one brief, horrified look into the pharmacy area; then, for the next ten minutes, they went from room to room. The other locks were intact and nothing appeared to be missing. But the last area to be inspected was central supply, where many of the sterile supplies were gone.

"Who'd want hospital supplies?" Pete asked. "No resale value in bedpans and IV tubing."

"But it looks like they cleaned us out of disposable syringes," said Dina. It was typical of Dina that she knew what had been stored on each shelf, in every drawer.

"It may be ages before we can get replacements," Burt said, dejected now as well as angry. "How can we care for our patients with no supplies?"

"But look, Burt," said Dina, "it all works out. We won't need any syringes until we can get some more medicines." Her cynical logic drew a sardonic smile from Pete.

Burton was not amused. "How can people steal drugs from the dying? What's the matter with people?"

"People are just people. How'd you live over forty years and still believe people are trustworthy or decent? They're just as selfish and immoral as any other animal."

Burt shook his head. "I'll never agree with that point of view. But we need to be dealing with this situation, not arguing the nature of humanity." And he turned back toward the requisition room.

Somehow Dina's cynicism served to bolster his own conflicting views. He would never relinquish his faith in mankind, his firm conviction that honesty and decency lay at the heart of every human being. Why, human beings had the very spark of God within; it was just that negative situations clouded and diminished it. Undoubtedly that was true in the case of the ones who had robbed and killed here today. In a way they were victims, too.

He walked through the door and was glad to see that the wounded had been moved. A masked and gowned cleanup crew was disinfecting the places where blood had spilled, operating as always on the assumption that there were many varieties of the virus that caused AIDS and that no one needed a second strain of infection. A policeman with a clipboard was talking to Ski, filling out a report, and Pete joined them. Burt stood by the door and watched, mentally listing the next things to do.

It was easier to think about work, in any case, than continue pondering Dina's appalling ideas. Burt could not admit even the possibility that she was right, because that would lead only to despair. If he were wrong and humanity had no inherent goodness, how could the world's current struggle ever be won? What other hope was there?

"We gotta clean 'em up. Nobody's gonna want them stinking like they do."

Otto Krause was refining his plans. He did not appear to be looking for recommendations from Stoney Hickman. Indeed, Philip suspected that any suggestions would infuriate him. But he seemed to enjoy thinking out loud.

"Maybe clean clothes, too," he continued. "Yeah, that's good, we'll get some new clothes, maybe stop somewhere and give 'em a bath. We want to get as much as possible, right?"

"Right. All the traffic will bear."

Philip Tyler listened as well as he could over the rattles of the aging truck. On this, their second morning, he was both more terrified and more sanguine about the situation he and his sister faced.

On the one hand, they were farther from home, and he was increasingly afraid that if anything were to be done to effect their rescue, he would have to do it himself. Philip was all too aware of his inadequacy for that job. On the other hand, their two abductors were increasingly familiar, and for that reason a little less fearful. Stoney—the children now called the men by name—had fed them again and even cleared some of the clutter from the floor of the truck so they could sleep more comfortably. There had been no more slaps, no more threats. Philip, of course, was obeying perfectly and invoking no anger.

Also, the two men, like everyone else in creation, had apparently fallen for Sara's charm. Stoney seemed to find her enchanting, and even Otto had smiled once in response to something she said. Sara was an adaptable child and seemed to know instinctively how best to respond to their difficulty. At the same time, she was more and more unpleasant to her brother, increasing her demands that he do something to end this ordeal.

Otto continued his discussion with occasional feedback from Stoney. Where should they get new clothing for the kids? Shoplift it? Ask for a handout at a government "Shelter and Supply" for the homeless? Otto even proposed buying it—evidently a major deviation from policy. And how to bathe the children: Was there a river or pond nearby? Should they risk a home invasion in some nearby town? But a home invasion, he pointed out, usually ended in having to kill somebody, and killing might put on the heat.

Philip liked the idea of a bath and clean clothes; he thought there might even be an opportunity to get word to his family or to the police, while Otto was finagling all these improvements, but he was increasingly uneasy about the motive behind the proposal. Why was Otto going to such trouble to

make them more presentable? Certainly not from any interest in their comfort or welfare. As he listened, it became obvious. He and Sara were merchandise, and Otto was concerned about the packaging.

"Hey, I know where we are," Stoney chirped. "We're nearly
to Tampa. You can get it all here."

"Yeah. There's houses and stores and the river. Yeah. We
can get 'em fixed up here. I think that's state road 54; I'm getting off 19." Otto turned the truck onto a smaller road.

One of the few remaining highway signs read *Odessa, 16
miles.*

The Army car had been assigned a place in the convoy immediately behind the first truck. The van was far back, somewhere near the middle. Their route was logical: 41 to 491 to
490 to 19. With a group this size there would be almost no
danger, even on 19, which was a major highway and often hit
by gangs of carjackers. They had a straight shot into Tampa—
a piece of cake.

Each passed the time in his own way.

Sergeant Paul Cordray maintained the proper interval behind the lead truck. He thought about Aaron Tyler and his
crisis. What agony that man was suffering! Maybe it was better to stay single, have no hostages to fortune. Or was that
the coward's way?

Major Ed Shearson was reviewing the records of the rest
of his team—a squad of Air Police, eleven men, under the authority of a sergeant. A sociologist; a criminologist with advanced degrees in police science; a long-time civil servant and
expert in city management; a think-tank guy with experience
in planning the Quarantine Zones; and additional medical
personnel. All of them good people with excellent experience,
but he was disconcerted to realize that with the exception of
Dr. Kovaks, all of them had been drafted for duty. Even she

was fulfilling the terms of a student loan contract. As recently as a year ago, he would have had at least a few volunteers, people who cared a little about making the scheme work.

But the major had dealt with draftees before; he could make it work.

Let's see, he thought, beginning to plan the order of the next convoy from Tampa to Belle Glade. *Four private cars, a large bus, a personnel carrier, his command car. . . .*

In the van, Aaron drove as usual, with Carly Jenson sitting beside him as second man. The sisters had the swivel armchairs in the back; Olivia was now talking constantly, obsessively, about the children. Iris listened as her sister moved from story to story without pause, luxuriating in the particulars of each reminiscence.

"And he was singing louder than everybody else put together—yelling, really. And it was so cute, everybody laughed out loud. He was singing, 'The first Noel the angels did say was to frighten poor shepherds in fields where they lay.' He said it so clearly, there was no misunderstanding him; he said *frighten.*"

Iris listened with compassion, wondering vaguely if this new behavior was a healthy sign.

Aaron and Carly were talking steadily, covering the few subjects they had in common—Carly because he was uncomfortable with silence and Aaron because he wanted to be polite.

Carly, for his part, felt rootless, removed from home, routine and all the accouterments that made life worth living. He was enduring a climate of perturbing emotions—anxiety about the dangers they faced, unsettledness over his role as purveyor of silver, loneliness at the new sense of not belonging. He had no high-flown motives like the Tylers, no solemn purpose like the soldiers, no ax to grind like Iris. He had been sent by a callous father to gain a profit.

Aaron, for his part, conversed with part of his mind and used the rest to plan his strategy for rescuing his children. The first and most significant item on his agenda was to locate them. Maybe in Tampa there would be some news of the painter's truck. Oh, please, God! Somebody must have seen it somewhere. And it was only an hour and a half to Tampa.

In the 1500s Tampa was known as the best port in the world; now it is known locally as the Big Guava, an overgrown cracker town with a Latin accent.

Ponce de León was probably the first white man to set eyes on Tampa Bay, in about 1513. But he is not the hero chosen to be honored by the citizens who now inhabit that fair city, nor are any of the other dozen or so bold and bloodthirsty Spanish sailors who explored Florida's west coast. No, modern-day Tampans choose to celebrate the memory of José Gaspar, one of the most successful, colorful and brutal pirates who ever plowed the seas.

José bloomed early. It was only twelve years after his birth in 1756 that he kidnaped a neighbor's child and held her for ransom. For this escapade he was given a choice between prison and the Spanish naval academy. He proved to be a superb naval officer and achieved the rank of admiral by the age of 28.

Things went smoothly for a while; then romance blossomed. A high-ranking lady of the court fell in love with him, which displeased her husband, while José fell in love with one of her ladies-in-waiting, which displeased the high-ranking lady. Once again he escaped arrest and imprisonment by the skin of his teeth. With the help of a gang of escaped convicts, he stole a naval vessel, sailed from the harbor and began the reign of the pirate known as "the scourge of the Spanish Main."

Seldom has there been such an effective combination of the man, the times and the role. José Gaspar was renowned for courage in a time when *most* men were fearless. He was a notable buccaneer at a time when enterprise was booming and opportunities for success abounded. And his name stood for brutality in an era of widespread cruelty.

Because of his success, Gaspar soon needed a land-based headquarters—stockades for his prisoners, warehouses for his plunder, land for growing fresh fruits and vegetables. He chose Florida, sailed up the bay into Tampa and claimed his spot.

To this day the residents of Tampa honor this man. Every February a group of men dress as pirates, complete with eye-patches and swords, sail into Tampa Bay in great pirate ships and "capture" the city. The mayor smilingly capitulates, giving the keys to the city to the invaders. The week-long celebration includes parades and a lavish pirates' ball, as well as much "yo-ho-ho and a bottle of rum."

Thus is there a spirit of piracy over Tampa Bay. Robbery by violence, theft of the property of others, inventive lawlessness as a means of livelihood—all these are found in abundance in Tampa.

A suitable destination indeed for kidnapers.

Telephones still worked in Tampa, electricity still hummed, grocery shelves were still stocked, gas stations still pumped gas, even restaurants, bars and movies still catered to those seeking an evening out. All these societal benefits rested on the foundation of dependable police protection. The men and women charged with keeping the peace in Tampa were still at work, and crime was not much higher than it had been before the Order of Quarantine.

Aaron pulled his van into the parking lot and approached the large, one-story, lushly landscaped headquarters of the Tampa Police Department. He had left Livvy with the others at the Ramada Inn; she could rest and get a bite to eat while he checked on the panel truck (which almost certainly belonged to the kidnapers of the children). If there were no news, Aaron preferred to handle his disappointment alone.

He crossed the terrazzo-floored lobby, passing glass cases of crime-stopping memorabilia: guns, bullets, knives, weapons of all kinds, newspaper clippings and photographs all pointing to the success of the Tampa police. Aaron passed police officers, attorneys, prisoners, confused-looking citizens holding summonses, and a nearly somnolent brigade of cleaners.

"Help you, mister?" asked a heavy-set Hispanic man in a spotless blue uniform at the information counter.

Aaron explained, speaking deliberately. So much rode on this, on top of so much other tension already, that he was having trouble with his respiration. He would stop breathing, it seemed, if he did not concentrate on it. "I want to find out if you all know anything about a certain truck. The sheriff in Lafayette County sent an inquiry. . . ."

The desk sergeant listened, nodding at intervals. As Aaron wound down, he nodded again. "Lemme check." He picked up a phone and talked for some time, then hung up and shook his head. "Sorry, 'fraid not. I can check with the Highway Patrol?" He made it a question and Aaron nodded numbly. The man picked up a different telephone.

Aaron leaned against the counter, suddenly too weak to stand without support. He had counted on getting some word of the truck's location. He had even dreamed that the kidnapers were in custody and his children waiting for him to collect them. How could he tell Livvy the police had no news? There was almost no chance of spotting the truck south of Tampa, where there was little police activity and almost all the Highway Patrols used helicopters. Safer for the patrolmen, certainly, but not nearly as good for spotting kidnapers.

The desk sergeant shook his head again, hanging up the receiver. "Sorry."

"Well, much obliged."

"Look, keep in touch with us," the officer said kindly. "We might spot them anytime. Only been a coupla days." He scribbled on a small notepad and handed the paper to Aaron. "Here's my name; call any day between eight and six. I'll remember and keep an eye out."

The sergeant's kindness encouraged Aaron. "Like I said, we're part of an Army convoy, and they have radios and cellular phones and I don't know what all. Maybe you could call us?"

"Sure. If you got some way we can contact you, I'll keep you posted."

"O.K., I'll get back to you with whatever you need."

The policeman nodded. "And don't give up hope. Even nowadays sometimes people get lucky."

Aaron nodded without speaking; he was afraid if he tried to thank the man, whose kindness was a partial balm to Aaron's discouragement, he would break into tears. He pocketed the note and headed back to the van.

The rendezvous for the Finger Squad's convoy was set for 9 A.M. Sunday, so they had Saturday evening and night to do as they pleased. Dr. Kovaks called a friend from her undergraduate days at the University of South Florida and accepted an invitation for dinner. Major Shearson called his family, talked happily with his wife and two daughters, then retired to his room with a rented movie, a favorite World War II epic.

Aaron insisted that Olivia eat well; then, over her protests, gave her two of Dr. Kovaks' sleeping pills. He spent a contented hour watching his wife sleep soundly. Then, feeling unmanly, he swallowed one himself. He barely had time to undress before he, too, slept.

Paul Cordray declined an invitation to join the major and his movie. Instead he took a long walk, then showered and read.

Because Carly generally allowed life to happen to him, he made no plans for the evening. But when he ran into Iris at the ice machine, he asked her out for dinner. Her nonchalant acceptance motivated him to action. He unpacked the Armani suit, consulted the desk clerk about restaurants and nightclubs, and ordered a taxi (at an ungodly price!) to pick them up at 7:30.

When they met in the lobby, Carly was disappointed in Iris' appearance. She was plenty good-looking on her own, of course, and her makeup and hair looked as great as usual. But jeans and a cotton shirt were not exactly appropriate for an evening at an expensive club.

She was not unaware of his disapproval. "I'm sorry about the jeans, Carly, but I didn't pack anything dressy. Who knew we'd be going out on a date? *You're* pretty fancy!"

"You look fine," he soothed her, glad to divert any questions about his own clothes. "I got us a cab and reservations at Los Dos Gatos. Cuban food, Latin music, drinks, dancing. One last night of civilization before we leave."

A horn sounded at the front door. The cab carried them through brightly lighted, palm-lined streets to the night spot that was everything the desk clerk had promised. The decor was aggressively Latin, the food exotic and spicy, the combo inspired. Carly's dancing was only fair, but Iris was so proficient she made them both look good—in spite of her attire—and he knew all watching eyes must admire such a handsome couple. They teased, they flirted, they imbibed any number of rum drinks as the night passed, and played the game adroitly, as befitted their long experience.

It was almost one o'clock when Iris said, "We ought to be thinking about going. It's pretty late."

Carly felt offended. He had paid through the nose for this night of forgetfulness, and it ought to last as long as he wanted. "Aren't you having fun?" he asked stiffly.

"Well, sure, Carly, I've had a great time. But we ought to get some sleep. Tomorrow may be really rough."

Tomorrow and all the rest of the foreseeable future, he thought with irritation. He had pushed the facts down for a while, and blocked active awareness of the task his father had set him to do, with good food and rum and a pretty girl. He had even forgotten, briefly, the heavy metal suitcase locked and hidden in his motel closet.

But the fragile period of tranquillity was broken. He signaled for the check.

7

Sunday morning, September 12, 1999

Philip was getting used to sleeping in the truck, though it was hot and uncomfortable and he was unspeakably lonely. Sara slept restlessly beside him. He continued to be grateful for her company but resentful of his responsibility for her.

On Sunday morning Stoney awakened him and the others for a breakfast of stale cinnamon rolls and cola. Philip was sick of the cloying sweets and longed for the granola and fresh fruit his mother served. Sara was upset about her long hair, which had not been brushed since after her bath at home Thursday evening. But the men ignored her and Philip had no way to help her.

"This is really bad, you know?" Sara grumbled. "I want to go home! I want Daddy!"

"Come on, Sara," Philip soothed her. "You don't want to make them mad."

"I don't care about them! I think they're hateful and I wish they'd just—I don't know, *explode* or something!"

"We just need to stay safe till Dad gets here. I know he's coming after us, and we want to be—you know, safe. We don't want anything else to happen till he does."

The two men had been leaning on the truck talking. The

children stood as far from them as possible, while Philip kept a wary eye in their direction. Otto tossed aside the wrapping from his roll and opened the driver's door.

"Load up, kids. Time to go."

Stoney opened the rear doors and helped Sara into the back. She thanked him automatically, the etiquette dear to her mother's heart deeply ingrained. Philip refused help and settled as comfortably as possible on the floor.

A delicate morning mist hung over the ground as the white panel truck drove steadily south. Even Stoney was quiet. Their surroundings were surprisingly rural considering they were within the circle of the Tampa Bay area, home to an estimated two million souls. There were no houses or vehicles in sight, only flat land with tall grass, palmetto scrubs and an occasional pine grove. None of the passengers in the truck knew they had crossed from Pasco into Hillsborough County. They were within twenty miles of Tampa.

"Hey, look, Otto," Stoney cried suddenly, "a pond and a trailer." He pointed to a bucolic scene on the right. An aging but well-preserved mobile home stood in a copse of stunted pines, its modest screened porch facing a narrow lake.

"Yeah, we can scrub off the nippers and maybe get a bite to eat from the trailer," Otto exulted.

He turned off the road without further discussion onto an almost indiscernible driveway through the sandy soil. "Hope they're in the mood for company."

The similarity of convoys to the wagon trains of the old West had been apparent from the beginning, and several of the same terms were used. The person in charge of the formation was the wagonmaster, and the person in the seat beside the driver was riding shotgun, even if the weapon he held was an Uzi. Defensive maneuvers were inevitably called *circling the wagons.* But the days of the autocratic wagon-master were gone. The governmental philosophy of the present-day wagon trains was democracy; it was customary to make decisions jointly on issues like route, timing and the possibility of rest stops.

On Sunday morning Major Shearson met with all the drivers, guards and passengers for the Finger Squad convoy, making every effort not to issue orders. Paul Cordray, who knew him well, was amused at his struggle. A major in the U.S. Army was unaccustomed to considering command decisions a collaborative effort.

"I think Interstate 75 to Ft. Myers, then 80 to Belle Glade," he began. "It's roughly 140 miles to Ft. Myers and another 75 to Belle Glade. We'll be there mid-afternoon, even if we stop."

"It's shorter to take 70 over to 27," suggested one of the passengers, the think-tank representative, who was young, brilliant and cocky. He was obviously used to being the smartest fellow around.

"We need to consider safety as much as speed," the major said reasonably. "I did take advice from the Highway Patrol and the sheriff's department."

"I don't think there's much danger," another man, a driver, spoke up. "You get that olive drab Army color on enough of the vehicles and the gangs don't mess with you."

"I hear different." This was from one of the medical people, a tall, middle-aged man riding as a guard. "I hear they wiped out a whole convoy of military up by Jacksonville."

"Sometimes they seem to *look* for authority figures," another guard agreed.

Major Shearson was quiet. Paul caught his eye and smiled. None of these easy opinions came from the other military people, of course, who (including the sergeant in charge of the Air Police squad) would have accepted the major's first plan without argument. No, these comments came from the so-called experts on the team. Civilians! Not the vaguest concept of order and discipline, and the major would be dealing with them for months.

Give him strength, Lord, Paul thought with humor.

The day was hazy, already warm, with the humidity around eighty percent. The day promised to be hot with the "feels-like" temperature even hotter. Paul hoped tempers would stay cool.

Decisions were made at last and positions assigned. They pulled out one by one from the parking lot of the Ramada Inn onto the street that would lead them to Interstate 75. The major had prevailed.

Will Stoddard found himself drawn to Micah Boyd. At first he thought Micah provided comfort because he was living proof that people did, in fact, return from south Florida whole and healthy. But it was more than that. Micah had a way of looking at life that was immensely comforting to Will, somehow. Over the past two days he had visited the Boyds as often as he dared.

He came again to the Boyd home at 10:30 Sunday morning. Micah and his wife were walking down the porch steps as Will drove up.

Of course! he thought with annoyance. *Church.*

Micah walked over to Will's truck, hand extended, a look of concern on his face. "Hi, Willy. Any news?"

"They called from Tampa about suppertime last night. No news about the kidnaper's truck, but they're still assuming they're on their way to Belle Glade."

"How's Olivia holding up?"

"Hard to say. She put on a good front for me and her mama, but I know it's just killing her."

Micah smiled gently. "Not really, Will. She's in great pain, but she's not being killed."

"Mebbe not." Will sighed. "Well, I'll get out of your hair, let y'all be on your way."

How little he wanted to return home to his heartbroken wife, his unknowing horses and the weight of having nothing whatever to do.

"I can stay home if you'd like to talk."

"Really? I'd hate to impose."

"No problem. Nora can go on without me."

Micah walked back to his wife waiting by the car, pulling off his necktie as he went.

The two men sat in the sunny kitchen drinking strong coffee, talking on a level that surprised Will. He was a private person and Micah was little more than a long-time acquaintance, yet Will found himself opening up.

"I feel so blasted helpless. I didn't go with them, I wasn't invited, and Charlotte says that's Aaron's place anyhow. But to just sit home and wait—it's what women do! Men *do* something."

"You think you could do a better job than Aaron of hunting the kidnapers down, getting the kids away from them? Even getting through all the hazards of going that far south?"

Will thought and answered as honestly he could. "Not really. I'm older, used to bossing people around, and I got 'way yonder more money. But Aaron's O.K. He's sharp and he's clever. Mainly I guess it's that he don't ever know when to quit. He, uh, what's the word? Perseveres."

Micah nodded. "I know him a little, from church and around town. I got a lot of respect for him. And they're his kids. He's the head of that family, and that means God's going to use him."

"I hope so."

"No hope about it, Willy. It's faith you need."

Suddenly Will felt an overwhelming hunger for the kind of faith Micah had. It would be wonderful, he thought, to believe as Micah did, that there was a Source of infinite power and wisdom and goodness available to help. To have this supernatural power accessible to work on his behalf. In short, to have confidence that if he prayed, it would really have an effect.

Micah shook his head in bewilderment. "You know, Willy, I don't see how people stand things like this when they don't know God. I don't understand how they can even get through life without Him."

"You really believe it works? That praying'd make a difference?"

"Absolutely. It's not a matter of theory with me; I *know* it works."

"That must be wonderful." Will heard the self-pity in his voice. And something else. Was it jealousy? Was he jealous of Micah?

"It's available for anybody, long as it's on His terms. You have to belong to Him, but when you do, why, He's on your side! He's *for* you. And the Bible says He's the God of all flesh and there's nothing too hard for Him."

Will sat very still while his thoughts raced. He did not want to be like Micah, all Baptisty and self-satisfied with plaques by the door, making other folks feel uncomfortable if they should happen to slip and curse. He did not want to give up beer, sit in church on Sundays, sing songs to organ music and listen to over-long sermons. And he did not want to talk as they did with "Praise the Lord!" and "God bless you!" He wanted nothing to do with churchiness and all it entailed. He had tried that when he was a kid and it was no good for him.

On the other hand, he did want to hook into the supernatural power Source Micah seemed to have at his disposal.

"Don't think too much about the religion part," Micah said,

as if he were reading Will's mind. "Think about the Lord. Churches and Christians and all that can be pretty annoying, but He isn't."

Will was startled and wondered if that all-powerful Source could read his mind, too. At first the idea made him feel invaded; then it made him feel strangely comforted. Maybe the Source would cut him some slack if it really could see deep within. Wouldn't expect too much of him. He was pretty old to do much changing.

Finally Will mustered a response. "Don't seem right to me to wait till you're desperate."

"God doesn't care. He wants those kids safe more than you do. Remember, He created them in the first place. And make no mistake about it, He can protect them. He just needs somebody to pray, to loose some faith and set things in motion. You're not dealing with a cold, reluctant God, Willy. *He's on your side.*"

Suddenly something inside Will broke and he felt vulnerable, excited, frightened, hopeful, embarrassed, scared, all at the same time. He was uncertain how to do this thing, but confident that he must do it. It was the right, the only, thing to do. No longer would he sit in misery, unable to do a thing to help his family. He would do something almost unprecedented in his experience: He would pray. He would tap into the Source and loose the power on the behalf of his daughters, his son-in-law and his grandchildren.

"Micah, let me ask you something . . ." he began hesitantly.

The woman was in her 70s, tall and sturdy, with cropped gray hair and steady brown eyes. She held a shotgun cradled with familiar ease in her right arm. As Otto stopped the truck and opened the driver's door, she stood at the door of her mobile home and raised the shotgun chest-high.

"Back in your truck and on your way," she called. "I don't mind shooting."

"Please, ma'am," Otto answered in a docile voice. "We don't mean no harm. I got my two grandkids here and we sure could use some breakfast and maybe a dip in your lake."

"I got nothin' for strangers," she replied. "No food, no welcome. Go on, mister. I mean it. I'll shoot."

Otto spoke quietly to Stoney. "Get Sara, let her out your door." Then he spoke again to the woman. "We'll pay you, ma'am. We got cash. Just a chance to clean off and we'll be out of your hair, no harm done."

Stoney pulled Sara roughly over the back of his seat, opened his door and pushed her out. She stumbled and almost fell, then turned to glare at Stoney.

"Start walking toward the house," Otto said in a harsh whisper. "Talk to the lady, tell her you're hungry."

Sara stood undecided while Philip gripped both fists.

"Run, Sara," he muttered. "Run, scream, tell the lady to shoot them."

"Move, dammit," Otto whispered. "Don't try no tricks. I still got your brother, you know."

Sara started forward slowly. The old woman looked at her in surprise and lowered the gun a little.

"Please, lady," Sara said in her sweetest voice. "Please don't shoot us."

"Lord, child, I wouldn't hurt you." The gun came down. She held it loosely in her right hand and watched as Otto advanced. Stoney climbed out of his door and Philip followed.

She's going to let them in, Philip thought. *It'll be my chance.* How often he had seen it in movies. The victims left a note somewhere, and after the crooks made their unsuspecting departure, the note was passed along to the police. He could do that, they would be saved and he would be a hero. All he needed was some time alone with the woman.

As they approached the mobile home and she could see them more clearly, she raised her gun again. "Stay right there. Don't come no closer. Tell me what's going on with these children." She shook her head in disgust. "They look awful."

"That's why we stopped," Otto whined. "Their parents just tested positive and I'm their only other relative. I'm their grandpa. I live in Sarasota and I drove up to take them home with me. We didn't have time to get their clothes or food or anything. I was afraid they'd get quarantined, too, so we hurried."

Philip watched the woman closely. It looked as though she was not buying. The gun stayed steady, the twin barrels pointing squarely at Otto's chest. Her face was tight. Then Sara spoke again.

"Please, ma'am, I'm really hungry. Let us come in." She smiled her sunniest, don't-you-think-I'm-cute smile. "Please, my grandpa wouldn't hurt anybody."

What is she doing? thought Philip in fury. She was betraying him, whether she knew it or not, joining the enemy and making Otto's lies believable.

The woman stared at her for a long moment, then dropped the gun again and nodded. "O.K., you can bathe in the lake and I'll fix you a meal, but you'll have to leave as soon as you've eaten."

"We'll pay you," Otto said.

The lady shook her head. "Keep your money. I don't charge for feeding hungry children. My name's Parker, by the way." She took Sara by the hand and smiled for the first time. "You like biscuits, honey? And guess what else I got? Blackberries! And good fresh milk from my own cow." She opened the screen door and they all trooped in.

Now that nice old lady will end up dead, Philip thought in fury, *and all because Sara wants the tangles out of her hair!* Was he the only one in the world to realize what a jerk his sister was?

❖   ❖   ❖

Burton Chancey had taken another shower. Although he had not come near the spilled blood, he felt contaminated. Now he wore belted white shorts and a bright pink T-shirt with the legend *I can't even THINK straight*. He usually hated the gay-pride cutes, but had been sent this shirt as a gift, and it did look good.

He returned to the office after lunch. Dina was drinking coffee and glanced at his shirt with a raised eyebrow. She herself was now wearing a dress, stockings and heels, with even a trace of lipstick—dressed up, Burt realized, for the arrival of the Finger Squad.

"Don't you look nice," he said dryly.

"And don't you look gay," she retorted.

"Maybe we both feel like making a statement."

Dina smiled. "Mostly I want to say, welcome and get to work. It's really getting desperate."

Burt sank into his chair, suddenly weary and depressed.

"Their rooms all ready?" he asked. "Remember, they're all negative, supposedly, and we have to use the disposable stuff. It's silly, but nobody'd ever come if we didn't make a point of treating them different from the infecteds."

"People don't think it's silly to take precautions, Burt. You're the exception. Most people don't want to get AIDS."

"You think I do?" He was astonished.

"Certainly. Everybody knows it. You self-destruct every chance you get." Dina leaned back, smiling a little. "Like that shirt. You don't do things like that, push your homosexuality in people's faces. But now we're getting this crew of people— some of them *soldiers*, for heavens sake!—who are probably crawling with homophobia, and you pick today to wear pink! Why? Do you feel the need to punish yourself?"

"Look, Dina, it's Saturday. We're supposed to be off-duty. I can wear what I want."

"Sure you can. It's just the timing that's interesting to me. But what do I know?" Her eyes twinkled with amusement.

Burt walked out of the office; he could not abide her smug, laughing face right now. What did she know? She thought he wanted to get AIDS. That was nonsense!

But his brain was whirling. Why *did* he wear the pink shirt today of all days? Had there been an ulterior motive? Did it have anything to do with soldiers?

The day grew warmer as the sun rose; heat waves off the highway blurred the distance into shimmery ripples. Nor did a fitful breeze bring coolness. The car's air conditioner hummed steadily. The major was driving now and Paul sat to his right, holding a rifle loosely across his chest. They were not first in the column, but there was still a need for vigilance. Then the major spoke.

"What in blazes are these bugs? I never saw anything like them. If they were any thicker, they'd clog up the radiator."

Paul had noticed the numbers of these insects they were encountering. The windshield was smeared with sooty black bodies, about the size of mosquitoes but heavier. There were dozens of them.

"They're called love bugs," Cassandra Kovaks answered from the back seat.

"Why love bugs?"

"That's all they do. They spend their whole lives making love. They appear, like, from out of nowhere a couple times a year, procreate like mad and then disappear."

"Are they some kind of fly? Mosquito?" the major asked. "I've been all over the world and have never seen anything like them."

"I think they're just here, you know, in Florida. Word is

they were, like, created here." She leaned forward and laughed lightly. "There's a rumor to that effect, anyhow."

Paul turned to look at her. She was dressed in shorts, a man-style shirt and high-top tennis shoes. She wore no makeup and her hair was tied back in a ponytail. She looked as little like a doctor of medicine as anyone he could imagine. Her face was open and innocent, and she seemed too—well, what was it? He finally defined it: too untouched.

"Created?" the major asked.

"Well, sort of. There was some kind of genetic experimentation going on. Some say in Miami at the university there, others say at USF. I went to USF and I know there was genetic research, like, six years ago, but of course love bugs have been around a lot longer than that. But anyhow, they say something went really wrong and some of the bugs got loose, and now they're, like, part of our ecology."

Major Shearson was amused. "Do you believe that?"

"Well, we didn't used to have these bugs when I was a kid. They just suddenly appeared—like, from out of nowhere. A brand-new bug! I mean, what other explanation fits?"

"I don't know. Mutation, maybe? The idea of science gone mad, that's pretty hard to swallow."

The doctor shook her head. "It could be. I know they're doing some pretty wild stuff with genetic engineering."

"Making giants," Paul said softly. "As in the days of Noah."

Dr. Kovaks glanced at him curiously but continued talking. "We have human cells, estrogen receptor cells, implanted in beef cattle now to make it more tender, and genetically engineered mice that are actually patented. We can produce male mice from female embryos by injecting a sex-trigger gene into the fertilized eggs."

Paul had noticed that the doctor's use of the jargon of youth—*like* and *you know* and *I mean*—diminished when she was talking professionally. He remembered being told once that speech full of nonsense was a sign of a chaotic thinking. That might explain the doctor's case; she seemed mature and confident in her professional role, and her speech disclosed the contrast.

"We're working now to engineer dairy cows with extra genes," she was saying, "so we can give the cows certain drugs, the drugs get into the milk, and patients can get medications directly, you know, in the milk they drink. And you remember the transgenic mice?"

"Doctor, I don't even know what that *is!* But you'll tell me, I'm sure." Major Shearson was apparently amused by Dr. Kovaks' fervor.

"They made them at Bethesda, the National Institutes of Health, for AIDS research. They bred a female mouse, harvested her fertilized eggs and injected the viral genetic code for the HIV into the nucleus of the egg and reimplanted them in another female mouse. Some of the babies were born with the AIDS virus in every single cell. They had a lot of negative publicity, you know, like—well, what if they escaped and started breeding little AIDS carriers in the community? That kind of thing. Obstructionist publicity."

Major Shearson had stopped smiling. "What happened? Did they stop?"

"I don't know. I never heard any more about them. Probably just got a gag order and, you know, kept it quiet."

"I'm not sure I like the sound of that."

The doctor shook her head. "Well, America is still fighting for a standing in the field of experimental biotechnology, and we have an awful lot of hindrances. There's still a ban on some kinds of fetal transplantation research, and—"

"This is beginning to sound like science fiction," Major Shearson broke in. "I can't even understand what you're talking about."

Paul spoke into their laughter. "Are there any other rumors of things gone wrong? Besides the love bugs, I mean?"

"Oh, I guess so. But you can't stop progress."

"You call it progress? Engineered animals? Animal organs in human beings? Human cells growing in animals?"

"Not cells, really," corrected the doctor. "Just genes."

"Human tissue, anyhow," Paul insisted.

The major turned on the windshield wipers and dispensed the washer solution; the wipers smeared the insect bodies in arced streaks across the glass. Paul felt uneasy. Both his companions would be considered good, decent people; they would even qualify for the greatest accolade of the '90s—being sensitive and caring. But neither of them had any inkling of the potential for evil in the subject under discussion.

If it concerned science, most people believed, it must be good. Research and scientific advancement had as its goal the meeting of human need and the enrichment of human life; and neither the major nor the doctor saw anything but good in that perspective. If it helped human beings, it must be good.

Even Christians fell for that deception, Paul thought. Somehow the Church had been suckered into responding to human need instead of to the will of God, failing to see that the two were not the same thing at all.

"You know, some people think the HIV started that way, like, in a scientific laboratory." Dr. Kovaks was thoroughly enjoying the talk; usually both men avoided her.

"I've heard that," the major agreed. "In smallpox vaccine. But it was too technical for me."

"The idea is that because Koprowski's vaccine was manufactured by culturing attenuated polio virus in monkey kidneys, maybe some batches of it were contaminated with a simian AIDS virus. Actually, contamination happened a lot. As many as 30 million kids were infected by a monkey virus,

SV 40, between 1954 and 1963, when they were vaccinated for smallpox. That's documented. So maybe the HIV, too. Anyhow, Dr. Koprowski's vaccine was given by squirting it into the kids' mouths, which would give the virus time to enter the bloodstream through, you know, cuts in the mouth, and it wouldn't be killed by the stomach acids.

"The most significant fact is this: He tested his vaccine in what was then the Belgian Congo, the exact place where AIDS started and where it's killed nearly everybody by now. Koprowski gave his vaccine to over 200,000 people in 1957."

"That so?" The major was frowning. "I heard whispers. You know, everybody does. But I didn't know the details."

"Well, smallpox vaccine is one possible way, very possible. It's logical and some of the evidence supports the theory. But even if it was true, it wouldn't be anything more than an accident. Like a mistake. But some people think AIDS was constructed deliberately, made on purpose by some unknown group for some unknown objective. I find *that* really hard to believe. Nobody could be so evil."

Paul smiled without humor. Humanists want to believe humans are good, but he marveled at the ease with which they swallowed this particular lie. The deliberate construction of a death-dealing microbe, using human intellect and technology was, in his opinion, exactly the kind of thing unregenerate mankind could accomplish. One had only to look around to see the depth and scope of the evil that humanity could and would do—with proficiency. The Bible said it: The heart of man is desperately wicked.

And mine, too, he thought. *I'm no better than anybody else without the Lord.* The conversation in the car faded, each retiring into his own thoughts.

We'll be there soon. In a place of disease and death and desperately wicked hearts, I wonder if there's enough Light in me to make a difference.

✤　✤　✤

Taxi drivers and bartenders were his best bets, Carly decided. They know about the dark side of life in any town. You want a gun, some light little recreational drugs, maybe a guy to do some shady chore that might bend the law—whatever you need, you can find through a taxi driver or bartender. Maybe tonight he could take a walk around Belle Glade and get a notion about how to sell the silver.

He hoped devoutly he could finish the business in Belle Glade and not have to go on to Miami. He was not afraid, exactly. He had enough money to make the trip and even hire protection if he wanted to. Nor was he afraid of Miami, despite its reputation. No, what it actually came down to, the thing he did not want to face, was trying to explain to Aaron Tyler why he would have to go.

Carly stared out the window at the hot, flat terrain that flashed past. Iris Stoddard was silent in the companion chair beside him; Olivia and Aaron were quiet in the front seat. What possible reason could he give these people for a side trip to Miami?

He continued thinking about finding a taxi driver or bartender, about the technicalities of a negotiation new to his experience, about anything at all except his father, and how his father had sent him into danger—known and unknown—without a thought for his son's well-being. Thinking only about money.

Once again Carly cut short this line of thinking. Still, a hint of that theme was always there, flowing through and around his thoughts. He resisted it with every force at his disposal.

The pond water looked brown, but it was clean and Philip enjoyed the swim. He and Sara wore their pajamas into the water. After three days they were filthy. Otto Krause and Stoney Hickman joined them, stripped down to their shorts.

Sara was a cautious swimmer who hated water in her face and avoided splashing. She paddled alone happily near the shore while Philip swam vigorously out to the center of the pond and back. The clean water and exercise were wonderful. Otto cavorted like the out-of-shape whale he resembled, while Stoney swam back and forth intently with his head held high out of the water, an absorbed look on his face. There was no conversation.

Philip's mind was busy with plans. He would keep an eye out for pencil and paper and find an opportunity to write a note. They would have to maintain the pretense Otto and Sara had begun. If the truth came out, Philip was sure, Otto would kill Mrs. Parker.

"Food's ready!" The old lady stood on her porch and beckoned to the swimmers.

They made their way, dripping, to the trailer. She handed out clean towels and walked back inside as Otto and Stoney pulled on their shabby clothes over dripping underwear.

"Food's ready when you are," she called.

There were only two chairs at the small table in the kitchen, so Otto Krause and Stoney Hickman sat awkwardly on the sofa in the adjoining living room. To Philip's frustration, Otto could still see his captives. The home was shabby but spotless. The shotgun lay on the kitchen counter; Mrs. Parker had swallowed the story but did not completely trust them. Even if she believed Otto was their grandfather, he still looked disreputable and dangerous. And Philip was sure she was no fool.

It was wonderful to eat sitting at a table again. Philip was so comforted by the homelike atmosphere, by being served real food on a plate by a woman, that he was almost ready to cry. The only thing that restrained his sentimental tears was his fury at his sister.

His mother would certainly approve of this wholesome food. He recalled some of her little sayings about food: "God made honey; man makes sugar" (he had never quite had the nerve to ask her where the bees fit in); and one that reflected her great regard for fresh fruit: "An apple tastes plenty sweet if you're not in the habit of eating ice cream." His love for her was so strong and gripping that he could hardly swallow.

I'll never fuss about food again, he vowed. *I'll eat anything she gives me. Even lima beans.*

Sara sat across from him, savoring her blackberries in milk and hot biscuits with jam. She was chattering around the food in her mouth, charming their hostess.

"My hair is all tangled," she complained. "My mama always brushes it every morning, and again at night, and it hasn't been brushed for days." Sara's hair, dark-gold, thick and slightly curly, had never been cut, only trimmed, and Sara was inordinately proud of it. Philip agreed, it did look awful now.

"I got shampoo and conditioner. They'd do better than pond water," Mrs. Parker said. "Soon as you're done eating, let's go fix you up."

Otto raised his head from his plate of food and stared at Sara, his little eyes tight with suspicion. But he did not come up with a reason to refuse Mrs. Parker's offer.

Sara finished her food quickly and took Mrs. Parker's hand. "I'm ready."

The old woman picked up the shotgun with her other hand and led Sara down the hall toward the back of the trailer.

"This won't take long," she told the others. "Help yourself to more food if you want."

As soon as they had disappeared behind a closed door, Philip was hit by fear. For all his irritation with his sister and the distress of the responsibility she represented, he was suddenly aware that Sara's presence strengthened him. Her sunny cheer held at bay some of the evil within their captors; and her ability to charm the savage hearts of these unfeeling men had been a wall of protection—not only for her but for Philip. Now that she was gone, he was suddenly alone feeling younger, more helpless and much, much more afraid.

8

Sunday afternoon and night, September 12, 1999

B elle Glade is situated three-quarters of the way down the peninsula of Florida, forty miles west of Palm Beach. It has a history as a farm town with a mostly non-white migrant population. Like the rest of south Florida it is flat, sandy and fertile, with a humid, semi-tropical climate. This small, impoverished town has made headlines several times in public health matters.

In the 1940s Belle Glade was the site of a flourishing syphilis epidemic, the case numbers out of all proportion to the population. The government launched an investigation, built a hospital and improved housing conditions. But the inevitable official interest was temporary; efforts dwindled quickly. Things in the small town returned to what passed for normal.

Belle Glade made the charts again in the '80s, ranking with (and later even above) San Francisco and New York City in the percentage of its population testing positive for HIV. The demographics of this little town made this peculiar. Without a large number of homosexuals, intravenous drug-users or even a particularly reckless or promiscuous population, the incidence of AIDS soared. The conclusion of a scientific study published by two M.D.'s was frightening but, they claimed, inescapable: The HIV was being spread by mosquitoes.

This information hit the so-called AIDS experts like a bombshell, and those in charge moved quickly to suppress the material. The American public had been told repeatedly that the transmission of AIDS in this way was so unlikely as to be impossible; and few Americans were privy to the data from Great Britain and elsewhere indicating that it was indeed possible. Few Americans learned about the Belle Glade controversy.

The Centers for Disease Control did their own investigation of Belle Glade, investigating the previous investigation. Not surprisingly, they disparaged the earlier study. The original researchers sued the CDC, asking that the different test results be reviewed independently. But the courts ruled that releasing the data would violate the privacy of the participants, even though no names had been used. Preserving the privacy of AIDS patients still had a far higher priority than protecting society from the spread of the disease.

The CDC explained the unusually high incidence of AIDS in Belle Glade as a result of the usual things—sexual intercourse, IV drug use, blood transfusions. It was worse here, they said, because of poverty and crowded living conditions.

But this bewildered the few citizens aware of this dispute. Even the public was beginning to question what living conditions had to do with a blood-borne virus. Hadn't the experts told them that factors like how you lived and who you lived with had no effect on the incidence of AIDS? And what of other locations with similar poverty and overcrowding? Why no alarming rise of AIDS in those places?

For the most part, however, questions about Belle Glade were dropped. It had a disproportionate incidence of AIDS but people no longer asked why. That high incidence was one of the factors that led to its being classified as an infected area and the center of a Quarantine Zone for AIDS carriers.

Sara returned from the back of the trailer with Mrs. Parker, who still held the gun.

"Don't she look pretty?" the old woman asked with apparent pride, while Sara smiled her agreement.

"Look, Grandpa!" She pranced into the living room and pirouetted in front of her kidnapers. "She used a hair-dryer."

"Real pretty," Otto sulked, still suspicious. He peered intently at the old woman, trying to read her face.

"You're a regular little Barbie doll," Stoney said with enthusiasm. "We gotta get you a brush."

"Time to go."

Otto stood up and Philip felt his heart begin to pound. There had been no chance for him to leave a note and now they were going. Would Otto leave Mrs. Parker alive or eliminate her as a possible witness to his crime?

It did not occur to Philip that Mrs. Parker might shoot both men. He was so sure of Otto's power that he assumed his abductors would win any conflict, even against an armed opponent.

Mrs. Parker stood by the kitchen table, gun in hand, eyes fixed on Otto. For one frozen moment the kidnaper and the woman with the shotgun stared at each other. Stoney's bright brown eyes flashed back and forth between them.

Philip could sense Stoney's longing for the battle. He wanted bloodshed. He held his breath and prayed as hard as he knew how. *Jesus, let us walk out of here without them hurting her.*

Time stretched like a rubber band. Someone would have to move soon or they would be unable to continue the charade. At last, when Philip thought he would scream, Sara broke the impasse.

"Thank you for the food. I enjoyed it very much." Her obedience to her mother's oft-repeated instructions restored the illusion of normalcy to the group.

"You're welcome, honey. Good luck on your trip."

"Yeah, thanks," Otto muttered, opening the door. "Come on, kids."

Stoney bobbed an awkward little bow. Some of the gleam had gone out of his eyes. "Much obliged, ma'am."

Philip pushed Sara ahead of him, then followed her out the door. Her curls bounced against her back. Otto took her hand in his and hurried toward the truck.

Philip looked back toward the old woman. Could he possibly go back, say he needed to go to the bathroom, whisper a plea for help? But that was fantasy, beyond the capacity of a ten-year-old boy. His head drooped as he followed his captors and sister back to the truck. He crawled into the back without being told.

The town of Belle Glade sits uncertainly on the southeastern shore of Lake Okeechobee within hailing distance of the unthinkably expensive real estate along Florida's gold coast, at most an observer of—never a participant in—the good life there.

The Indians rightly named this lake by their word for *big water.* Okeechobee is the second-largest freshwater lake in America. It is 35 miles long, 730 square miles in area. It is the wellspring of the Florida lowlands, the great liquid heart of one of the most fertile regions in the world. Lake Okeechobee is fed by the Kissimmee watershed, a chain of lakes that feed into the Kissimmee River. The river flows south 100 miles to Lake Okeechobee, and beyond the lake by means of canals, dams, streams and rivers into the Everglades to the south and the Big Cypress Swamp to the southwest.

These watery lowlands include about one-fifth of the area of the state, over 12,500 square miles of land and water that cover what was once a hollow in the sea floor. The area encompassed by Florida's waterlands is greater than that of Connecticut and New Jersey combined.

Lake Okeechobee is shallow, usually only twelve to seventeen feet in depth, but this measurement is altered by erosion, the deposit of sediment and by rainfall.

Before the canals were built, Lake Okeechobee exhibited a volatile and deadly nature. In 1922 the lake rose more than four and a half feet in less than three months as a result of heavy rainfall. Two years later it gained a depth of nineteen feet, and finally in September 1928 it revealed its true temperament. A hurricane swept across the peninsula of Florida, dropping many inches of rain over a short time. The water level in the Everglades rose from four to eight feet in the first hour and almost 2,400 people drowned.

Something must be done, everyone agreed, to tame this monster lake, to bring him to heel and pull his fangs. The answer: a clever network of manmade canals built to work either way—water could flow from the Glades to the lake or from the lake to the Glades. Man could respond to potential danger in one of several ways in order to prevent a repetition of the death and damage of earlier days.

But control of this immense and unstable marriage of land and water was not easy to achieve. The security of locks and dams and canals was more presumed than actual. And the numerous conditions influencing the lake, the Glades and the expanse of flat land surrounding them, while touched by man and his efforts, were in no way dominated by him. There were too many other powerful factors, too many irresistible natural forces, for man to claim mastery.

There is a reason, after all, that natural disasters are called "acts of God": because it is beyond the power of man to initiate them.

Or to control them.

✤　✤　✤

The convoy arrived at the Belle Glade Quarantine Zone Barrier about 3 P.M. The travelers climbed out of their vehicles and stretched. The hazy heat seemed to intensify the glare of the sun. The testing committee was competent and their procedure remarkably efficient—a quick fingerstick, a drop of blood on a glass slide and a rapid scan by the medical computer, with the result appearing almost instantly. There were no surprises; all the team members were still uninfected.

No one was completely comfortable being within an infected area, in close contact with so many sick people, but at least it was temporary. They climbed back into their trucks and cars and drove into the Zone.

The hospice was situated about a mile north of Highway 80 and a mile west of Route 175, putting it about halfway between Belle Glade and the neighboring town of South Bay. The original buildings, like most structures in Florida, were made of concrete blocks low to the ground, painted in pastel hues and landscaped with more money than concern. The buildings had been outgrown within eighteen months, and the necessary additions were prefabricated metal warehouses erected hastily on concrete slabs.

The vast patient-care facility sat in the midst of numerous outbuildings: clinics, recreational facilities, living quarters for staff and guests, and garages and repair shops for the fleet of vehicles. Less than three years old, the place already had a look of neglect.

The dormitories were five rectangular four-story buildings with high, narrow windows. All were painted a dispirited beige. The members of the Finger Squad, being uninfected, were housed on one of the top two floors of the building officially designated as "Temporary or Semi-Permanent Housing Facility Number 4." It was known familiarly as "Dorm 4."

None of the hospice administrators seemed to care—if indeed they even realized—that the Tylers, Iris Stoddard and Carly Jenson were not part of the official team. They were given lodging without comment.

Room assignments were handled with disinterest, and in the end the hot, tired guests simply took what seemed convenient. So it happened that Iris Stoddard and Dr. Cassandra Kovaks were once again roommates. Carly Jenson took the second bed in the room already chosen by Sergeant Paul Cordray. The major, of course, had his own room and bath. The Tylers took the first room they walked into, shut the door and clung to each other in wordless desperation.

Dinner was set for six in the hospice dining room, followed by a meeting with the hospice managers for those on the investigative team. The Pine River contingent would have the evening free.

The sun beat down on the metal body of the truck, making the interior extremely hot, and the smells of chemicals, vomit and bodily wastes sickened Philip. He lay in a stupor of depression. He had failed to improve their chances for rescue and knew he probably never would. No matter what the opportunity, he would be too afraid, too hesitant, too much a child.

Sara sat immediately behind the front seat perched on a large, upturned paint can, high enough to see through the windshield but far enough back not to be seen easily by anyone outside. She often sat here chattering away to Stoney. But the men were talking to each other now, discussing plans for the afternoon.

"Been a long time since we had any feminine companionship," Otto had begun. "Maybe we ought to see to that while we're still in Tampa. Much farther south and we'll hit the Infected Zone."

Philip listened passively, unable to boost his flagging hopes that there might be some opening for escape.

"Lots of places along Nebraska Avenue," Stoney said.

"What about the kids? Can't hardly take them with."

Stoney waited in silence.

"I guess we could lock them in the truck," Otto continued thoughtfully. "Put the truck somewhere nobody could see in, no way they could signal to anybody." He paused. "Or we could just knock them out."

Philip stirred in consternation and sat up.

Otto snapped his fingers. "I know, Stoney! We'll go to Halley's. She's got a garage and we can just drive in and shut the door. Leave the nippers in the truck with no worry."

"She got a friend for me, Otto?" Stoney asked.

"Sure. Halley's got lotsa girlfriends. We'll have the whole afternoon, maybe all night." Otto stopped again to think. "We might oughta get a coupla bottles. Or maybe she'll have some."

The discussion continued during the search for the residence—with its all-important garage—of Otto's friend Halley. There was no problem with signs, since Tampa had most of its street markers intact, but the kidnapers had a hard time finding exactly where Halley lived. They drove back and forth for more than an hour, finally recognizing familiar landmarks.

Philip was stirred by the idea that once again they would be in the company of a third party, but had no confidence in himself now to act, and little confidence that the unseen Halley would undertake any action to help them, even if she knew their plight. *Jesus, please help us.*

Suddenly Otto announced excitedly, "There it is, Stoney. Hop out and open the garage."

Stoney jumped eagerly from the truck and Otto turned to the children. "We're gonna go see some friends. You kids just wait here. Don't do anything foolish, hear? We'll be keeping an eye on you."

Sara crawled back toward Philip as the truck drove into the dark garage.

Otto climbed from the truck, slammed his door and locked it, then walked around to lock Stoney's door and the rear doors. The children could hear Stoney greeting someone and a robust female voice answering. The light dimmed as the garage door was pulled down behind the truck. Then the two men disappeared, accompanied by feminine laughter.

"Let's sit up in their seats, Philip," Sara urged. "It's nicer than just being on the floor."

"You go. I don't feel like it."

"Oh, Philip, they're gone! We can talk out loud or whatever we want. Don't be in a bad mood."

A bad mood! That showed how much *she* understood about the situation. He was so homesick he could hardly bear it, and on top of that they were both probably going to die. And just because he had enough sense to know it, she thought he was in a bad mood. What a flat wave she was.

"We'll be rescued real soon now," she said happily. "I told Mrs. Parker about how we were kidnaped."

Philip turned to her in astonishment. "You *didn't!* Why didn't you tell me before?"

"I knew you'd holler like you always do and they'd know. You always get so excited. Anyhow, I'm telling you now."

Sara was so satisfied with herself he wanted to shake her. "What did you tell her? What did she say?"

"I told her all about it and she said she'd call the police. And I gave her the phone number."

"What phone number?"

"Our phone number in Pine River, of course. Then I thought, in case nobody's home, I should give her Grandpa's number, too. She wrote them down."

Sara's self-esteem, always high, was currently soaring. Philip was in emotional overload—thrilled that the message might go out, anguished that he had not been the one to give it, jealous that Sara *had* been, uncertain that the message would be sufficient to effect their rescue, anxious that they keep this news from Otto and Stoney.

But more powerful than all these was an incredible puzzle: Had Sara really been clever enough to plan this? Had she schemed from the beginning of the visit, calling Otto "Grandpa" in order to get help?

"O.K.," he agreed. "Let's sit in their seats and you tell me every single thing you said to that lady and she said to you."

Will was mucking out the stable as Joe Jenson drove up. At first he thought Joe might be bringing some news of the kids, but he decided quickly that was unlikely; Will communicated more with the travelers than Joe did. Maybe Joe had come to *get* information.

"Hey, Willy." Joe stepped out of his gleaming silver New Yorker, dressed impeccably in pale gray slacks and a long-sleeved silk shirt the color of sweet burgundy. He removed his silvered sunglasses and walked toward Will.

He's a handsome guy, Will thought. Tall and erect with those smiling blue eyes.

Will wore faded jeans and a worn cotton work shirt, both dirty, and an old Miami Dolphins cap. He removed the cap to wipe sweat from his forehead with his shirtsleeve.

"Watch where you step, Joe," he warned. "I'm not done here yet."

Joe stood a careful six feet from the stable and grinned. "I know that must be fun, Willy, but do you think you could knock off for a while and let's talk?"

"Sure. Want a beer?"

"Got anything with a little more muscle?"

"How about bourbon? Seems I heard that's your drink."

"You can't be in politics in the South without loving bourbon."

"So I hear. Loving money, too."

They fell in step walking toward the house. They had known one another all their lives, were as familiar to each other as the town itself, but they had never been friends. Will voted for Joe on the rare occasions when his opponent seemed even less a statesman, and he gave Joe some of his legal work. He knew Joe to be wily, adroit and securely connected to the power structure. But Will had not trusted Joe since grade school.

Joe considered himself superior to Will Stoddard in every way: He was richer, smarter, better educated, from a higher social stratum; and while Joe was a player in life, a mover and shaker of things around town, Will was merely a spectator. But then, Joe felt this way about nearly everybody, not just Will, and he was shrewd enough not to let it show. Both men disapproved of the relationship between Iris and Carly, and both took comfort in the knowledge that it was almost certainly temporary.

Now they shared the uncommon experience of having children in danger.

Will was fixing drinks in the kitchen, Joe sitting at the kitchen table, when Charlotte came in. "Do you have news?"

"No, I came to see if you all had heard anything." Joe the politician knew how to act like plain folks. He accepted a hefty bourbon on the rocks from Will with a nod of thanks. "I thought maybe Carly'd phone, but I haven't heard a word."

"I talked to Aaron last night," Will said. "They were leaving Tampa this morning so they're probably in Belle Glade by now. No word on the truck, but he's still hopeful."

Charlotte poured a cup of coffee from the pot she had brewed at lunch and put it in the microwave oven to heat. It was very black, almost viscous. "We're just hanging on, going through the motions. How are you managing?"

"Well, I miss Carly, of course. We work together, live to-gether. I'm used to having him around. But he isn't *missing*, you know. Not like your grandkids. I know he'll be back."

Will popped the tab of a beer and joined the others at the table. "That may be overly optimistic, Joe. I don't want to be negative, but I been talking a good bit to Micah Boyd, and he says it's dangerous down there for everybody." His thoughts jumped back to the extraordinary interlude he and Micah had shared that morning. He wasn't completely sure what had happened, but *something* sure had.

"Oh, Micah's an old woman," Joe said. "He says things like that because he wants everybody to admire his courage to keep driving down there."

"Most folks do," Will shot back. "Just like folks think it was pretty great of Carly to go along with Aaron and the others."

An odd look crossed Joe's face.

What's the cagey old guy up to? Will thought. The attorney looked amused, secretive, even triumphant. *There's a fox in the henhouse somehow.* But Joe's intrigues were of little interest compared to the pain of his loss and the new wonderment of whatever it was that had happened at Micah's.

"The thing I hate is, now they might not be able to call," Charlotte complained. "Though I guess the hospice will have *some* way to communicate."

"We can trust Aaron," Joe said. "I'd say he's pretty re-sourceful."

Will wondered: Should he mention his prayer with Micah? On the one hand, it would be embarrassing, although he knew enough about these fanatical Christians to know they did not mind saying things that would mortify normal people. On the other hand, it would probably make the thing more real to him if he admitted it openly.

"Well, yeah," he said. "Aaron's solid. But he's not the one I'm putting my confidence in."

"You mean the soldiers?" Charlotte asked.

"No, I mean the Lord."

"Who?" Joe and Charlotte spoke in unison, looking at him in amazement.

"You know, God. Jesus."

He had been right—it was almost painfully embarrassing. But now that Will had started, it was too late to back down. "I prayed this morning and asked God to bring them home, and you know what? I believe He will."

"You sound like Olivia," Charlotte said, shaking her head. "I can't believe it's *you* talking."

"Funny the different ways people respond to stress," Joe said with a tolerant smile.

Will was suddenly furious. They had nothing to offer: Charlotte had cried till her cheeks were chapped and her only solace was the giant-sized prescription bottle of Valium by her bed, while Joe Jenson denied he had anything to worry about. Besides, Joe had his own crutch: His triple bourbon was almost gone already.

"Look, you can act smug if you want to, but it seems to me if there's anything God knows about, it's having a Son in danger. Maybe Jesus wasn't exactly kidnaped, but—"

The telephone rang.

Dinner was over before seven and Iris faced an evening alone in a strange town where almost everybody was infected. She sat on the bed in her assigned room contemplating the prospects. Her roommate was busy with the rest of the medical personnel, touring the hospice. *That sounds jolly*, Iris thought with distaste.

Carly had disappeared somewhere right after dinner and she certainly did not intend to hunt him down. What night life there was in Belle Glade was almost certainly too earthy for her liking, anyhow. Should she seek the Tylers out for companionship? They invariably preferred each other's company to anyone else, and she would only intrude into their privacy and grief. Both Major Shearson and Sergeant Cordray were busy with some official activity.

She was on her own.

O.K., she said to herself. *I can handle this. I can spend this time trying to figure out what in blazes I'm doing here. Then I'll reward myself with a drink before I try to sleep.*

She kicked off her shoes and stretched out comfortably on the narrow bed.

First thing I need to know: When I decided to come along with Livvy and Aaron on this little safari, was I running away from something or running toward something?

As exhausted as Burton Chancey was, he reviewed carefully (as almost everybody did these days) to be sure there was a genuine cause, that he was not manifesting one of the early signs of AIDS. But today it was easy to see real reasons for fatigue. He sat in a comfortable chair by the window in his bedroom.

The building known as Dorm 4 was the nicest of the staff quarters and housed not only guests from outside the Zone, but also the upper-level hospice personnel. As director, Burt had his two-room apartment on the first floor rear, next to the kitchen. It was not always quiet, but it was very convenient.

Because of Dina Hawk's efficiency, the dinner for the Finger Squad had gone well. The food was tasty and nobody had shown too much reluctance to be in a room full of infected people eating the same food. The guests used disposable dishes and silverware, of course; and most people could (when necessary) still behave as though AIDS could not be transmitted by casual contact.

They want to believe it so badly, Burt thought. *Most people have a marvelous ability to deny what's becoming more and more obvi-*

ous. Since they're all ordered here anyway and have no choice, denial is a great way of coping.

He tried to work up some optimism. Maybe this team of experts would make a difference. If they could establish security and control the crime, he could handle the rest of it. They all seemed to be top-notch people with impressive credentials.

And talk about impressive! His mind drifted to Sergeant Paul Cordray. Young, handsome, fit. Masculine strength and grace; authority in sharp, starched khaki. Very impressive indeed.

He jumped to his feet, annoyed with his reverie. More than a waste of time, it was dangerous to let his thoughts drift along these lines.

I need sleep, he thought firmly. *I'll have a couple of drinks and get to bed early for a change. Tomorrow will be rough enough.*

Double-occupancy rooms were built with bathrooms between them, so Carly Jenson and Paul Cordray shared a bath with two other members of the Finger Squad. It meant some crowding and delay, but it was all done with good will. Paul was preparing for a meeting the major had called involving all military personnel in Belle Glade. It was expected to be brief; there would be far less discussion than with the other specialties. It made you appreciate one of the many benefits of military life—no "rule by committee"!

Carly was going to town; he planned to hit the night spots, hoping to meet that bartender or taxi driver who could direct him to parties interested in buying silver. A town the size of Belle Glade offered little in the way of entertainment, but there were many bars and Carly dressed with care. He did not want to look rich to the patrons of the bar; that might be dangerous. As he brushed his hair back from what he considered an exceptionally noble brow, he found to his surprise that he was almost pleasurably excited.

There was no reason in the world, of course, why he should not do a good job of this business. He could meet the right people, make a good profit, then go home and spit in old Joe's eye.

"I'm trying to reach Will Stoddard." It was a woman's voice unfamiliar to Will.

"Speaking."

He was eager to get back to his talk with Charlotte and Joe Jenson. He was just warming up to telling them about the exhilaration of tapping into the Source.

"I'm Jessie Parker from Citrus Park, down by Tampa, you know? I got a message for you from your granddaughter."

Will sank back against the counter, suddenly too weak to stand. "You what? You mean from Sara? You talked to Sara?"

Charlotte jumped up from her chair and grabbed at the receiver, but Will pushed her away. Joe flashed a sharp look in their direction, then rose to pour himself another triple bourbon.

"Yes, sir. They were here this morning."

"Where are they now? Were they all right? Her brother was with her, right?" Will was almost shouting.

"Yes, sir. You just calm down and I'll tell you all about it."

"Wait, wait just a minute, let my wife get on the other phone." He motioned to Charlotte, who ran toward the living room. An instant later he heard Charlotte pick up the other line. "Now, start at the beginning."

Mrs. Parker told the story well, chronologically and succinctly. But both Will and Charlotte interrupted her again and again with questions.

"I called the police right after the truck left, and they took me to Tampa to look at pictures."

Will started to interrupt again but she raised her voice to override him. "Yes, I identified both of them. Both men have

criminal records but nothing to do with children before. The
police think that's a good sign. Anyhow, I only just got home
and had to feed my chickens and milk my cow and this is the
first time I had to call you."

"Can you believe they're still in that truck? Can you beat
that for being stupid?" Will was soaring. The children were
all right, not abused—or worse. And how about that Sara?
Smart as a whip, getting alone with the woman to get her help.

"I don't know if I done right," Mrs. Parker was saying. "I
thought about it and it seemed right at the time."

"What do you mean?" Charlotte asked.

Charlotte was crying again, Will could tell. Good news or
bad, she cried. That was Charlotte for you, the city waterworks.

"Well, I could have killed them, of course. I had my shotgun in my hands, two barrels, all ready to shoot. But I never
killed people before, never a human being, and I wasn't absolutely sure I could do it. And also, I thought about what it
would do to them kids, watching the men die right in front
of them. It's a messy thing with a shotgun, and I thought that
might be worse for them kids to forget than being with the
men a little while longer."

"Oh, I see." Will wanted to reassure the woman that she
had done the right thing, but the idea that the kids might be
free, that he might be driving south right this minute to pick
them up, stopped the words in his mouth.

"I had to decide on the spot," she continued. "I couldn't
let them get suspicious."

"Of course not," Charlotte said stoutly. She was still crying but at least she could talk. "You did what was best and
we're very grateful. It was wonderful of you to take them in,
at a risk to yourself, and feed them, and—oh, you even fixed
Sara's hair. She cares so much about how she looks, sometimes I think too much, actually. . . ."

Will broke in. "Do you have the name of a particular police officer in charge, or a case number or anything? I'd like to call them."

Mrs. Parker gave him some information and he thanked her again profusely, then hung up the phone with a shaking hand.

Charlotte came back into the kitchen and hugged him exuberantly. Her face was radiant though tear-streaked, her posture erect again, her voice bubbling with joy. "Oh, Will, isn't it wonderful? They're O.K.! And the police know all about the truck. . . ."

Joe raised his glass in salute.

"Great news," he beamed. "Too bad Aaron and them already left Tampa."

Don't throw cold water on it, Will thought in annoyance. "This is good news, Joe. Shows we have good reason to hope." Then he stopped himself, then spoke with delight: "Not hope. It's like Micah said, it's faith. This is a sign my prayer's being answered! Sara was talking to that lady just about the same time I was praying."

Charlotte looked at him with teary-eyed perplexity, Joe with amused superiority. But Will did not care. He knew what he knew.

"You'll see," he said happily. "My prayer's going to be answered."

Iris had dozed, read a magazine, washed and set her hair and dozed again. Finally at 11 she realized that her plan to think through her motivations had failed. She would get a glass of juice and go to bed. She walked down three flights of stairs.

Two people were in the little kitchen. The hospice director sat at the round table that graced the center of the room, nursing a cup of tea, while his assistant was stirring something on the stove. Iris hesitated at the door, but they made sounds of welcome.

Mr. Chancey looked up from his cup and spoke. "Come on in. Have some tea, or maybe you'd prefer hot chocolate? Dina—that's Dina Hawks, my inestimable helpmeet—makes hot chocolate to die for." He gestured toward a chair. "Sorry, love. I forgot your name."

"Iris Stoddard." She sat down across from him, trying to decide if he were drunk or merely whimsical.

Dina smiled and held up a cup and saucer from the cabinet. "What's your pleasure?"

"Hot chocolate sounds good, if there's enough."

Dina poured Iris a cup of dark, fragrant cocoa, then poured her own cup and sat down. "You're the aunt of the kidnaped children."

"Yes. My brother-in-law went down to Security Headquarters after dinner, trying to decide the next step. We know the vehicle they're in."

"I hope those people do better for you than their usual mediocre standard. They're not noted for excellence." The director sneered delicately. "All guns and guts but no glory."

Dina smiled sadly at Iris. "You'll have to forgive Mr. Chancey, Miss Stoddard. He's having one of his bad days. They often come when we have guests. Something about not being able to play with his toy soldiers."

Iris was uncomfortable. She was sure the director was a little drunk and there were undercurrents of meaning in the conversation she could not interpret. She had just decided to finish her cocoa quickly and leave when a new factor entered the equation: Paul Cordray walked into the room.

All three sat up straighter. Burton Chancey looked at the soldier in surprise and brushed a smoothing hand over his hair. Dina glanced from Paul to Burt and back again with bright eyes.

Iris felt a fluttery weakness and wondered how she looked—disheveled, probably, but still attractive. Paul, on the other hand, looked simply smashing; his tie was loosened and his sleeves rolled up.

He smiled at them impartially and nodded toward the refrigerator. "May I get some milk?"

"Certainly," Burt said. "Anything else you want?"

Dina made a choking sound and took a delicate sip of her cocoa. "Anything at all, Sergeant?"

"Just milk is fine." Paul found a glass and poured. Then he leaned against the counter, ignoring the empty chair at the table.

"This place is quite an operation," he commented. "Even knowing the statistics, I had no idea it was so big."

"Big and deadly and out of control," said Burt. "We're counting on you to bring some order from the chaos."

"Well, hold the good thought. Major Shearson's an efficient man and we'll do what we can." Paul finished his milk, rinsed the glass and put it in the dishwasher. "Well, good night."

He walked out and Iris felt diminished by his leaving. If she had looked, she would have seen the very same emotion mirrored on Burt Chancey's face.

Dina wore a mischievous smile as she rose to clean up the mess from the cocoa.

The bar was named "Mama's Boys." A twenty-foot strip of violet neon ran along the roof in front proclaiming itself to Belle Glade. It was the fifth bar Carly had visited that night and he was beginning to feel the effects.

The lighting inside was dim and the music loud. Carly took a seat at the bar and ordered a bottle of beer. Bottled beer, he figured, might be just a little safer than tap in an infected establishment.

Most of the crowd was either sitting at tables along the dance floor or in booths opposite the bar. Only two other customers sat at the bar, and Carly was quickly able to get the bartender's attention.

"Like to get a little information," he said confidentially.

The bartender was large, pale, balding and expressionless as he faced Carly. "Yeah? Like what?"

"Suppose a guy was looking for some action. You think you could help?"

"What kind of action?"

Carly leaned forward, closer to the man's ear. "Suppose he has something to sell. You know, privately."

The bartender wiped the bar in front of Carly with a soiled rag and nodded. "What kind of merchandise?"

Carly hesitated. This was the closest he had come; only twice before had he reached the questioning stage and both times he had been shut off immediately. This man seemed shrewder than the others and more venal; Carly knew he represented danger. But this man was interested and would hardly negotiate without information.

"Well, if I tell you," Carly answered cautiously, "let's agree there won't be any questions asked."

"Just tell me, buddy, whatcha got? Drugs, weapons, kids, information?"

"Silver."

Now the dye was cast. Carly relaxed a little.

The bartender's eyes opened a fraction. "Yeah? How? Coins, bullion?"

"Bars."

The dirty rag made its circuit again. "Gimme 24 hours. Come back tomorrow night. Price'll be set by the buyer, but he guarantees about thirty points over the London close and you avoid paying sales tax. I get ten percent from you and you deliver. That O.K.?"

Carly managed to keep his face as expressionless as the bartender's. He nodded abruptly. "See you tomorrow night."

As he walked out he could hardly keep from grinning. A man among men, able to wheel and deal with the big boys. He walked through the lavender glow from the neon sign and read it with amusement. Mama's boy? Not Carly Jenson! He was Carl Joseph Jenson, Jr., and he was his *father's* boy.

Halley Cain had begun life as Havia Canerra, born into the group known locally as Tampanos: Cuban-Americans born and raised in Tampa. Her parents had spoken Spanish and Italian but prided themselves that they had never learned English. They had owned a small mom-and-pop café that served excellent Cuban food. On the side had taken bets on horse races, jai alai and the numbers.

Halley's parents were dead now and her three brothers had migrated south, attracted to the easy money available in Miami. They made their muscle and knowledge of south Florida available on the open market and became involved, not surprisingly, in the drug trade. Halley kept the café, augmenting the marginal income it provided by arranging what she euphemistically called "parties" at her house for visiting gentlemen. Otto and Stoney had enjoyed her hospitality before.

The music was loud and the drinks flowed freely. Otto sat with Halley and drank while Stoney danced with several of Halley's other friends who joined the festivities. It was late in the evening when Halley broached the subject of the children.

"Whose kids ya got?"

Otto's arm encircled Halley's shoulders as she turned to look at his face. She was in her mid-40s, still attractive despite increasing girth. Her eyes were dark brown, her hair dyed a vehement and uncompromising black to subdue the encroaching gray.

"Belong to a friend of mine," he replied casually. "I'm taking them to their grandparents down in Sarasota."

"I guess you don't care much about them, to just shut them up in a truck." Halley was looking at Otto curiously.

"They'll be fine. They're probably asleep."

"I know another guy who's interested in kids." Halley's voice sounded carefully neutral.

"You mean a dealer?"

Be careful, Otto told himself. In a world that tolerated almost any perversion, this was still a practice most people condemned—the marketing of children to adults whose objective was to abuse them.

"No, my guess is he's a user." Halley sounded careful, too.

This was new territory for them. Even though she probably knew him to be the last person who would criticize any kind of behavior, people were funny, and even the most debauched of men could occasionally feel tender toward children.

They looked at each other for a long time, evaluating any possible risk. Then, simultaneously, they smiled.

"I could call him," Halley offered. "I get ten percent."

"I'll listen to his offer. But, look, these ain't just any kids. They're smart and real good-looking. A little blonde girl, prettiest thing you ever saw."

"I'll tell him." Halley left the room for a more private phone while Otto poured himself another drink. What a break! He had dreaded driving through south Florida, and now maybe they could take their profit without leaving the relative safety of Tampa. He wondered what sort of money was involved in this racket. If it paid well, he and Stoney might have found themselves a new career.

Halley returned within twenty minutes. "He'll be here in the morning. And he'll bring cash."

Otto smiled. "So let's celebrate."

9

Monday, September 13, 1999

The low-pressure trough traveling westward, carried along on prevailing easterly winds, was showing signs of increasing intensity. The number and severity of thunderstorms that it spawned had increased, the barometric pressure in the central core was falling and circulation around this core was better organized. A hurricane-spotting plane was dispatched from the National Oceanographic and Atmospheric Association at MacDill Airfield in Tampa to locate the center. It clocked the circular winds at forty miles per hour. So the area of unstable weather was upgraded to a tropical storm, the first of the season, and it was named Ariel.

None of those responsible for compiling the yearly lists of hurricane names knew that this storm had been named "The Lioness of God."

For many, Monday signals the beginning of the work week, the return to routine. But not so for eight people who awakened in Dorm 4 of the housing section of the Belle Glade Hospice. For them, the most outstanding characteristic of this day would be its total lack of routine.

Paul Cordray and Ed Shearson rose early, shaved, dressed

160

and met at the hospice dining room for breakfast. The major had appointments throughout the day with various people in charge of keeping the peace within the Belle Glade Quarantine Zone. The sergeant would accompany him.

Dr. Cassandra Kovaks was scheduled to meet the chief medical officer at 9 A.M. to receive her first assignment and begin briefing for her new duties. Last evening's orientation had told her that nothing at the hospice was up to standard—personnel, equipment, level of care—and that the results were well below par. Even for one so sunny and optimistic as Dr. Kovaks, a deficient building filled with dying patients cared for by a hopeless staff with insufficient equipment was depressing.

Iris Stoddard did not know what she would do that day, other than try to help her sister and brother-in-law. She was relieved when her roommate left so she could get ready for the day in solitude.

The Tylers had slept together on one of the twin beds, clinging to one another for emotional, if not physical, comfort. Aaron planned another visit to the security guards this morning, as his visit the previous evening had availed nothing. He had encountered a different mindset here: In a town composed almost exclusively of those living under a death sentence, the kidnaping of two young children was small potatoes. Purposeful activity was dampened by the climate of despair. Nevertheless, after breakfast Aaron and Olivia would solicit help from those assigned to give it.

Burton Chancey woke with a splitting head and raging thirst. His body was accustomed to moderate alcohol consumption, but yesterday from dinner on he had drunk steadily. He staggered into the bathroom, drank two full glasses of water and pressed a damp cloth to his forehead. Then he lay back on the bed and waited till his dizziness passed.

Despite his tortured body, however, he faced the day with

anticipation. He would see the young sergeant again; he would make sure of it.

Carly Jenson also felt the effects of too much alcohol. And like Burton Chancey, he anticipated the day. If he could sell old Joe's silver and avoid the back-breaking taxes that a legal sale would involve, he would have navigated a tricky rite of passage and would return home better equipped to handle life and the practice of law, not to mention old Joe Jenson. But nothing demanded his attention till night. He turned over to sleep again.

Stoney Hickman blinked against the light and stumbled from the couch where he had slept to the bathroom, moaning softly.

"Here, catch." Otto passed in the hallway and pitched the truck keys at Stoney. "Get dressed and get the nippers. Halley wants to give them a good breakfast before the man gets here."

Neither found any inconsistency between Halley's concern for the children's immediate nutritional needs and her lack of concern for their overall well-being—or indeed, for their lives.

All three were part of a society that had to accommodate an AIDS epidemic touching every facet of life. Thus Halley could know genuine pleasure in feeding the children, then forget them without a qualm. It was just one more way to survive.

The Roy Fitzgerald Memorial Hospice was run as well as any other patient-care facility in a Quarantine Zone. In fact, the staff and administration were a cut above average. But the seemingly endless rows of emaciated, despairing and dying people horrified young Dr. Kovaks. Nothing in last evening's orientation lecture had prepared her for what she saw this morning.

Nothing in her past had, either. Her medical experience had begun in her father's practice, which was modern, immaculate and caring. She had been trained in large teaching hospitals fully funded at public expense. She had neither seen nor dreamed of unwashed patients on filthy sheets, or of the odor that hung over the hospice like a cloud. It was as uncivilized as a scene from a horror movie.

The doctor who had been assigned to escort her through the wards this morning, Martin Kilgore, was nonchalant, seemingly untouched by any of these deficiencies. He had been on staff at this hospice (which he liked to refer to as "Roy") for almost two years now. No more than 35 years old, he already had a cynicism that showed in his wry humor. It suddenly occurred to Cassandra: He himself was probably HIV-positive. But wouldn't that mean he should care *more?* Before long he himself would be lying in filth and neglect.

They walked from a large terminal ward and stood in the hall outside the door. Patients in terminal wards lay in the last stages, many comatose, and Cassandra watched in revulsion as a male nurse walked along the rows of cots, listening briefly through a stethoscope for heartbeats, occasionally pulling the sheet up to cover the patient's face.

"Did I come at a bad time, maybe?" she asked at last. "Or are things always this awful?"

"You mean not much nursing care?"

At her nod he replied, "I guess they do the best they can. You'll have to lower your standards, I'm afraid."

Dr. Kovaks drew herself up to her full five feet eight and met the other doctor eye to eye. "Never! I wasn't brought up to compromise and I wasn't trained to accept conditions like this with no reaction."

"You don't understand things here. This really is a death house straight out of the Middle Ages. Here's a for-instance. Here at Roy we have almost no drugs and no means of ad-

ministering them. The storerooms and pharmacy were bur-
glarized this weekend, so Burt Chancey got the idea of getting the sterile syringes and needles that were supposed to be
given out to drug addicts on the street. He pointed out that
a sterile needle exchange is pointless when everybody's already infected. But you know the drill: 'We may have our own
HIV, but we don't want anybody else's.' So he got turned
down. The street addicts keep their goodly supply of sterile
syringes while dying patients lose out."

"That's awful! It doesn't make any sense."

"Merely one example of the triumph of folly around here.
And your only protection is to quit caring." Dr. Kilgore smiled
sadly. "You have to learn to stand back and watch the game
without caring who wins."

"I can't do that. I won't. We're doctors and we're supposed
to make things better, not just watch things get worse."

"My dear, how very young you are. I really must help you
appreciate reality. First realize this: For right here and right
now, doctors are redundant. Superfluous. Supernumeraries.
We do nothing to help these patients. The boy who wheels
the trolley in from the kitchen is of more value than we are.
At least he brings them food. Learn this if you learn nothing
else: We will cure nobody here. We do precious little even to
ease them. We are worthless. We are *powerless* against this disease. They will all die soon and if you don't know that—and
act like you know it—you'll go crazy."

He smiled suddenly and made a deprecating gesture, dis-
counting his own fervor. He leaned back against the wall and
resumed his posture of cool irony. "Forgive my ardor. I get
caught up sometimes appreciating the incongruity. My own
personal incongruity. Seventy thousand dollars in debt, twelve
years of study and training, all kinds of hopes and plans for
living the good life and maybe even a little bit of healing people
along the way. Then I get one tiny little needle stick in the

emergency room. I'm just about to begin my life's work and I get one needle stick. So I'm infected. I get shipped here to Roy where I will never, ever, ever heal or cure one single patient. Don't you see the irony? The beautiful, symmetrical irony?"

"I'm so sorry," Cassandra said, putting a consoling hand on Dr. Kilgore's shoulder.

He jerked away. "Don't be silly. I'm fine. I just don't want you to break your heart here. Because it's really true, doctor. Folly does triumph, and the only way to survive is to learn to appreciate the irony."

"Never!" she said again.

But there was a cloud in her eyes.

"Back again, are you?" the officer smiled.

Aaron was surprised to see many of the same people who had been working the night before still on duty this morning.

"You work long hours," he commented. "This is my wife, Olivia. We're here to talk about my kids."

"The captain's here. I'll see if he's busy."

Aaron was pleased to hear this. One of the hindrances last night had been the absence of a ranking investigator.

The building housing the security forces for the Quarantine Zone had obviously been the police station in earlier times, and most of the personnel had just as obviously been the policemen. The building was low and rambling, constructed of the ubiquitous concrete blocks, showing wear but also good maintenance and housekeeping.

"The captain'll see you."

The officer held the office door open and Aaron let Olivia enter before him. It was a smallish room, cluttered but clean, furnished with filing cabinets, a desk with computer console, two telephones, a swivel chair and two plastic chairs for visitors. The Tylers scrutinized the man who had stood to greet them. (Shaking hands was no longer customary in this time of AIDS.) He was fortyish, Hispanic, heavyset without being fat, with a calm, kind face. He would be vital to their purpose. Was he bright? efficient? willing to help? *Would* he help them?

He seated himself behind the desk and spoke in a deep, vibrant voice with a noticeable accent. "My name is Santiago. How may I help you?"

"I came by last night," Aaron began, "trying to get some help in finding my two children."

"And you are?"

"Oh—I'm Aaron Tyler, and my wife's Olivia. We're from Pine River." He launched into his story.

"I was given a report of this," said the captain, "and we will certainly do whatever we can to help you. There are limitations, since we have no indication that your children are actually in the Belle Glade area, and since we have limited resources. We are limited these days in much of what we can do. We struggle to hold back the tide of crime and violence in an area given over to it. We can no longer consider that we fight in a battle between good and evil, but between evil and worse evil. We seldom conclude our cases having accomplished anything moral. Many of our staff have more or less given up. Still, it would be wonderful to find these children and return them to you safe."

The captain's mellifluous voice and pessimistic appraisal rolled over them. Aaron hardly knew what to say.

"We'd like that, too," he said at last.

"I presume that you, at least, believe that your children are here. You have made some considerable effort to get here. Do you have any reason for believing this?"

"The police at home thought it was logical. Like you said, it's an evil place—the kind of place that would attract evil, especially if they're planning to sell the kids. I stopped and talked to the Tampa police and they sort of agreed."

"I do, too. We have people here we know trade in human flesh, and others we suspect do so. If your kidnapers are looking for a market, this is a likely place. Also, we are the gateway to the Miami markets."

"How would you begin?" Olivia asked. "We have pictures if you want to make posters."

"It wouldn't be worth the effort, ma'am. I'm sorry. Even if someone saw the poster and knew the whereabouts of your children, the odds are small that they would tell us." Santiago leaned back in his chair, assumed even more of a soothing tone and continued, gesturing occasionally with a pencil.

"You see, almost all the people here are dying. They have only a few years at best, with no hope of cure. In addition, most of them have been brought here by force, held in this area against their will, so now anger marches with the hopelessness. Not one in ten thousand feels he might be responsible for his own condition—and indeed, many are not. But instead of trying to make the best of their few years, they seek ways to vent their hatred. They are full of resentment, against fate or God, against the government or doctors or whoever else they think has failed them. But above all they resent those who are not sick.

"The population of this town, as a whole, would rejoice to know that you have lost your children. It would tend to balance the scales, don't you see? They have AIDS, you lost your children. Balance, justice. It was your remarkable good fortune that you found me. I have another way of finding balance."

Aaron was horrified at this speech, so Olivia spoke first.

"We're very grateful," she said.

Captain Santiago nodded in her direction. "We will begin by asking our informants about new arrivals at the corrals of the so-called chicken hawks. We can check for the truck. I have a colleague in Miami I will contact." He smiled suddenly. "I can be a policeman again."

"We really do thank you," Aaron said. "I'm gonna sort of drift around, too. Ask a question or two. I don't think I can just sit on my hands and wait."

"Be very careful. When a man is under penalty of death, there's little we can do to deter him from evil. If he has no internal control, no bridle on his own behavior, we're helpless."

"I see what you mean."

"And remember, my friend: If you walk in life, and they are already in the realm of death, they will hate you."

Philip Tyler was startled from sleep by the noisy opening of the rear doors of Otto Krause's truck. As dim light filtered in, the children clambered out, to be greeted by Stoney.

"Chow time," he said brightly.

"I thought y'all forgot us," Philip complained. "We never got any supper and we had to go to the bathroom in the truck again."

"Otto won't like that," Stoney said darkly.

Too bad about Otto, Philip thought indignantly. *What else could they do?*

He followed Sara through the door from the garage into a fragrant, old-fashioned kitchen where an energetic dark woman was cooking at the stove. Otto was nowhere in sight but Stoney took a seat at the table. Philip felt relieved that there was no possibility of asking the lady for help. No need to compare his courage with Sara's.

The woman smiled. "My name's Halley," she said. "What's yours?"

Sara spoke first. "I'm Sara Angela Tyler. I need to use your bathroom, please."

"Right through the living room." Halley gestured through a second door. "And you?" she asked Philip.

"He's my brother. We call him Flip," Sara answered for him.

"My name's Philip," he said stiffly.

"Go wash up; it's ready." Halley began to serve up scrambled eggs while the children took turns in the bathroom.

Once again they sat at a kitchen table eating real food on a plate, which someone had really cooked. But this time Philip found no comfort in it. This woman, for all her smiles and interested questions, frightened him. He said nothing, although Sara chatted with her naturally.

When Otto joined them, Philip understood his own reticence. The woman kissed the kidnaper casually and served his eggs with a smile. She was no possible source of help! Whereas Mrs. Parker had been suspicious, an adversary to Otto and Stoney, this Halley must be Otto's girlfriend.

Sara seemed oblivious to the distinction. It made the woman seem less threatening, as though Sara's not seeing evil were a defense against it. As in the cartoons, where the characters could walk on air and fell only when they looked down and realized their danger, so Sara's apparent inability to recognize the evil around her seemed to render it impotent. Sara's acceptance of the woman made Philip feel safer.

He was hungry. The scrambled eggs had onions and green peppers in them and tasted hot like chili, but they were good and everybody ate a second helping. There was toast and milk and the men had coffee.

But Otto kept looking at the clock on the wall, which increased Philip's dread. He wanted to leave this house immediately, even if it meant getting back into the truck.

"Fix 'em up, Halley, why don't you?" Otto said finally. "Wash their faces and maybe brush out her hair. She's got nice hair when it's brushed."

"O.K., Sara, let's go get prettied up."

Sara followed the woman willingly and Philip felt his stomach begin to knot. Something was very wrong. Why did they want Sara pretty?

"You, too, Philip. Come with me," the woman said.

Philip began to pray again as he obeyed reluctantly. He had done more praying since the kidnaping than all the rest of his life put together. Never had he needed it so much!

Two phone calls could have done the job—one call from Mrs. Parker to the Tampa police and one call from them to the police in Belle Glade. As it was, it took almost 24 hours for the Tylers to get the information about their children.

When the word came, it was via radio to Ed Shearson from a concerned-sounding desk sergeant in Tampa who said he had talked with Mr. Tyler on Saturday. The major rushed up to Aaron and Olivia's room on the top floor of Dorm 4 late Monday afternoon. He knocked quickly, then burst in, full of his news. But as the Tylers turned to face him, he could not help noticing the increasing stigmata of their pain. Every time he saw them, they looked more ravaged by the effects of the loss of their children.

"Word from Tampa," he said quickly. "A lady called the TPD yesterday evening. She saw the kids and they were fine."

He was cut short by their reactions. Olivia grabbed him with surprising strength and began to shake him. "Where are they? Can you go get them? Tell me everything." Her eyes glittered like the eyes of one obsessed. Aaron sank onto the bed and began to cry, gently at first, then with abandon. He sobbed, gasping for breath, his shoulders heaving.

"Now calm down, both of you. Let me tell you about it." Ed Shearson pried Olivia's hands from his arms and pushed her down next to Aaron. "Hush, Aaron. You won't be able to hear."

He told them everything, gratified to see their faces respond to the news. "They seemed healthy, and Sara told the lady they hadn't been abused. Maybe slapped around a little, but apparently no—you know. Nothing serious. They left all cleaned up and fed, and Mrs. Parker said they seemed to be coping well."

"Still driving that same truck," Aaron said in amazement. "Are those men absolute fools?"

"Certainly inexperienced, at the very least. But I think it's more being just scattered and thoughtless. Drifting along, looking for the main chance. Maybe they *can* think and plan and just don't."

"Oh, they're alive!" Olivia cried in ecstasy. "They're alive and well and not defiled. Thank God!"

Defiled, the major thought. What an odd word. But it told of the mental agony this mother had suffered. He thought of his own little girls safe at home in Baltimore. The worst they had suffered, that he knew of, was being called dirty Jews by an eight-year-old Nazi. Their confusion and hurt had rent his heart, and he had raged against the evil that lashed out at children for circumstances beyond their control.

But racial intolerance, an evil he had always despised, was insignificant compared to the greater evil that still possessed the Tyler children. Now Ed regretted not letting Aaron cry longer, washing out some of his tension and pain.

"You need to call the local police," he suggested kindly. "It might stir them up."

"Right," Aaron grinned. Standing up, he looked younger, taller and full of authority. "Guess I oughta wash my face first."

Paul Cordray was looking for a desk or flat surface on which to do paperwork. The only place he knew of within the hospice that had tables, chairs and a modicum of privacy—excepting mealtimes—was the dining room, which he found after several wrong turns.

He chose a place in a corner, hoping to be overlooked by anyone who came in. He poured himself a cup of coffee from the pot sitting at the end of the counter, unconcerned that there were no disposable cups available, and sat down to study his papers.

The team, in his opinion, had its work cut out. Despite the billions of dollars poured into the Belle Glade Quarantine Zone and the efforts of many well-meaning administrators, the place was in chaos. Those of its population who had good will and good intentions were a small minority whose purposes were constantly thwarted by two other population groups—those ordered here because of disease and those who had come willingly, drawn to the climate of license and villainy. The conditions in this society were similar to (or an exaggeration of) conditions in areas designated "clean," where there was nonetheless a growing polarization of society into good and evil. Good citizens were better, the criminal element far worse.

The criminal factor had become the problem of the military. No other organization could maintain the peace in the face of the AIDS epidemic, yet peace had to be maintained if the nation—indeed, the race itself—were to survive. If for some reason certain people would not govern themselves, then control must be imposed from without.

Most people recognized that if certain elements of the population would not refrain from criminal behavior simply because it was wrong, they would have to be compelled into refraining through the fear of punishment or through incarceration. It sounded simple. In fact, it was almost impossible, especially when the criminals increasingly outnumbered the law-abiding. The problem was exacerbated by the element of society that denied the concept of culpability. Every form of evildoing, to them, contained some exonerating ingredient, and the criminal was not to be punished but cured. If society did enough, paid enough, cared enough, there would be (according to this theory) no criminals.

Paul's thoughts were interrupted as two women entered the dining room from the hall. He glanced up. They had left the dining room door open and its angle partially protected his table from their view. He recognized one of the women, the assistant to the hospice director. The other was a young woman of about 25 who carried a baby in her arms.

"Coffee or tea?"

This was Dina Hawks. When there was no answer, she persisted, "Come on, Holly. You need to face reality and I'll help all I can. But mostly it's up to you."

"Is there any milk?" The other woman had a high, wispy voice, vibrating with emotion.

"I think so."

Paul leaned around the angle of the door to observe Holly more closely. She was turned away from him, watching Dina pour a glass of milk, but he could discern instability even from her quarter profile. She was jiggling the baby continually.

Paul ducked behind the door again as Dina returned with the milk and a cup of something hot.

Holly took a long drink from the glass and looked at her. "I wish I were dead. This is a calamity."

From the fruit of his lifelong habit of reading, Paul heard Shakespeare's fateful words spoken of Romeo: "Affliction is enamored of thy parts, and thou art wedded to calamity." But Romeo hadn't contracted AIDS.

"Do you know how it happened?"

"I have absolutely no idea. I thought it was Ryan; he'd been unfaithful. But he's clean. Just me, and they say probably the baby. From the hospital, you know, when he was born. I've been breast-feeding him. It's supposed to be so much better for them to breast-feed; their immune system, even their IQ. I was trying to be a good mother, but I've probably killed him." Holly's voice rose. "And Ryan chose not to come with me. He's going to stay there with our other kids, and I can't do a thing about it."

"You still have a life—"

"I want you to tell me everything you know about this disease. You're well educated. Give me the benefit of all those expensive years of education. Tell me, do you all still say our number-one weapon against AIDS is education? That's so ridiculous I wonder how you have the nerve! Do you really think knowing about it is the same as curing it? Or not getting it?"

"What do you want to know?" Dina asked quietly.

"What's going to happen to me? I want the truth."

"O.K. The truth. First of all, you don't catch AIDS; you get infected with the Human Immunodeficiency Virus. That's testing positive. It becomes AIDS when your immune system is so weakened it can't fight off the infections and cancers anymore. Usually your blood will test positive about one month after infection, but in some cases it's much longer. The symptoms start showing up anytime from three to maybe seven years later—coughing, flu-like symptoms, fatigue, weight loss, fever, enlarged lymph glands, diarrhea.

"And then you have full-blown AIDS, with pneumonia, different kinds of cancers, all kinds of severe common germ infections affecting the whole body and, of course, affecting the brain directly, so there's maybe dementia. Death usually comes within two years of the diagnosis of full-blown AIDS.

"At this point, they figure one person in thirty is HIV-positive in America, maybe one in twenty worldwide. There is still a slim chance, a very slim chance, that we can stop it before the race is extinct, but human beings are definitely an endangered species.

"For you personally, it may be years before you even notice any symptoms. You can have a pretty good life here, go back to school, meet people. You can work as long as you want to, and when you get sick, there are people to take care of you. When it comes right down to it, Holly, we're all going to die someday, not just people with AIDS."

The young mother's voice was bleak. "My life is over now, whether I'm dead or not. My life is dead without my children. Ryan wouldn't even get near me. He backed off and pulled the kids away. Wouldn't let them touch me. I'm one of the untouchables. He yelled at me to just take the baby and go, he'd keep the other kids. Then he shut himself in the den; he was still in there when they picked me up."

Holly's voice was fading. Paul had to strain to hear her last words. "It's over, the marriage, the family, everything."

"You still have the baby, and you're all he's got. You have to keep going for him."

That sounded like a platitude, but Paul knew it was true. Maybe, come to think of it, that's why it was a platitude—because it *was* true.

He heard the women scrape their chairs back.

"Bring the baby and we'll go see your apartment. You're in what we call a quad, a double-wide mobile home shared by four people. They're real nice apartments with television and VCR and a screened porch. You'll have your own room and bath, share the kitchen and living room. . . ."

Dina's voice faded as they left the room.

Paul looked down at the papers spread out before him on the table. Full of facts, statistics, plans and programs to improve conditions, but devoid of the human element, the people who suffered and died who were the central reality of this epidemic and all the evils that stemmed from it. This one woman, with her almost certainly doomed baby, had touched Paul as none of the statistics had. She would probably never see her other children again; would certainly never see grandchildren. And that poor infant! He would never survive to fulfill whatever purpose and potential his Creator had planned for him. He would live a short, sad life and die in torment.

It's time for me to start doing whatever it was I came here to do, Paul thought fiercely. *It's way past time.*

The buyer had not come by mid-afternoon, by which time Philip was terrified. As the day had stretched on, Otto's patience had grown thin, while Philip agonized over whatever it was Otto had planned for his and Sara's future.

The concern that had led Halley to prepare breakfast faded by mid-morning, and all pretense of friendliness left with her when she departed for work at the café. The men sat commiserating about headaches and "hangovers." For Sara, who was irritable, Philip found the cartoon channel on TV, which soon had her absorbed. In the days they had been with the kidnapers, Philip had learned he had a certain freedom to act if the goal was Sara's diversion. Her whining annoyed them as much as it did Philip.

Lunchtime came and went. Otto had fallen asleep sitting up in an easy chair, snoring rhythmically. Stoney ate some of the nachos and pretzels that had been opened the night before, washing them down with a beer from the refrigerator and watching the cartoons along with Sara. Philip found cheese and bread in the kitchen and made sandwiches for himself and his sister. They were not very good since he could find no mayonnaise, but it did not seem to matter as much as it once would have.

All four of them jumped when the doorbell rang. Otto roused with a snort, wiped his mouth and brushed at his rumpled clothing. "Get that, Stoney."

Three men stood at the door. The man in the middle, well-dressed in a dark suit, was old, short and emaciated. Philip stared at him from the living room in alarm. He had long, thin hair and noticeably yellow skin. The other two men, much younger and dressed in jeans and T-shirts, supported him under each arm, and he smiled politely, revealing teeth whiter than any Philip had ever seen.

"Mr. Krause, please. I am Carmine Capovilla. I have an appointment." He gestured vaguely toward the other men. "My nephew Joey and his friend—uh, Randy." The short speech seemed to have exhausted the old man. When Stoney stepped aside, he tottered into the house and took a seat on the couch. The other two men lingered in the doorway till he wiggled a yellowish hand in their direction. Then they came in and stood side by side against the wall.

"I'm Krause. These are the kids." Otto gestured toward the Tyler children, and the old man turned to see. His eyes passed over Philip without pausing but stopped at the sight of Sara.

"Oh, yes indeed. I see what Halley meant."

Sara had turned from the television with some annoyance at the interruption. Now she turned it off to observe the visitors. Philip walked over and stood next to her.

"Come here and let me see you, little girl," Mr. Capovilla said gently.

Sara crossed the room obediently and stood in front of the old man. Stoney was watching with bright-eyed interest. Otto remained in his easy chair, keeping an eye on the two younger men.

"What's your name, dear?" Mr. Capovilla asked.

"I'm Sara Angela Tyler, sir."

Philip was frantic. He was positive that this new man represented a far greater evil than Otto or Stoney. There was something repulsive about him—his scrawny body, yellow skin and watery eyes. Philip felt the same kind of skin-crawling revulsion he would at a poisonous snake, while his sister stood right in front of the man apparently unaware of the aura of depravity.

"You're a pretty thing, aren't you? You ought to have a pretty dress, Sara. I'd like to buy you a brand-new dress; would you like that? What color do you think we should get?"

"I like yellow best."

Then this guy's right up your alley, Philip thought with a sudden, almost irresistible urge to giggle. *He's the yellowest person I ever saw!* He was sick with dread, trembling with fear, but almost unable to control his laughter. Was he going crazy?

The old man extended a yellowish hand and touched Sara's hair. "Do you ever wear ribbons in your hair?"

"Sometimes. I have hairbands at home and barrettes, but I don't have anything here but this old nightgown." She turned to glare at Otto.

The old man smiled and nodded, his withered hand still on Sara's head. "Mr. Krause, I was told this was a special child, and I agree. You *are* special, aren't you, Sara?" He patted her head.

She stepped back.

"Do you know how to sing?"

"Yes."

"Would you sing something for me?"

"I guess."

"If I'm going to buy you a pretty new dress, you ought to sing for me, don't you think? Isn't that fair?"

She hesitated. "I guess."

"Very well, sing."

Sara took another step back and made sure everybody in the room could see her. "What song do you want me to sing?"

"Anything will be just fine."

She'll do "The Frog on the Lily Pad," Philip thought, *or maybe "The Bluebird of Happiness."* They were her usual performance numbers.

But Sara seemed undecided. She paused a long time, then began to sing unself-consciously. Her voice was sweet and true and she seemed confident that anyone listening would enjoy hearing her. But her very first words seemed to strike the old man like a blow: "Jesus loves the little children, all the children of the world. . . ."

Philip stared in amazement. Whatever had made her pick *that* song?

Otto and Stoney watched Sara with a kind of proprietary pride. The two young men stood expressionless. The old man stared at her without moving a muscle, eyes riveted on her face, while she moved into the second verse.

"Jesus died for all the children, all the children of the world. Red and yellow, black and white, they are precious in His sight. . . ."

Suddenly the old man made a choking sound and began to shake his head. All eyes moved from Sara to Mr. Capovilla.

Sara stopped singing. "Are you all right?"

The young men moved in but Mr. Capovilla waved them away and continued to shake his head. "Not this child, Mr. Krause. No. Not this little girl."

Otto fumbled for a response, but Mr. Capovilla was focused only on Sara.

"I enjoyed your song, Sara. Thank you." He gestured at Philip. "Is that your brother?"

"Yes, sir."

"Is he a good brother?"

"Yes, sir. He takes care of me when my mama and daddy aren't around."

"You know, when I was just a little boy, about the age you are now, my grandmother told me I had a guardian angel who would take care of me. I remember it quite well, her telling me about it. Do you know what an angel is?"

"Yes, sir."

"Do you think that's true?"

Sara nodded seriously. "Your grandmother wouldn't lie to you."

"No, of course she wouldn't."

The old man was leaning toward the little girl, absorbed in their conversation. The two young men had moved to the wall again. Otto looked agitated.

"Let me tell you something, Sara. I have cancer of the pancreas. Do you know what that means?"

"Cancer is a disease. I don't know what pancreas are."

"It means I'm dying. I have very little time left. You have pointed me in a direction I've not gone for sixty years. I am very grateful." He gestured to his nephew and the two men jumped quickly to help him stand.

"Mr. Krause, I cannot do business with you. Not for Sara or even for her good brother. We'll go now. Joey, the door."

The old man struggled out as quickly as his infirmity permitted, leaning on his companions. One of them pulled the door shut firmly behind them.

Sara went back to the television, sitting closer than her mother would have allowed. Philip, suddenly weak, flopped down beside her. Otto sat back down in the easy chair.

"Now what you reckon happened?" he asked, aggrieved. "Seemed like he liked her for a while."

For once, Philip thought, it sounded as though Otto really wanted an answer.

Stoney must have thought so, too.

"He got religion," he said, nodding his head wisely. "That's it."

"Oh, don't be a bloody fool! Go get me a beer."

"No, Otto. I seen it before. He got religion and then he couldn't do a bad thing. Didn't ya hear him talking about angels?"

"Shut up! I don't want to hear any more about it."

Otto slumped into his chair and Stoney disappeared into the kitchen.

Philip was breathless with relief. So enormous had been his fear of this new threat that the captivity they had known with Otto and Stoney now seemed a minor inconvenience. He looked at Sara in wonder, but she was absorbed once again in the unending futility of the Coyote's hopes of victory over the Road Runner.

Had she planned her strategy to achieve the result it had? Was Sara that smart—to select a song that would evoke such a change in the old man? Or was she just incredibly lucky?

It had been a rotten day for Carly, boring and tense. He had no way to prepare mentally for his meeting at "Mama's Boys" but spent the day trying. It was awkward figuring out how to deal with Aaron Tyler, too. Carly's avowed reason for making the trip was to be helpful to Aaron, but he had little interest in Aaron's problems and avoided the Tylers all day.

The hours finally passed until he was once again crossing the parking lot of the tavern, trying as before to be unobtrusive. He stepped under the glow of the sign and entered. The place was more crowded tonight, for some reason, and all the stools at the bar were occupied. It was more than a half hour before Carly was able to press through the crowd to get a place at the bar. Again he ordered a bottle of beer. The bartender served him with no sign of recognition.

He sipped the beer slowly, watching the activity around him and wondering how and when to proceed. It was an acrimonious crowd. Most of them were drinking heavily, calling impatiently to the barkeep for more rounds, and their conversations sounded belligerent. He had heard the phrase *looking for trouble* plenty of times; now he was witnessing it. This whole roomful of people was looking for trouble.

Then the bartender began wiping the counter in front of
him. He leaned down toward Carly and spoke in a confiden-
tial voice: "I got a name for you in Miami. Delivery no later
than midnight Wednesday. Do you have my fee?"

Carly nodded.

The bartender motioned him to the end of the bar, where
he raised a hinged portion for Carly to walk through. As he
followed him through a back door, the customers at the bar
raised a howl of protest; service was already inadequate. The
bartender threw a curse over his shoulder and led Carly
through a door in the building's rear wall, which opened into
an untidy, dimly lit room.

Carly's only information about silver came from high school
chemistry: that it had the highest thermal and electrical con-
ductivity of all the metals; and that it was a precious metal
used in jewelry, tableware, the minting of coins and in more
practical applications like photography and dentistry and electrical circuitry. None of this helped in his negotiations with
the bartender, who was demanding to know the level of purity of Carly's silver and its provenance. Carly did the best he
could, struggling to hide his ignorance and dickering over the
price, until at last a deal was struck. Everything was settled
but the final price; that, within certain preset limits, would be
decided by the buyer.

He paid off the bartender and walked back through the
anger-filled bar with conflicting emotions. He was glad the
negotiations were over and felt he had done a good job so far,
but now he dreaded the actual exchange. And how would he
get to Miami? No one could just rent a car and drive there,
not from a Q. Zone. The whole point of these places was to
keep you *in*. And what about security? It was dangerous to
drive around south Florida, especially alone—most especially
with a fortune in silver. The trip from Pine River had not exactly been a picnic. And he had no guns or loyal family, as

Aaron had, no armed soldiers to protect him. He would have to manage this thing on his own.

He walked beneath the purplish glow from the sign on the tavern's roof and thought for the first time in fifteen years of his mother. He remembered her death vividly and his eyes stung with tears. Suddenly he missed her desperately.

Mama's boy!

10

Tuesday, September 14, 1999

Will Stoddard woke to brilliant sunshine and light breezes following the first good night's sleep he had had since the children disappeared. Charlotte was still sleeping peacefully beside him, so he rose quietly. Impatient to be outdoors, he dressed quickly and deferred shaving. Early mornings were pleasant year-round in Pine River, the country air clean, the animals raring to go.

The kitchen was awash in cheerful light as he plugged in the coffeemaker that Charlotte always prepared the night before. He waited as the coffee dripped, enjoying the return of peace. After four days of agonizing uncertainty, Mrs. Parker's phone call had brought a blessed release of pressure. The children were alive! For the first time in four days he was able to let down the guard around his thoughts. He could plan for the return of his family.

He poured a mug of coffee and walked out toward the stable. The world was waking up, the birds singing, the breeze dancing. The horses heard him coming and whinnied in welcome. What a wonderful day to be alive!

He thought of each individual in his family: his wife, his two daughters, his two grandchildren, his son-in-law. He felt a warmth for Aaron—approval, admiration, gratitude, kinship—he had never felt before. In fact, it was as though he were seeing Aaron clearly for the first time. All the competition and striving he had felt for years were simply gone— gone so totally that he could not understand why he had ever felt that way.

It was a glorious release. Will even felt *physically* lighter. How delighted Olivia would be at this new attitude! No more the tightrope she must have walked trying to mediate between the two men she loved most.

He smiled as he opened the stalls and let the horses out to pasture. They trotted past him through the barn door, eager for freedom and fresh grass; only Ginger stopped to greet her master. She nuzzled his shoulder and tossed her head flirtatiously. He reached into his pocket for a lump of sugar and held it out to her.

"Won't be long now, old girl. Flip'll be home soon."

He walked beside her out into the yard and they stood together, horse and man, basking in the peaceful landscape and the beauty of the day. He thought of something Aaron had quoted; was it Shakespeare? (With Aaron it was usually either Shakespeare or the Bible.) How did it go? "Where every prospect pleases, and only man is vile."

And in my own prospect, at least one of the vile men has been me, he thought with a grin. *But no more!*

Suddenly he gripped the horse's mane and leaped onto her back.

"Let's celebrate, Ginger," he laughed.

Leaning low over her withers, he held the long hairs of her mane with both hands, while Ginger, understanding something of his joy, responded to his mood if not his words. She surged into a rollicking canter across the pasture, head high, hooves dancing.

Will rode with total delight. Never had life seemed so full of promise. His family was coming home!

I think I'll go see Micah after while, he decided. And then the thought struck him: *Maybe this isn't all the result of the phone call!*

Otto Krause was the leader of the criminal enterprise of Krause and Hickman, not because he was a good commander, but because he was better than Stoney. He was, in fact, more of an opportunist than a strategist. When the proposed sale of the Tyler children fell through, he had no contingency plan. And lacking anything better to do that afternoon, he did nothing.

The men continued to drink and the children continued to watch television in something akin to the law of inertia. As objects at rest tend to remain at rest, and objects in motion tend to remain in motion, so Otto and Stoney and their two young captives continued in these prevailing activities until they were acted upon by an outside force.

The outside force was Halley Cain.

She was furious, on her return from work, to find that no big exchange of cash-for-children had taken place, for no comprehensible reason. Instead of having shared in a profitable business venture, she showed a dead loss. For two days she had fed and housed two men and two children, throwing in alcohol and feminine companionship. Because they were fugitives, she had undergone some risk to do so. And all she had to show for it was a messy house and an empty refrigerator. Now Halley showed her Latin temperament with gusto.

The kidnapers and their victims were ejected from the house and on their way within ten minutes.

"Man, she gets fired up, don't she?" Stoney laughed.

"Witch!" Otto snarled. He careened down the street. "I'll fix her. Wait'll next time."

"She says ain't gonna be a next time!"

"Put a sock in it, Stoney. I'm warning you."

"Sure, sure. Take it easy. Don't get mad at *me.*" Stoney waited a few cautious minutes. "What'll we do now?"

"Let's go somewhere different. Let's go south."

"We got enough money left?" Stoney never had money of his own, never carried cash or credit or debit cards. Otto paid all the expenses, and in return Stoney contributed one hundred percent of any earnings, legal or illegal.

Otto grinned suddenly. "We got plenty. We got all Halley's bank cards." He laughed. "She left her handbag in the bathroom and I helped myself."

"You're a bleeding wonder, Otto!"

"Yeah, well, that'll teach her to watch what she says to me. I'm stopping to cash in right now, get as much as I can before she gets wise." Good humor restored, Otto called back to the children, who were listening with interest from the rear of the truck. "How'd you like burgers? If I go to a drive-in, you promise to keep your mouths shut?"

"We promise," Philip replied.

"I'll be quiet, but you tell them I don't want any onions," Sara said firmly. "If I get 'em, I won't eat 'em"

Otto laughed cheerfully for once at her attitude. "Hey, Miss Priss, who's running things around here? Somebody die and leave you in charge?"

The three chuckled companionably.

But Philip shook his head. The longer this thing went on, the less he understood it.

How much of the significant activity of life takes place in kitchens? Paul Cordray wondered. Not in bedrooms, not in boardrooms, but in warm, safe, full-of-loving-and-life, heart-of-the-home kitchens. He sat now disconcerted in the kitchen of Dorm 4, across the table from Dr. Cassandra Kovaks, watching her cry.

Like most men, Paul was upset by tears. They made him feel inadequate, strangely guilty and in danger of being manipulated.

"You want a drink of water?" he asked. Anything to stop the flow!

She reached out blindly for napkins. He grabbed several from their holder and put them into her hand.

She mopped her face, blew her nose and peered at him self-consciously from red eyes. "Sorry. I don't usually lose control this way."

He murmured soothing words.

I wish you'd find a less embarrassing way to lose control, he thought.

Cassandra gulped, hiccuped and swallowed. "I'm fine now."

"Want to talk?"

He had found her on the walkway outside the hospice, pacing and crying. He had taken her arm and led her back to the housing area, where she had continued to cry even after they had taken seats at the kitchen table.

"It wouldn't help," she said mournfully. "I just feel so awful. I mean, it's going to be terrible, and I have six months here."

"You knew what it would be like, didn't you? Danger of infection, lots of patients dying. Hard for anyone not to find it awful."

"But I thought they'd *try,*" she wailed. "You know? Everybody's just, like, given up trying."

"You mean research? Trying to find a cure?"

"They're all saying they'll never find a cure. Because it's a virus, you know, and we've never defeated any virus. But no, I mean more like trying to make things comfortable, helping people through it. Not giving up."

"You think the researchers have given up?" Paul persisted. He knew this would be considered heresy in most medical circles.

"They're just going through the motions. Like everybody else."

"Who else has given up? The staff? The patients?"

"Everybody! The patients think they're going to die and the doctors and nurses, like, agree with them. Nobody fights here. They all just give up."

Paul got a glimmer of what the young doctor's problem might be. She was seeing a comet fall—the ancient sign of the death of kings displayed for all to see right here in the Roy Fitzgerald Memorial Hospice.

"What do *you* think they should do?"

"Fight!"

"How?"

"They don't have to just lie down and surrender to it. They can fight." She was getting angry now, looking at Paul with annoyance.

"It bothers you that medical care isn't helping them, doesn't it?"

Cassandra seemed not to hear. "I've been with Martin Kilgore and he's just awful. He has no faith and no hope, and he's just, like, given up. Let them all die, you know—that's his attitude. And pretty soon it'll be him dying and even *that* doesn't bother him. I can't stand it!"

"You still have faith and hope, Cassie?" he asked gently. He had never called her by this name before, but she seemed not to notice.

"Certainly. You never know when somebody'll make a breakthrough. It could happen anytime, if they don't give up."

Paul nodded. He was almost certain he knew the root of the doctor's distress.

"Cassie," he said quietly, "I want you to listen to me. Don't get angry and don't turn me off. I have the answer to your problem, but you're going to have to get through some preconceived notions first."

Even two days ago he would have prayed for her but probably not spoken out. But he had been stirred by the conversation he had overheard in the dining room the day before between Dina Hawks and the newly admitted young mother, and now he was willing to risk rejection, rebuke, even being reported to Major Shearson, in order to try to help Dr. Cassandra Kovaks.

She sat up straighter. "Shoot."

"O.K. Everything in this world is going to pass away, right? As somebody said, this world is a sinking ship and we will never patch up the leaks. Nobody is going to cure AIDS. It doesn't really matter whether they try or not; this disease is incurable."

She frowned.

"I think you're upset," he went on, "because you can't stand the idea that science can fail. You had faith that science could solve all the world's problems, save you, save lives, save the rain forests, save the whales, save the world. Now you're beginning to see that it can't, and that's frightening. You want to see everybody still trying, still having faith that the medical system will conquer this enemy. But in your heart you know it can't, that all their efforts are futile. And that's horrible, because you believe that if medicine can't win over this plague, then *nothing* can. If medicine fails, then the human race is without hope.

"And Cassie, that's just not true. Medicine *will* fail. Science will fail. They're human efforts trying to meet human need, and they will always fail. You need something new to put your faith in, something that won't fail."

She was looking at him intently. "You're right about what upsets me. It isn't working and we're losing the battle. But what else is there?"

"There's Jesus Christ."

There was a long pause. "Are you serious?"

"Completely."

"What does religion have to do with AIDS?"

"I'm not talking about religion. I'm talking about a Person."

She stared at him again.

"I'm listening," she said at last.

Aaron spent the morning at the police station. Santiago was cautious and pedantic, but he seemed genuinely pleased at the news of Mrs. Parker's phone call. Aaron left in time to meet Olivia and Iris for lunch in the hospice dining room.

Everything was better today. The food tasted better; even the air he breathed seemed lighter. At the same time, despite the joy of the news that the children had been alive and well Sunday morning, Aaron realized things might well have changed. The children were, after all, still in captivity.

"I'm going to walk around town this afternoon, maybe go into some bars and see what I can find out," he told Olivia and Iris. There was no likelihood that he would discover anything of value, but he could not tolerate the idea of doing nothing.

The sisters agreed to spend the afternoon catching up; hair and clothes needed washing, and they planned to try to telephone home.

"I won't be late," Aaron promised.

He drove through the little town slowly, sensing the atmosphere, observing the few pedestrians. In the heat of this post-prandial hour, everything was sluggish. He drove out along the highway where a strip of seedy little bars drowsed, hunkered down in the heat.

I can spend the afternoon pub-crawling, he thought. *I'm sure these kidnapers drink.*

It happened in the third bar he hit, an establishment almost indistinguishable from the others—an over-warm concrete block cube with one of its few windows blocked by an air conditioner rattling thunderously and ineffectively. The walls were a dingy grayish beige, decorated with calendars, posters and tattered bits of erotica. Aaron wondered how things could possibly have become so dirty in only a few years.

Customers and employees alike matched the setting. There was a weariness about them that might have moved Aaron to compassion had he not been so absorbed in his own predicament.

He fit in easily enough. He had the clothes, the accent, the vehicle (if not a truck, at least a van) to blend in. He slumped on a stool at the bar, nursing a beer. It was a fair-sized crowd for early afternoon, and unfriendly—silent and self-contained. Aaron was silent, too, thinking his own thoughts.

He had never loved the taste of beer. Actually, he preferred iced tea, like most Southerners, or cola, or even plain water. But Will Stoddard drank beer and had always made it plain he considered drinking beer part of being a real man. In the beginning Aaron had taken up beer-drinking as a way to win Will's approval. Now he felt ashamed; he still did not like it that much, nor had it won him Will's approval.

No more, he decided. *No more beer, and if Will doesn't like it, well, too bad.*

He noticed activity stirring among the patrons. Several men were moving through a side door to another part of the building. What was happening? If he were to get information, he would have to talk to people who knew what was what in Belle Glade. Was this such an opportunity?

Then a young fellow sitting next to him turned and spoke. "Can you let me have fifty bucks?"

The fellow was typical of the bar's customers—poorly dressed, not particularly clean, obviously not well. Aaron guessed he was HIV-positive, in the process of developing full-blown AIDS but not sick enough yet to be hospitalized. Aaron also guessed he was pursuing drug and alcohol highs to dampen the emotions that anyone would experience in such circumstances—emotions like anger and hopelessness. As it was, the fellow looked bewildered, even shell-shocked, though he had not yet reached the zombie-like state of many Belle Glade residents.

"What for?" Aaron asked.

"They're having a contest tonight. Death games. Tickets on sale in there." He jerked his head toward the side door. "Gladiators from Miami, I hear. I can get you in if you'll pay for me."

Aaron was torn. This was definitely an in-crowd kind of thing, and if he were accepted by these men, he might gain valuable knowledge about Belle Glade's traffic in children. But death games were still illegal in most states, including Florida, and besides, he was not sure he could stand to watch.

But desperate situations demand desperate solutions, and he found himself nodding. "I'll pay."

"I'll have to vouch for you, so tell me your name, in case they check. We'll say you're my cousin. Where you from? My name's Clement, by the way, Bobby Lee Clement. I'm from Valdosta."

Aaron nodded and gave Clement the necessary data, in accord with his driver's license and Certificate of Health. Then they joined the line that had now formed at the side door.

Aaron felt slightly nauseous. He was going to pay a hundred dollars so he and this stranger could watch one man kill another. No matter what good he hoped to derive from the men he might meet at the games, it sickened him.

Lord, if this offends You, forgive me, he prayed silently. *And please keep the law away. I don't have time to waste going to jail.*

Carly Jenson had decided to steal a truck. An Army truck would be best, of course, but difficult to steal. He would do better taking one from the hospice. He spent the morning

checking things out—"casing the job," he thought dryly—
and it looked not only possible but simple.

Hospice security was laughable. If he had the proper uniform, he could easily walk into the hospice motor pool, get
an authorized permit and drive away with a full tank of gas.
It was the perfect solution to his problem. Marked hospice
trucks could pass through the checkpoints around the Zone
perimeters with only a routine glance at papers; and he would
probably be safer on the road, too.

He would take the truck later, well after dark, load it with
his things—his good suit, the silver, maybe one of Aaron's
guns—and hide it somewhere. He would leave for Miami just
before dawn. He had till Wednesday midnight to make his
connection.

How much driving time? he wondered.

It was about 85 or 90 miles each way, if he took Highway
27. To allow four hours driving time would be generous. Then
he would have to find the meeting place once he got to
Miami—probably not a simple matter. Then the wheeling
and dealing and home again, safe and successful.

Now that he had turned the corner on his fear, he could
not help thinking of the operation as a television show. He
was the handsome hero, rich, educated and urbane but street-
wise and savvy. He might run some risks, maybe a setback or
two, but to fail was unthinkable.

The hero on television never fails.

After spraying the washing machines in Dorm 4 thoroughly
with disinfectant, Olivia and Iris put in the clothes they had
worn since leaving Pine River. They dared not leave their
things unattended in this environment of widespread crime,
so they sat on the straight plastic chairs to wait as their clothes
swished and spun.

"Aaron said he's calling the Tampa police as soon as he gets back from town," said Olivia. "Let's call the folks after that."

Iris was glad her sister still sounded hopeful. The news that the children had survived the first few days had been an enormous boost to Olivia's spirits, although she was still stretched tight. But a lifetime habit of "bursting Livvy's balloon" prevailed and Iris murmured without thinking, "If the phone lines haven't been cut."

"If they are, we'll radio or use the major's cellular," Olivia responded wearily.

After that first day, things had been very different from what Iris had expected. Instead of extreme deprivation, heart-thumping danger and demands for courage, fortitude and sacrifice—all of which she was prepared to handle—Iris had battled boredom, dull food and a too-soft mattress.

Now she sat in a hard chair in a hot, noisy laundry room trying to carry on a conversation with her sister who was intensely stressed from an overwhelming catastrophe, and most of her thoughts revolved around her distaste for communal life, her disappointment at seldom seeing the sergeant and the sorry condition of her nails.

Olivia fell silent and Iris listened to the churning of the washers. Maybe Carly would come around later. She would accept a date tonight, as little as she cared to go out anywhere in Belle Glade. Even Carly Jenson and this little town would be better than another night in Dorm 4.

Joe Jenson had been busy at work these past two days covering Carly's duties as well as his own. He welcomed his usual drink at the cocktail hour, but for the second day this week he was alone. They had often been apart before, of course. Carly enjoyed an active social life and Joe's practice (at least, before the spread of AIDS) had often required him to travel around the state. But this separation was different. He was troubled by the lack of communication and the additional element (however unlikely) of danger.

And there was something else. Joe felt guilty.

The visit with Will and Charlotte Stoddard had touched something in Joe. For the first time, for some unexplainable reason, he felt twinges of envy toward Will. Why, he couldn't imagine. But Joe recalled Will's response to the telephone call: a flood of joy and—well, glory—that had plainly transformed the man. Despite Joe's considerable successes, despite his honors and rewards, he had never experienced anything like the emotional phenomenon Will had exhibited Sunday when he learned his grandchildren were alive.

Joe suspected that this lack revealed some kind of diminished faculty within *him*, connected somehow to his sending Carly to sell the silver. Maybe it wasn't that he had sent Carly, but that he was *able* to do such a thing. He felt very sure Willoughby Stoddard would never deliberately expose his children to risk.

He swirled the ice cubes in his chunky glass full of twelve-year-old straight Kentucky bourbon, suddenly irritated. He had always been a happy guy, appreciating the good things of life. Every picture taken of him showed him smiling! Why should he be wondering now if Will Stoddard had something Joe himself lacked? Preposterous. Joe sat in serene power, in the office of the senior partner of the most successful law firm in the county. Will Stoddard was probably shoveling out horses' stalls.

He sipped bourbon and laughed.

But underneath he wondered if anything in creation could ever bring him the glorious joy he had seen on Will Stoddard's face.

Otto Krause's white panel truck exemplified his policy of graduated neglect. It got gas when it ran dry, repairs when it broke down, water and oil rarely and cleaning never. This was the fifth day the Tyler children had used the interior of this truck for eating, sleeping, playing, bickering, relieving themselves when unavoidable and—at least in Philip's case—praying. The truck was filthy.

Philip was praying off and on now as Stoney was driving and Otto was snoring in the passenger seat. Sara clambered into the back from the large up-ended paint can behind the front seats where she had been perched.

"There's nothing to look at," she grumbled. "I wish there was something to do."

"Stoney bought you some comic books," he replied. "You could read."

"They're too hard. I just looked at the pictures. Flip, where are we going?"

"They said south. Later they said Miami."

"That's a city like Tampa, isn't it?"

"Even bigger."

"What's going to happen there?"

"How am I supposed to know? I don't even think *they* know."

Philip scorned these two men who held them. His ideas of manliness came from what he knew of his father and grandfather, both of them methodical, thorough, purposeful, competent, trustworthy—the antithesis of Otto and Stoney.

"Flip, you think we'll ever get home again?"

"I think so, Sara. I know Dad's looking for us, and they're praying. I think we'll be O.K."

"It's just been so long. I miss Mama and our house. . . ."

Philip had less trouble relating to his sister when there were only the two of them and he did not have to be reminded that everybody in the world preferred her to him. *He* had never stopped conversation by merely walking into a room. Strangers seldom approached his parents to rave about *him*. But if Philip could get past how others were charmed by Sara, and if she did not try to boss him around, they got along pretty well. He felt tender toward her now.

"Don't think about missing things. Think about how great it'll be when we get home. What's the first thing you'll do?"

"I'll get Buffalope and hug everybody and Mama'll make chicken and dumplings and I'll take a bubble bath." Her eyes shone. "What about you?"

"I'll go see Ginger and Grandpa and make sure nobody moved the stuff in my room, saying they were just cleaning! And I'll eat, too. I bet Mama'll let us eat anything we want, at least for a day or two."

They laughed so spontaneously that Philip gave a nervous glance toward the front seat.

"And you know something else I'll do?" he whispered. "Go to the police and tell them all about those guys so they can catch them."

Sara grinned in mischievous delight. "Yes, and put them in jail for a hundred years!"

11

Tuesday night, September 14, 1999

Burton Chancey had made a firm resolution to curtail his drinking for a few days. He was feeling the effects not only physically but in his work, too, and *that* he would not tolerate. To Burt, the job was not something he did; it defined who he was.

For years he had had a love-hate relationship with alcohol—a friend and comforter when used in moderation, an enemy and harsh taskmaster when taken in excess. For now, no more excess—at least until the Finger Squad left.

Dina bustled into the office. "Sorry I'm late. I just finished supper."

"I appreciate your coming in after hours."

Burt knew that Dina, like him, had little to do with her time besides work, although neither liked to acknowledge this.

"I thought we could review some of what the team's done so far," he explained, "see which of our recommendations they're following up on."

"Fine. I made some notes at this afternoon's meeting. It looked like maybe the best you could manage was to stay awake."

"Very amusing. I've been a little under the weather the past few days."

"And there's no medicine like Chivas, right?"

"Drop it, Dina, do you mind?"

"Right." Dina shuffled her papers and began in a brisk, businesslike voice. "Let's take them in the order they were presented. First was transportation and supply. They wanted more equipment, more personnel, the team said no.

"Then utilities. They say most of their stuff is falling apart, especially electric. Rolling brown-outs will increase unless things improve. Water supply: The lack of contamination most of the time is debatable. And the telephone system problems. Overall, their main complaint was about vandalism and sabotage. The team said they need to improve their routine maintenance. Then we had the comptroller and his little gnomes from accounting. The accountants say we're hopelessly over budget, and the team says we spend more per capita than any other Zone and we'll have to cut the waste."

Unbelievable. "Just get to medical, please. And security."

"You *were* asleep, weren't you? We never got that far. Tomorrow, maybe."

He shifted self-consciously. "It isn't working, is it? They're not doing anything to help."

Dina looked up from her notes. "Not so far, but I didn't really think they would. They have people to answer to, you know. And remember, America is broke. Tax riots all over, government buildings bombed. Healthy people don't want to support us anymore."

"But they have to. It's the law, an entitlement. If they're going to lock us up, they have to take care of us."

Dina looked at him shrewdly. "While you've had your head stuck in the sand—or in a Scotch bottle—I've talked to some of these people to get an idea of the political climate in the clean areas. There's more and more talk about Cuba, how

America should have tested and quarantined fifteen years ago, how Cuba's the only place in the world that has reversed the spread of AIDS."

"But the Cubans violated the civil rights of the people they quarantined. They probably locked up people who weren't really infected."

"Healthy people don't care about AIDS carriers' civil rights anymore, Burt, you know that. They're concerned with survival. There's a movement afoot to kill us all, have you heard that? It's organized—marches, lobbyists, everything. Their logo is an iceberg, from the Eskimo custom of putting old people out on an iceberg to float away and die. I'm sorry, boss, but this little Finger Squad isn't the answer to your prayers. They're going through the motions and they'll leave ASAP. Believe me, this team doesn't give one hairy rat's behind about us."

Burt stood up, despite his aching head and unsteady stomach, to pace across the office. "What's going to happen to us, Dina? There's all this havoc—what the sociologists call social unrest, like it's some kind of mild disturbance. Crime and drugs and senseless violence. We can't function without more peace officers, social workers and counselors. If we don't get them, we'll need more jail cells. It's just not working." He looked at Dina bleakly. "What's going to happen to us?"

"That's simple, boss," she said. "We're going to die."

Long before it was time to get the truck, Carly Jenson was excited. The theft of a hospice uniform—as simple as walking into a linen storeroom and helping himself—would be invigorating.

He recalled a bit of advice given him by old Joe when he first began practicing law. Joe believed that success was primarily a matter of displaying purpose and assurance. "Act like you know what you're doing," Joe had said, "and you'll convince other people, and when they believe it, they'll convince you." The world is full of sharks, Joe believed, who love to attack those who are crippled or weak. The best defense is to appear strong and whole.

Of course, it's better to become a shark yourself, Carly smiled to himself.

His mind played the audio of his drama: "He had become a shark, a creature conceived and designed for destruction, perfectly adapted to his murky underwater world."

Murky underwater world. That was good. Yes, this would be an exciting show.

One of the worst parts was how her emotions fluctuated out of control. Olivia tried hard to stay calm, rational, able to function. But her emotions swooped and soared, controlling her mind and body. She had actually shaken the major!

Tonight she sat alone in the Dorm 4 bedroom assigned to her and Aaron, overwhelmed again by events and forces over which she was powerless. Earlier concerns like the danger of being infected with HIV were dwarfed by the enormity of losing the children. But tonight she had an additional concern: Aaron. He would not change his mind: He was going to a death game contest.

It was abhorrent. For one thing, he would be breaking the law. While that might not be unusual for Belle Glade, it was unusual for Aaron. And what sort of residue might it leave in his mind and spirit? He had shot a man their first day out from Pine River; Olivia had not forgotten that. But that was in self-defense. This was capricious, cold-blooded murder.

The experts, those who presumed to describe social phenomena, explained these games as an outgrowth and refinement of many theatrical predecessors. For years violence and death had been portrayed on screens and written into books, which had the result of desensitizing, even brutalizing, the public. Now life was imitating art. Aaron would return to her from a crowd of men—women, too?—who had paid money to witness a murder, people stimulated by watching another human being die by violence.

They had had no contact with Pine River since Tampa. Telephone time was (inexplicably) being rationed now. Her lack of contact with her parents was a sore trial. Her sister was little comfort, and now Aaron was acting in a way that alarmed her.

Maybe I'm supposed to be getting comfort from God, she thought in surprise. *I might as well try; I have no one else. And isn't the Holy Spirit the Comforter?*

But how to go about it? Cuddling Buffalope, she walked the narrow confines of the room. Then she took Aaron's Bible and sat in the only chair. Holding his Bible made it seem that he were part of this experiment. There was a technique she had heard of; somebody had laughingly called it Scripture Roulette. You opened the Bible at random and pointed to a verse and that was your message from God for the occasion.

Olivia still held Sara's stuffed animal as she shut her eyes, opened the Bible awkwardly, flipped to the middle and pointed a hesitant finger. She opened her eyes and looked at the top of the page: Isaiah 49. Isaiah was a prophet, she knew, a spokesman for God. Good so far. Then, hope rising above the doubt, she looked at the verse where her finger pointed: "I will contend with him that contendeth with thee, and I will save thy children."

Goose bumps rose along her arms. She read verse 25 again. *I will save thy children.* What a coincidence!

Or could it possibly be more than that?

She closed the book slowly, her mind a jumble of conflicting thoughts. Still clutching the stuffed bison, she stroked the cover of the Bible. Then she saw as if for the first time the familiar round sticker that adorned the front of Aaron's

Bible. She recalled the day more than a year ago that he had applied it.

They were coming home from church. Sara was chattering in the back seat about a prize she had won in Sunday school. She had known her lesson well or memorized a Scripture and was acting vain about her accomplishment. Aaron fussed at her gently about her pride, and somehow the incident had ended with Sara giving the prize to her father.

"Do you really think you ought to take her reward?" Olivia had asked him later.

Aaron had said Sara needed to learn to give.

"She gets so much, Livvy," he explained. "We can't let her grow up thinking she's *entitled* to awards and prizes, that she's better than everybody else. That'll destroy her character."

Sitting in the quiet room now in Dorm 4, Olivia smoothed the edges of the little round sticker, worn from its year's residency on the cover of Aaron's Bible. She read it again. And for the first time she received into her soul the message on the sticker: *The Bible is God speaking to ME.*

She sat in absolute stillness reading the words over. This was *not* another coincidence. It was God telling her, "Yes, the Bible verse you turned to in Isaiah was from Me."

And without further deliberation, she knew that God had guided her finger to that particular verse, and that when she doubted He had shown her the sticker. Maybe the sticker had been put there a year ago for this very night!

"He will save my children," she said aloud. "I believe it."

And peace flowed over Olivia's wounded spirit like a fragrant, healing ointment.

Halley Cain spent most of the afternoon cleaning her house. She changed the sheets, scrubbed the bathroom with disinfectant, vacuumed, washed dishes and pitched out every trace of her visitors.

You always were a fool, she told herself furiously. *A trusting fool.*

But the idea of reporting Otto's crimes to the police violated her code. His kidnaping was less heinous by far than ratting, snitching, being a stool pigeon. She might rail at how she had been used and abused, but she would never believe that Otto's offenses gave her the right to bring in the law.

Then she discovered that her bank cards were missing.

She might not even have noticed the theft until morning, but this outrage had given her an intolerable headache, and her medicine was in her purse hanging on the back of the bathroom door. As she dug through the bag for the pills, she noticed all the contents of her wallet—pictures, driver's license, Certificate of Health—loose in the purse, and she knew.

Halley thought back to her arrival home from work, the explosive confrontation with Otto and Stoney and their precipitate withdrawal. Even in the turmoil she had left her purse (like a fool) hanging in the bathroom, available to anyone. Otto had obviously helped himself.

Otto had made a big mistake.

Halley was so angry that, without even taking time to pop a pill for her headache, she grabbed the ravaged purse and drove in fury to the Tampa Police Department. Under most circumstances, given her position on the fringes of the law, she avoided contact with cops. But she was a businesswoman, after all. A taxpayer. A property owner. She had a right to police protection.

Her mind was red with rage but functioning sharply. Not only would she report his theft; she would also, without exposing herself to prosecution or revealing her own culpability, let the police know that Otto had abducted and was still holding two young children.

Kidnaping was a capital crime in Florida. And Florida had the electric chair.

✤   ✤   ✤

It was still light enough by 8:30 P.M. to see the crowd gathering in and around the ballfield. Aaron and Bobby Lee Clement trudged across scruffy grass to the bleachers and took a seat on an upper row.

"How can they play out in public like this?" Aaron asked. "It's illegal."

"No problem; the fix is in."

Bobby Lee was still shabby and unclean, but he was animated now. He was one of those people, Aaron realized, for whom excitement substituted for happiness.

"How many games?"

"Three or four. Only one ring."

Aaron nodded, pretending he understood. His knowledge of the revived gladiatorial games was minimal, mostly what he had seen on the news.

Apparently the managers—they called themselves *impresarios*—recruited from the ranks of young, strong and still healthy HIV-positives. They offered contracts varying in length from six months to two years, during which time the young "gladiators" were given a life of relative luxury—all the drugs, women and excitement they wanted. At the end of the contract, they were set one against the other in combat, to the death.

The appeal of the games was astonishing. Since many INFECTEDS were suicidal and all feared the lingering, tormented death of AIDS, impresarios had few problems recruiting. Lately they had added female contestants, although Bobby Lee reported regretfully that none was playing tonight.

The gladiators were trained in various killing arts; some proved skillful and survived their contracts by consistently winning their matches. Many had thus become stars with loyal (not to say rabid) fans. The public flocked to the games. And betting on the matches was both popular and profitable.

America, after all, had worshiped the god of sports for decades. Athletic stars were likewise worshiped. With the decay of society, what had been wholesome and clean in the sports world also decayed. Concepts like sportmanship, decency and fairness had been supplanted by widespread corruption; and violence (among both players and fans) was common if not condoned. Today's sports reflected today's world. No more simulations; now they actually killed each other.

Aaron estimated a sizable crowd, maybe as many as 3,000. At fifty bucks a head, Aaron figured, that was $150,000, and the crowd was still coming.

And three or four young men would die.

Vendors moved through the stands, hawking homemade liquor and a variety of drugs with the same festive air that Aaron had once seen in the sellers of hot dogs, peanuts and beer. When the field lights came on, there was a scattering of applause. The excitement intensified. There was a shriek of feedback as the public address system was turned on and the play-by-play announcer began, "Testing, testing, one, two, three. . . ."

The similarities to the hometown baseball and football games of the past were extraordinary. *Everything but "The Star Spangled Banner,"* Aaron thought.

Almost all other athletic competitions had been halted in this era of AIDS. When the medical community finally admitted that the virus lived—indeed, seemed to thrive—in human sweat, the reign of sports dwindled and died as surely as if sports, too, had been infected with a deadly disease. For some of these gladiators already infected with HIV, it was a moot point whether AIDS could be transmitted via human sweat. They were under a sentence of death anyway.

The crowd roared and rose to their feet as five men exited

a large trailer parked at the edge of the field. It was wired up to one of the light standards to obtain electricity, and armed guards were stationed around it. The words *Sid Galen's Games* were painted along its sides. The first man was clad in a well-tailored dark suit, and he walked with brisk confidence.

"That's Sid Galen," Bobby Lee said excitedly.

The impresario waved to the crowd which roared back its admiration. Two of the other men were in long black pants and black and white striped shirts, obviously officials; the final two were the gladiators.

One of them, thought Aaron, *will not walk back after this encounter.*

"That last guy's Tim Baker," Bobby Lee said. "He's a real stayer. This'll be his sixth fight."

The fighters were dressed in athletic garb, shorts and high-topped canvas shoes, each with his own colors. Tim Baker, the favorite, was wearing black and yellow, his opponent two shades of blue.

The announcer gave the contenders' backgrounds and past records, ending with the statement that the weapons for this contest would be knives. The crowd shouted its approval. A circle about twelve feet in diameter had been chalked onto the grass, into which one of the officials escorted the fighters.

"The rounds will be seven minutes, with one-minute rests between. If there has been no victory at the end of five rounds, the contestants will be bound together by their left wrists. We caution all spectators to remain at least fifteen feet from the circle."

The crowd was electrified. One official was checking the weapons, long-bladed knives that appeared to be identical; the second was arranging additional equipment on one of the benches behind the circle—other weapons, towels and water bottles and a short stack of neatly folded body bags.

"Two minutes till the first contest," the announcer proclaimed.

Ten other contestants, meanwhile, had left the trailer and were taking seats along the bench.

Bobby Lee grinned wolfishly. "This is gonna be great. Tim'll slice him open in the first round."

Aaron was already on the verge of being physically sick, swallowing back the almost overwhelming urge to vomit. It was not just the games, although they were evil enough. It was the crowd gathered to enjoy the pain and savagery and death. It was breathing out its communal blood-lust so forcefully it was almost palpable.

He rose suddenly and started down the bleachers, bumping into spectators who turned angrily as he passed. Nothing mattered but getting out as quickly as he could. Murmuring continuous apologies, he forced openings between the closely packed fans. Not even Bobby Lee's calling him could deter his headlong push down from the bleachers and away from that evil.

It seemed at one point, as a roar rose and he realized the games had begun, that he would be a part of the crowd that witnessed Tim Baker's murder of his opponent. But once he was off the bleachers he broke into a run, out of the field area and down the now-darkened street toward town. As he increased his distance from the field, he slowed his pace, pressing a hand to his right side, now a knot of pain.

He stumbled and almost fell, then slowed to a walk. Others on the road were headed in the opposite direction, hurrying toward the scene of death he had just escaped. His flight, he realized, had been just that: an escape. He had avoided by the skin of his teeth a contamination more deadly than AIDS.

Crying, teeth chattering, he was whispering the same words over and over: "Forgive me, Lord. Forgive me, Lord."

✣   ✣   ✣

Carly Jenson stole the uniform without a hitch. Just walking out of the hospice with the white pants and shirt under
his arm had indeed been exhilarating. He had hidden them
between his mattress and box spring with a feeling of victory.
So this is what they meant by high-adrenaline situations. By
golly, he liked it!

He confronted other pulse-pounding events that evening
as he transferred first his clothing, later the suitcase of silver,
to a hiding place outdoors. Each trip carried the risk of discovery. All the Pine River people lived in the same building—
Sergeant Cordray shared his very room—and Carly had no
way of knowing where each one was at any given moment.
But the risks brought him wonderfully alive.

He sat now in the dark, leaning against the building across
the road from the hospice motor pool. Apparently all the car
and truck keys hung on hooks on the wall behind the desk
where a guard sat. Twice today Carly had watched a uniformed
man enter the building, exchange a few words with the guard
and help himself to first the key, then the vehicle it fit.

The truck would be no problem.

He watched in silence, his strong and handsome face creased in
thought. The planning done, it would soon be time for Carly to act.

No, not *Carly;* that was almost a diminutive. The hero of
this electrifying drama should have a forceful, utterly masculine name. Rock? No, that was too completely Rock Hud-
son. How about Brock? Not perfect. Brick? Buck?

Suddenly he knew. The hero of this production would have
none of those names; he would have a title. For the purpose
of this adventure show, he would become the Shark. No longer
would he be Carly, the junior partner, the junior Jenson. Carly
was usually weak, sometimes ineffectual, occasionally a failure. The Shark was powerful, durable, savvy.

He considered the question of a gun. He knew Aaron had stored his rifle and one shotgun in the van. He had wrapped them in old towels and put them into the well that held the spare tire. It would not take much of a tool to pry open the van doors and uncover the tire well. But would Aaron discover it and suspect him? Was it likely that a thief would find the guns by accident, or should Carly take everything else from the van to cover the fact that the thief knew where the guns were hidden?

He rose slowly and walked across the street. It did not matter what he decided—gun or no gun, strip the van or take only the gun. Whatever he did would work. The Shark was invincible.

He entered the brightly lit garage-like building and smiled at the seated guard.

"Hot for September, isn't it?" he asked casually.

"You got that right," the guard answered, hardly lifting his eyes from the pornographic magazine he was looking at.

Carly took a key from a hook labeled *Pick-ups and Long-beds* and strolled toward the parked vehicles, smiling triumphantly to himself.

Invincible!

They were back to Twinkies and soda and Philip found it hard to believe that only a few days ago he had been thrilled at that diet. Today had been hot and uncomfortable and he was feeling more and more dejected. He slouched next to Sara in the rear of the white panel truck and contemplated his distress.

So many new things were bothering him. He wanted to brush his teeth, for one thing. His mouth was coated with an unpleasant layer of something—probably the sugar his mother so opposed. Right now he would rather brush his teeth than ever eat another Twinkie. It made him want to cry, thinking how pleased his mother would be to hear that.

Otto pulled the truck off the road and stopped with a jerk. "That's the barrier," he said to Stoney.

"Ain't we going in?"

"Let's get some sleep first."

It was fully dark, a quiet and rural place. Philip slapped a mosquito and settled himself as comfortably as possible. Might as well get some sleep; it made the time pass faster.

Barrier to where? he wondered. *And to keep people in or keep them out?*

"I appreciate your seeing me, Micah," Will said. "You could be getting a little sleep, I know."

"No problem. Come on in." Micah opened the door, clad in a bathrobe. "Nora's in bed."

Will took the now-familiar walk through Micah's old-fashioned home to the big, friendly kitchen. It was almost 11 P.M. Darned if he knew why he had waited this long. But Micah planned to meet a convoy at eight the next morning in Gainesville and he wanted at least one more visit before Micah left town and he was "on his own."

"Going all the way to Miami?"

"No. I unload in Lauderdale, reload with produce right after. Then I line up with another convoy heading back. Should be home Friday if I'm lucky."

"I'll miss you." Will smiled sheepishly. "I been depending on you. I guess you noticed."

"Nothing wrong with that. You want a drink or something?"

"No. I just wanted to say things are going real good. It's like you said, maybe circumstances haven't changed much yet, but I have. I'm different, I know I am."

Micah smiled. "Give me an example."

"Aaron, for one thing. I used to resent him; he stole my little girl from me and maybe I been jealous of him, I don't know. But it's gone."

"Wonderful!"

"And I don't get so irritated with Charlotte." Will grinned, his face full of mischief. "That's not to say I don't get irritated at all. Just it's better."

"You *are* seeing changes."

"I wish I'd done this a long time ago, Micah. It's really great having God on your side to help you."

"The Bible says the Lord is a present help in time of trouble. That means you have a Savior, Someone to save you."

"That's what I wanted."

"You're going to need to move on from here, of course."

"Move on? I got saved, didn't I?"

"Sure. You accepted Jesus as Savior. What I mean is accepting Him as Lord."

"What's the difference?"

"Well, you're talking about asking the Lord's help in getting what you want. He's going to ask you to let that go, help Him accomplish *His* will."

His will? Things had been going fine. Will knew the kids would return safely from their hardships and exploits, and until then he could wait with composure because he was seeing improvements within himself. Always a pragmatist, he had no interest in fixing what was not broken.

Micah was smiling at him. "Don't worry, Will. It's a simple matter of growing in your relationship with God."

"Does everybody do this?"

"Good heavens, no!" Micah laughed. "Almost nobody does. Most Christians think of God as a spare tire, and they keep Him in the trunk until they have a flat."

"So how would you describe the other way, the making Him Lord thing?"

"Well, I guess that's when He climbs into the driver's seat and takes over."

"Oh, I follow you."

"Not many people really want that," Micah added.

Will laughed. "I can appreciate that!"

Help Him accomplish His will, he mused. *Wonder what that might involve.*

12

Wednesday, September 15, 1999, dawn till twilight

When the sustained winds within tropical storm Ariel reached an average speed of 76 miles per hour, she was upgraded to the status of hurricane. Her center was located about 500 nautical miles east-southeast of Miami, her forward speed was about 18 knots and she was moving in an easterly direction.

The responsibility of tracking and projecting the hurricane's progress was held by the six-man crew of the National Hurricane Center in Miami, a branch of the National Weather Service. They had an impressive volume of data at their disposal coming from an array of technological and scientific resources. This included weather satellites, land-based radar, and computers furnished with databases and statistical models (by which they could make projections based on the performance of past storms as well as current information) and the hurricane-tracking plane, a P-3 Orion flying laboratory filled with delicate sensing devices. She flew directly into the storm to locate its eye and measure the central pressure in millibars. They were a dedicated and efficient group of men with an enviable record for accuracy.

No matter how much they knew about a hurricane, however, they had no way to control its power. Information, they were well aware, was never tantamount to protection.

Wednesday dawned humid and overcast. The four people who climbed stiffly from the white panel truck and walked toward the restaurant were quiet. They had slept in the vehicle again which, as usual, had taken its toll.

They were inside the Belle Glade barrier now. Getting in had not presented a big problem; the trick was getting out again without having your blood scanned. Otto Krause knew the children's blood would probably trigger all kinds of alarms in the fully integrated computer system. Just about everybody was hooked into the blood scanners: schools, hospitals, restaurants and, of course, the police.

Well, maybe they would get lucky and get rid of the kids here inside the Belle Glade zone. If not, they would cross that bridge when they came to it.

Otto shut down the thinking process.

Philip walked behind the kidnapers. Despite his fatigue, he was full of tension. He and Sara would be around people again, inside a restaurant full of customers. There might well be an opportunity to escape, and he was breathless with the thought. He also recognized the very real possibility that anything he did might make the situation worse.

His sister was walking next to Stoney, chattering cheerfully.

"Is Philip right—we don't have to test clean to eat here?" she asked.

"Yeah, we're in an Infected Zone. I hope they got grits."

"I want berries, like we had at Mrs. Parker's," Sara responded. "What do you want, Otto?"

"I want the address of the guy I'm looking for," he answered shortly. "Do our business and get outta the Q. Zone."

Another man who used children, Philip realized. Like Mr. Capovilla in Tampa. They had escaped him only by luck, or by Sara's cleverness, and now Otto was looking for another man. Philip was not sure what these men did with the children they bought, but it must be terrible.

He began praying again as they entered the restaurant. How long would their luck hold?

Or was it luck?

Burt drank coffee as he ran a weary eye over the midnight report that had been left on his desk by the night shift supervisor. Computer printouts offered statistical summaries of admissions, transfers, assisted and unassisted deaths in the last 24 hours. In addition, copies of all the Infraction Records (official forms that catalogued anything employees did wrong) and Incident Reports (official forms to cover any mistakes for which employees could not directly be blamed) made for a tall stack of bad news. What a day it promised to be!

Anything that can go wrong *will*, Burt thought. Was that the Peter Principle or Murphy's Law? Actually, maybe one of the laws of physics (he forgot which one) said it better: Everything is hurtling toward increasing chaos.

Burt had been strongly tempted for some time now to quit trying—to withdraw his finger from this inadequate dike and let the destruction pour in. His stand against the reign of chaos was a washout. Might as well try to control the devastation of a hurricane! It was always smart to recognize the truth. Sometimes the better part of valor was flight.

He wondered at the implications of this uncharacteristic line of thinking.

Paul Cordray looked around the dining room for Major Shearson. He was either already at work or had not yet arrived. The idea of eating alone appealed to Paul, but it died aborning as Dr. Cassandra Kovaks hurried up to him.

"You're just the man I've been waiting for."

He nodded pleasantly, balancing his breakfast tray. "Here I am; what can I do for you?"

He was surprised to see that instead of the regulation white pants and lab coat, the doctor wore a soft dress of light blue. A blue ribbon held her dark hair back from her face. As usual she wore no makeup.

"Hurry up and eat. I want you to go with me to the suicide room. Seems I have that duty today. I'm supposed to be a consultant, you know. Not just another one of their employees."

Paul led the way to an unoccupied table and set his food out: eggs, toast, grapefruit, coffee. Dr. Kovaks sat opposite him; everything about her expressed impatience.

"I know you have your own things to do, but after our talk yesterday, you know, I wanted you to come in that room and, like, tell me how you feel about the suicide machine."

"You can probably guess how I feel," he grimaced, attacking his plateful of eggs. *That* was certainly going to help his appetite.

"Yes, but I don't want just to know how you feel. I want to know why you feel that way." Her usually cheerful face was intent.

He ate as quickly as possible and skipped his usual second cup of coffee. Within fifteen minutes they were standing outside a door labeled

SUICIDE ROOM
Authorized Personnel Only

Dr. Kovaks took a key from her pocket and unlocked the door.

❖   ❖   ❖

The Everglades, Florida's "river of grass," extended originally from just south of Lake Okeechobee to the southern
tip of the peninsula, stretching almost from coast to coast.
Florida's Everglades is like no place else on the planet. Count-
less miles of breathtakingly beautiful, uninhabited, inhos-
pitable land, it is untamed, stunning, dangerous.

But when men originally settled in that part of the state,
because this environment did not accommodate human comfort, and because its almost primeval beauty was largely un-
appreciated, they began scheming to drain it.

The scheming and drainage continued for decades. Much
of the gold coast of Florida—some of the most valuable real
estate on the planet—was later built on the sandy land re-
sulting from man's "reclamation" of the Everglades.

Even so, the Everglades remain the largest freshwater marsh
in the world, over 5,000 square miles of wet prairies, swamps,
marshes, sloughs, areas of jungle and low islands. The majority of the expanse is covered with sawgrass—hence the
name river of grass.

Sawgrass grows from roots sunk deep into the fertile bottom muck, below the shallow, brackish water, flourishing to
a height of ten to fifteen feet. Its blades are as tough as bam-
boo, with razor-sharp edges; the roots lace together into a
matted whole, separated into clumps by channels of slightly
deeper flowing water. The grass waves and dips like the ocean.
Also like the ocean, it is dotted with islands, called hammocks.
This novel terrain spreads mile after mile, from horizon to
horizon.

It is frighteningly easy to become lost in the river of grass.
The blades grow so tall that there is no way to see ahead, and
they cannot support a person's weight to allow a climb up for
a look around. The grass blades also slash anyone who tries
to walk through them.

The usual means of transportation across the grass are air-boats, flat-bottomed skiffs with curved prows that skim along the surface of the grass as easily as they do on water. Powered by airplane motors and propellers mounted on the rear of the boat, they can easily achieve 70 miles per hour.

The Everglades are almost completely flat. The highest elevations are its islands, only about seven feet above sea level. These small islands support an abundance of plant and animal life. Orchids grow wild and with their profusion can transform a hammock into a magical hanging garden. Tropical birds like the pelican, ibis, egret, crane and spoonbill thrive. Occasional trees—mango, palm, mahogany, palmetto, strangler fig—ablaze with wild orchids, teeming with brightly colored, raucous birds, stand like ancient sentinels over the unending vistas of flowing grass.

The higher regions, with a more solid foundation of sandy soil, nourish more than ninety varieties of trees, including three kinds that form forests: mangrove, pine and cypress. These forests and veldts support the remnants of Florida's deer, panther, black bear and bobcat. Nearby, hidden from sight in the shadowy world of jungle swampland that lurks just behind the beauty, dwell the man-killers: snakes and alligators.

Recently another killer was added to the Everglades' roster: mosquitoes. Now, passing from one blood source to another, carrying the HIV as in times past they carried malaria, mosquitoes have become potential killers more deadly than alligators or snakes.

On Highway 27, Carly Jenson would drive his stolen truck across a bit of the remarkable terrain of the Everglades, then skirt its eastern border on his way to Miami.

❖   ❖   ❖

Since daytime was safer than night for driving the highways, Carly had driven off the road into a thicket of palmettos and slept until morning, slumped behind the wheel of the truck. He was enjoying his role as the Shark and looking forward to his appointment that night with representatives of drug lord Julio Renata. His mind played the voice-over narration for the scene of the meeting: *As the Shark entered, his impact was felt by every man and woman in the room. No one doubted that this handsome young Anglo was a force to be reckoned with.*

When he wakened to a gray and blustery morning, he sought a highway sign to guide him, even though for years Carly had read about the antisocial customs adopted by the gangs who lived outside the law—stealing, plundering, ravaging, killing. When for some reason they could not do anything really harmful, they contented themselves to do things that were at least annoying. One of the most famous of these was their practice of either destroying or altering highway signs.

Carly knew this happened, but for some reason it never occurred to him not to trust the markers along the roads leading from Belle Glade. When he encountered a sign that said *U.S. 27 Andytown 41 miles,* he drove on, confident it would lead him to Miami.

Had the weather been better, with sunshine and shadows to give him directional clues, he would not have made such a mistake. But the approaching storm was preceded by a heavy overcast, and Carly had no indication that he was driving not south toward Miami but west toward Fort Myers.

Dr. Kovaks opened the door and stood back as the sergeant entered before her.

"There aren't any nurses or orderlies to help here," she explained. "The doctor does it all."

It looked about the same as any other room: a regulation hospital bed; a small table next to it with the usual plastic water jug and glass; an armless straight chair beside the bed; a small cart with IV solutions, tubing, syringes and needles, and such paraphernalia as tourniquets, tape and arm boards. The only window was covered by a dark green shade. Across the room a counter ran along the wall with cabinets above it. A small desk had stacks of papers and printed forms neatly arranged on it. Beside the desk on a rolling standard was a sphygmomanometer.

Cassandra pointed to this last item. "You just do BP and pulse to declare death. No brain-tracing or EKG."

Paul recognized that the sphygmomanometer was one-half of the equipment (along with a stethoscope) required to take blood pressures.

The young doctor took a seat next to the bed. "I really believe in rights, like the right to choose, you know? Each person is entitled to decide when they want to die. But I never did this before and—I don't know, it almost seems like I'm actually killing somebody. You know?"

"You *are* killing somebody," said Paul. "Even if they want to die, it's still killing them."

And that's murder, he finished silently.

"But if doctors don't help these people, who will? If they try to do it without our help, they may fail. Most medical ethicists say it's normal medical care. It's just sort of new, like abortions were at first."

"Yes, exactly like that."

Paul was suddenly furious—at the absurdity of the human race, at the foolhardiness of making life-and-death decisions based on what so-called ethicists said, especially *some* of them. Talk about walking in the counsel of the ungodly! But, of course, these people didn't read Psalm 1, nor did they consider what God might think about this horror.

Jesus had said, "I hold the keys to death and hell." And Paul knew that fulfilling one's so-called right to die was an abomination in God's eyes. But he had no interest in discussing it with this confused young woman when he felt as agitated as he did. He wanted out of this room right now, even while he knew Cassandra was looking for a response.

Then he saw a small, framed quotation sitting on the desk: *There is a time to die. Ecclesiastes 3:2.*

He whirled around to face her. "Remember what I said yesterday? Man wants to be his own god; he ignores the Creator, makes his own laws and rules and decisions, and this is the result—a dying world where man is given over to desperate evil. A world without hope or peace or security. And we're so blind and foolish we can't even see that everything we do fails. It doesn't work! I want to shout it from the rooftops: What human beings do *doesn't work!* We have an intellect that is darkened, hearts that are wicked and deceived, and bodies that are dying. Yet we want to create our own laws and programs, and we keep thinking we can save ourselves. Can't we see? The very best we can have is the intellect of fallen Adam."

He paused and pointed at the quotation. "That's the very thing Satan did in the Garden of Eden to beguile Eve. It's a distortion of Scripture. He convinced Eve to disobey by confusing her about what God said." He shook his finger angrily at the offending quote. "God does say there's a time to be born and a time to die, but He means *His* time, not man's!"

"I guess you think I oughtn't to do it, then?" Cassandra asked.

Suddenly he was unwilling to battle the bland ignorance that faced him. Where was the zeal for her that he had had yesterday?

"Killing people on demand is just one of many things that are part of the world today. It's unspeakably evil—but I don't see why you should shy away from a little professional mur-

der when things like abortions and organ transplants and genetic engineering don't bother you." He knew his sarcasm
was cutting but couldn't seem to stop himself. "I mean, why
draw the line there? Why draw a line at all?"

Cassandra spoke defensively. "They save lives, and that's a
good thing."

He pointed again at the Bible quote. "Read that! There *is*
a time to die, and God alone knows when it is. It's not right
to *extend* life by doing things God has forbidden any more
than it's right to *end* life by doing things He has forbidden.
Why don't you just quit trying to be God?"

He knew he was focusing his anger on her. How would that
help her toward salvation? He shook his head, drained of passion. "I'm sorry. I shouldn't talk to you that way. You certainly
aren't required to walk in my beliefs." He managed an apolo-
getic smile and she smiled back.

"I don't mean to blame you for all the faults of this wicked
and perverse generation. It's just that here in a hospital it's so
clear how medical people are trying to be gods. But it's true
in every other field, too. Everywhere that we ascend the throne
of our own lives, ignore God and live in our own light, the
result is chaos. When we're unwilling to yield control of things
to God, we're doomed. Blind. We lead other blind men and
we both end up in a ditch. We both end up in hell."

He sat on the bed across from Cassie. "Forgive me for
yelling at you?" he asked.

"Oh, sure. I kind of see what you mean. I mean, things are
pretty bad. I just never thought of it as a religious problem."

He smiled ruefully. He was too overwhelmed at the height
and breadth and depth of her ignorance to try to explain how
"religion" was no solution. It was, in fact, a big part of the
problem. How few people could see the difference between
a religious system organized to try to meet human needs, and
the God of the universe reaching down to reveal Himself and

redeem sinful, fallen humanity! The difference between the true Church—a living, breathing, procreating organism, full of beauty and wisdom and power—and the counterfeit of the Church, an organization operating in merely human wisdom and strength.

Paul rose again. "Let's get out of here, O.K.?"

"Sure. I'm going to, like, think about what you said. I agree with a lot of it. But you have to admit, people do have the right to choose. I mean, after all, it's their life. I mean, you know, their *right*. Isn't it?"

The restaurant was crowded and noisy. Philip followed Sara, Otto and Stoney to a booth toward the rear of the room. Otto sat with his back to the wall and scanned the room suspiciously. But the crowd was lighthearted, calling back and forth, joking and teasing.

A large, unkempt waitress approached their table and dealt them each a grubby menu. "What'll it be for you folks?"

Philip made no attempt to read the menu. He ordered dry cereal, a whole-grain his mother approved, then offered to help Sara.

"I want cereal, too," she said virtuously, her thought of berries apparently forgotten.

As the men ordered, Philip turned to look at the roomful of people and was immediately discouraged from seeking help. No single face invited approach. He was disappointed but relieved; it was safer to do nothing.

Their food came quickly. The children poured milk onto their cereal while Otto talked quietly to the waitress. "I was told about a guy sometimes comes in here. Older man, name of Kibbee. Ever heard of him?"

"Could be."

Her broad face was closed, her eyes narrowed. It was obvious to Philip that she knew the man. Was she hesitating from fear or was she hoping for money?

Otto took a bill from his pocket; the waitress slid it into the front of her blouse. "That's him at the counter, got on the Hurricane shirt. Poor old geezer. His son used to play football for the Hurricanes; now he's dead."

"Wait for me," Otto commanded Stoney. "Watch the nippers."

He walked toward the counter.

It seemed a long time before Otto came back. The other three had finished eating by the time he took his seat. He began to eat and talk at the same time.

"We deliver them to a fish camp down in the 'Glades. I got directions how to get there; shouldn't take more than an hour or so. He says he'll come pick them up tomorrow night. He even told me how to get out of the Zone without passing a checkpoint." He grinned around a mouthful of egg and toast. "Real handy guy."

"Sounds good, Otto," Stoney nodded.

"What say let's go on down? We could do some fishing."

"Yeah, I don't like this town. Everybody's infected, and I don't like eating after them."

Sara and Philip exchanged a nervous look. Time was running out.

Julio Renata had been born into grinding poverty. His native Cuba had long been poor and his family was one of her poorest. He had been raised in a shack without adequate food or clothing, toys, games, friends or formal education. But even more impoverishing was his deprivation of soul. He had been given no love and no hint of morality.

Julio was the fifth and last of his mother's children; no one knew who his father had been. His mother was a dark, angry woman who had made her submarginal livelihood as a prostitute, her clientele the day-laborers in the sugar cane fields of Cuba's Oriente Province. Her scant income was allocated first for rum, then for the small cigars she loved, and finally (if anything remained) for food for her children.

From earliest childhood, Julio hated his mother. The strength of his hatred grew so great that it seemed to develop a life of its own. He spent hours daydreaming of escape from his appalling life and of revenge against his mother. In what might have been compensatory fortuity, Julio had been gifted with a quick intellect and unbridled ambition. He thought long and well. When the time was right, he took action.

He was only eleven when he set fire to the shanty that was the only home he had ever known. His mother, brother and three sisters died in the fire. He walked away from the smoking ruins and from his past with no shred of regret. He had proved his mettle; he had the skill to plan and the fearlessness to act.

Julio discarded his surname—his mother's name—and chose instead the name Renata, meaning newly born, or born again. He was born anew of his own power. Nothing could deter him from his destiny. No accident of birth could hold him back. No political turmoil or social strife was sufficient to hinder his rise.

This was the man Carly Jenson hoped would buy his father's silver.

Paul Cordray finally got his second cup of coffee. He sat alone in the hospice dining room and thought of modern society. Incredible! If anybody had written a book twenty, even ten years ago detailing American society as it would become in this time of AIDS, no one would have believed it.

I'm living in it and I can hardly believe it, he thought.

Then he caught sight of Aaron Tyler pouring himself a cup of coffee, and motioned him over. Aaron's coffee cup shook in his hand as he joined Paul at the table—a sign, no doubt, of unremitting emotional pressure.

"Any news?" the sergeant asked.

"Nothing. I'm going out to ride around town, just to feel like I'm doing something. And so I won't have to face Olivia."

Paul wondered whether it was better to let Aaron talk or try to divert him. He decided on the latter.

"I had a guided tour of the suicide room this morning. Reminds me of the execution site I saw once in a stockade. Exact same feeling to the place."

"I guess it's pretty busy in a location like this. The so-called easy way out, huh?"

"Yeah. It's pretty obvious life isn't working real well for most of the people around here." Paul shook his head. "And of course, they think this is all there is."

"How do they stand it without God?" Aaron said softly. "It's rough enough knowing the truth and having the comfort of that 'sure and certain hope of the resurrection.' How can anyone face waking up each day when this world is falling apart and not know there's another world waiting?"

Paul nodded. "And I wonder how they can fool themselves into thinking they might have answers. Solutions. It's unbelievable that they've been running things for all these years, and it gets worse every day—especially here in America for thirty-odd years—yet they keep doing their same things, apparently unaware that it's only making things worse."

"I've wondered the same thing. Olivia works in a school clinic, and you wouldn't believe the stupidity of what she has to do. With teenagers doing crimes, killing each other, committing suicide, taking drugs, hating their parents and every other kind of authority, and seemingly not learning a thing in class, these school officials never stop to realize it's a result of their programs—that what they're doing is not helping."

"Same thing everywhere. The theory is, if it isn't working, do it more. Blind leaders and blind followers."

"Well, one consolation." Aaron smiled tautly. "It can't go on much longer."

"That's true." Paul rose reluctantly. It was a pleasure to talk to someone with whom he was spiritually compatible, to be able to say what he felt without offending.

"Is there anything I can do for you?" he asked. "I really do care, and I feel so helpless."

"Thanks. I wish I knew something for *me* to do," Aaron replied. "But I'll remember the offer."

Carly was fighting panic. It was late morning before he realized his mistake. When he entered Fort Myers, he realized the truth of his situation and pulled off the road to think. Almost noon now; he had wasted hours!

Although he had only a hazy mental map of this part of the state, he knew he was limited in his options. He had only three possible routes to Miami. He could cross the Tamiami Trail, also known as Alligator Alley, which bisected the Everglades. He could go farther south on Highway 41 and cross the Big Cypress Preserve. Both these routes would put him in wild country, full of lawless gangs. But his third choice was little better: He could retrace his path across the state on Highway 80 back to Belle Glade, back to the Infected Zone with its barriers and checkpoints, back to the site of his "grand theft auto."

He pounded the steering wheel in frustration. He still had time to make his nighttime meeting in Miami, but the extra mileage meant he would have to buy gas, and that might prove tricky. There were few gas stations in the really lawless areas.

It was this factor that finally decided his route. Better to deal with guards and blood scanners than run out of gas somewhere in the watery no-man's-land of southwestern Florida.

That would spell disaster. And maybe the theft of the truck had not yet been reported; things in Belle Glade, after all, were pretty slipshod.

He turned the truck around and headed back east. His cheerful optimism, in the face of his blunder, had been replaced by desperation.

Even as far north as Pine River, the afternoon was cloudy and the wind gusty. Feeder bands of wind and rain were thrown off from the leading edge of Ariel's swirl, so that even northwest Florida felt her presence.

Joe Jenson sat in his office ignoring a desktop full of work. He always made a point of not drinking before the cocktail hour—usually no sacrifice. But today was different. A strange feeling of dread lurked in the shadows behind his thoughts. He felt haunted.

There's no reason to be worried, he told himself firmly. He was confident Carly would return safely and soon, no doubt a better man for his experience.

But if he was not worried about Carly, and felt no anxieties about the practice, why was he so jumpy?

Suddenly an idea struck him. Without thinking he telephoned Will Stoddard.

"Willy, whatcha got on for tonight? Nothing? Great. Let's get together, have a couple of drinks and some dinner. What do you say?"

They set the time and Joe hung up, feeling a remarkable release of tension. Will might have word on the Belle Glade folks. If not, they still had things to talk about. At least it would be better than sitting around worrying—especially when there was absolutely nothing to worry about!

Certainly not the appointment he had later this evening for his routine blood test for HIV. He had no cause for concern on that front.

✛ ✛ ✛

Dina Hawks squatted in front of the last and least accessible filing cabinet. In one of these files was a written procedure about responding to a hurricane. She had been looking for it for hours, and still it eluded her.

Lots of it was common sense: Store drinking water, be sure radio batteries are fresh, bring in or tie down outside equipment that might be blown away, prepare for a shutdown of electrical power, check food and pharmacy supplies. Nothing she could not figure out on her own. But the procedure was there and she should be able to locate it.

Burt entered their common office and stared at her owlishly. "Playing jacks?"

"No, but if you can find a set, I'll beat the tar out of you," she snapped, rising from her squatting position. "In my day I was great at jacks. Also marbles, softball and Frisbee."

"I, on the other hand, hit my peak when I finally managed to ride a bicycle without training wheels at age eight," Burt said mournfully. "I was such a stereotype!"

He turned and stood to look out one of the windows. "They say our weather is now 'tropical'; we're going to have 'tropical' rain. That means very big drops, air that's buoyant, winds shifting erratically and low barometric pressure. Aren't you glad I learned all this?"

Suddenly Burt beat his clenched fists on the windowsill. "I hope it gets so savage it tears this place down!"

Dina studied him from the side. His reddish complexion was even redder than usual. He was on *something*, no doubt about it, but it did not seem to be alcohol. Well, whatever it was, it wasn't right of him to get high or stoned with the Finger Squad here and a hurricane on its rampaging way.

"Do you know where the hurricane procedure is?" she asked.

"No, and I am supremely indifferent to its whereabouts. There are not enough words in the English language to tell you how little I care about the hurricane procedure." He waved his hand in a grandiose way.

"Are you drunk?"

"No, I am not drunk. I am dissociated. I am hanging onto sanity by a tenuous, almost gossamer, thread."

"Want to tell me why?"

"Because in a world that glories in rights and choices, I am beginning to see that every single choice I have ever made was wrong. Counterproductive, don't you see? Designed to bring the most disastrous and deadly results."

Dina cocked her head. "Not every single one, surely."

"Oh, yes." Burt nodded in a conspiratorial way. "I've batted a thousand. A perfect record. And I reach the summer of my days without family, without success, without a future, without hope. Surely it could not have come out so totally wrong by accident, could it?"

"Let's don't worry about that now, Burt. Let's get some coffee and see if we can't jot down a few guidelines for the staff for the hurricane. It might be really bad by morning."

"Well, maybe I can arrange not to be here by then." He sat down with a thump on his desk chair and immediately fell asleep, his head lolling back.

Dina kept looking at him curiously, then walked out of the room.

It never rains but it pours, she thought. *And this time it's going to be a deluge.*

A hundred—no, a thousand—things had to fall in line perfectly, he realized, for the two vehicles to have met. Carly was not a deep thinker and had always felt irritated with people who expended time and effort trying to find deeper meanings for the inexplicable phenomena of life. But the coincidence was so compelling, the meeting such an against-all-odds fluke, that he was shaken to the core.

It was late afternoon. He had made the return trip to Belle Glade, even driven through it, without incident. The hospice truck and the now wrinkled and dirty white uniform had apparently been sufficient authorization. And since his blood scanned as uninfected, he had sailed through the checkpoint and was finally on Highway 27 to Miami. He had treated himself to a good meal, both his confidence and his good humor largely restored.

It was growing dark, mostly because of the overcast, but he still had plenty of time to make the rendezvous, even though he would need to get a room somewhere to shower, shave and metamorphose from a poorly groomed hospice orderly into a well-dressed, astute attorney. A Shark.

The incredible event happened at the intersection of Highway 27 and Alligator Alley. In the past this area had bustled with toll booths for the turnpike, restaurants, gas stations, two motels and a string of small shops specializing in Everglades mementos and bric-a-brac. It had been an energetic island of commerce in the midst of a natural wilderness. In the wake of the AIDS epidemic, things had calmed down somewhat. The toll booths had been closed but there were still tall lights (lit now against the dark, stormy sky), one functioning gas station, a drive-in food-and-drink establishment and much activity. Carly pulled off the road to top off his tanks with gasoline.

Three large trucks were parked together, obviously part of a convoy, and a half-dozen men stood nearby, drinking soft drinks and laughing. There was a flatbed truck with a load of produce; the driver, a second man and three others were waiting for an available gas pump.

Carly parked directly under one of the tall light standards and looked around for restrooms. Finding none, he walked beyond the sphere of brightest light and behind a clump of palmettos. It was then that he saw the other vehicle—hidden, like his, behind the foliage. A heavy-set man sat behind the wheel. It was just as Carly had heard it described: a white panel truck with a sign reading *Otto Krause, Tip-Top Painting.*

The kidnapers.

He crouched down quickly and began furiously to think. What should he do? Confront the driver? If he rescued the Tyler kids, he would be a hero of major proportions. But these were felons, possibly armed, and he had no desire to get shot. Then there was the fact that he had stolen the truck, not to mention the fact that he had an appointment in Miami.

He considered just driving on. That was certainly the safest course. But the enormity of the coincidence argued against that plan. If Fate had led him to the kidnapers, he was probably supposed to take some action.

Maybe he could follow them, get a fix on their location and telephone back to the Belle Glade police. Yes, that sounded best.

A short, dark-haired man walked out from the bushes and climbed into the front of the truck. The driver started the engine. Carly heard him call out, "Get a move on! I want to get there 'fore the rain starts!"

The driver's voice lowered as he addressed remarks to his companion. "We'd of been there this morning if we didn't have car trouble. Blasted stupid radiator."

Carly listened with amazement. They had been delayed, too! That made the coincidence even more remarkable. But his heart almost stopped as the bushes parted and out of the wooded area walked Philip Tyler. He was thin, bedraggled, listless, but unmistakable even in the dimming light. The boy paused and looked over his shoulder. "Sara? You through? We gotta go."

Carly heard a rustling again, this time nearby. Philip turned toward the noise as Sara Tyler emerged from the bushes not fifteen feet from where Carly crouched.

"I'm coming. I got bit by an ant." They walked toward the truck, which was now backing out from its nesting place behind the bushes.

When it stopped, Philip walked behind it to the double doors and stretched up to reach the handle.

"You want to sit in the back now?" he asked his sister. "It's almost too dark to see out the window."

He turned to look at her, and without conscious thought Carly straightened up and began to walk slowly, deliberately, back into the light. His motion caught Philip's eye, and Carly was happy to see a look of astonished recognition cross the boy's face as their eyes met.

He shook his head briefly in warning. Then, with a feeling of indescribable joy, Carly nodded once and winked. He strolled beyond the children and kidnapers back toward the stolen hospice truck.

Talk about your adventure shows! This was a sure award-winner. Once again he was invincible.

Paul Cordray was eating an apple on a concrete bench next to the walkway in one of the rest areas dotting the hospice grounds, when Iris spotted him on her way from the dining room to Dorm 4. What a stroke of luck! She stopped in front of him and smiled.

"Is that your supper?"

"At least my appetizer."

"Looks good. The original forbidden fruit, right?"

"Not at all. Apples got a bum rap; it wasn't a natural fruit at all, you know."

"Well, that isn't my area of expertise." She knew more about *being* forbidden fruit, she thought dryly.

"The fruit Adam and Eve weren't supposed to taste was

really the ability to make their own evaluations. It was the knowledge of good and evil that was forbidden, not the poor old apple."

She sat down next to him, not too close but not too far. A shiver of excitement went through her. At last they were alone, as she had pictured so many times, just the two of them, in a quiet spot where interruption was unlikely. And she was dressed in flattering, if not elegant, apparel.

"You look tired," she said sympathetically. "Was it a busy day?"

Her mind translated the query: *Hard day at the office, dear? Here's the loving little woman, ready to make it all better for you.*

"Not especially. If I'm feeling the effects, they're emotional, not physical."

A breeze gusted from the east, pushing stringy gray clouds along and rustling the palm fronds above them. The sky to the west was still reddish but dusk was falling rapidly in the east. The concrete bench was still warm from the heat of the day.

Iris smiled to herself, anticipating the pending encounter. "So how do you plan to unwind tonight?"

"I have piles of paperwork," he answered.

"That's relaxing?" She smiled wickedly. "Can't you think of anything better than that?"

"I enjoy reading," he said courteously.

She could not tell if he was being deliberately obtuse or if he was really so innocent he did not recognize a come-on.

"You sound like Aaron. He reads all the time. Olivia gets fed up sometimes, and she isn't the type to get upset. He reads highbrow stuff—classics, like Shakespeare."

"Some of the most profound words in the English language came from that man."

"And the Bible. I guess you read that, too."

"Absolutely. Words of life."

Iris was getting annoyed. Here was another cool and superior being, like the Tylers, all satisfied and confident and patronizing. Once again she felt put down, tried in the balance and found wanting. Suddenly she wanted to spoil his serene self-possession.

She leaned closer and looked ardently into his eyes.

"I can show you a better way to relax," she murmured.

"Sorry, I can't." His words were blunt, not cold but absolutely uncompromising. No doubt he had known *exactly* what she meant.

"You can't?"

"Well, I won't, at any rate. I'm afraid I'm just too old-fashioned."

Iris straightened up and wished she had not started this exchange. But now that she had, she could not help probing. "You're not serious!"

"Very. It's nothing to do with you, just I've made a commitment."

Iris shook her head. "My God."

Paul laughed shortly. "No, not your God. Mine. He's very old-fashioned, like what He said about four thousand years ago."

"You don't mean the Ten Commandments?"

"Yeah. The Law shows us how God feels about things, and I want to please Him. Plus it's so much better. Every law God made was for our good, you know—not just because He wanted to throw His weight around."

Iris wasn't listening. An almost unbelievable idea had occurred to her. "Do you mean you never. . . . You're a—?" Her face was full of wonder as she stared into his kind brown eyes.

"That's right. I never." He was smiling at her, amused.

She shook her head in amazement.

"Not that I'm so holy; a lot of it is just enlightened self-interest. I care about *me* too much to let such an important ingredient of my life be soiled or damaged. And there's always AIDS, you know."

"You're unreal."

"Not really. Look. There are laws that govern how the universe operates. I don't mean laws like the Ten Commandments; I mean what you could call principles. Laws of physics, say—you jump out of a tenth-story window and you're going to smash. And mathematics. If you want to land a rocket on the moon, you'd better get the math right. There's no margin for error.

"The same thing is true of spiritual laws. You do something God has forbidden and bad things happen—not just occasionally but every time. Like the law of gravity. It always works and there's no way to repeal it. God knows what works for us, and out of His love He's told us how to live our lives to avoid violating spiritual principles."

Paul's eyes regarded her warmly. "If you want success in life, peace of mind, the ability to recognize truth when you hear it, protection from harm—all that and a whole lot more come from obeying the spiritual principles.

"And one of those principles concerns physical love. God says it's for marriage only. Not before marriage and not outside of marriage. I intend to line up with what He says. When the right woman comes along, I don't want to miss the moon because I've loused up the math."

Iris stared into his handsome face without speaking, her mind in a turmoil. The horror of rejection was hovering nearby, waiting to pounce. Just beyond that, a flood of regret for what she had so willingly thrown away, and envy at what he still possessed. And over all, the wonder that such a man existed in this day and age.

There seemed to be little for her to say. Was an apology in order?

"I'm sorry," she said quietly.

"Please don't feel bad. And please don't think I don't like you. I know I'm not your usual breed of cat, but maybe we can be friends anyhow." He smiled engagingly.

"I just feel incredibly old and—I don't know. Used, maybe. You're different from anybody I've ever met."

"I know." He stood up and offered her a hand up. They stood close without touching. "This way of looking at life isn't typical of our generation, but that doesn't mean it's wrong. Actually, just from a pragmatic standpoint, it's more necessary now than ever before."

He threw his apple core into a thicket of slash pines beyond the border of the hospice grounds and smiled at her. "I was planning to take some time off tomorrow. Maybe we could take a walk by the lake, if weather permits. How does that sound?"

She was feeling awkward but wanted to see him alone again. "Fine. I'd like that."

"I'll be in touch, then." He smiled again and walked off toward Dorm 4.

She watched him with a lump in her throat. How incredibly lucky the woman who helped this rare and princely man get the math right and find the moon! But it could never be the likes of Iris Stoddard. Iris was damaged goods. The lump in her throat was an ache of remorse; tears stung her eyes. Suddenly she sank onto the bench and began to sob.

She was mourning her lost innocence.

13

Wednesday evening,
September 15, 1999

Philip made a fist of his right hand and bit the knuckle hard, trying to control his reaction to a miracle. Fortunately the light in the truck was faint, and the others were too busy watching the highway and the weather to be aware of Philip. But his heart was racing and his breathing ragged. He had seen a man from Pine River, Carly Jenson, who had nodded and winked at him!

Philip was thrilled by the promise of rescue. He was also confused. Why Mr. Jenson? Why not Dad or Grandpa or one of their close friends? Although Philip knew more than his parents suspected about Carly Jenson's relationship with Aunt Iris, that didn't explain why he would be out hunting the Tyler children. And what was he doing in south Florida, hiding in the bushes? How could he have known they would be there then? Well, it had to be part of a rescue attempt; there could be no other reason for his presence at the highway plaza.

Philip ached to share his good news with Sara but was sure she would let the cat out of the bag. His sister was notorious for her inability to keep a secret. So he chewed his knuckle and hugged his secret to himself as they drove southward toward the fish camp.

Iris Stoddard would probably never have asked Cassandra Kovaks if there had been any other way to get a sedative; she shared a room with the lady doctor but almost nothing else. But Iris needed a full eight hours of sleep and saw no way without some chemical assistance.

When she reached the room in Dorm 4, Iris was happy to see that her roommate was preparing to go out. She was already dressed in a short skirt and bright cotton blouse, leaning over from the waist to brush her hair upside-down. She stood up, shook back the dark curls and smiled at Iris. "What's the latest weather?"

"More of the same, getting worse through the night," Iris answered. "The thing they're worrying about is the water level—how far will the lake rise, or the Everglades."

"I guess that depends on the amount of rainfall, doesn't it?" the doctor asked.

"That's apparently only one factor. There's also the direction of the wind, how low the barometric pressure gets, and something they call a tidal surge." Iris kicked her shoes off and sat down heavily on the edge of her bed. "Look, I don't want to put you on the spot, but is there any chance I can get a couple of sleeping pills?"

"I suppose so," Cassandra answered without enthusiasm. "Long as it doesn't get to be a habit."

Iris was annoyed at Cassandra's patronizing tone, but wasn't it typical of drug dealers to lord it over their customers and demonstrate their position of mastery? Nevertheless, she accepted the pills with thanks, then swallowed them with a sip of water from the bathroom.

"You going out?" she asked, reaching into the closet for her nightgown and robe.

"I'm watching a movie with Kilgore, one of the staff doctors. He's just somebody to pass time with."

This last remark struck Iris as somewhat defensive. "Well, I'm going to sleep. This has been a week from hell, or almost a week, and I need some R and R." Iris turned down the covers and crawled under the sheet. "Just turn off the light and shut the door when you go."

"Sleep well."

Carly Jenson had seen hundreds of television and movie scenes in which the hero stalking the bad guys was discovered only if it served the story line. Fictional heroes, on the other hand, seldom had such unfavorable conditions as those suffered by Carly in his alter ego as the Shark. For one thing, traffic was scanty and the road almost untraveled. Aside from their two sets of headlights, there was almost total darkness. The wind was increasing and it had begun to rain, lowering visibility. He tried to keep a safe distance behind the kidnapers' truck but could not risk losing sight of it.

It was a good thing the truck was heading south, the right direction for Carly's purposes. He was well aware of time passing; he could not miss his appointment in Miami with Renata's men.

Suddenly he saw that the truck had slowed, stopped, then turned west off the highway. He braked and eased slowly forward, peering through the rain for signs of a road. He found it, a narrow dirt road leading off to the right, marked by a sagging wire fence and an aging gate, now slightly ajar. A hand-painted sign was nailed to the gate:

Naylor's Fish Camp
Posted, No Trespassing
This Means You

Carly grinned. Mission accomplished. He checked the odometer so he could give the police the exact mileage from the intersection with Alligator Alley. They could pick up the kids, get the glory (if there was any), and no one could fault Carly for failing to do more.

He checked his watch and saw with satisfaction that he still had plenty of time to get a room and clean up, grab a bite to eat and meet his contacts on time.

He was obviously on a winning streak.

The sergeant knocked politely, though the door was open, and saw the major smile wearily, looking up from the desk in his bedroom.

"Come on in, Paul. Care for a drink?"

"No, thank you, sir. I just wanted to see if there's anything else you need me for tonight. If not, I might turn in early. Tomorrow could be demanding if the met boys are right about the hurricane."

"Sounds like it's already started. But they don't expect it to get really bad till tomorrow. So go ahead, get a good night's sleep if you can."

He rose, stretched and moved away from the desk. "This whole business"—he gestured impatiently toward the desk and its stacks of papers—"is an exercise in futility."

Paul sat down on the edge of the bed. "Sorry to hear that, sir."

"I go over and over it—the requests from the Belle Glade people, the team's recommendations, what's actually possible in terms of money and personnel, and, of course, the various regulations. We're going to leave these people almost exactly like we found them, and that's a shame."

"I imagine it's hard for them, trying to do anything purposeful in a climate of lawlessness."

"A lot of them have quit trying. The hospice people, law

enforcement, some of the ones involved in the educational system, maybe a few others—they still seem to be trying. Seem to care about what they do. Others have given up."

"Do you think it'll hold together?" Paul felt sure no other teams would follow theirs. Whether they failed or succeeded in solving the Zone's problems, this was probably Belle Glade's last chance for outside help.

"Maybe, for a while longer. But if we look at it like a battle, which in a way it is, then the forces tearing things apart are far more powerful than the forces trying to hold things together. It's hard to get people to care about the future, let alone sacrifice to make it sound and stable, when they know they won't be around to enjoy it."

"Well, don't let it get you down, Major. You can only do what you can do."

"I just hate to admit to myself that it isn't working. This is—or at least used to be—the most prosperous, powerful nation the world has ever known, and if *we* fail, our whole civilization is probably down the tubes."

"You see it as a sort of 'Today Belle Glade, tomorrow the world'? That our Finger Squad is a microcosm or prototype of all the efforts everywhere?"

"Oh, I don't know, Paul. It just gets me to sit here and see that the whole strength of the United States of America, all its resolve and endeavor and wealth, can't help." The major sat on edge of the desk. "I always thought we could do anything if we'd just quit bickering and feuding among ourselves. Now I see that isn't true, and it's something of a shock."

Paul watched his superior with something like tenderness. Here was another colleague whose bubble had burst, a close colleague facing the reality that the organization he served, in which he had trusted, to which he had given his life, was failing. Paul saw Ed Shearson, like the good doctor, over-whelmed by the realization that "it just isn't *working*"!

What it meant, Paul realized, was that the combined might of the U.S. government and her military arm, along with an advanced medical system, was impotent in the face of AIDS and its havoc on society. What, if anything, should he say to this man who had become almost a friend?

The major looked up with a wry smile. "I don't mean to dump all this on you, Paul. I'm just tired."

"Maybe you should get a good night's sleep, too."

"Well, you go on. Don't worry about me."

Paul could see the major was embarrassed, regretting what he perceived as a lapse of control. Not the time to attempt evangelism. But he left the room with a feeling of incompleteness.

Miami is one of the least-typical American cities on the continent. Situated on the southeastern coast of Florida, it rests on porous, sandy soil on top of reclaimed swampland. It is more than the pastel Miami many people know, with art deco architecture from the land boom of the '20s, and more than the drug- and crime-ridden Miami depicted on television.

It is large, tropical, beautiful, wealthy, corrupt and dangerous, with an enormous community of politically active Hispanic refugees and a growing influx of professional criminals, both foreign and domestic. It has Salvadoran death squads, the Mexican Mafia and superbly organized, tightly run Colombian "business" cartels with no-holds-barred, no-rules-apply methods of conducting their "business." Miami plays reluctant hostess to pitiful Haitian refugees who reflect the misery of a land formally deeded to Satan in return for his protection from American slave-traders. Miami harbors aggressively patriotic, relocated Cubanos, many of whom love America with a right-wing, white-hot fervor. And, finally,

Miami has an assortment of retired Americans (many of them Jewish and Italian), rich and otherwise.

The city of Miami has been called many things. Some say its name originated from two Indian words, *maiha*, meaning "very large," and *mi*, meaning "it is so." Others say the name derives from other Indian words meaning "sweet water." A folksy explanation of its name says that an Indian chief was walking along the beach when a wave broke over his feet. A brave called out, "Hey, Chief, you're getting your feet wet!" The chief answered, "My, am I?" And thus he named the magic city.

Today Miami is also called Little Havana: Over half its population is Cuban. Miami is only 140 miles from Havana, closer than it is to Florida's own capital, Tallahassee. Calle Ocho, southwest 8th Street, which is the Miami end of the Tamiami Trail (Highway 40), is not just reminiscent of but almost identical to Main Street, Havana. Many of Miami's Cubans remain first and foremost Cuban.

Most Cubans came to Miami to escape political oppression—breaking free of a dictatorship, later a Communist regime, bringing with them families, morals, strongly conservative politics, staccato Spanish and a boundless potential for success. They brought hope, ability and perseverance. In the thirty-odd years that Cubans have been a vital factor in Miami's economy, almost 700 of them have become millionaires. The city is full of not just the usual American "Anglo" yuppies, but the newer yuccas—young up-and-coming Cuban-Americans.

The president of Ecuador has called Miami "the capital of Latin America." As evidence, the Miami airport hosts more international flights than any airport in the world; and the port of Miami, if both cargo tonnage and passenger miles are tallied, is the most active in the U.S.

Thus is Miami the pot of gold at the end of the rainbow to South and Central American entrepreneurs, both legitimate and otherwise. It is the full trough at which the avaricious can feast, a glory of free enterprise and open markets. After all, if crime is merely capitalism run amok, it is logical that crime will flourish in the same soil that nourishes free enterprise.

Miami is a haven of political freedom for those oppressed by both left- and right-wing tyrants. It is a place to recover fortunes, recruit followers and plot overthrows. It is, more than New York, Los Angeles or Washington, D.C., the most international city in the United States.

Caucasian Americans, third- and fourth-generation Americans—what some think of as "regular" Americans—are a minority in Miami; more than sixty percent of Miami's population is foreign-born. And more South and Central Americans keep flocking to the city of sun and fun every day. Some come to survive. Others come to seek prosperity. Still others come to devour. As a result of this influx, there is a common, somewhat exasperated saying in south Florida: "Will the last Anglo to leave Miami please bring the flag with him?"

Miami is called both America's Gun Belt and her Military Supermarket. Foreign buyers can shop not only for guns and ammunition but for missile parts, bulletproof vests, helmets, listening devices and "interrogation apparatus." And they can hire mercenaries, of course—soldiers who will fight for any cause if the money is good.

Finally, most significant of all, Miami is named the Corner Drugstore.

For hundreds of years, the Caribbean Sea has been a lake of smugglers. It still is. Miami has a history of relating companionably to criminals. In the 1920s and '30s, Chicago mobster Al Capone bought an estate on Palm Island, followed by other criminals fleeing the icy winters of the North. In the wake of improving communications, they could run their felonious empires from the warmth and beauty of Miami.

In the 1950s, Meyer Lansky controlled the syndicate's Cuban operations from Miami. And by the 1970s, an estimated two-thirds of all American drug traffic was funneled through Miami. New *capos*, gangs and gangsters had found their niche in Miami.

The drug of choice has changed from the liquor of Capone's day to narcotics. The dealers are now Hispanic, not Sicilian. The dark suits, snap-brim hats and spats of Prohibition days have been replaced by loose jackets, aviator sunglasses and high-heeled cowboy boots—well-known as a handy repository for plastic baggies full of dope. Revolvers have matured into automatic weapons, and the soldiers and "button men" of the past are now called mules or smurfs. But the mating of Miami with powerful criminal organizations continues. Miami in the 1990s has again become the Queen of Crime.

Carly Jenson—whose goals were to find a functioning telephone, a drink, a shower and supper, in that order—entered this bold and bustling city as a lamb to the slaughter.

The plan had been for drinks in the office, then dinner; but somehow they had not progressed beyond the drinks. Will Stoddard, never much of a bourbon drinker, prided himself on being a genial fellow and believer in "when in Rome. . . ." So he had accepted Joe Jenson's expensive bourbon, then more of it, with aplomb.

The law office of Carl Joseph Jenson, Sr., was old-fashioned and (like its owner) expensive and pleasing to the eye. Joe Jenson sat in a large leather chair behind his impressive desk looking relaxed and smiling. He was working on his third drink. Will sat across the desk from his host, snug in an upholstered armchair. Unlike many armchairs, it was large enough to hold his bulk comfortably. The room was lit softly by lamps, and Will was surprised by the pleasant, intimate atmosphere.

The two men remained separated, of course, by the width and mass of Joe's expensive mahogany desk, and Will knew this was no accident. The desk symbolized something to the wily attorney. Protection? Control? A difference in caste?

"They're coming later to check my blood," Joe said idly. "I really hate that, needles and all."

"At least they come to you," Will said with some annoyance. "I guess rank still has its privilege."

HIV-testing was refined now, a quick and simple procedure. An essential part of the process was the establishment of the person's identity. Then the test results were fed into a nationwide computer network. For the next three months computer terminals everywhere in the country would report the results of this test. Most institutions had terminals that could check this "confirmation of negativity" either by a fingerprint or by blood obtained from a fingerstick. The so-called "window of error"—the interval between infection and positive testing that produced false negatives—was for the most part ignored. What could not be helped was best denied.

"Looks like south Florida's getting a bit of weather," Joe said. "I saw the news at six."

Will took a tiny sip from his glass. "I suppose that'll slow down the hunt for the kids. Can't do much of anything in that kind of blow. I tell you, I'm ready to hear some good news. This has stretched out long enough."

"I thought you were all secure now, having God on your shoulder and all that." Joe smiled like a sly child, but Will sensed something defenseless and sad behind the mocking words.

"Well, it sure helps. Doesn't mean I'm not still worried. Or maybe just weary of it—weary and ready to see the end of it."

"Tell me, Willy. How do you pray?" The attorney's smooth

voice was naked; for the first time in their lives, Will sensed total honesty from old Joe.

"Oh, mostly it's just talking. Saying how you feel, what you want. Saying thanks."

"Like you would with a person?" Joe had finished his drink and was busy pouring another, not looking at Will.

"Pretty much." Will hesitated, wondering what course the conversation should follow. Finally he asked, "Why?"

"Just wondered. I never did, you know. Pray, I mean. I just wondered how it worked." Joe was seating himself again, still not looking at his companion.

"Micah Boyd says it isn't so much how you do it, but what you believe and what the attitude of your heart is. The most important thing of all, of course, is who you pray *to*."

Will cringed inwardly. A week ago he would never have talked about heart attitudes! A few weeks ago, in fact, this whole conversation, like so much else in his life, would have been unthinkable.

"But praying does make a difference, Joe. It has for me. It changed things; it was my prayer that changed circumstances and we heard from that lady in Tampa who'd seen the kids. I believe that as sure as I believe my name's Will Stoddard. But more than that, prayer's changed *me*. Inside. I'm just different."

"And that's good?" Joe finally raised his eyes. Will was surprised at the pain he saw there.

"Oh, yes! Everything is—"

A knock on the front door of the office silenced Will. Joe walked through the reception area, then returned leading two medical people wearing white lab coats marked *U.S. Public Health Service*. One of them carried a tray for venipunctures.

"Vampires, Will," Joe laughed. "Here to suck out my life's blood."

Once again he was the charming, urbane attorney radiating confidence and success. The revelation of the inner man, the exposure of his weakness and need, had been swallowed up by the public persona. Joe rolled up his sleeve and joked with the medics as they pulled on plastic gloves and prepared to draw his blood.

Will finished his bourbon and made his farewells.

Burt was making a mess of things. He spilled milk on the stove, cut his finger on the soup can and dropped crackers on the floor.

"Just like everything else," he muttered. "One big mess. I'm not even worth shooting anymore."

The food, he hoped, would counter some of the effects of the alcohol. If alcohol is a depressant, as he well knew, he had been nursing from a bottle of liquid depression for days.

Tomato soup made with milk had been his mother's remedy for colds and flu—a real comfort food when filled with crushed saltines. Warm, mushy, simple carbohydrates. He picked up the pan, burned his thumb and released a few choice words. He propped a two-day-old copy of the English language edition of *The Miami Herald* against the napkin holder and arranged his food in front of it. Then he sat down, pulverized a double-handful of crackers into his bowl, and began to eat and read.

Nothing new in the paper. Tourism down even more this year; riots among the Haitians; vandalism on the increase. There were the usual howls from conservative politicians about the influx of HIV-positive illegal aliens who came ashore and were eligible immediately for free education, public housing, welfare benefits and health care. The price of plywood had increased 600 percent in Miami in the past two days as homeowners and shopkeepers prepared for Ariel. A psychic claimed he controlled the path of Ariel and offered to divert the hurricane away from the area—for a price.

"Mind if I join you? I never got any supper and I thought I'd have a snack." Paul Cordray stood in the doorway holding a plastic bag.

"Please, be my guest." Burt was flustered, embarrassed by his sloppy meal. "There's cheese and peanut butter, bagels in the fridge."

"Thanks. Fruit will do, maybe a glass of milk."

The sergeant still wore his uniform, shirtsleeves rolled up, collar unbuttoned. Burt thought he looked magnificent.

"The weather's getting interesting, isn't it?" the director asked.

"Yeah. A hurricane's a new experience for me."

Burt watched as Paul pulled a peach from his bag and washed it. *Such a lovely man*, he thought. *That's what the Irish would call him, lovely.* He averted his eyes as Paul turned to lean against the counter and took a bite from his peach.

Burt smiled and quoted, "And you ate a peach and I ate a pear. . . ."

" . . . From a dozen of each we had bought somewhere," Paul finished with a grin. "Good old Emily. She had a gift, didn't she?"

"I'm not sure we got that just right," Burt said.

"Maybe not." Paul smiled again. "I think I'll have a glass of milk."

As he turned to open the refrigerator, Burt watched him with wistful eyes. The long, lean curve of the soldier's back was splendid. "So, what do you think of the hospice?"

Paul shrugged. "I don't know. It's obvious you're fighting an uphill battle, one you'll never win, and I'm sure you're doing the best you can. It's pretty discouraging. But then, it would be, wouldn't it? Pain and illness and death."

"I know. I feel that depression every day."

"And there's nothing so lonely as constantly being in a crowd." Paul finished his milk and rinsed out his glass.

Now he'll be leaving, Burt realized, desperate to prolong the conversation. *I must keep him here.*

"But we do have ways to assuage that loneliness," Burt said. "We make human contact, sometimes briefly, but still a comfort. We sometimes manage to really console each other. You know?" He was quiet, watching the sergeant closely.

Eye contact, he pleaded silently. *Just look up at me, look into my eyes.*

Then he heard himself speaking again. "I'm not infected, you know. I still test negative." He waited, breathless, for an answer.

Paul looked up. His handsome face was terrible.

"No," he said with finality.

Burt thought Paul might expand on the rebuff. The young soldier appeared to be thinking, reaching a conclusion. Then he shook his head slightly.

"Thank you for the milk," he said formally and walked from the room.

Burt crumpled over his bowl of soup, now cold, and succumbed to tears of disappointment and rejection.

The wind howled. The rain rattled against the windowpanes.

"I wish I were dead!" he whispered.

The house was not the most expensive in Miami but unquestionably one of the most opulent. Owned by Julio Renata, it had been built to his specifications.

It was large, pastel, surrounded on three sides by cypress fencing and on the fourth by the waters of Biscayne Bay. It had the obligatory tropical gardens, pool, Jacuzzi and sauna; an elaborate security system merging electronic surveillance with trained dogs and armed men; and the obligatory blonde, complete with tan and bikini. She was perfect for her role. She never expressed an opinion, was decorative when guests came and walked among them with a tray of what appeared to be talcum powder.

The décor was what one woman visitor had described as "Drug Dealer Dreadful." The decorator had called it Moorish—a conglomeration of heavy, dark woods; red velvet everywhere; thick carpets dotting the parquet floors; oil paintings of ancient Spanish warriors; and authentic artifacts of appalling expense. It was tasteless and inappropriate for life in the semitropics.

Julio loved it.

His house made a statement. It told everyone who saw it that here lived one of Miami's most influential men. It was about as far as he could get from his origins—his revenge for having been born in a prostitute's tin shack in Cuba. This was the castle, the seat of power, of one of the city's most successful entrepreneurs, a Cuban expatriate who dealt in controlled substances and other interesting commodities.

Like his home, Julio Renata was almost a caricature, an exaggeration of the newly rich, newly Americanized, wildly successful drug lord. But there was nothing about him to inspire ridicule; he was both menacing and exceptionally attractive. Slender, handsome, of medium height, Renata exuded an aura of danger that almost everyone found fascinating. He was the focus of attention in most gatherings. Both men and women were drawn to him.

On this stormy night—raindrops drumming at the windows, the wind rattling the panes—Renata stood in his living room discussing business quietly with two of his men. He was dressed in gray silk slacks and a soft shirt of pale green. His dark, wavy hair was long and he wore jewelry: a two-carat diamond stud in one ear, two heavy gold chains around his neck and a thin platinum watch. His boots were handmade of elephant skin with high heels and pointed toes. His slender brown hands were manicured but strong and masculine. There was an aura of stillness and control about him, like a dynamo humming at idle.

He spoke grammatical but somewhat stilted English. "It is important that we know this man's relationships. Specifically, is he working alone? If we find he is a lone wolf, perhaps we can have his silver without giving up our money."

Both the men nodded a quick understanding.

"Leave now. Be there before he arrives and watch his behavior as he waits."

Again the two men nodded, then left the house for their rendezvous with Carly Jenson.

Paul closed the door to his room and sank into the chair, relieved to have some privacy.

What in blazes is going on? he wondered.

He thought through his encounters with Iris Stoddard and Burton Chancey and could find nowhere that he had stepped out of the bounds of proper behavior to invite such a reaction.

Paul was no fool. He knew other people considered him attractive physically. He was also convinced that a person's outward appearance has no enduring value. Character and accomplishment count for far more than physical attractiveness, or lack of it. Far from being flattered at this recent pattern, then, he was disturbed. He had treated both Iris and Mr. Chancey with casual friendship, and their reactions to him were out of line.

"How come I'm suddenly so irresistible?" he asked out loud. "Am I being set up?"

There was a polite knock on the door and a man's voice: "Phone call for Aaron Tyler."

Aaron left the room with a sense of relief. It tormented him to see his wife's face daily more ravaged, daily more desperate.

The spiral cord of the telephone that hung on the wall outside the kitchen in Dorm 4 was long enough to reach into the kitchen. Aaron took it and sat at the table. "This is Aaron Tyler."

"Captain Santiago here, Mr. Tyler." The rich and melodious voice of the Belle Glade policeman flowed like warm honey from the telephone.

Aaron's heart jumped. Because he had initiated every other contact, he felt sure the captain would not have called without news.

"I have had two different bits of information about your children today," Santiago continued, "the last just a few minutes ago."

"Tell me." Aaron bumped the table as he jumped to his feet. He could hardly breathe.

"First was a routine report from Tampa, a complaint from a woman there about Otto Krause. It seems this man and his companion, Mr. Hickman, had been guests in her home, and they robbed her before leaving. She was angry enough to report the theft, and she mentioned that two children were traveling with the men. Mr. Krause claimed they were his grandchildren, and she said she believed him. She says she became suspicious only after they left, but it seems clear they were your children. They were traveling under their own names and they match the descriptions. She gave the same description of the truck the men were driving, and said she heard the men discussing the idea of coming south, probably to Belle Glade."

Aaron was gripping the receiver. "When was this? Were the kids O.K.?"

"That report was misplaced. It took longer than it should for the information to reach me and I am sorry. It is out-of-date in any case. I received another telephone call just now, anonymous but credible. This man saw your children only a short time ago—the children, the men, the truck—and he gave us their location."

"Thank God," Aaron whispered. "Can I go with you to get them?"

"Well, this presents something of a dilemma, I'm afraid. We can't go get them."

"Why not, for heaven's sake?"

"We can't leave the jurisdiction, for one thing. Most of our people are infected, you see—under quarantine." The detective spoke soothingly. "And the hurricane is almost on us, and the truck is at a fishing camp in the Everglades—an unsafe place at any time, but doubly so during a hurricane. They are 'way south, in Dade County. I am forbidden to leave the Zone even for a cause such as this."

"I'll go," Aaron said. "Tell me where they are."

"Certainly. Is there anything else we can do for you? Do you have weapons and ammunition?"

"I'll be fine. Just tell me where they are."

Santiago relayed directions and Aaron wrote them down, his hand shaking almost beyond control. Then Santiago spoke again cautiously. "There was something odd about this anonymous caller. He had no clear explanation as to how he knew we were looking for this truck or the men or the children. And he referred to the children by name. He said specifically that he had seen both Philip and Sara, and I got the strong impression that he knew them. Personally, I mean. That he was acquainted with them."

Carly Jenson, Aaron thought. Who else could it be? They had all discussed Carly's absence and decided it was more likely that he had abdicated—cut and run, for some reason—than that he had been abducted. But Aaron did not begin to worry about Carly at this point.

"I can give you a Certificate of Safe Passage to get out of

the Zone if you come by the station. Save you some time at the barricade."

"Thanks. Get it ready; I'll be there soon."

Aaron's mind was moving fast. What he decided first was that he would not take Olivia along. He would ask Paul Cordray to be his second man.

It was almost impossible to see the building through the rain as Carly Jenson dashed from the hospice truck to the door of the bar. He had tried to keep his suit dry; he had looked sharp, maybe even dangerous, when he left the hotel. Now he was damp and disheveled. He felt a rising panic; he had to get hold of things, keep his plans from unraveling. He had to be in control.

He was in Little Havana, that section of Miami that is identical with its Cuban namesake in almost every way. Surely this was Renata's turf. But if Carly could maintain his Shark persona, that advantage would not matter.

He rubbed a palm over his dripping hair and shook water from his fingertips. Then he opened the door and stepped into the dark, smoky interior of Tia Maria's Cantina, the site of his appointed meeting with Julio Renata's men.

The bar was narrow and deep, with weak strips of fluorescent lights along the middle of the ceiling, augmented by dim lamps on small tables. A long mahogany bar ran along the right wall, with backless stools in front of it. Red and black vinyl tiles checkerboarded the floor; the walls were plaster, painted shiny brown. Dusty artificial palm trees stood wearily in corners and beside the cash register. A dozen or so patrons were quiet, keeping to themselves.

A large Hispanic man dressed in an aging tuxedo moved ponderously from behind the cash register and approached Carly with a question in Spanish.

Carly shrugged and answered in a loud voice. "I am meeting two men—dos hombres—here. Aquí I'll just wait. En la mesa, por favor."

The man crooked an amused eyebrow and led Carly to a table about halfway to the back of the building. He stood briefly, apparently awaiting an order. Carly flipped an impatient hand and the man moved back to the cash register.

"I hope these guys'll speak English," Carly muttered aloud. He was angry with foreigners who came to America, legally or illegally, and refused to learn the language.

He looked around with distaste. Hunched groups of swarthy men spoke in whispers, sneaking stealthy glances around. Must be some kind of political club, hashing and rehashing the delicate diplomacy of Cuba or some Central or South American country. Or of drugs. All these things were significant in Miami, he knew, far more than the politics of the U.S. or even the politics of AIDS.

Time stretched beyond Carly's comfort zone. He wished he had ordered a beer to pass the time. He was debating about ordering and checking his watch yet again when two men appeared and took seats at his table. They were so similar as to be indistinguishable; burly, dark, emotionless, somewhat menacing.

"Señor Jenson?" The man pronounced the *J* somewhere between a *W* and a *Wh*.

Carly nodded.

The man motioned with his hand. A waiter brought three drinks, set them on the table and withdrew. The man took a neat sip of his drink and turned an expressionless face to Carly. "So. You have something to sell?"

"Yes. Silver bars."

"You have them with you?"

"I have them where I can get them quickly." This dialogue was so typical of a television show that Carly found it hard to consider it real.

"You expect to be paid in dollars?"

"Certainly. What else?"

"Some people wish for drugs, firearms, whatever they might need."

"Well, I want money. American money."

And I'd prefer to deal with Americans, he thought in annoyance.

"My principal has checked the current price for silver and arranged the surcharge as agreed. For seventy pounds of silver, this is our offer." The man extracted a small notebook from his suit pocket and wrote a figure in it with a gold pen. He tore out the sheet and handed it to Carly.

Carly read the figure and almost whistled. Wow! That would make old Joe's eyes gleam.

Carly had no idea how much his own eyes were gleaming, and he missed a quick, knowing look that passed between the other two men.

"You accept our offer?" the speaker asked. He continued to take meticulous sips of his drink.

"Yes. Where can we make the exchange?"

Carly's mind was soaring. He could not wait to return to the privacy of his purloined vehicle and narrate to himself the latest episode in *The Adventures of the Shark.*

The men held a short conference in Spanish, too fast and quiet for Carly's minimal language skills. Then the spokesman said, "Two A.M. at Mr. Renata's house. I will draw you a map to find it."

Again he withdrew the little notebook and hunched in concentration as he wielded the small pen. The result was an impeccable map with street names, landmarks, distances and directions.

"No problem," Carly smiled. "I'll be there with bells on."

Four Latin eyes stared at him and he ducked his head with some embarrassment.

"Small joke," he muttered. "I'll be there with the silver."

They all rose, nodded without shaking hands and left the Cantina. No one, as far as Carly could tell, paid for the drinks.

"Blasted door's locked," Stoney grumbled. "Want me to break the lock?"

The kidnapers and children stood on the narrow front porch of a ramshackle one-story wooden building—apparently the fish camp lodge.

"We're getting soaked," Otto grunted. "Break her down."

Philip stepped back as Stoney slammed the sole of his right foot against the lock, splintering the door and shattering the closure. Then he and Sara followed the men into the dark but blessedly calm and dry room.

"Strike us a match, Stoney. Hurricane's coming—power's supposed to be down. See if you can find a kerosene lamp." Otto moved to open a closed door to the right. "Maybe it'll be in here."

The children followed the two men from the living room. As their eyes adjusted to the dim light, they found themselves in a large, old-fashioned kitchen with shuttered windows on two sides. Philip stood by a square wooden table in the center of the room while Stoney opened cabinet doors and groped inside in search of a lamp. Otto unlatched and opened the back door; when a rush of wet wind surged through he slammed it shut.

"Getting rough out there," he said anxiously. "Hope there's a portable radio we can get working." He laughed shortly. "We're too used to electricity, I reckon."

Stoney cried in triumph and extracted two lamps, filled to the brim, from beneath the kitchen sink. He set them on the table in front of Philip, lit them with his cigarette lighter, then adjusted the wicks.

The darkness and foul weather were driven back as the room was suffused with a warm, golden light. All four stood in the circle of the lamps' glow, responding to their civilized promise of protection from the elements. Philip stared into the flickering light and felt the retreat of the enemies.

"What they got in the way of food?" Otto asked finally. "We got 24 hours to wait, and that's assuming he can make it here through the storm. Might's well be comfortable."

"Lotta canned goods." Stoney nodded toward the cabinets. "Is it a gas stove?"

"Of course it's a gas stove. What are you, blind?"

Hot food, like the light, would be a comfort, thought Philip.

Stoney moved around, locating pans, dishes and a can-opener, while Sara helped him in an obscene parody of how she helped her mother in their Pine River kitchen.

"Do you think there are real beds here, Stoney?" she asked. "I'm sick of sleeping in the truck."

"I guess so," he answered, reading soup can labels painstakingly. "We got tomato, chicken noodle and bean with bacon. What should we fix, Otto?"

"Chicken noodle. Look, I'm going take a walk around outside, check things out. I won't be long." Otto pulled his collar up around his neck and hurried out the back door.

Philip felt a release, as always, when Otto was gone. He could think, even breathe, a little easier. He huddled close to the table and watched his sister helping Stoney cheerfully, chattering away.

This was the last night. Someone would arrive tomorrow, either rescuers or the unknown man-who-used-children. Philip vacillated between certainty of deliverance and a dark hopelessness that denied he had ever laid eyes on Carly Jenson. *That's just wishful thinking,* this despairing mood taunted. *Someone who looks like the lawyer, maybe, but certainly not him.*

Sara bustled around the table, scolding Stoney with a patient superiority. "Spoons go on the right. If we had forks, they'd be on the left."

Stoney nodded humbly.

Once again Philip began to pray silently. *Lord, don't let that man get here. Stop him somehow and bring my daddy here. Please, God. In the name of Jesus.*

He mumbled the Bible words again that he had remembered the first time he had prayed: "I will not leave you comfortless. I will come to you."

The sounds of the rising storm blended into Iris' dream. Despite the iron fist of the drug she had taken, the tumult and noise of Ariel's advance penetrated her senses. Her dream, like all of Florida's peninsula, was full of sound and fury.

She dreamed she was in a cavernous subterranean room, vaguely Scandinavian in construction and décor, rather like Gepetto's shop in the movie *Pinocchio*. A few people sat on long wooden benches. Then she realized it was a waiting room in an underground railway station. A man in front of her looked like the stationmaster. He was dressed in Alpine garb— *lederhosen*, thick walking shoes and a short jacket decorated with braid. He sat in an intricately carved wooden rocker smoking a long-handled pipe. He smiled broadly, which terrified her.

"I am the Doll-Maker," he said softly. "Have I met you before?"

She backed away, bumping into one of the benches. When she turned to apologize to the waiting people, she discovered with horror that their flesh was turning to wood. The ones in the back row had already become wooden dolls, and the ones in front were in various stages of petrification. They appeared to be either asleep or anesthetized.

All the while, the sounds of violent nature punctuated the horror around her. The wind howled and she heard the unmistakable rattle of palm fronds above her. Suddenly she looked up and saw a way out—a round hole in the ceiling with a straight wooden ladder leading up. She could see the stormy sky through the hole, while the old man in the rocking chair continued to call her.

"Come and let me meet you, Iris. You're such a pretty girl; you will make a beautiful doll! I'm the Doll-Maker, Iris."

Nothing in her life paralleled the sheer heart-pounding terror of this moment. She hurried toward the ladder and her chance for escape.

"Look what I have," the Doll-Maker called.

She turned to see that he was holding Sara Tyler asleep in his lap.

With a groan of agony, Iris turned from the ladder and forced herself to approach him. She saw with revulsion that Sara's eyes were stuck together and that there was webbing growing between her fingers. She was being metamorphosed into a doll before Iris' eyes.

The Doll-Maker smiled at her with monstrous malice.

Gathering all her courage, Iris rushed at him with a scream of defiance. Fighting back her terror, she snatched Sara free from his arms and raced toward the ladder.

It was almost impossible to climb. She had to support Sara's heavy, unyielding body while grasping the rungs above to pull them both up. She shifted Sara onto one shoulder, hoping that would free an arm, but this position threw her dangerously off-balance. But she made slow, agonizing progress up, hearing the rain and wind more clearly each moment.

Then she felt the Doll-Maker pulling on her skirt, dragging her and the hapless Sara down into his chamber of horrors. She felt herself toppling backward and sensed her hold on Sara loosening. Then she screamed in despair, "No-o-o!"

Her cry awakened her and she leaped out of bed. She was terrified, her heart pounding, her teeth chattering.

"I need to talk to Livvy," she whimpered.

Dressing hastily, she rushed toward her sister's room.

Aaron burst through Paul's door without knocking. Paul was in bed.

"Somebody called about the kids. Called the Belle Glade police. Probably Carly Jenson, but that doesn't matter. He saw the truck, saw the kids themselves, says they're at a fish camp in the Everglades. Will you go with me?"

Aaron did not need to say anything about the danger, the threatening weather, Paul's lack of obligation. Paul knew all that.

"Of course," he replied, jumping out of bed. "I need to tell Major Shearson and get my gear organized. Say fifteen minutes."

"I'll go tell Olivia. She won't like being left here, but that's O.K. When push comes to shove, she'll do what I tell her."

"A woman more valuable than rubies," Paul smiled. "You really are blessed."

Excitement bubbled up inside him, the adrenaline kicking in. Soon he would settle down—a calculating, precise, professional soldier.

"Come to my room when you're ready."

"Right."

Paul hesitated, then asked as Aaron was leaving, "You do want guns, don't you?"

"Damn right. Bring whatever you can get hold of." Aaron's face was resolute. "I meant it when I said I'll do whatever it takes—up to and including murder."

"Right."

Aaron shut the door sharply behind him.

And me? Paul wondered. *Am I willing to kill to set those children free?*

He opened the closet even as he pondered this question and took down a holster and box of extra ammunition from the shelf. He also took down the .45 caliber automatic resting there.

He was fully armed when he left to see Major Shearson.

14

Wednesday night, September 15, 1999, until 2 A.M. Thursday, September 16, 1999

The massive, whirling disc of Hurricane Ariel moved across the Florida peninsula.

She was not, as hurricanes go, a killer storm. The velocity of her sustained winds was only around ninety miles per hour. But she contained the power to destroy indigenous flora and fauna and flatten houses and other buildings. She could flood farmlands, tear down electrical lines, wipe out dams and levees, rip off roofs, overturn cars. The low pressure that accompanied Ariel could exacerbate infections, even hasten the onset of childbirth.

What Ariel devastated—both natural and manmade—would take years to restore.

Iris ran to the Tylers' room, thumped on the door and flung it open. The scene inside stopped her in her tracks, her dream for a moment forgotten.

Aaron was sitting on one of the beds loading a .38 revolver while Olivia stood watching him. Both seemed unaware of Iris' entrance. The room was packed with tension.

"Livvy, what's going on?" Iris demanded.

Olivia looked up, startled. "Oh, Iris, you're here. Good."

Aaron, concentrating on the weapon, glanced up briefly to flash a tight smile. Iris was shocked at the sight of his glittering eyes. He appeared in the grip of some fiercely controlled obsession.

"What's happened?" she repeated.

"The police called," Aaron answered tautly. "They know where the kids are and Paul and I are going to get them."

Olivia spoke, her voice filled with emotion. "I'm not allowed to go."

Her face was still ravaged by the agony of the past six days, but Iris read newer feelings, too: anger at being excluded from the rescue; a glistening bud of hope that the ordeal might soon be over; fear that this last do-or-die encounter might fail.

"We won't discuss that," Aaron said shortly.

He rose from the bed and pulled a knee-length yellow poncho over his head. He pulled on a rainhat and shoved the gun and additional ammunition through the slits in the poncho's sides, struggling awkwardly to find his pants pockets. The protection offered by the raingear was offset by the loss of mobility.

Paul Cordray walked through the still-open door. He wore Army fatigues, boots and a rainproof poncho. He carried a hat and a two-quart thermos in one hand. In the other hand he held a revolver. Like Aaron, he appeared to have a tight rein on his emotions.

Paul nodded to the women, then spoke to Aaron. "Ready when you are. I brought us some hot coffee, black and sweet."

"Let's go." Aaron kissed Olivia with passion, but his attention seemed to be focused elsewhere. Was he feeling inadequate on what might be the most significant night of his life?

Paul waved and the two men walked out.

The sisters looked at one another.

"Now we wait," Olivia said in a flat voice.

"I need to talk to you, Livvy," Iris responded. "I had a nightmare and I need to understand what it meant."

"Not tonight. Sorry, but my resources are totally depleted." Olivia grimaced. "It's taking everything I've got just to hold on. Why don't you talk to a counselor at the hospice? They're on call 24 hours a day."

Iris stiffened. The wounds from a lifetime of rejection, both real and perceived, attracted more wounding like a magnet.

"Well, I certainly don't want to impose," she said in a strained voice.

"Darn!" Olivia moved to the dresser to pick up the little stuffed bison. "I wish I'd thought to make Aaron take Buffalope. Sara would be so happy to see him again, to hug him and know he's safe." She clung to the toy fiercely and sank into the chair.

"Well, I might as well go," Iris said, ashamed at her selfishness but angry at Olivia's unconcern.

"O.K. I'm going to sit here and pray. You go find a counselor to help you." And Olivia began to rock gently in the chair, cuddling Buffalope.

Iris shut the door behind her.

Julio Renata held a small wooden figure in his hand. It was the crude but beautiful representation of a sleeping dog, painstakingly carved from some reddish, veined wood.

"I have collected artworks from this tribe since I arrived in Florida. A very ancient people. They had only the most rudimentary tools, but a very keen eye, as you can see." He turned the figure lovingly in the light while the small group of Atlanta bankers murmured with appreciation.

The two men who had been Renata's emissaries to Carly Jenson entered from the hall, damp but quietly triumphant.

"Will you excuse me?" Renata asked politely. The bankers nodded. He joined his men in the hallway.

"He is ripe for the plucking," said one subordinate. "Inexperienced as well as foolish."

"In what way?"

"Our offer overwhelmed him. He was practically dancing with delight. It never occurred to him that it was too good to be true."

"He did not even pretend to have backup," added the second man. "There will be no one to protest if we do away with him, help ourselves to his silver."

Both avarice and savagery rose within Renata. "And how was it left?"

"He's coming here at two, alone, with the silver."

"Ah, good. I want to see him myself. Here first, then the office."

"Yes, boss."

The two aides walked away and Renata smiled in anticipation. This was not a big deal. Seventy pounds of silver were insignificant in the light of his wealth. And the death of one more blessed-from-birth, born-with-a-silver-spoon Anglo was but small payment on the debt Renata felt life owed him.

But it was something. Every bit of money acquired pushed back a little more of the specter of poverty that had greeted him at birth and walked with him through his childhood. And it seemed to help each time he could confront one of those lucky ones who had been welcomed into life—loved and nourished and valued; each time he could challenge that assumption of privilege and watch their eyes change as their luck altered, moving from inevitably good to unspeakably bad. Doing away with this lawyer and appropriating his black market silver would even things up a bit more.

The only problem was that the feeling of relief was so temporary.

Renata returned to the living room. "I'm sorry, gentlemen. Let's get down to business, shall we?'

Joe Jenson could remember opening a second bottle. Was it possible this was number three? He poured a hefty drink, plopped in two fresh ice cubes and settled back in his chair.

The room swirled around him. He was really quite drunk. He peered at his watch and, after an effort to focus, saw to his shock that it was almost eleven o'clock. He had been sitting in this chair drinking steadily for nearly five hours.

Joe considered himself a moderate user of alcohol. Although he drank every day, he was almost never fully intoxicated. But he certainly was drunk now.

His mind roamed around the corners and borders of his life. What was happening, and where, to cause him to drink this way? Was it Carly's absence and all that implied? Or was that just a symptom of a deeper problem?

Some of Will Stoddard's words came back to him: "There comes a time—at least there did for me—when I realized my life wasn't working. No matter what I did or what I had, there was a hollow. Now that hollow is filled."

Will had said that days ago. That eminently self-satisfied, I've-got-it-all-together statement was the real reason Joe had wanted to talk to Will again. He also wanted to be absolutely sure he himself had no hollow. Willy was a country man, rustic and unlearned. He had friends but no real honor among the men of Pine River. Nor did the name Willoughby Stoddard mean anything in Tallahassee.

The name of Joe Jenson, on the other hand, was well-known and respected. No hollows in *his* life.

He poured another three fingers of bourbon. Then the phone rang. He concentrated on his articulation as he answered, to conceal his inebriation.

"Mr. Jenson, this is Dr. Sherman at the Public Health lab. I'm afraid I have some bad news for you."

"Can't you at least make it the good-news-bad-news thing?" Joe asked, attempting an amused tone. "Bad news alone isn't fair this time of night."

"Sorry, sir. We just ran the final blood tests for the day. It is my unhappy duty to inform you that you have tested positive for HIV." The doctor began chanting what sounded even to Joe, in his inebriated state, like an official refrain. "In compliance with Public Health regulations and policies, you will be taken into custody so that your medical needs can be met while the public's safety and welfare may be protected. A second, confirming test may be done. . . ."

Now there's a hollow, Joe thought calmly. *My life is over.*

" . . . And you have been assigned to the Belle Glade Quarantine Zone. You will be flown there in the morning. The airport van will pick you up at ten A.M. and take you to the airport in Gainesville. You are allowed two suitcases and one carry-on. Your family may ship other belongings at a later date. . . ."

Joe switched off the monologue. Everybody knew all this. What was new was the victim of the proclamation. It was a good thing he was drunk!

The flow of words continued but Joe, numb, heard only two things: "You are diseased. You will eventually die of an AIDS-related complication."

He wondered if he would see Carly. Was Carly still in Belle Glade or had he moved farther south? Would he be horrified by the news or would he relish being promoted to senior partner? Being the heir instead of the heir apparent?

Unhealthy blood. Defiled, dirty, dangerous blood. Would anyone truly mourn for old Joe Jenson?

✢   ✢   ✢

The blast of the wind and the surprisingly warm rain struck Iris forcefully as she left Dorm 4. She bent her head and stumbled along the concrete path leading to the hospice.

She was furious with Olivia, of course. After Iris had humbled herself to seek help, tacitly acknowledging for the first time that Olivia was more successful than she in handling life, it was insulting that Olivia had refused her. Sent her to a counselor!

Both Stoddard girls had been exposed for years to their father's scorn for professional counseling. "They've got as many problems as I do," he grumbled. "What makes them think *they* got all the answers?" His daughters had acquired a certain skepticism. Even Iris was enough Will's daughter to doubt that professional counselors were the best possible source of wisdom, help and comfort.

She also happened to know Livvy shared this doubt. She had heard her express it often enough. If objective reality no longer undergirded society, Olivia would say, if absolutes no longer glued civilization together, then human opinion reigned. Ethics replaced morality, "positive" and "negative" supplanted good and evil, and behavior was never wrong, merely "inappropriate."

Iris had little trouble looking beyond her own moral deficiencies and recognizing that psychologists and psychiatrists, by virtue of their degrees and titles and licenses to practice, had been elevated almost to godhood—society's answer to all human dilemmas. No matter that these gods regularly contradicted one another. No matter that a school counselor was considered better equipped to address kids' problems than the parents of the kids. In everything from sex therapy to suicide prevention—despite a degenerating world—the counselor reigned supreme.

Still, Iris was irked enough by her older sister's rejection, and driven by her horrifying, still-vivid nightmare, to pursue any course to get help, even one in which she had little confidence. Olivia had sent her to a counselor; to a counselor she would go.

She was soaked to the skin within seconds and buffeted by the fretful wind. The surrounding buildings provided no real shelter from the fury of the storm. It seemed to take forever but at last she reached the hospice. It took all her strength to open one of the heavy glass doors against the force of the wind. Then the door thumped behind her, bringing some relief from the noise.

The entire complex was operating on emergency generator power and the result, as in Dorm 4, was almost a brownout. Half the hall lights were off; the remaining lights had been dimmed. She hesitated while her eyes adjusted. This was a familiar part of the hospice; the dining room was located along the hallway to her right and the business offices to her left. The hallway directly ahead, which she had never followed, led to patient areas. The counselors' offices were in that direction.

She started down the hallway with some trepidation. The lack of light and the uncertainty of her destination summoned the horror and helplessness of her dream.

At least I'm not underground, she thought stoutly. *And this is all concrete block, not wood.* The memory of the dream brought Sara to mind, and Iris spared a thought from her own distress to hope fervently that Aaron and Paul would rescue the children.

The hall intersected another corridor. Iris looked in vain for a directory, then turned to the right. This new hall was identical to the first—dingy, dim and deserted. She saw not a living soul.

Suddenly a door opened and a crowd of young men stopped in sudden silence to stare at Iris.

She could tell by their garb that they were patients—green

cotton pajamas, bedroom slippers made of raffia and wrist-bands stamped with the usual patient information. They were also discernibly ill—thin to the point of emaciation, hollowed eyes, prominent cheekbones and a kind of physical guarded-ness, as though they were accustomed to pain.

"Look what just come in out of the rain," leered a small, dark man in front. An IV was running, the bag attached to a rolling standard that he grasped in one hand as if for support.

The rest of the group murmured approvingly. Iris straight-ened to her full height.

"I want to see a member of the counseling staff," she said in a calm, firm voice. "Where are their offices?"

"Maybe we can help you," a second man said suggestively. "Right, Larry?"

Larry nodded his agreement, looking around. "Let's see, there's five, six—eight of us. What we'll do, lady, we'll take turns. If one of us can't help you, maybe the next one can."

The men laughed humorlessly and began to discuss the order in which they would "help" Iris.

Iris was in a panic, feeling the same emotions she had felt in her dream—revulsion at the unspeakable things an enemy had in mind for her, the horror of a trap closing, a wild de-sire to escape, fear for her very life. Had she fled from a prophetic dream only to walk into the reality?

The eight men edged around her in a circle—each of them skeletal, unsteady, feeble, but in aggregate far stronger than Iris. Terror paralyzed her as Larry shuffled toward her.

Burt could hear the feral cacophony of the storm but tuned it out.

It has nothing to do with me, he thought. *I have things to de-cide and I don't need to think about the weather.*

What he did need to think about was the smothering blanket of depression that had settled over his mind like a fog, obscuring reason, destroying hope.

What have I done wrong? he wondered. *Why has nothing worked since I came here? What's the missing ingredient? Not motivation, not ability, not commitment, not effort.*

Had he walked away from a successful career in politics, throwing away all the compensations that kind of life might have brought, only to be buried alive here? He thought back to Dina's comment days before. Had he chosen this course because he really did want to die, and this was the quickest way? This life, this place where death reigned—was it his own personal suicide machine?

The suicide machine.

Burt sat at his desk in the director's office. The room was dim. He listened to the primal sounds of Ariel's increasing passion.

"Don't think of it as death," Dr. Jack had said. "Think of it as the dying process. Use it to enhance life."

Burt could not quite fathom how death enhanced life, but the thought held comfort for him all the same. Besides, enlightened people knew that the time and method of departing this life—of shuffling off the mortal coil—should be at the discretion of the individual. The right to choose for oneself is as inalienable a right as any that exists. And when things get too bad, when the pain builds up beyond your ability and willingness to bear it, you have the right to end it.

Burt had heard the arguments from the other side, of course—including the ravings of religious fanatics about some God whose rights superseded his own. He rejected that God and anyone who believed in Him.

Some of the more rational arguments did need to be addressed. "A permanent solution to a temporary problem," for example, might have a grain of truth. And what exactly was on the other side? What lies beyond, as Shakespeare wrote, does serve to give us pause. Could he be perfectly sure what he was going *to* was better than what he was running *from?*

Burt's mind skittered around the fables and legends about a fiery hell where eternal punishment was meted out to the unworthy. Stories to scare naughty children! He rejected such a concept out of hand.

I am weary of hunting and fain would lie down, he quoted to himself. *I am ready to rest from the battle and be at peace, finally.*

The decision, he realized, had been made.

And this bright, well-educated, experienced, capable, compassionate, accomplished man rose from his desk and walked with determination down the eerily lighted corridor toward the suicide room.

The size of the house overwhelmed him. Through the raging weather, Carly could dimly see the bulk of the three-story home, the extent of the manicured grounds and the almost tangible expense of Julio Renata's estate.

Two taciturn men in yellow rain gear stopped him at the gate, checked his identification and telephoned the house before finally opening the wrought-iron gates barring the driveway. A circular gravel drive led to the front of the house and a large parking area. He parked, grabbed the case full of silver and dashed through the rain to the porch. Standing under its inadequate roof, he rang the bell.

The door was opened almost immediately by a middle-aged Hispanic woman in a black dress and low-heeled shoes. Her dark hair was pulled into a firm bun at the nape of her neck, lending her an air of both submission and composure.

"Yes?" she inquired with genteel distaste.

"Name's Jenson," Carly said. "I'm expected."

"Come with me."

He put the case of silver on the floor next to the wall and followed her through various rooms and halls. The rooms were colossal in size and full to overflowing with furniture, pictures, statuary and mirrors.

At last they arrived at a brightly lit room full of rich furnishings, soft Latin music and more than a dozen well-dressed gentlemen. The woman gestured toward a bar along the far wall.

"Serve yourself a drink, if you'd like. I will tell Señor Renata that you are waiting." She moved away silently.

Carly walked across the room with as much poise and assurance as he could summon while his mind soothed him with stirring words: *The Shark moved with the grace of an adagio dancer toward the bar. He might as well enjoy the man's Scotch while he waited to enjoy the man's money.*

But somehow the Shark persona failed to calm Carly's increasing disquiet. He poured a hefty shot of liquor, added soda and ice, then turned to survey the room. Perhaps twenty men in all. Several stood in small groups talking quietly, but the majority (were they guests? employees?) were clustered around a large oval table at the far end of the room. Some were seated at the table; others watched over their shoulders.

Carly thought at first they were playing poker. The seated men all appeared to be shuffling cards. Then he realized they were counting money. Four men were counting stacks of currency, each man finishing his count and passing the stack along to the man on his right. The final man banded the bills into bundles about five inches thick, marked the bands with a grease pencil and packed them neatly into a large suitcase.

Then Carly noticed that several of the men watching held weapons, standing relaxed but alert. What a scene this would make in a television show! Millions of dollars, maybe, representing untold luxuries and pleasures and indulgences, all piled in nonchalant self-confidence on the table. Untouchable. The power of this one man, Julio Renata, provided security as great as a bank vault.

Carly considered the other half of the lifetime of the money—not only its potential for future happiness, but its past and the almost certain pain, degradation, even death that the acquisition of this money represented. Maybe the depth of the misery that had produced the fortune would exactly equal the life and pleasure it would bring. Could it be that the money itself, these green and gray slips of printed paper, was a repository of dormant or potential experiences? What was the opposite of kinetic energy? Was it potential energy?

His elbow was jostled and he turned to see one of the two men he had met at the cantina.

"Come with me, please."

Carly turned reluctantly from his contemplation of the paper fortune and followed his guide to meet the drug lord.

The men, all eight of them, were ringed around her. Although Iris was aware of their disease and horrified by the thought of infection, she was equally repulsed by their bodily filth. Vivid was the rank odor of unwashed bodies. She stood frozen, knowing instinctively that any show of fear would heighten her danger.

Suddenly a door opened behind her and she heard steps approaching. The faces of the young men looked beyond her and changed from glee to sullen resentment.

"What's going on here?" snapped the hospice director standing behind her, swaying slightly, arms folded across his chest. He was unsteady and his voice was somewhat slurred, but his authority transformed the situation.

"Just a little harmless fun," whined Larry, still leaning on his IV standard.

"You men get back to the ward," Chancey ordered. "It's past lights out and there's a hurricane to boot. I've got no time to waste with the likes of you causing trouble." His voice changed and became gentler, placating the now-hesitant men. "You know this woman isn't a patient. This kind of thing can cause you real trouble. Wise up."

Several of the men began to mutter.

"We already got real trouble," growled one. "What can *you* do to us?"

Murmurs of agreement.

But the momentum of attack was lost, and one by one they turned, grumbling, and moved back through the doorway.

Iris heaved a sigh of relief and leaned feebly against the wall.

"Thank goodness you came along," she said fervently. "I was scared."

"I'm sorry it happened," the director replied. "I don't know why, but one thing all Infecteds have in common is a hatred for the clean. The sicker they get, it seems, the more they want to contaminate what's still unpolluted. What they really wanted, whether they realized it or not, was to make you contaminated like them."

Iris shuddered. "Whatever it was, you saved my life."

"Glad I could be of assistance." He ducked his head awkwardly. "You had better return to your quarters. Watch the storm now."

Iris watched him walk away unsteadily before turning back down the hallway, her quest for a counselor abandoned. The reality of danger had diminished the illusion of danger she had felt in her dream. She considered what the director had said about the group's goal to infect her with HIV. If true, did they know that was their true objective? Did they know they wanted her contamination—and ultimate destruction—more than they wanted sex?

She stopped suddenly as a thought hit her. It arrived full-blown, a complete and perfectly drawn parallel, logical and devastating.

The same principle had been operating earlier that evening when she sat outside on the concrete bench with Paul Cordray and tried to seduce him. Even before they talked of his commitment to purity, something in her had known of his resolution and been determined to break it. Like these sick, terrifying patients, she herself had stalked and threatened Paul Cordray, determined to besmirch his offensive cleanness. That had been more important than the sex. Her goal had been to impose her will on his, to prove that her desirability was stronger than his integrity.

She had thus been saved twice this day—once from being the villain and once from being the victim—of an evil force that hated virtue and sought to destroy it. Iris felt an uncleanness every bit as foul as what she had seen in the sick men in the hallway.

Had her flirting and posturing with Paul been as offensive to him as the eight men had been to her? She had exposed him to the manifestation of disease and death that she knew now were resident in her own soul—the same filth and stench of corruption as the AIDS patients manifested in their flesh. Had Paul turned from her in revulsion as she had turned from her tormentors?

Iris reached the double glass doors that opened to the yard, and she pushed her way out into the raging storm. She was crying now, the weight of emotion beyond her capacity to bear—the residue of fear from the dream redoubled by the incident with the eight men; perceived rejection from Olivia; ongoing anxiety about the children; concern for Paul and Aaron in the Everglades in a hurricane; guilt that her life was so centered on herself. Even tonight with the children's lives in the balance, she had tried to take from Olivia rather than being willing to give. And over it all was hatred for the filth and contamination in her own soul.

How she longed with all her heart to be clean, to be uninfected by the disease so much worse than AIDS, the disease of—what? Was it impurity, or was it some greater evil? She knew she must add the disease of selfishness to the disease of immorality. And hatred, certainly. And anger. And jealousy.

Could it all be summed up as sin?

She sank to her knees on the sopping, spongy grass lawn and lifted her face to the tumultuous weather. Rain streamed over her head and down her face. She lifted her hands to the raging heavens and cried aloud, "Lord, save me! Save me from *me!*"

The dream had been a parable of reality—perhaps even a warning. There really *was* some subterranean realm where a wily enemy sought to kill her. First he would bind her, then blind her, then cast her into a stupor. Finally he would own her, then kill her at his pleasure.

The child Sara, representing all that was good and wholesome and decent, already showed signs of the enemy's campaign. But the way out was too steep and too hard to climb without help. No bootstrap operation could save those pitiful souls in the underground kingdom of the enemy. Without outside help, they were all damned.

"Who will deliver us from the realm of disease and death?" they cried.

Only one Being could truly answer, "I will."

Iris remained kneeling on the ground for a long time. The wind caught away her words as the rain washed away her tears.

Much later she rose—drained, empty, at peace—and walked slowly back to Dorm 4.

Joe Jenson drove home through the rain feeling little evidence of his long hours of drinking. Maybe the shock of his test results had sobered him. He pulled into the driveway of the house that had been his home all his life, and walked through the front door with disbelief nipping at his heels.

He climbed the stairs to his bedroom and turned on the light. Moving like an automaton, he collected his luggage and opened the two largest bags on the bed. He emptied his bureau drawers and transferred the neat stacks of socks and underwear to the suitcases. Next he opened the door to his well-stocked walk-in closet and began packing shirts and pants. He made no conscious choices, merely took what came to hand first, aware that under the restrictive baggage regulations he could take less than a tenth of his expensive, well-coordinated wardrobe.

His mind swerved back to the early morning almost a week ago when he watched his son pack for his trip south. His heart contracted in pain.

Ironic, he thought. *I've been caught in my own plot.*

What his Sunday school days—and probably Will Stoddard—would tell him was that he was reaping what he had sown. Joe had sent Carly into the danger of south Florida, and now an even higher Authority was sending Joe himself.

The thought reminded him of his talk with Will a few hours ago—a lifetime ago. Will had talked about a hollow in the life of a man that could be filled only by God. Should he make some sort of move toward God now? Certainly there was an enormous hollow. And just as certainly there was nothing else that could help.

But no, that would be cowardly and unfair. After a lifetime of denying God, how could he change his mind now that he was desperate?

No, he would go on as he had begun, with his hope and faith and future in his own hands. It was the only way he knew.

✢   ✢   ✢

Burt unlocked the suicide room and snapped on the over-head lights. It was tidy, chilly and surprisingly welcoming. He looked around, organizing his thoughts.

He switched on the light on the bedside table. The head of the bed was rolled up to a semi-sitting position and he lowered it a bit. Collecting a blanket from the cabinet, he spread it on the bed.

Next he moved to prepare the injection. Funny, he had not considered the difficulty of starting the IV. But it was a fairly skilled procedure and he was untrained in the technique. Nor had he ever taken IV drugs. There was a real chance he would make a shambles of the whole thing. But he got the tubing attached at last, keeping things as sterile as possible. He took care to expel all the air from the tubing to protect himself from infection or air embolism—the irony of this lost on him.

He chose potassium chloride and injected it into the bag of fluid. Then he wheeled the IV cart to the bedside and attached his bag of fluids to the standard. He sat down heavily on the side of the bed. Then he wrapped the tourniquet tightly around his left upper arm and watched as the veins engorged and rose prominently within the hollow of his left elbow. He took the needle and started to insert it. Then he realized he had prepared no tape to hold it in place. He removed the tourniquet and shook his arm a few times to restore circulation. Then, finding a roll of tape on the IV cart, he tried to tear the tape into strips as he had seen the doctors and nurses do. This was another skill he had not mastered. Finally he gave up and cut the tape with scissors. Then he reapplied the tourniquet.

He inserted the needle backwards, toward the upper arm, and had no real problem puncturing the skin. But it was difficult to penetrate the vein. It seemed determined to thwart his efforts, rolling away from the needle point as though in fear of the approach of the poison. It was an awkward, one-handed effort and Burt was sweating in frustration when he finally felt a delicate *pop* and saw blood flowing through the needle back up the tubing. He jerked one end of the tourniquet loose. Blood and fluid flowed into his arm. Next he applied the strips of tape carefully, securing the needle and tubing, and relaxed.

Done, finally. Now it was only a matter of waiting.

The IV dripped steadily as Burt lay back on the bed. He welcomed the song of the storm as a lullaby. All his adult life he had advocated the right to choose. This final act was merely the ultimate affirmation of his right.

His eyes fell on the framed quotation on the desk across the room: *There is a time to die.* From the Bible, of course. He had often wondered who in the world had brought such a thing to this of all places! But no one had ever removed it.

Everyone agreed on the fact that there was a time for death; the only conflict was who chose that time. He laughed softly. If there was a God, Burt had beaten Him. Certainly God was having no part in choosing *his* time to die. This thought was immensely satisfying.

Burton Chancey never knew that the God he discounted stood beside him now in grievous, agonizing accord. God had exhorted Burton Chancey, as He exhorts every human being, "I have set before you life and death, blessing and cursing: therefore choose life. . . ." But God agreed with Burt, on a very deep level, that he did indeed have the right to choose.

The Lord of Life watched with infinite sorrow as this beloved child moved to embrace death.

"Can you see?" Paul asked.

The rain swept in almost solid sheets across their path, reflecting the van's headlights as it fell.

"Well, actually, no. Occasionally I get a glimpse of the side of the road." Aaron grinned without taking his eyes from the road. "At least we don't have to worry about traffic. Nobody else is fool enough to be out in this."

"Any truth to the stories I heard about the water level rising? I mean really rising, really fast."

"Probably. I've never been in the 'Glades before. I know this kind of storm can drop an inch and a half, maybe two inches of water every hour. When it's falling on water—like a lake or this marsh—it's certainly not going to drain into the ground. All it can do is raise the level of the lake."

"That might frighten the kidnapers."

"But not the rescuers, right?" Aaron smiled again.

Paul nodded. "We're the fearless heroes, didn't you know?"

Looking into the side-view mirror, Paul saw huge wings of water flying back from the tires. The highway was probably two inches deep in water now, and Ariel had not yet arrived in full force.

"Tell me your plans," Paul said. It was easier to think of the rescue operation, over which they had some control, rather than the hurricane and its effects, over which they had no control.

"I don't know enough to make any plans," Aaron replied apologetically. "Find this fish camp and take the kids away from the bad guys—that's all the plans I have. That's probably hard for the military mind to handle. Sorry."

Paul laughed. "I don't know. Lots of times our plans get blown first crack out of the barrel, and we're left to improvise. That works, too." He paused briefly as a sudden gust of wind rocked the van wildly. "But I want to talk again about how far you're willing to go to accomplish point number two, taking the kids back. Would you sneak in and kill these guys in their sleep? Or do you feel obligated to give them a fair chance?"

"I don't know, Paul. That's something else I don't have much of a plan about."

"But you must have a principle. You said once you'd do anything to get your kids back. I wonder now if that was just hyperbole, and maybe there are some things you won't do."

"I wish I knew. I've heard that lots of soldiers trained for combat can't really fire a weapon at the enemy—that when it comes down to it, they can't actually look down the barrel of a gun at another human being and pull the trigger. I don't know how it'll be with me." Aaron wiped condensation from the inside of the windshield, marginally improving the view of slashing rainfall. "Is it true? That lots of men can't fire?"

"Yeah, I think it's true." Paul spoke thoughtfully. "I talked once to a fellow who was a total pacifist. A Christian who said the 'resist not evil' Scriptures were as much a commandment as anything else in the Book. I argued with the usual theory about how we don't resist attacks on us but we do defend others. And with the idea that we don't fight back against human beings but we do fight evil spirits.

"But he had a whole new slant on it, something I'd never considered. He said if we resist, it limits God on our behalf. This guy believed that anytime we add the arm of flesh—the natural efforts of man—to something we should be getting by faith, then that faith is diminished. He said that faith plus human effort does not produce something bigger and stronger and more effective than faith alone. And he applied it to everything we can want from God—protection, provision, healing, whatever—"

"So if you want healing," Aaron interrupted, "you have a better shot at it if you *don't* go to a doctor? Prayer alone is more powerful than prayer plus medicine?"

"So he said."

"Well, it has a kind of logic. What can we do to add power to an omnipotent God? And maybe that arm of flesh we add means we're double-minded, not operating in faith."

Paul shook his head. "I don't know."

"If it's true," persisted Aaron, "then the kids are safer if I don't pull out my gun. I can go that far. But if you follow this to its logical end, it means they'd be better off if I'd stayed in Pine River, and I don't believe that. Did your friend have an answer for that one?"

"I never asked him. Never thought it out."

As the howl of the storm rose, Aaron leaned forward and peered at the speedometer.

"About ten more miles, I figure. How about pouring me a cup of that coffee?"

15

Thursday, September 16, 1999, 2 A.M. through 7 A.M.

Paul poured another cup of coffee and secured the thermos under the front seat.

"You tired of driving?" he asked. "I don't suppose you can sleep."

Aaron laughed shortly. "Lord, no. If you want to catch a nap, fine. I can't."

"Me neither."

The van offered some protection from the storm, but the noise of the rain and wind seemed even louder within the tinny shell. It was warm and unpleasantly humid.

"Did you always want to be a soldier, even when you were a kid?" Aaron asked.

"Never considered anything else." Paul sipped his coffee thoughtfully. "My dad was in 'Nam, a real hero. His father was a career Army man, served in the big one, the second World War. His father was in WWI. Actually, there have been Cordrays in military service in every war America has ever been in. It's even how we got our name. Kind of an interesting story, true or not.

"Legend has it, in some battle 'way back in the Middle

Ages, the king was wounded and they dumped him into a wagon. Going to haul him off to get doctored up. He kept saying he couldn't leave, that the army would be discouraged and wouldn't fight well without him to inspire them. So an ancestor of mine took the king's cloak and his horse and took his place in the battle. He rode out into the thick of the fighting, and was evidently such an inspiring sight they won the battle. The king got well and knighted my great-great-great-whatever he was and gave him a new name: Cordray. It means 'the king's clothing.'"

"Do you believe that?"

"More or less. But I wanted to be in the military not just because of family tradition. I honestly think it's a good thing to be a soldier, a noble thing. It's sort of in disrepute in America right now, but historically soldiering has always been a profession of honor and duty and importance to society."

"Historically mandated, too," said Aaron. "Remember the Preamble to the Constitution? One part talks about 'provide for the common defense,' and that's you all."

"But since the rebellion of the '60s the military has lost respect," returned Paul. "There's a feeling there's something immoral about self-defense."

"I wonder why. People who hold that point of view aren't particularly concerned about any other kind of morality."

"I think what they can't stand is the order, the discipline and rules and the fact that we see a duty that's worth dying for."

"Yeah, that crowd really doesn't want rules and regulations. They prefer the concept of 'whatever's right for *me.*' So instead of the idea that some things are right and some things are wrong, everybody can reach his own conclusion. No absolutes, nothing higher than your own opinion."

"What about you, Aaron? I never heard what you do for a living."

"I'm a mechanic. I can fix cars, of course, but I can also fix any kind of machinery man ever made. Not very aristocratic as a career, but I really enjoy it." Aaron was silent for a moment. "And you know what? My boy Philip's just like me. He has very clever hands."

They fell silent as they drove on through the rain.

"Mr. Jenson, welcome to my home." Renata extended a hard brown hand and gripped Carly's firmly. "I see the weather did not deter you. Good."

Carly looked at the drug lord with interest. He was smooth and Latin and quite well-dressed, a strong presence. The man's self-assurance was monumental. But Carly was a good three inches taller than Julio Renata, and he tried to use his height to gain some psychological advantage over the drug lord.

It was useless. If Julio Renata measured five feet nine inches, then that must be the perfect height. It meant that Carly was too tall.

The two men Carly had met at the cantina stood close by, silent, secretive.

"You brought the silver?" Renata asked.

"It's in the hallway, by the front door."

Renata nodded briefly to one of his subordinates, who slipped out.

"Let's move into my office," Renata said. "It's more private."

The three men crossed the room, passing by the table of money with the counting men, guards and spectators. Renata nodded regally. They passed through a doorway into a gracious office with desks, filing cabinets, telephones and computer terminals. Renata took a seat behind the largest desk and motioned Carly into a facing chair.

The silent guard stood directly behind Carly's chair. For the first time, the young attorney felt a whisper of fear.

They waited without speaking for several minutes, until the assistant entered with Joe's metal case. He deposited it on the desk in front of Renata, flashing Carly a look of triumph.

"Seventy pounds, you said?" Renata asked.

"Just about. I'll throw in the case for free." Carly grinned. No one returned the smile.

"Actually, I was considering just taking the silver—getting it free." Renata lit a slim cigar, turning it carefully in the flame from his lighter. Finally he looked up. "Or 'for free,' as you put it."

Carly felt a stab of fear. He was at the mercy of these men.

"That's not funny," he protested. "If you want to talk price, fine. That's negotiable."

"The price is settled. I will pay nothing."

"Well, I guess that means our meeting is over." Carly laughed ruefully, groping for some way to relate to these men.

"Perhaps even more than that is over."

Renata looked full into Carly's eyes, apparently in search of something. When he spoke again, it was in a measured, sibilant whisper. "I see you're beginning to realize the danger you're in. A bit foolish, was it not, to walk into my domain with no protection? Were you so naïve as to trust me?"

Carly could hardly believe his ears. "I thought you'd keep your word as a businessman."

Renata smiled.

Carly knew he was in peril. But the cavalry still had time to charge in with trumpets blasting. Surely this man would not do what he was threatening. He was only toying with him.

Life had not taught Carly—because of his money, because of his family's position of influence, because no one had truly said no to him—that consequences follow actions.

"So what next?" Carly asked with as much aplomb as he could muster.

Renata was staring at him deeply, almost hungrily.

"Tell me about yourself," the drug dealer said. "Where were you born? What is your mother like? Does she cook for you?"

He's crazy, Carly thought. *Totally wigged out.*

But as long as he could stay alive, there was a good chance his circumstances would improve. So he answered, "Well, my mother is dead. . . ."

It was a miracle they saw the gate.

By now the rain was virtually a solid wall of water and the headlights could not penetrate more than a few feet. It was a miracle they had stayed on the highway at all. For the last hour they had traversed a flooded highway in winds gusting to nearly a hundred miles an hour. Aaron had fought to keep the van on the pavement, but occasionally a particularly violent gust would hit the vehicle and shove it sideways.

It was during one such swerving skid that the wild arc of the headlights passed over the gate and its sign, illuminating their goal:

Naylor's Fish Camp
Posted, No Trespassing
This Means You

"That's it!" Aaron shouted. "Paul, we found it!"

"Incredible," Paul laughed. "In the dark, in this weather, we look up and there's the sign."

Aaron had braked and they sat in silence in front of the sign.

"What now?" he asked more quietly.

"Maybe it's time to make some plans."

"We still don't have any information. What's the place like? How many men do they have? Are there any other roads in or out? I don't see how we *can* make plans." Aaron shook his head. "The most important undertaking of my life, and I'm just drifting. I want to take charge, make decisions and plans, but I'm too scared I'll do it wrong."

Paul nodded. "It's not just an exercise or an adventure; it's life or death."

Aaron switched off the headlights and the engine. They listened to the pounding rain and the gusting wind.

"Look," Aaron continued. "Don't be afraid to say what you think. I don't have an ego about this thing. You have a lot more experience and I want to hear your opinion."

After a few minutes Paul spoke again. "We could park the truck a little ways back, maybe turn it around in case we need to make a quick getaway, then walk back and take a look around. What the Brits call a reccy, a reconnoiter. We can tell something about the lay of the land even in the dark and rain. Then maybe we can make some decisions."

"Sounds good."

"O.K. For now let's get the van turned around, as out of sight as possible. Then let's slip through the fence and see what's what."

Aaron started the engine, made a three-point turn to face north, drove about fifty yards up the highway and pulled the van as far as possible off the road.

"What about the key?" he asked. "Leave it in?"

"Maybe under the seat or in the ashtray. Just in case I get back here before you."

Aaron stared at his companion, seeing little in the inky blackness. "You mean if I'm killed and you're coming back alone."

"Or with the kids." Paul paused a long time. "We might as well get going, Aaron. Just waiting'll kill you."

Aaron watched him get out, kneel and smear his hands in the sandy mud around his feet. "Probably won't last in this rain, but let's try and darken our faces."

Aaron complied, daubing his face with the cool mud. It was

too liquid to adhere well, and he was distressed to feel it flowing down his neck to dampen his shirt.

"Ready?" Paul asked.

"Let's pray first. Like they say, it can't hurt."

They stood with heads bowed in the whipping wind, under the pounding rain and spoke simply and briefly. Then they moved to the gate and opened it wide enough to slip through.

Will Stoddard awakened only two hours after falling asleep. Wide awake, he knew he would be unable to sleep again. Too much to think about, for one thing. And his drinking bout with Joe Jenson had left him dizzy and nauseous.

He left the bed quietly and walked downstairs to the kitchen in the dark. He switched on the overhead light, then peered into the refrigerator for inspiration. It seemed unwise to add beer to the uneasy reservoir of bourbon already on deposit in his unhappy stomach, so he took a Coke and poured it over ice. Maybe the sugar, caffeine and fizz would bring solace to his digestive system. He sat in his usual place at the table and sipped the cola cautiously.

Although Ariel was making landfall just north of Miami, almost three hundred miles from Pine River, the local weather was affected by her advance. The air was boisterous and gusty, and he heard the occasional patter of fretful rain. They had almost no danger in this part of north Florida, and only a wildly unlikely turn in her course would bring the storm into local territory; but she was still making her power felt.

Will listened to the weather and tried to imagine the more violent effects being felt in Belle Glade. Slashing winds, pounding rain, rising water, damage to both natural and manmade objects, danger and destruction brought about in a climate of fear, death and disease—this is what faced his daughters, grandchildren and newly esteemed son-in-law. All his cherished ones at risk in south Florida, while he sat untouched and comfortable in his own home, seeing just a smattering of foul weather.

There was a tidy parallel, he realized. The younger ones bore the brunt of both weather and emotional torment, facing the dangers and battling the enemies, while he was distanced and protected from both. It made him feel old and useless.

Then he recalled something Micah Boyd had said. Micah had been talking about his many long drives to Miami and how he spent the time.

"I pray all the way down and back," he said. "Pray for every member of my family, all my kin, from the oldest to the youngest. Nobody can interrupt you and nothing can distract you."

I don't even pray, Will thought. *Not much, anyhow. But better late than never. I can pray right now.*

Where should he start? Aaron was the oldest. Or maybe he should begin with Sara because she was youngest.

With some timidity he turned off the bright kitchen lights; this was a thing best done in privacy. He sat down again, folded his big hands awkwardly and bowed his head.

"Lord, I want to ask You to go to Sara right now and take care of her. Comfort her and keep her from being afraid. Help her remember she belongs to You and that You love her.

"Give Philip courage, Lord. Give him gumption and show him exactly what You want him to do. . . ."

As his whispered prayers continued, Will realized he had been wrong in his assessment. Maybe he was not experiencing the tropical hurricane as fully as his children were, but he had been wrong to think he was removed from the pain of losing Philip and Sara. That pain was so real and strong he was sobbing as he prayed.

Philip Tyler sat beside his sister on one of the aging rattan couches in the main sitting room of Naylor's Fish Camp. The room was large and cluttered, with a shadowy bar along one wall, gun racks with shotguns and rifles chained inside, and plenty of chairs and sofas for tired sportsmen to enjoy after a day's excursion.

Sara was sleeping fitfully, stretched out on the couch. Philip sat protectively close to her. Their captors sat on the far side of the room, lounging in two upholstered chairs angled toward one another across a small table. In the course of checking their provisions and making a desultory effort to render the building as weatherproof as possible, Otto had discovered a cache of gin, almost a full case. For the past two hours he and Stoney had been partaking freely.

Philip had seen them drunk before, and kidnapers drunk were more frightening than kidnapers sober, with even less judgment. And with the storm on them, it was scary to think there was no rational adult to handle things.

The only light came from one of the large, old-fashioned kerosene lanterns sitting on the table between the two men. The sound of the hurricane drowned out their murmured conversation.

Philip ached with fatigue but he was far too frightened to sleep. He was wondering for the hundredth time whether he had truly seen Mr. Jenson from back home, and what it might mean if he had, when Otto shouted out.

The sudden cry shocked him, and roused Sara to a state of confused wakefulness. The children huddled together as Otto howled in rage.

"Blast you, Stoney! I blistered my hand! Why'd you set the stupid bottle right next to the lamp? Look there, the whole back of my hand is burned."

"I'm sorry, Otto. Want me to get some medicine?"

"We ain't got no medicine, you jerk."

"Yeah, Otto, there's a first-aid kit in the kitchen." Stoney,

having accepted the blame without question, was eager, placating. "It's got all kinds of stuff in it."

Otto nodded, still angry but somewhat mollified. "Hey,
kid. Philip. Go get me the first-aid kit in the kitchen, and another bottle of gin while you're at it."

"The kit's on the bottom shelf by the stove," Stoney added
helpfully. "And the booze is on the counter."

Philip patted Sara's hand, then walked through the dim-
ness into the kitchen. It was lit by the other kerosene lamp;
he could see well enough to find what he was looking for. He
carried the first-aid kit, a white metal box a little larger than
his school lunchbox, to the table and opened it in the light.
There were bandages, tape, a tourniquet (probably for use in
case of snakebites), several syringes full of medicine, tubes
and jars of ointments and several bottles of pills. He lifted one
to see the label, and with a sudden thrill read *Empirin with
Codeine*.

By the strangest coincidence, he had recently heard his
mother discussing this very medicine with one of their neighbors. The neighbor had been given this drug for pain following a tooth extraction, and Mom was warning her about
the danger of driving after taking it. "It's pretty strong," she
had said. "Really makes you sleepy."

What if I put some pills into the liquor? Philip asked himself.

If the men were drugged into a stupor, maybe he and Sara
could run away. It also might help in case Mr. Jenson did come
to rescue them. Also, of course, time was running out. Otto
had talked openly of the man who was coming as soon as the
weather cleared. The children were to be sold to this man,
and Philip knew without doubt that this would spell disaster.
If an escape or rescue were to take place, it had to be soon.

He no longer considered whether or not he possessed the
courage, maturity and cunning to be effective. He was caught
in the web of circumstances. He *must* act.

With trembling hands, he struggled to open the child-proof cap on the bottle. He had to hurry. Otto would probably weigh his own basic laziness against his impatience, but sooner or later one of them would come to check on him.

The cap popped open and he poured out a heaping handful of fat white tablets. Next the top on the square bottle of gin—much harder to manage with one hand full of pills. Philip was shaking like an aspen, terrified of being caught in the act.

At last the deed was done. Holding the bottle cap in one hand, he poured the tablets into the bottle with the other. Two pills fell onto the table; he snatched them up and dropped them in after the others. His whole body was trembling and he was gasping for breath.

Just as he was reclosing the bottle, Otto's furious voice rose from the other room over the clamor of rain and wind. "Get in here, you little brat!"

"Coming," Philip called shakily.

He snapped the first-aid kit shut and took it, along with the drugged bottle of gin, back into the sitting room.

Iris was soaking wet, cold, shaking with fatigue, yet strangely at peace. She made her way through the dim halls of Dorm 4, up the stairs to the room that had been home for three days. The door was unlocked. Hearing gentle snoring from Cassandra Kovaks in the far bed, she moved quietly to strip off her sodden clothes and pull on a dry nightgown.

I need to go check on Olivia, she thought. *I can at least be company for her. It must be horrible sitting alone in the storm, not knowing what's going on.*

It was rare and satisfying to stand at a distance, undisturbed and safe, from her older sister's predicament. Usually Iris was the one in distress and Olivia the one looking on with tranquil sympathy.

Then a strange thing happened: Iris felt a genuine contact

with her sister's pain. Gone was her sense of lifelong rivalry and the nudges of resentment she always felt toward her more-favored sister. How Olivia must be hurting!

She pulled down the covers, and lay down on the cool dry sheets.

I'm just going to lie here a minute, she thought, *and warm up a bit. Then I'll go see Livvy.*

She was asleep in two minutes.

Aaron waited for Paul to reclose the gate. The road ahead of them was unpaved, basically two grooves worn over time by the tires of trucks going to and from the fish camp. They could follow it by skirting the strip of foot-high grass along the center and walking in one of the shallow, rain-filled furrows. Aaron hunched against the weather. In the darkness he could see the outline of saw-tooth palmettos and stunted oaks lining the road.

They had walked about ten minutes when they saw the faint glow of orange light flickering ahead of them through the storm.

Paul stopped and put his mouth close to Aaron's ear. "Firelight, probably a lamp. I think we're seeing it through a window."

"Can you tell how close?"

"Pretty close, I'd say. Be real careful from now on."

It seemed impossible to Aaron that anyone inside could spot them outside in the dark and rain, but he hunched over and walked more slowly. His pulse pounded and his mouth was dry with anxiety. This was the final scene, the showdown.

"Look, it's the lodge," Paul said softly. "Two different lights in two different rooms. I'll see if I can look into a window. You wait here."

"I'm coming, too."

"Stay close behind. We may need to confer," Paul said.

Aaron put a hand on the sergeant's shoulder and together they crept forward.

Otto grabbed the white metal box without a thank-you and rooted clumsily for burn ointment. Stoney left his chair to look on.

Philip placed the bottle of gin on the table, careful not to put it too close to the lamp, then saw with horror that the mound of white tablets lying on the bottom was revealed clearly by the lamplight. He grabbed the bottle back without thinking and began to jiggle it violently.

Both Otto and Stoney, trying to medicate and bandage Otto's hand, stared at Philip in bewilderment.

"What's got into you, boy?" Otto asked.

Philip gave a sickly grin and put the bottle back on the table.

Jesus, melt those pills, please, he prayed fervently. *Don't let them see what I did.* Then he moved closer to Otto, standing in a position to screen the bottle from the two men.

"How's your hand?" he asked.

"Hurts, what do you think? The whole back of my hand was right on the glass, and it's hot as a stove." He glared at Stoney.

"This'll help," Stoney soothed. He had smeared yellow ointment on the blistered skin and was wrapping Otto's hand in gauze bandaging. He added pompously, "This'll keep it from the air and prevent infection."

Philip looked at the none-too-clean hands that had applied the medication and wondered.

"Did you get the gin?" Otto demanded.

Philip nodded.

"Pour me some."

Philip picked up the bottle, relieved to see that the tablets had dissolved. He shook the bottle, poured two big drinks and sat down by his sister.

Joe Jenson was furious. There was no way any plane would fly into south Florida today, but the quarantine regulations allowed no loopholes for logic. He had been put into their computer as positive, and must therefore be taken forthwith to a place of quarantine. They would pick him up and transport him to the Gainesville airport, where he would have to sit until the weather cleared to the south. Neither rain nor storm nor ninety-mile-an-hour winds could stay those bureaucrats from the swift completion of their stupid regulations!

His packing completed, he sat in his darkened living room with a bottle of Seagrams VO. A raging fire of indignation served to mask his grief and anguish. There was the shock and pain of the lab results that clamored loudly for his attention. There was the humiliation and grief of losing his position as a man of honor in the community. There was the unbelievable outrage of having to leave his own home. But the most compelling subject, and the most powerful emotions, concerned Carly.

Joe drank steadily, waiting for the precious blurring of all these distresses, while a sequence of memories paraded before his mind's eye of his son, each more painful than the last.

Joe Jenson had lost his health to HIV. He was losing his career and his livelihood because of quarantine regulations. But the son he had lost and might never see again—the son who represented Joe's only hope for immortality—had been sent away. He had no one but himself to blame.

The future waited, grim and menacing and lonely.

He poured another drink.

✤   ✤   ✤

In America there are more than thirty legal definitions of death. The old equation of "no heartbeat and no respiration equals death" was nowhere near sophisticated enough for modern American medicine.

But by any possible definition, Burton Chancey was dead. The course of decay had begun; the body was cooling and all the processes of anabolism had ended. The blood had stopped flowing when the heart stopped and was pooling, in response to the pull of gravity, in the lower parts of the body. Rigor was setting in and the body was stiffening in its position of final repose. The IV, now stopped, had done its work.

The storm raged, the rain fell, the winds blew, but the being who had been named Burton Chancey was gone. Only the outer husk remained, still uninfected by HIV.

And that was a hollow victory.

The weather, a perfect screen for their actions, also served to hinder their progress. But finally they reached the main lodge of the fish camp.

The fish camp had been built on the shore of a broad expanse of water, the shoreline screened by mangroves. The camp itself consisted of the one large building and other, smaller structures that Aaron could barely make out in the darkness—a boathouse, some storage sheds and a short dock along which a number of rowboats and small skiffs were moored.

Two different rooms were indeed lighted, each room with several windows. The two men approached the closer of the two lighted areas and crouched beneath the windows. Paul gestured to indicate that he would look. Aaron nodded.

Standing with his back to the wall next to the window, Paul turned slowly and moved his head into position. He looked, then crouched and reported in a whisper to Aaron.

"It's a kitchen; nobody in there. Let's try the others."

Again they made their way, bracing against the powerful wind. What seemed to be the main sitting room ran along the south side of the building. Aaron crept forward behind Paul for about thirty feet. He could see dimly beyond the edge of the building to the wide sweep of water, now a heaving turbulence. Then they reached the second set of lighted windows and hunched beneath them.

Paul positioned himself again. Again the slow movement to look and a wait, longer than before. Then Paul dropped down to whisper in Aaron's ear: "Two guys sitting together drinking, and two kids across the room."

Aaron stood up without thinking and peered into the window. He scanned the dimly lit room, looking beyond the table and chairs that flanked it, where two men sat, to a sagging sofa on the far wall. There he saw his own children looking helpless and scared, and his heart constricted with pain. The vision blurred through the rain and his tears as Aaron groaned inwardly.

It's inexplicable, he thought, *this love that I have. I cannot believe how much I love them. This is a father's love. I love them because they're mine.*

Victory was within sight. The chances had never been so good for success. But Aaron was more frightened and less confident than ever before.

After a few moments he was aware of Paul pulling on his arm, trying to drag him down from the window. He was unwilling to budge. Finally Paul overwhelmed him, and the two men huddled together beneath the windows.

"Follow me," Paul whispered, and slunk quietly along the side of the building, away from the windows.

They crouched together again and Paul spoke softly. "Let's get away from the lodge."

"Are you crazy? I'm not leaving my kids! I'm going in to get them."

"Aaron, wait. Think. We don't know if they have others helping them, maybe asleep in a bedroom. We've got to check for other cars, plan how we'll get away."

"I can't leave them. What if they take them away from here?"

"They're not going anywhere tonight, Aaron," Paul said reassuringly. "By morning we'll be able to see better, and we'll be able to drive off after we get the kids."

"I know, it's all perfectly logical. But how can I just walk away and leave them? Even a few more hours is almost more than I can stand."

Paul pulled him up. "Come on, let's check around the back."

Paul led the way and Aaron found himself reluctantly following.

"You're making a mistake," Carly blustered. "I'm not some nobody you can kill without a second thought. I have friends and family. I have a position. . . ."

"Quite the contrary, Mr. Jenson; you are the one who is mistaken. You are precisely the kind of man I can kill with impunity. Even with delight, if I may say so."

Renata sat behind the desk, calm and reasonable and utterly malignant.

"Look, you got the silver. Just let me go."

Carly tried desperately to think of some way to bargain. Begging would only rouse Renata's contempt. "Why do you want to kill me? What good will my death do you?"

Renata frowned.

"It makes me feel good," he said finally. "I enjoy it. I get pleasure from killing and from the fact that you are dead and I am still alive."

Carly listened, appalled. Reasoning with this evil man would never work.

"But why?"

"I really don't know. It probably has its roots in my unfortunate childhood." Renata smiled slightly. "I have enjoyed killing almost as long as I can remember."

I can't believe this is happening, Carly thought wildly. He looked toward the two men now standing in silence by the door. No hope for help there. They viewed the scene with indifference.

I am going to die, he thought. *This is it.*

Then the truth of the situation invaded and changed him. The loss of hope brought a semblance of calm. Gone were the conflict and frenzied striving to change things. He was left only with regret for his wasted potential and unfulfilled dreams—and the ardent hope that his death would be painless.

"Well, go ahead and get it over with," he said finally.

Renata peered at him. "You are giving up?"

"I don't see any choice."

"Very well, then. I see no reason to prolong things." The drug lord slid open a desk drawer and withdrew a small silver pistol. It was so tiny it looked like a toy in Renata's hand. "Would you like time to prepare?"

Carly wanted to die with dignity and impress these men with his bravery and fortitude. Maybe he was no leading man, but he would not whimper. "No. I wouldn't know what to do."

"Very well." Renata rose and walked around the desk to stand behind Carly. The two aides approached and stood on either side of their prisoner.

Carly gripped the arms of the chair to control the shaking of his hands. Then he felt the pressure of the metal mouth of the gun against the back of his neck and stiffened involuntarily. The two aides closed in and gripped him by his shoulders and forearms, restraining him in the chair.

"Good-bye," Renata whispered.

Suddenly Carly plunged and jerked against the restraining

hands of the men. He shrieked in terror and fought to free himself. Then he heard the blast of the gun. A hot, bright redness filled his mind and he was swallowed up by its crimson swirl.

It was the last thing he knew.

Paul was soaked to the skin, bracing against the powerful wind, straining to see through the downpour. He led the way with Aaron close behind. He crept around the lodge building. No other rooms lighted and no evidence of other inhabitants. Only the white truck, and no other vehicles.

The plants along the southwestern edge of the property had been bulldozed and removed in order to form a shallow beach. The water pounding along this narrow shore was heaving and foamy, and they skirted it quickly. At the westernmost edge of the beach, the waves were battering the aging wooden underpinnings of the short dock, threatening its integrity.

Paul spoke directly into Aaron's ear: "Wait here. I want to check out the boat situation." He took off before Aaron could protest and returned in a few moments with a report. "There's a few boats, but no outboards in them. Maybe they're put away for security. But it doesn't matter. There's no way anybody's going to travel by water tonight. The boats are all sinking. I think we're safe in assuming there are just the two men. Now, do we make our move now or wait till it's light?"

"Now."

"There are some reasons for waiting."

"I can't wait, Paul."

"All right. Then we need to talk. Let's go back to the van."

They struggled, gasping for breath, back along the ruts that connected the fish camp site with Highway 27, exited through the sagging gate and made their way northward along the highway till they reached the van. Its familiarity, shelter from the rain and relative quiet were a relief.

"It's rubber-meets-the-road time, Aaron," said Paul. "Time to decide just what you will and won't do."

"Maybe we should wait till they're asleep. Then we can just walk in and take the kids." Aaron looked calm, but Paul noticed his hands and voice were shaking. "That's what they did to me in Pine River. Just walked in and took the kids."

"I'm not opposed to waiting."

"But the weather may get worse and we need to get back to Belle Glade before the water rises."

"We ought to discuss some particulars. How does this sound? First we put their car out of commission, slash a couple of tires. Next, go in through the back door into the kitchen, wait, listen to what's happening in the next room. Then we go through into the sitting area where they are." Paul tried to contain his excitement. "I'll keep my gun on the men; you get the kids and bring them back into the kitchen. Keep them calm and under control. Then we'll decide whether we want to tie up the kidnapers, depending on whether they're full of fight or whether they're more afraid of *us*. We'll see."

"I never thought of that. What could we tie them up with?"

"I have some nylon rope. It doesn't take much. But we don't want to immobilize them unless we have to. There's not much chance of anybody happening by to let them loose."

"Anything else?" Aaron sounded unsure of himself.

"It's your call. Now or later, guns or no guns, whatever you say. I'm with you." The sergeant spoke solemnly into the darkness.

The long silence was punctuated by the beat of rain and the gusting winds.

"You're used to obeying orders, aren't you?" Aaron asked abruptly. "Well, I'm getting an inkling of the load an officer carries."

"So how's it going to be?"

"It's going to be right now. It's going to be armed with

everything we can carry. And it's going to be whatever it takes. We're going to walk out with both kids—no matter what happens to the kidnapers."

Paul smiled grimly in the darkness. "Let's go, then."

Yes, Aaron was right; those who made the decisions did carry a heavy burden. But that did not remove accountability from the followers. No one but Paul himself would answer for the actions taken this night by Paul Cordray.

And was he still the same, or would he find he was no longer willing to shed blood?

"You may remove the trash now," Julio Renata told his men.

He stood in his office looking out through a broad window toward Biscayne Bay. Usually the expansive grounds of his estate were spotlighted after dark so he could enjoy his view day or night. Tonight, however, the view was dark and the visibility doubly blocked by the storm. No matter. At this moment he was so placid and satisfied he scarcely noticed.

"It's too wet to dig, boss," one of the men protested.

"How about dumping him in the bay?" the other asked.

Julio shook his head. "There is no way to predict where the body might turn up." He was eager to celebrate his victory in solitude. "Find a dumpster."

"Really, boss? He might get found real soon."

Renata's voice turned ice-cold. "Do as I say."

The two men wrapped Carly Jenson's lifeless body in a tarpaulin and carried it awkwardly between them out a side entrance into the stormy night.

16

Thursday morning,
September 16, 1999

Aaron and Paul reached the fish camp quickly, where Aaron disabled the white truck. Then they crept along the wall of the lodge to the back door. It was locked, but Paul took a strong, thick-bladed knife from his belt and broke the lock easily. He opened the door as narrowly as possible against the wind to reduce the noise of their entry, and they slipped inside.

There they stood a moment, allowing their eyes to adjust to the light flickering from the kerosene lamp on the table.

"Through there," Paul whispered, nodding toward the door that led into the sitting room where they had seen the children through the window. He extracted his .45 through the slit in the side of his poncho. "Remember, bring the kids in here. See if they're injured or anything. I'll cover the men."

"I'm ready." Aaron had drawn his own gun and was relieved to see that he held it steadily.

From that point for Aaron, time and perception changed. He felt as if he were walking in slow motion or dragging his feet through thick mud. The next few minutes would remain forever etched on his mind.

Ahead of him, Paul reached the door, paused, then burst into the lounge. He extended his arms and gripped his gun with both hands.

"Hands up!" he shouted.

The kidnapers, still sitting on armchairs, looked startled and groggy. Aaron maneuvered around Paul and turned toward the children. His heart contracted again with pain and joy.

Philip sat erect, one thin arm around his sister's shoulder. "Dad!" he shouted triumphantly. "I knew you'd come!"

Sara, roused from sleep, saw her father, blinked in disbelief, then burst into tears. With rescue and remedy at hand, she crumpled under the weight of her emotion.

As Aaron moved toward them, focused on the sight of his children alive and well and here with him, Paul shouted again. Aaron heard a crash from somewhere behind him.

Paul had theorized to Aaron that the kidnapers, surprised from sleep by two armed men, would probably divine the hopelessness of their situation and surrender quietly. But Otto Krause responded like a cornered rat. In danger, even in his grogginess, he lashed out with the only weapon at his disposal—the kerosene lamp. He grabbed it and hurled it at his attackers.

The lamp flew past Aaron and Paul, spraying hot kerosene as it passed, and struck the far wall. Fuel spilled onto the floor and burst into flames. Aaron ducked instinctively and turned in horror as fire ignited the curtains and spread across the floor. In the shouting and confusion, a large figure charged by him, shoving him to the floor. A spasm of pain shot from his knee.

"Get the kids!" he heard Paul cry out, and he struggled to regain his feet.

The man who had pushed him down had reached the children, hoisted Sara over one shoulder and was yanking Philip by the arm. A second, smaller man had joined him. Both children were screaming. Aaron lunged after them, but the pain in his knee brought him again to the floor. He raised himself to his good knee, ignoring the flames licking around his feet, and raised his gun. He peered through the smoke-filled room to take careful aim. He must not shoot the children.

As he squinted to sharpen his vision, he saw with clarity, for one miraculous instant, the four figures across the room. Sara was slung across the shoulder of the larger man and was pounding his back with her small fists, screaming in fear and rage. The smaller man was pulling Philip along.

Aaron had no doubt he could kill these men. Nonresistance had been part of neither his religion nor his code of honor. But he simply could not pull the trigger. He lowered the gun without firing and heard himself shrieking, more in desperation than in pain.

The two men opened a sliding glass door and made off once again with his children.

Moments later, when they reached the dock, Philip stopped trying to fight Stoney's viselike grip. He was haunted by the horrifying vision of his father on his knees amid the flames and the certainty that he was dead and all hope was lost. The stress of the past week and the despair of the last few minutes were finally too much for a ten-year-old boy.

The storm around them raged unabated. Philip wondered dully how Otto could even see to lead them along the flooded length of the dock.

"We can't take a boat, Otto," Stoney protested over the roar of the wind. "The weather's too bad."

"Weather ain't as bad as guns," Otto said shortly. He pointed to a lone fourteen-foot skiff, almost awash from the rainfall. "Everyone get in."

Stoney's desperate fear overrode his usual submissiveness.

"It'll sink with any more weight, Otto. It's nearly under water now."

"You can bail as soon as we get in. It's either that or those guys shooting us." Otto was losing control. "Didn't you hear— he called him 'Dad'! That's the kids' father, you idiot, and they're not giving up on account of a little fire. They'll keep coming. Now get in that boat."

Stoney stepped gingerly in, moaning in fright but pulling Philip in, too. Otto handed Sara to him.

The skiff teetered wildly. Now there was even less freeboard visible above the churning water.

"You, Philip," Otto commanded, "grab that bucket and start bailing."

Philip obeyed instantly. There was no fight left in him.

Otto clambered aboard, almost capsizing the small craft in the process, and settled himself on the central seat. He slipped a pair of long oars into the oarlocks and pulled away from the dock into the teeth of the storm.

Sara was huddled beneath the prow, sobbing.

"Did you see, Flip?" she asked in a ragged whisper, leaning close to be heard above the wind. "Daddy was on fire!"

"Maybe he'll get out," her brother answered, trying to sound hopeful. Flames licked in the windows of the lodge behind them. He longed to shout it out: Yes, their father would die; there was no longer any chance of rescue. But something inside him held back the death-filled words.

Instead he echoed Otto: "He'll never quit coming after us, Sara. He's our dad."

And somehow, in spite of everything, the faith-filled words intended to hearten his sister encouraged Philip's own soul. He began to bail faster.

"Just think how close he is!" he murmured to her. "They know we're alive and they know where we are. Keep praying, Sara! It's not over till the fat lady sings!"

Philip found a new spirit of expectation in his heart. Despite the danger and pandemonium surrounding them, hope had been born anew.

He bailed—and prayed.

Only minutes had passed since their escape from the lodge.

Iris slept like a baby for several hours, then awakened to the sounds of the storm, refreshed. Cassandra Kovaks' bed was empty and made up.

Iris jumped out of bed to dress. There was much to do. She wanted to find out if Olivia had heard anything about the children, but first she had an idea.

She pulled on jeans and a cotton shirt. Makeup? There wasn't time. She quickly applied lipstick and, for the first time in more than fifteen years, left the privacy of her room to face the world without cosmetics.

She dashed through the still-violent rain to the hospice and entered through the same glass door she had gone through last night during that strange, impassioned interlude. She felt a touch of shame at the memory, then realized that it was the first unpleasant emotion she had experienced since waking.

She stopped short. It was true! She had felt no hint of disquiet or the free-floating sadness that usually greeted her upon awakening. No resentment, no anger, no depression lying in wait to seize a resting place within her. In fact, since she woke up she had felt serene, with maybe even a hint of joyful anticipation.

I'm really different, she thought in amazement. *Something really happened.*

In a world in which expectation always exceeded actuality, in which nothing lived up to its promises, in which disappointment was the rule rather than the exception, this experience was even better than she had hoped. She wanted to sing or clap her hands; instead she hurried down the hall to the dining room.

The man behind the counter frowned and spoke defensively.

"Nothing hot but coffee," he said. "All we have is cereal and bagels and such. And fruit."

"That'll be perfect," she beamed.

The attendant looked at her suspiciously.

"It's the power," he explained. "We're still on emergency."

"Don't worry on my account," she smiled.

She collected a disposable tray and piled two plates with bagels and individually wrapped servings of cream cheese and jelly. She selected two bananas, two big Granny Smith apples and an assortment of wrapped packages containing silverware, napkins, sugar and cream. Then she poured two steaming mugs of coffee. A second tray served as a cover for the first.

"It's not all for me," she explained to the attendant, still watching her. "I'm taking some to my sister."

He actually laughed.

Was it possible the change in her was so great that it changed others, too?

Iris hurried back through the rain, trying not to spill the coffee, trotted upstairs to the Tylers' room and tilted the tray to knock awkwardly on the door.

"Open up, Livvy," she called. "Breakfast."

Aaron's mind was filled with dread. He was convinced the children were lost and that further pursuit was almost certainly futile.

It had taken him and Paul several minutes to get out of the lodge, and then to beat the flames out of Aaron's clothing. His right knee was throbbing and both legs were burned.

He hobbled painfully, desperately, through the stormy night after Paul. Action, even hopeless action, held at bay the despair of final and irreversible failure.

The fire threw an indistinct light through the windows and

patio doors of the lodge but could not penetrate far through the dense rain. Aaron staggered to keep up with his companion, who sprinted toward the boat dock.

It was apparent that the kidnapers would leave by boat. Even assuming they did not know their truck had been disabled, they would certainly realize that in order to reach it, they would pass the line of fire of the two armed rescuers. The only other escape route was the water.

The wind had whipped the lake into a frenzy. Choppy waves were breaking on the shoreline, battering the border of reeds and cattails growing in profusion along the verge. The tiny beach that had been cleared next to the dock was littered with branches, palm fronds and small trees that had fallen to the wind and been deposited here by the surf.

Paul stopped abruptly and held out an arm to restrain Aaron. "Watch out! The waves are hammering the dock. It could collapse any minute."

The waves were indeed battering the ancient wooden underpinnings, threatening its integrity. High water had almost swallowed the narrow beach.

"Then we'd better hurry," said Aaron.

He pushed past Paul and ran painfully onto the flooded dock. It shifted under him, unstable but still standing, while water sprayed him from the crashing waves. He strained to see the posts to which the boats were moored and tried to remember what they had seen on their earlier scouting trip. Three boats or four? More? He made his way with dwindling hope to the end of the short, unsteady dock.

There were no boats left. If the kidnapers had escaped this way, they had taken the last vessel. He stood at the end of the wooden quay, peered into the murky vista of darkness, rain, wind and boisterous waves, and realized it was over. He could go no farther. There was no more dock, no more boats, no more hope.

Turning in anguish to Paul, close behind him, he reached out a hand. "I'm afraid—"

The dock heaved once again, more violently this time. A loud *crack!* sounded from below. The short wooden expanse that was visible in the dim light was buckling and splitting apart.

Aaron had a sensation of falling. Then he was gasping, choking, frantic in the surging water. He struggled for a lungful of air.

"Paul!" he screamed.

But the wind snatched his voice away. This, too, was a futile effort.

The water was alive with menace—swirling, sucking, immensely powerful. It battered him as he grabbed at broken timber from the splintered dock. He was able to keep his head above water but was tiring rapidly. He had to reach shore while he could still swim. Which direction was right?

Disoriented, he looked around in panic, then saw a dusky orange glow behind him—the light from the fire inside the lodge. It was succumbing now to the torrents of water from Ariel's abundant bosom, but still gave enough light to guide him to safety. He shoved through a heaving mass of broken timbers and pulled for the shoreline, only a short dock's length away.

It seemed a long time before he reached his goal. The twenty minutes Aaron spent fighting Ariel in this dark and watery arena would seem to him for the rest of his life to have lasted for hours. He was sobbing with pain and hopelessness and exhaustion when finally he pulled himself over a strip of broken reeds onto a littered, storm-tossed but blessedly fixed and motionless strip of dirty sand.

He collapsed on his stomach, coughing and retching, praying and moaning. Only vaguely was he aware of Paul flopping down next to him. He rid his protesting stomach of its load of brackish water, relieved to be alive and heartbroken because he feared his children were not.

He picks the worst times to nurse a hangover, Dina Hawks thought, looking around the director's office in annoyance. *I'm going to have to make a formal complaint about him if this doesn't improve.*

She collected the midnight reports from Burt's desk and carried them to her own.

Maybe after the Finger Squad leaves he'll get back to normal— or what passes for normal with him. She laughed shortly to herself.

The office door opened and a uniformed security guard entered, full of suppressed excitement. "Got a problem, Ms. Hawks. Dr. Kilgore said I should bring you right away to the suicide room."

"What's the matter?" she asked. "I'm waiting for a report of any storm damage and I need the latest weather forecast. I don't have time this morning to indulge the young doctor."

"Please, ma'am. He said it was real urgent."

"Oh, all right."

She got up and walked briskly down the hall. It was a poor time to leave the office unattended and she was going to be incredibly busy today with her own work plus the director's. On the other hand, it might be quicker in the long run to get Dr. Kilgore's problem out of the way.

The door to the suicide room was closed. She opened it without knocking.

Shades were drawn over the windows and the lighting was dimmed with the restriction of electrical power. But she could see well enough to grasp the situation immediately.

The young doctor stood uneasily by the head of the bed. "I'm sorry, Ms. Hawks, but he's dead. Looks like he fixed his own cocktail and started his own IV. I thought you ought to know."

Dina approached the bed and stared soberly at the remains of her superior. Maybe Burt had found release at last. Maybe this had been a wise move in his battle against depression.

He looked awful. He was still husky and strong, still favored with thick hair and solid musculature, for the evidence of his physical health had not been obliterated with his death. But the expression on his face was one of dread. He looked haunted, shattered, undone. There was a tension, almost a withdrawal, in his frame. Whatever his suicide had accomplished and wherever he had gone, he had not departed with peace and joy.

She spoke calmly to Dr. Kilgore. "Go ahead and sign the death certificate and issue a burial permit. Wait—he wanted to be cremated, I believe. Look into his living will and see what disposition of remains he favored. And get it done ASAP."

"What about a memorial service or something? He was a pretty important guy around here."

"I don't see how that would serve any good purpose," she said. "There's enough homage paid to death around here. Just dispose of the body and get on with your work."

The doctor seemed to recoil, and the security guard kept his face tactfully averted, but Dina turned and left the room. Why worry what people thought? There was work to be done. With the death of Burton Chancey she was once again in charge—the CEO, the main honcho of an important establishment. Even in a death house there was some pleasure to be gleaned from being in the seat of power.

She smiled and quoted to herself: "Power is delightful, and absolute power is absolutely delightful."

She had become like the Pope or a justice of the United States Supreme Court: Only death could remove her from office.

❖   ❖   ❖

The sun struggled with a sky full of boisterous, unruly clouds, and an occasional yellow beam penetrated the Stoddard kitchen to herald the beginning of another day. Will lifted a weary head from its resting place on the table and began again to assault the throne of God.

"Father, You stay right with them. Guide every single thing they do, every word they say, even what they think. Don't let them give up! Send your angels to guide their path. . . ."

It had been hours but he was unable to quit praying and go to bed. Exhausted in mind and body, he kept at it—with the exception of those moments when his aging body failed him and he dozed off into a shallow, troubled sleep.

"Your Word says that You are the mighty God, and right now I pray that You will win this battle against the enemy. I don't know what's happening down there, but I know there's a struggle going on. Don't let the bad guys win, Lord!"

He gripped his head between his work-roughened hands and massaged his temples. Such a headache!—the result of alcohol, emotional effort and lack of sleep.

But Will would not quit. He closed his bloodshot eyes and continued to petition heaven for his family.

Most experts identify four separate hazards from a hurricane: high winds, heavy rains, tornadoes and storm surge—a great dome of water, often fifty to one hundred miles wide, that sweeps across the coastline near the location of the landfall of the hurricane's eye. It is the most dangerous of the hazards, causing nine out of ten hurricane fatalities.

Those who have witnessed this terrifying wall of water approaching at thunderous speeds from the sea can testify to the panic it generates. Like a horizontal Niagara, this overpowering, uncontrollable liquid mountain covers cars, roads, homes, trees and puny human beings.

The storm surge (or tidal surge) originates in the ocean and is therefore confined to coastal areas. But a counterpart can arise inland and wreak almost as much destruction. It has no fancy name; it is called simply "rising water."

Ariel had deposited more than seven inches of rain on the lower third of Florida's peninsula when the kidnapers rowed away from Naylor's Fish Camp, still holding the Tyler children prisoner. The uncommonly low barometric pressure had raised the water table another several inches. And once they left the shelter of the shoreline, the little group found that savage winds were whipping up waves of four to six feet. It was obvious the skiff was in trouble.

Through the slashing rain, they could see a fitful orange glow in the direction of the fish camp. Ahead they could see the turbulent, flooded surface of the Everglades. It was a forsaken and desolate scene.

The kidnapers were losing control. As the rough water tossed the boat, Otto and Stoney began to fall apart. Years of predictable actions and reactions between them were being reversed.

"You bloody fool, Otto," Stoney shrilled as a particularly forceful wave threatened to capsize their craft. "You head *into* the wind, not meet it broadside."

"Since when did you get to be an expert?" Otto gasped, fighting manfully with the inadequate oars, despite his burn, to maneuver the boat. He had ripped off the soggy bandage and thrown it overboard.

"Go back to shore while we still can. We're gonna drown if we stay out here."

"Look, Stoney, I'm running things. You want to go back? Then swim."

Neither man was aware of the drug Philip had added to their gin, and neither had any knowledge of the effects produced by mixing the two. They were aware only of fear and fatigue reacting with the gin, along with confusion, anger, insecurity and great physical discomfort.

"I can't see the camp anymore," Stoney wailed. "The current is taking us *north*, for heaven's sake!"

"How do you figure that?" Otto said contemptuously.

Stoney was too unnerved to answer.

Philip had stopped bailing; it was pointless to try to reduce the amount of water in the bottom of the boat when more sloshed over the gunwales with every wave. Neither man noticed his dereliction of duty. He scooted forward toward Sara and squatted next to her, protected somewhat by the prow.

"It's going to be O.K.," he said encouragingly. "Don't be afraid."

It felt funny to talk this way when he was himself shaking with fear, but his sister looked at him trustingly and tried to smile. Philip took one of her small hands and held it tightly. "Whatever happens, we need to stay together. If we turn over, remember Grandpa always said stay with the boat."

"You know there's snakes in this water, you jerk," put in Stoney. "And 'gators, too, and I don't know what all."

Suddenly Otto let out a howl. Following his trembling finger, Philip looked aft, in the direction of the camp. What he saw terrified him.

A swelling wall of dark, tumultuous water was rushing toward them. This solid wave had no topcurl like a breaker; it was an eight-foot-high rampart of water moving toward them at an incredible velocity.

"Jesus, help us!" Philip cried aloud. "Hold onto the boat, Sara!"

She grabbed the gunwale as a last bulwark of safety.

Stoney stood up behind Otto and began to pound him on the back with furious fists. "You fool! You blasted know-it-all! You got us all killed!"

Otto ignored him. He had dropped the oars and was staring, frozen in horror, at the racing wall of death.

The wave hit the stern of the skiff with a thunderous *whack* and tilted it up on its prow. It was propelled forward in an upright position, perpendicular to the lake, so that it danced on the point of its prow like an overweight ballerina. Cushions, bait cans, oars and oarlocks toppled into the water.

With one arm, Philip clutched his sister around the waist so tightly that she cried out in pain, but he did not loosen his hold. With his other hand he gripped the gunwale with all his strength.

Otto and Stoney were pitched forward from the boat, falling together into the roaring torrent. Philip saw them pulled beneath the surface of the water. The boat swept by.

Moments later Philip realized the boat had righted itself. Now it bounced atop the tempestuous water, keel down, none the worse for its battering by the wave. In fact, the main result from the boat's gyrations with the wave had been to empty it of most of its cargo. Not only were he and Sara alone in the boat, but the floor was now clear of water. The wave had done the bailing for him! Philip scanned the roiling water behind them. Otto and Stoney were nowhere to be seen.

Philip laughed. "They're gone, Sara. We're free! All we have to do is wait till we hit land and call home."

"Did they drown?" Sara asked hesitantly.

"Sure they did!"

"Is it all right to be glad?"

"I don't know if it is or not, but *I'm* glad. We're free, Sara! We're going home."

"Well, isn't it about time!"

Philip grinned at her with total joy and leaned over to hug her.

"You know, Sara, you really are a little jerk," he said.

When Olivia opened the door, Iris hurried in, full of vitality and good cheer. She shopped short as she saw her sister's face. Olivia was stretched to the breaking point and it showed.

Iris put the breakfast tray down on the bed and grabbed her sister's hands. "Oh, Livvy, have you heard bad news?"

"I haven't heard *anything!* It's been hours, Iris. All night. They could have been there and back twice by now and I have no idea what's happened."

Her sister broke free and began to pace the cramped, narrow tract of a caged animal. Her cotton shirt from the day before was badly wrinkled. Her hair straggled loose from an untidy bun and she looked almost slovenly, certainly not the cool, serene beauty so admired in Pine River.

"I try to hold onto God, but I am about used up." She smiled weakly. "I'm glad you're here."

"Oh, me, too! I want to help. See, I brought you some food. Why don't you eat some breakfast?"

"Don't be silly. I couldn't possibly eat."

Could she divert her sister, Iris wondered, giving her a break from the mental pressure?

"I have some news."

Olivia looked indifferent. "What news?"

"I got saved, Livvy." Joy once again flooded Iris. "It's all so different now. Do you want to hear about it?"

Olivia stopped short. "Really, you did? Iris, that's wonderful!"

"It was all because you told me to go find a counselor. I went looking for a counselor and ended up finding God."

Olivia smiled a smile of genuine pleasure, oblivious to the

hurt her remark the night before had caused. "Maybe you don't know, but one of His names is Counselor. From Isaiah 9. Actually, it's Wonderful Counselor."

"And I say amen and hallelujah to that!"

The remark was so totally unlike Iris that both sisters laughed. Suddenly they were hugging and crying. Iris found that she was overflowing with love for her sister.

Olivia broke free first and wiped her eyes with the back of her hands. "Well, you certainly are full of surprises! And you know what? I think I might just be able to handle something to drink. Is there any juice?"

"Oh, come on, Livvy, forget about being healthy. Have some coffee."

"Did you bring decaf?"

"No, but don't let that stop you. I think, all things considered, you could use the caffeine."

"Well, maybe I could at that. And maybe I'll even put some sugar in it!"

They shrieked with laughter.

Considering all the emotional assaults they had weathered so far, unbridled laughter seemed appropriate.

They realized the new day was dawning when the black around them turned to dark gray, but rain was still all they could see. Paul sat with Aaron in the van tending to his burns with the first-aid kit they had brought from Pine River. They had the engine idling and the heat blasting for warmth.

Paul closed the kit and they sat without talking for several minutes. The next move might be up to him. Aaron's sense of failure had robbed him of initiative.

"I just couldn't shoot," Paul said at last. "I'm so sorry."

"I couldn't either. And I can't even tell you why. How in God's name can I tell Olivia?"

"What should we do now?" Paul asked.

"Whatever you want."

"We're going to have to decide our next step."

"I know. I just can't face it. Why did I just let them walk away? I could have shot them!"

"I know. Same goes for me. I can't pretend I understand it. But we have to deal with what's happening *now*, what's real *now*. Where do we go from here?"

Aaron looked intently at Paul. His eyes were tormented. "I just let them get away. How do I know I'd do any better if we found them again? Besides, how are they going to make it out there in this storm?" His voice broke.

"So what are you saying? Head back to Belle Glade?"

"How can I explain to my wife why I failed to protect our kids? I don't even understand it myself. How can I expect her to understand? I don't see how she can ever forgive me. I can't forgive myself."

Paul leaned closer to Aaron. "Look, don't get into a lot of introspection and guilt and trying to figure out the reasons right now. That can come later. Now's the time for action. If we're ever going to get them, now is the time."

Aaron considered briefly, then shrugged. "I don't know. I don't trust myself anymore. You decide."

"O.K. I say find a phone, wait till the lines are up, if we have to, try to get through to the Coast Guard, get the current and wind direction, see where they might put in."

"Whatever you think is best."

Paul watched him with pity, then pushed the emotion aside. Aaron's pain must not be allowed to interfere with the mission. Act now, sympathize later.

"Let's go," he said shortly.

With only cold food available, Dina Hawks was able to move quickly through the breakfast line. Her mind was already at work on strategies to overcome the enormous problems pinpointed by the Finger Squad—strategies that were likely to make her own career more rewarding.

Then she found herself behind Cassandra Kovaks. It seemed natural to find a seat with her at one of the few tables that appeared to be clean.

"I heard about Mr. Chancey," the young doctor said, slicing a banana onto cold cereal. "My condolences."

"It was his decision, and I suppose we have to honor his choices." Dina smiled ruefully. "Even if it leaves us in a bind."

"Does it? I mean, I'd have thought he was pretty much like, you know, a figurehead, and you did the real work."

"Well, it was heading that way. He had a lot of personal problems."

"This is a good place for them. Or I guess I mean a bad place for them. You know, everybody sick and dying."

Dina noticed that her companion chewed her cereal with gusto, full of life and appetite.

"He felt he was a failure," she confided. "His life was built around helping people—first his political life, later his commitment to AIDS patients. This institution became his reason for living. But the way things were heading, it just wasn't a good enough reason anymore."

"How sad!"

"Burton Chancey had no family," she continued, "no partner, no close friends, and he was facing the fact that he wasn't really helping anymore."

"You're like that—all alone." Cassandra looked at the older woman with frank interest. "I mean, does it bother you?"

Dina considered mentioning her children and grandchildren, but a basic honesty stopped her. They no longer had a place in her life, nor she in theirs. Certainly they were not important enough to constitute a reason to live. "I usually stay too busy to think about things like that."

"I had a couple of bad days when I got here. I mean, I was

like—wow, this is really bad news here." The doctor finished her cereal and wiped her mouth with her napkin. "But we still have to keep trying, doing our best, right?"

"That's what I'm going to do. Do my best to make some positive changes around here." Dina smiled proudly. No way would she buy the theory that this hospice was a star already burned out and plummeting to destruction. "It's time a woman had a crack at it."

"You sound like me. You like a challenge."

Dina smiled, surprised to find how much they had in common. "Anybody who likes a challenge has a real place here."

"That's how I'm going to look at it," Dr. Kovaks agreed. "I'll, like, you know, face the challenge to make things better."

"Then you'll have an impact. We women can make a difference if we try. Can I get you some more coffee?"

The skiff moved rapidly in the current of the surge as the sky began to lighten. The children sat together in the prow watching the remarkable panorama surrounding them. The water was frothy with swirls and eddies and flotsam. They passed limbs and branches and occasionally an entire tree toppled by the wind and snatched away by the water. Exhausted birds were using these casualties of the storm as resting places. Philip pointed out some large trees still standing upright, their trunks teeming with snakes seeking refuge, and Sara turned away, shuddering.

Perhaps thirty minutes after the swelling water had tipped their boat, low, sparsely wooded ground appeared to their right.

"I wish I had an oar," Philip said. "I could steer us there."

"Yeah, right," Sara said scornfully. "You always want to act so big."

Philip shook his head. "Look, Sara. We just went through

something really awful and it isn't over yet. Let's not be like Otto and Stoney. Can't we be nice to each other?"

She smiled sunnily. "Sure."

"I mean, it ought to be different after all we've been through."

"O.K. Hey, we're nearly to shore." Sara stood up to point to the land drawing closer. When the boat teetered she sat down again and snuggled up to her brother. They huddled together as the gap between boat and land closed.

"Here we go," he said, even as the boat scraped the shallow bottom near the shore.

Reeds grew along the sandy shoreline, along with a few mangrove trees. The water was crashing in small breakers. But the children clambered from the boat and waded safely ashore. Then they stood in the scanty shelter of a small tree and looked at each other questioningly.

"We need to find a road," Philip said with as much confidence as he could muster. "Let's go—"he looked around briefly—"*this* way."

He pointed in the direction that seemed the least obstructed and, wet and cold, they began to walk.

By some agency—luck, coincidence or a Force loosed by the words still pouring from Willoughby Stoddard—Philip had chosen the shortest, most direct route to intersect Highway 27.

The highway was flooded, its surface under several inches of water and its boundaries barely discernible. But Paul drove steadily. It was remarkable, he thought, that he could still maintain traction, and he toyed with the idea that this trip home contained some elements of the miraculous.

Aaron sat slumped against the door, his eyes closed. He seemed to have shrunk, and his face was set in lines of depression. Paul ached with compassion but could think of nothing to say to help.

Finally Aaron said, "Tell me again about the guy who thought helping yourself hindered God."

"Do you think that might be what happened?"

"No. I think we dropped the ball and I'm sure I'll never see my kids again. But that idea is the only thing that offers any light at all. And if I'm going to survive, I need some way not to hate God or the kidnapers—and especially myself."

"Well, he talked about not using a weapon to defend his children if they were in danger, because using a gun would be a sign he didn't trust God."

"You mean his objection to using force wasn't from pacifism but because it would show unbelief?"

"Right."

"I'm so afraid I'll lose my faith, start hating God. Abraham didn't. He was willing to kill his son to obey God. Surely I ought to be able to accept it."

"It's too soon to try to sort things out, Aaron. You're in too much pain to think straight. Give yourself some time."

"Oh, get real, Paul. Do you actually think the pain's going to go away? Ever?" Aaron passed a weary hand over his face. His eyes were still closed. "None of this matters. Nothing will ever matter again. I let them take my kids and I'll carry that knowledge for the rest of my life. In the final analysis it's my fault they're dead."

They fell into silence. Paul had no idea what to say.

He spotted them about fifty feet ahead, walking hand in hand along the edge of the highway. He was afraid of imposing even more emotional turmoil on Aaron, and their backs were turned, walking away from the van, but they appeared to be the right ages, a boy and a girl. Just how many children would be loose along the highway, walking through a hurricane?

"Aaron," he said gently.

"Hmm?" Aaron did not open his eyes.

Paul slowed the van. The children were about twenty feet ahead of them now. The boy had heard the sound of the vehicle and turned to look behind him. Paul recognized him immediately; it was the boy he had seen through the window of the fishing lodge. Besides, he looked exactly like his father.

"Aaron, it's *them!*" Paul shouted. He pounded the horn and yelled at the top of his lungs. "Praise the Lord! Thank You, Jesus!"

Aaron opened his eyes to stare at Paul in confusion, but Paul pointed ahead. "Look, man! It's *them!*"

Looking out the windshield, Aaron let out a deep, shuddering sob.

Philip had recognized his parents' van and was dragging his sister recklessly toward it. Then Sara began to shriek in excitement. The voices merged and blended in a cacophony of ecstasy as Aaron grabbed for the door and tumbled out painfully. They were all caught up in hugs and squeals that brought tears to Paul's eyes.

"Daddy!"

"Dad! You won't believe what happened. It was *wild!*"

"Philip, Sara! What are you *doing* here? I thought you'd be drowned!"

"I knew this was our van. Then I saw you!"

"Your mother's going to be so happy."

"Dad, they were awful men. They made us get in that boat."

"And they hit Flip and made us sleep in the truck. We had to go to the bathroom there, too. Where's Mama? I want to see Mama."

"Oh, Lord, You're so wonderful! Your faithfulness is truly astounding. Thank You for guiding us to these children."

"Philip was so brave, Daddy. He took good care of me."

"And she sang a song that made a man not buy us. She made him think about the Lord."

"Let's get in the van, kids. We can talk while we're driving back to Belle Glade."

"We were in Belle Glade already. We ate there."

"There's room for all four of us," said Paul. "You can stand right by your dad, honey. Brace yourself; it's kinda rough going."

"Daddy, you're hurting my arm. Let me down, please."

"Where are the men, Flip? How'd you get away? Ow—watch my legs."

And amid joy and laughter and gratitude and wind and rain and triumph, they drove back to Belle Glade to reunite the family.

17

Thursday afternoon,
September 16, 1999

The room was noisy, crowded, messy and hot, but nobody seemed to mind—not even the usually organized and tidy Olivia. She was propped up on one of the twin beds with her husband and two children, piled joyfully en masse in a never-ending, four-way hug. Actually, it was a five-way hug, since Sara was clutching Buffalope as tightly as her mother clutched her.

They were also passing the major's cellular phone back and forth among them, since one of the first things they had done on reaching Dorm 4 was to phone Pine River. Will and Charlotte Stoddard were on both extensions at their house, talking and crying at the same time. Articulate communication was hardly possible; everyone was too excited and drained to be coherent.

But emotions, if not words, flowed and overflowed between the two cities and love was communicated.

Olivia was radiant. Even though she still wore the same jeans and shirt, and more strands of hair straggled from her dwindling bun, the haunted look had left her eyes, and the lines of grief and torment that had marred her beauty only hours before were now crinkling with joy.

Aaron was awash in gratitude. He was exhausted, his knee was swollen and the burns on his legs were painful, but nothing could mar his happiness. There were things he would have to discuss with his wife and with Paul. But for now it was enough to bask in the achievement of rescue, no matter how it had been accomplished.

Philip was surprised to find that part of him would miss the mantle of responsibility. He had watched over his sister for nearly a week and felt he had done a pretty good job. Heady stuff for a ten-year-old! His parents were proud of him. But most of him rejoiced in being a child again—loved, comforted, protected, valued more than he had realized.

Sara was using words to battle the painful, frightening experiences of the past week. Talked about with her parents and integrated with the rest of her life's experiences, these experiences were rendered harmless. She especially talked about the scenes in which she had been heroic or successful. The small room, crowded with visitors, had already heard and applauded her conversation with Mrs. Parker and her song for Mr. Capovilla, which was gratifying. She snuggled close between her parents, squeezed Buffalope and began yet another anecdote.

Philip sighed patiently.

Paul Cordray, still in wet fatigues, sat on the floor in a corner of the Tylers' room, elbows on his knees, chin resting in his grimy hands, smiling but deep in thought. Like Aaron, he had unanswered questions about the mission. Even more, he had questions about his own performance.

Why had he failed to fire his weapon? He had not sent off even a warning shot—the most natural thing in the world.

He was not the father of the children, helpless in the grip of unmanageable emotions; he was a professional soldier, trained in the use of force.

None of the spiritual issues he and Aaron had talked about— not pacifism or unbelief or anything else—offered sufficient reason for his dereliction. So what if it had not been an Army mission? No, he had no excuse. The bitter truth was that he, Sergeant Paul Cordray, U.S. Army, had failed.

He would talk first to Aaron, then to Major Shearson. If this episode were more than an aberration and defined how he would conduct himself from now on, he would have to re-sign from the military.

But before making any life-changing decisions, he needed to figure out what had happened.

And even before that, he needed a bath, some food and sleep.

Iris sat propped up on the second bed, feasting her eyes on the Tylers. What a triumph! All their pain and fear were over, and their celebration was as deep and as powerful as their or-deal had been. Her sister was restored as the satisfied little hausfrau. Her brother-in-law was released from the impos-sible pressure. The children looked better than ever. The oh-so-fortunate Tylers were again in a position of blessing and favor.

But all this seemed very good in Iris' eyes—because the most miraculous thing was the fact that none of this bothered her anymore! The lifelong jealousy, the envy, the inner whine of "What about *me?*"—they were all gone!

Her eyes fell on Sergeant Paul Cordray, still wet and dirty, sagging with fatigue, looking totally depleted.

I wish I could talk to him, she thought. *I'd like to tell him about last night. But I'm probably the last person he wants to talk to.*

"Hang on, Grandma. Here, Aunt Iris." Philip reached

across the beds to hand her the phone, and his wide grin included her in the family jubilation.

Why, we're all different, she thought. *Not just me.*

She put the phone to her ear and heard both her parents talking at the same time and crying.

"Daddy?" she broke in. "Mama? One at a time, please."

"That you, Iris?" Will asked, sniffing. "Oh, it's good to hear your voice! I'm so grateful to God that you're safe!"

Grateful to God? Iris thought in astonishment. *Boy, have we all changed! Will Stoddard talking about God!*

"You ought to see them, Daddy. They're so happy it's hard to look at them without crying!"

Charlotte's laugh interrupted Will's response. "Oh, Iris, what a silly thing to say, but I know exactly what you mean!"

Only after they had depleted their exclamations of delight did Will mention the local news.

"Old Joe Jenson tested positive. He's already at the Gainesville airport waiting to fly down to Belle Glade. Can you let Carly know?"

"Daddy, Carly's gone. Missing. They think he stole a truck from the hospice, and nobody knows where he is."

"Can you figure that? Well, if he comes back, Joe wants him to know he'll be there in a day or so. You think I ought to tell Joe about Carly?"

This was a new wrinkle—Will asking Iris for advice! She took it in stride. "No, I don't think so. He's got enough on his plate right now, and maybe Carly will get back by the time Joe arrives."

"I just thought maybe he could leave the business in better shape if he knew Carly might not be coming home for a while."

"Daddy, you know they don't give you time to do anything like that. Joe can't change anything from the airport."

"You're right. And I shouldn't give him more bad news right when we're all so happy."

"Yes, isn't it wonderful! Did they tell you that Philip put sleeping pills in their liquor? What a brave kid."

"Sara, too—what a trouper! You heard about how she got that woman aside. And Aaron. It took guts to go into that country in a storm. You know, it's a lot like the Lord, when He came to earth to rescue us from captivity—the Father loving His children enough to face great suffering to set them free."

Iris shook her head in amazement. There would be a *lot* of catching up to do!

"Now, Mama, you get some chicken ready and some really giant dumplings, 'cause we're all coming home hungry!"

This is nice and I'm happy for them, of course, but I do have piles of work to do.

In fact, the exorbitant displays of affection that accompanied the narrative, as the Tyler children bounced between the two beds in their parents' room, were causing Dina Hawks acute discomfort. Her mind flashed old, old pictures of her own children at an early age, full of smiles and hugs and love. The display in front of her made her feel she was going to scream. Yet for some reason she had added to their joy by canceling the conscription order on Olivia.

Well, I'm director now, Dina reminded herself, *and I don't intend to whine and get drunk and botch things the way Burton Chancey did.*

Now if she could get Dr. Kovaks, smiling across the room— Cassie, as she apparently preferred to be called—as Chief of Medicine and get some discipline enforced, things would show some improvement.

She had *had* to work, she protested to herself. It wasn't that she didn't love her kids. But they could really drive you crazy, and of course that no-good Bob couldn't earn a decent living. If she had had to work, it only made good sense to do as good a job as possible. And commitment to her job had meant long hours.

Her children were grown now, married. The past was past, no going back. No use letting the accusing voices rise to torment her. Was it really so bad in this day and age not to know your grandchildren? People lived apart today, and travel was greatly curtailed anyhow. Besides, she had raised her own kids. What law said she had to lay down her life for yet another generation?

I'll stay five more minutes, she decided firmly. *Then I'm out of here. I've got work to do.*

Major Ed Shearson was another of the standing-room-only crowd in the Tylers' room. Like almost everyone who had heard about the kidnaping, he had put himself in the parents' role and found it unendurable. How could they stand the loss, the not knowing, the mental assaults?

He thought of his own two daughters and the incalculable catastrophe it would be if they were gone.

I wish I could spend more time with them, he thought with a tinge of an old, familiar guilt. *But what I do is essential, especially now. I do it well and I couldn't make much of a living any other way. They understand it isn't my choice to be away so much. It's just the way life is. At least I know they're safe, even if I'm not with them that much.*

He smiled at the Tylers' gaiety and, because he was a kind man and a family man, rejoiced at the children's rescue.

He was also aware that something had happened to Sergeant Cordray—something upsetting to the young soldier. He planned to address it first opportunity he got. This was what his job entailed—being a good officer to the men under him, performing his duties wisely and well.

I can make a difference, he thought. *I can make things a little better, maybe—if not for the world, at least for young Cordray.*

Cassandra Kovaks was the fifth outside celebrant in the Tylers' room. She stood by the window tall and robust, smiling benevolently.

This family thing was nice, and she was grateful for having been raised in an old-fashioned, two-parent household. Still, the call of something more rewarding and significant was pulling her away from the narrow confines of domesticity. Even this attractive family, seen at its best, offered little competition to the lure of—what? Well, whatever it was, there were other things besides a husband and children. For sure.

I said it this morning at breakfast: I want to face challenges and make positive changes in the world around me. That's my destiny. Maybe I won't even go back to Cross City. I'd like a little bigger pond than Daddy's practice.

She moved across the room to stand by Dina Hawks near the doorway. As everyone in the room was laughing and chattering, the two women smiled at one another in unspoken solidarity and understanding.

Dr. Kovaks had to resist the impulse to take Dina's hand.

Captain Santiago arrived as the others were leaving. He smiled paternally over the children and shook hands with Aaron. "I am utterly delighted that you succeeded, Mr. Tyler."

The deep, golden voice pouring into the room kept Paul and Major Shearson in the doorway.

"I wonder if you have any idea how remarkable an occurrence this is? In order for you to walk away from this place with your children safe and secure, a truly miraculous series of events must have happened, in perfect sequence and perfect timing. I hope you recognize and are grateful for your extraordinary good fortune."

"We believe in the Lord, Captain, and believe every bit of this is in answer to prayer."

"Oh, yes. I agree wholeheartedly. Now, I wonder if I might impose on you—and on you, too, Sergeant—to give me an accounting sometime? Nothing official, of course, merely to satisfy an old man's curiosity."

"Glad to, Captain. But I need a bath and a nap and maybe a bit of lunch." Aaron was almost staggering and his words were slurred.

"How about joining me at my home later this afternoon? I promise I won't keep you from your family too long."

Aaron looked at Olivia, a child under each arm. She nodded briefly with a wry smile, managing to convey in that simple gesture her resistance to the separation, her admission that it was the right thing to do, and her contentment with the restoration of her family that made everything else trivial.

"Fine, then," Aaron agreed. "Paul?"

"A good debriefing might help to answer some questions."

"Mind if I came along to listen?" Major Shearson asked. "I'm like you; it wouldn't be official. But we all like the happy ending and I'd like to hear, too."

"Certainly. Four o'clock, if that is satisfactory." The policeman took a business card from his coat pocket and sketched a simple map. "It's easy to find."

"We'll look for you later."

Everyone had gone but the four Tylers. Their catching up on the details of the week was without order or chronology or completion. There were showers, sandwiches in the room (nobody wanted to go to the dining room) and a three-hour nap in the afternoon.

Aaron was not sure how much Olivia understood about the rescue. Neither he nor Paul had made a big deal about their failure to reclaim the children at the fish camp, but it seemed obvious. She was bound to have questions, though she had said nothing. If anything, she was euphoric.

I'll have to tell her, of course, he thought. *Maybe that'll help me understand. But right now I need to sleep.*

He drifted into oblivion on a cloud of serenity .

The weather was improving, though far from pleasant. Lake Okeechobee was still rising in response to the rainfall as well as to the flooding that had traveled northward from the Everglades to empty into the lake. But Ariel was passing, heading toward the Gulf of Mexico and east Texas, her next predicted landfall. Without more rain, there was a good chance the levees and dams around the lake would hold.

Iris, too keyed up to sleep, borrowed an umbrella from the coat closet in Dorm 4 and took a stroll on the hospice grounds. Signs of the hurricane were everywhere. Palm frond, small trees, sheets from metal roofs, awnings and lawn furniture were strewn about in careless profusion. A glut of soil and other debris was deposited in rippled stripes across the soggy lawns—the evidence of standing water now decreasing. Iris was amazed to think she had walked through, then slept through the storm that had produced this litter.

She spotted Paul Cordray sitting on the very same concrete bench along the walkway to the hospice that had been the site of yesterday's humiliating encounter. Unshaven, he still wore his wet battle fatigues and poncho, and sat hunched in the intermittent rain. He looked up as she approached.

"Couldn't you sleep?" she asked. "I thought you guys were up all night."

"Can't stop thinking. Lots to figure out about last night."

"You mean the way you just 'happened' to run across the children walking down the highway? That's got to be a miracle."

"No, before that. At the fish camp." His head hung down as he stared at his hands clasped in his lap. "For some unknown reason, I just let them walk away with the kids. I had a gun and I didn't fire. I was ready to, and I never actually thought about it or changed my mind. It just happened. Like what they used to call buck fever."

"Well, that's easy to explain. It was God."

"What do you mean by that?"

Iris sat down next to him and he slid over to make room. She moved the umbrella over to protect both of them from the spatter of warm rain.

"Well, if you'd caught them by force, just scaring them or actually shooting them, then you'd be the heroes, wouldn't you? Everybody would be talking about how great Aaron and the sergeant were. They won this great victory. You'd get all the credit. This way, it has to be God. You didn't do anything that much to brag about."

He turned slowly and stared at her. She smiled back.

After a long time he nodded. "You may be right. It wasn't what we wanted or expected, but it was God's perfect will, which is what we prayed for." He was looking at her curiously as though he had never seen her before. "So we ended up with what we wanted—the kids safe and free. And God got what He wanted, which is always to glorify His name." He smiled. "Now tell me how in the world you figured that out."

"It's just logical, Paul. If we don't get what we want in answer to prayer, it means God wants to do something better, or He wants to go deeper. Which I guess is the same thing."

"Please don't take this as an insult, but you're really different from the way you were yesterday."

She nodded self-consciously. "I think you must have already left my sister's room this morning when I told Aaron about what happened to me last night. I'll explain again, if you're interested."

How very different I am, she thought, *from the tormented and selfish young woman who sat on this same bench, next to this same man, not 24 hours ago!*

Then she had been intent on breaking down his walls of integrity. Now she, too, had been given a position of righteousness and honor. She was *forgiven.* He was still almost unbearably attractive, and her heart longed for him in a way that was both joyful and aching, but she knew she would make no move toward him.

" . . . And when I woke up, I was all changed, and it's been that way all day."

He shook his head. "What a day of miracles!"

"Even the storm is passing," she agreed, pointing to the wind-lashed landscape with its clutter of debris.

Gale-force winds still gusted sporadically, and the clouds swirled and heaved, but the sky was a lighter gray and the rain had diminished.

"Say, we had a date, didn't we?" he exclaimed, straightening up. "Didn't we plan to walk along the lake, weather permitting?"

"I believe we did," she replied, almost unable to contain the delight bubbling up inside of her. "And of course, the weather has turned out simply gorgeous!"

Captain Santiago and his wife lived in a mobile home set among lush and obviously well-loved plantings on a wide lot on the south edge of town. He was in the yard raking up wreckage and trash as Paul, Aaron and Ed drove up.

He stripped off his work gloves to shake hands with Old World formality, and ushered them graciously inside. They took seats in the over-furnished but spotless living room. A quiet, plump woman with an abundance of graying hair stepped from the kitchen and ducked her head in shy friendliness.

"Gentlemen, this is my wife, Avilla. Will you have coffee? Tea? Perhaps some wine?"

Paul, who had not slept at all, requested coffee. Aaron, who looked punch-drunk, also requested coffee. Major Shearson joined Santiago in a glass of red wine.

The captain's wife served the beverages in silence, along with a tray of fruit, then scooted back to the kitchen.

The captain lifted his wineglass ceremoniously. "Let us toast your most impressive accomplishment. I am delighted to know that your children are with you once again, unharmed."

His three guests held up their drinks awkwardly.

"I have some news," continued Santiago. "It is almost certain that the two men who abducted your children did drown. Two bodies have been recovered in that area that match the descriptions, although I suppose it would not be wise for your children—your son, at least—to make formal identification. Or do you think that might help them write *finis* to this episode?"

Aaron shook his head. "I think that might be real traumatic."

"I am sure you are right." The captain settled himself elaborately in his deep velvet chair. "Please, tell us all about your adventures."

Paul and Aaron looked at one another.

"Well, where shall I start?" said Aaron. "Did Paul tell you about Captain Santiago's phone call, Major Shearson?"

"He did—and please call me Ed."

So Aaron started with their drive south, apparently reliving through his narrative the effects of the weather, the fear and tension, the danger.

Paul relived it, too, as Aaron recounted their discovery of

the gate with its sign; their creeping reconnaissance through the wet, turbulent night; the discovery of the children; their entry into the house. It all seemed as vivid in the telling as it had been in the doing. Then Aaron had them in the kitchen and in the sitting room, feeling the horror of those moments.

"The kerosene caught right away and the whole room was on fire. I got knocked down and hurt my knee and fell into the fire. . . . Just couldn't get through to the kids. But I had a chance to shoot the guys as they carried them off and I didn't take it." He stared in shame at the floor. "By the time we got outside, they had already taken the boat." He quietly sketched the nightmarish scene on the dock.

Paul longed to relieve Aaron of his guilt by repeating what Iris (of all people!) had said, but he felt intimidated by the major's presence.

I came down here for the specific purpose of proclaiming the Lord-ship of Jesus Christ, he thought. *And with very few exceptions I have failed to do that when I had a chance. Can it be that I'm ashamed?*

Captain Santiago's rich voice broke in thoughtfully.

"I hope you are not blaming yourself," he told Aaron gently. "Just consider how much more glorious this testimony is than one in which you killed or frightened these evil men. This is a miracle, not just a successful mission. Rejoice in this, young man. Don't let your pride as a man rob you of this victory, which is far, far greater."

"That's what Iris said," Paul broke in excitedly. "This way God gets the glory, not us."

Aaron looked up in surprise. "Iris said that?"

"Yes! We walked around all afternoon talking. Aaron, she's a different woman. You wouldn't know her. She's really—well, something!"

"Maybe I shouldn't have taken a nap," Aaron grinned. "I hate to miss any action."

He turned to the captain and spoke more decorously. "I'm sure you're right. Maybe it was just pride that got me so upset. Well, I'm going to forget about my so-called failure and give God the credit for protecting me from killing somebody in front of my kids."

"Or killing one of them," Major Shearson added. "Those men were moving targets, you had bad light, you were under great emotional tension, you had hurt yourself and you were standing in a fire. Not the best conditions for marksmanship!"

"I hadn't considered that. Captain Santiago, Ed, how much have you heard about the kids' side of the story?"

He filled in the narrative as he had heard it from Philip and Sara, while his listeners agreed that the boat righting itself was yet another miracle.

But Paul was listening with only half his mind. Something was coming together in his spirit.

O.K., so our notions and reasons and plans might very well be different from God's. That's not surprising. He says His ways are higher than our ways and His thoughts are not our thoughts. But that means we might well go into something with one goal in mind that isn't God's goal at all.

Paul tried to carry this thought to the logical conclusion. If this idea were true, maybe he had come to Belle Glade for some reason other than to preach the Gospel to dying AIDS patients. That had been *his* idea; God might have another. Certainly he had been almost as derelict at preaching as he had been with the shooting. Both his weapon and his voice had been pretty much on safety—maybe not quite in the holster, but almost.

Was it possible that his state of inertia had not come about because he was ineffective, but because he was here for a totally different reason?

Well, if he had not come to witness to the lost, why *had* he come?

Suddenly he knew. The words from Proverbs sounded not only in his mind and soul and ears; they reverberated throughout his whole being:

"Whoso findeth a wife findeth a good thing."

Dear God in heaven, I came here to meet Iris!

He was suddenly aware that the others were staring at him, and he wondered if he had spoken aloud.

But Aaron asked, evidently for the second time, "It was the only place along there where the kids could have made it through to the highway, wasn't it?"

"So it seems," he said quickly. "The undergrowth there wasn't nearly so thick. . . ."

The others took up the narrative and Paul returned to his amazing discovery.

So I didn't get what I expected, because God wanted to go deeper and do something better. Of course! But what about the practical side of things? Like my Army career. I can't take her with me all over the country. Am I supposed to resign? Besides, what makes me so sure she'll say yes?

Then he smiled broadly. Of course she would say yes. God would not bring him all the way down to Belle Glade, with all that that entailed, to meet a curvy little blonde who was only one day old in the Lord—and already presuming to instruct him!—and speak so strongly from heaven that this was *the one*, all to have her say no!

Besides, he was pretty sure she liked him.

More than an hour later, as they were leaving, Paul nudged Major Shearson. "Sir, I need to talk to you later. There are a couple of things I'd like to discuss."

"As soon as we get back. Incidentally, Paul, I was thinking it might be a good idea for you to drive back to Pine River with these folks. Jenson has not turned up, and it sure would be a shame, after all this, if they got shot down on the way home!"

"I think that's an outstanding idea, sir."

With a prospect like that, a man could enjoy a good dinner.

Aaron opened the door to their room in Dorm 4 and stood for a moment enjoying the sight of his family. The children were asleep in the beds, their faces above the covers flushed with sleep. Olivia was sitting in the only chair, curled up like a sleek cat, reading his Bible. Her long, golden hair was softly brushed, hanging loose and shining in the light of the table lamp. She looked up and smiled. Aaron thought he had never seen a lovelier sight.

He gestured toward the children and spoke quietly. "I thought you were seeing about getting another room."

"They didn't want to be separated from us. And to tell the truth, I wanted them right here where I could see them. We'll be crowded, but it's only for one night."

"Sounds good to me." He pulled her up from the chair, sat down in it himself and pulled her onto his lap. "Paul's riding to Pine River with us. The major's idea, but Paul seems pretty happy about it."

"You seem pretty happy, too. Did you get over feeling like you're a failure?"

"Did you know I felt that way? I guess I did get over it. It's all in how we look at it." He explained Iris' idea, confirmed by both Major Shearson and Captain Santiago. "And I agree with them. No need to take on all that guilt and condemnation. Who knows what God was about? He did it, and I'm going to concentrate on being grateful."

"Look how much good has come out of this," Olivia added. "Daddy got saved, Iris got saved, Philip has matured overnight, and how many people will hear about the miracles God did and be touched?"

"We'll never be the same again, Livvy. None of us. God willing, we'll never take our blessings for granted again." He looked with aching tenderness at his two slumbering children. "We've been so protected from the evils in life. We had our safe little world and thought nothing could ever touch us. Then something did touch us and we found that we were far safer than we had ever dreamed."

"We found out *eventually.*"

"But now we know. Now we can be confident that, no matter what happens—your getting conscripted, or whatever—God will take care of us. That truth never meant bad things couldn't happen. Instead it means that whatever happens will work for our good."

"So now I'm married to a philosopher, am I?"

"Livvy, I see there really is a fatal plague infecting more and more people. And there's a deep, black line of demarcation between those who are infected and those who are healthy. But the disease isn't AIDS, it's sin. So if anyone is wondering about the future, the important question isn't if he has AIDS, but if he has Jesus. That's the real dividing line. We're all going to die. The important thing isn't how soon, or under what circumstances. The important thing is, where will we spend eternity?"

"Oh, I get it. I'm married to a religious fanatic."

"Think you can handle it?"

"I reckon."

He leaned down for a kiss.

"Now how about a quick round of Scripture Roulette?" she asked.

"Sure—one for the road."

Olivia opened the Bible on her lap, looked up into Aaron's face and put her finger down on a page. She looked down. Once again she had turned to Isaiah, this time chapter 43. She read aloud, her eyes wide:

Fear not, for I have redeemed thee: I have called thee by thy name; thou art mine. When thou passest through the waters,

I will be with thee; and through the rivers, they shall not overflow thee: when thou walkest through the fire, thou shalt not
be burned; neither shall the flame kindle upon thee. For I am
the LORD thy God, the Holy One of Israel. . . .

She was crying softly. "Oh, Aaron, the fire and the water,
and neither one could hurt you."

Suddenly there was a knock on the door. Olivia wiped her
eyes hastily.

"Who's there?" Aaron called quietly.

"Us," answered a happy masculine voice. "We have news."

"Come in, then."

Iris and Paul stood side by side in the doorway, dripping wet,
holding hands. Their faces were twin pictures of radiance.

Paul looked down at Iris and she looked up at him.

Together they announced, "We're getting married."

Olivia emitted a happy squeal and began to cry.

"What?" Aaron protested. "Since when? You two hardly
know each other!"

"We don't have time to talk to you. We want to talk to each
other. But we wanted you to be the first to know."

Paul put a possessive arm around Iris' waist and they began
to move off, closing the door behind them.

The Tylers looked at each other in delighted amazement.
They could hear the newly engaged couple harmonizing as they
strolled down the hall of Dorm 4: "Fly me to the moon. . . ."

Then they settled in for a longer kiss.